THE LAST BOY

by ROBERT H. LIEBFRMAN

SOURCEBOOKS LANDMARK™
AN IMPRINT OF SOURCEBOOKS, INC.®
NAPERVILLE, ILLINOIS

Published by Sourcebooks, Inc.
P.O. Box 4410, Naperville, Illinois 60567-4410
(630) 961-3900
FAX: (630) 961-2168
www.sourcebooks.com

Library of Congress Cataloging-in-Publication Data

First Edition

Printed and bound in the United States of America
10   9   8   7   6   5   4   3   2   1

for GUNILLA

prologue

The pages felt like parchment but were not made of animal skin; they had the texture of a wood product yet were not paper. Tripoli remembered seeing some material like it once at an exhibition at the university museum. Tapa cloth, it was called, and it was made by the Polynesians from the bark of mulberry trees. The leaves of these ancient volumes sitting on Tripoli's kitchen table had the exact same feel. Tissue thin, yet strong.

Outside, the wind suddenly picked up and came whistling around his isolated farmhouse, rocking the trees as the sky darkened and flashes of electrical discharge illuminated the distant hills. Oblivious to the weather, he hunched over the books that sat nestled in the small ring of yellow light spilling from his lamp.

The bindings on the books—and there were five of them in all—were hand-sewn. Each gathering had been stitched together, then connected to make the whole. Tripoli's father had been a collector of old books. What a pity that he was no longer alive, he would have relished seeing these.

Tripoli began on what he guessed to be the first volume. It was not easy going. The books were in a multiple of languages, both ancient and modern. They were written in what looked to be Hebrew and Greek, English that spanned the gamut from old to medieval to modern. There were even portions written in Chinese-looking characters, other sections in what might be Sanskrit.

He concentrated on the portions that were in English. They were handwritten in a florid style that was difficult to decipher, and the language was old-fashioned and strange.

The first book appeared to be about the world, the greater world, not just the sun and planets but other galaxies and solar systems. There were drawings of orbits, endless charts with numbered entries. Interspersed throughout the book were elaborate illustrations adorned with gold leaf and colored with hues of lapis lazuli and the most dazzling of red-orange pigments. There were pages covered with what could have been mathematical formulas, though the symbols were like none that he had ever seen; and diagrams, too, plans and schematics for what looked like machines and odd contraptions.

Once Tripoli started, everything around him seemed to fall away: the day vanished into night, then dawn broke through with its early, pink light.

Slowly, very slowly, he began to understand—or thought he understood. Here, locked away in these precious books, was a virtual treasure trove of accumulated wisdom, a merging of philosophy and science, psychology and engineering.

Tripoli pushed on through the next day, breaking only to give the animals some water and fresh fodder, reading until his eyes burned and his brain ached. Jumping ahead to the more recent volumes, he discovered small inserts attached in strategic places where gaps had been left in the text. When he ran his fingers over the surface of these attachments, he discovered that the paper was different from the surrounding pages, crisper, newer. The ink, too, seemed fresher. When he put his nose close to the paper, it smelled of bark and berries. The notations contained some kind of ideograms commingled with numbers. One of the images looked like that of a little boy.

That evening as he wandered the fields and forests surrounding his home, he thought about the old texts, thought about himself, the transformation he was undergoing, he a streetwise, hard-boiled cop. He thought, too, about Molly. How she would somehow change, though she might continue to resist. How their lives would never be the same. And how it all began with the disappearance of a child.

POLICE EXPAND HUNT FOR BOY

Police widened their search this morning for five-year-old Matthew Roland who mysteriously disappeared from his Watertown Elementary School classroom. State Police have joined local authorities, extending their search to include a three-county area.

The boy was last seen two days ago in his kindergarten class. Shortly before noon the boy's teacher, Lydia Munson, noticed his absence and notified the school's principal, who then alerted the Jefferson County Sheriff's office.

"This is one of the most exhaustive searches we've ever done," explained Sheriff Dennis Holbrow. "If the boy is lost outside, we'd better find him fast. The weather's getting very cold."

The boy's mother was reported in seclusion and could not be reached for comment. Anybody with information concerning the disappearance is asked to contact the police.

-Watertown Daily Times,
November 5, 1938

BOOK ONE

chapter one

In Ithaca, New York, traffic signals today are controlled by a central computer that usually keeps traffic flowing. Local and state police agencies are linked by fiber-optic networks, and news now travels at the speed of light.

A small boy walks up the north side of Green Street past the photo store and Diamond's Indian Restaurant. Though the afternoon is chilly, in fact downright cold for October, the child seems skimpily dressed in his red flannel shirt with blue and yellow lines, bib jeans, and sneakers. Perhaps because he is so short, a little kid of five or six, no one appears to notice him. He walks with a determined stride as if he knows where he's going, has done this before—though neither is true. Reaching the safety of the sidewalk, the child wends his way through a small cluster of shoppers leaving the Woolworth's department store.

A frail old woman, with her once fine coat buttoned up against the wind, is standing on the sidewalk in front of the store, staring aimlessly at the sky. She lowers her gaze to watch the little boy as he darts diagonally across the busy intersection, the traffic swirling around him. Clutching her thin coat tighter to her throat, the old woman continues to peer at the child as he progresses up the street. Her skin stretches taut on the bones of her face, tissue thin, revealing the blueness of the veins that course just below the surface. She, too, appears to be out of place amidst the driving bustle of people on the street. And only she seems to notice the incongruity of the little boy's solitary presence.

Shoppers and workers rush past, hurrying to catch the bus that has just pulled up, nearly knocking the child over. Where's his mother? the old woman wonders. Her children would never be out alone like this, not at his age. She briefly tries to remember how old her children are, but becomes muddled as the memories wash over her. She knows they are a bit older. Maybe a lot older. Maybe not.

As he nears, she steps forward to meet him, her gait a little unsteady.

"Aren't you a little young to be crossing streets by yourself, young man?" she inquires as she tries to block his path.

"Huh?" says the little boy, looking up at her warily. His nose is running.

"What's your name?"

"Danny."

"Danny what?"

"Danny Driscoll." He starts to edge around her.

"Does your mother know where you are, Danny?"

"I'm okay," he says, wiping his nose with his sleeve and continuing his march up the street.

"Wait a minute!" The old woman calls after the little boy. She attempts to keep pace with him, but quickly tires and abandons the effort. She steps back to lean against the store's wall and catch her breath. A jet descending toward the Ithaca airport skims by overhead, the whine of its engines piercing the snowy clouds. It captures the old woman's attention and her eyes shift skyward. When at last she again looks up the street, the little boy is gone and she has already forgotten her purpose. Suddenly she remembers: "My little Mary is forty-six... no…forty-eight," she murmurs under her breath.

The sky broke open for an instant, yielding a chink of blue in the sea of heavy gray. Then the sun, half buried behind the western hills above the lake, suddenly bursts through the gloom. The sunlight flooded the valley with a final but fading flare, causing the maples behind the magazine's office to flame a spectacular red and splashing a blazing shaft of golden yellow against Molly's computer screen.

Molly Driscoll hadn't realized how late it was until that final flash of sun caught her attention. She had been so absorbed in work, putting out fires as Larry called it, that the day had just slipped by. The office was often a madhouse, but Molly loved it, thrived on it, fed on the excitement. Had Doreen not reminded her, she might have forgotten lunch. It was almost three before she had stopped for a quick sandwich. That was the way it was in this new job. Larry Pierce was the kind of guy who made you want to give everything.

It was only in the late afternoon that Molly began to think about Danny. They had both overslept that morning—the alarm had failed to go off, and she had had to yank Danny out of bed, frantically throwing on her own clothes while getting him dressed, too. She had packed a lunch and then stood over Danny in the kitchen of their trailer, rushing him through his oatmeal.

"Come on, Honey. You can eat in the car—we've got to run."

"It's too hot. I can't eat it!" he complained as she shepherded him to the old Chevy. She had run back to the trailer to pour on more milk to cool it. The runny cereal kept dribbling down his sleepy chin as they drove to town.

Shortly into the ride, Danny had a coughing fit and put down the half-eaten bowl. At first Molly thought that he was choking on the cereal, but then suspected that he was coming down with another cold. He always seemed to be picking things up at Kute Kids. A couple of weeks before, Danny had gotten a stomach bug and she had taken the entire day off. Last week her wreck of a Chevy wouldn't start and she lost half the morning. Well, she thought grimly, unless Danny had a fever he had to go to daycare.

The crew at the *Upstater* magazine pulled together as a team and she couldn't leave them in the lurch yet again. And these days, jobs in an Ithaca of darkened and emptied downtown stores were scarce. Especially decent-paying ones with a promising future. Day jobs. And working at the magazine was a hell of a lot more stimulating— not to say more respectable—than her nights cocktail waitressing at the Ramada where the construction workers from the new bypass on Route 13 stared down her top as she served them.

The publication was a small operation. Larry ran it with three editors, two editorial assistants, and the newest addition—Molly. She was essentially the secretary—with a fancier title—but the job came with the promise of advancement to assistant, then maybe, some day, to full editor. A dream job. People like Doreen and Sandy and Ben could come and go as they pleased, sometimes even work at home if they wanted to.

Now, as the sun sank behind the hills, it was nearly 5:30, and Molly was eager to leave but didn't dare until Larry started packing up or gave her the nod. Her boss was a tall man, somewhere in his forties, she guessed, an exuberant, entrepreneurial type with a head of dark, curly hair and strong, chiseled features—the kind of man who knew how to get things done. Before coming to Ithaca, he apparently had been a hotshot executive at *New York Magazine*. All it took was a call from him and he had a guy like Danny DeVito in town visiting the local wineries and generating a piece in the *Upstater*.

Molly thought him a bit vain: he worked out to keep himself trim and always had a bright-colored handkerchief folded into the breast pocket of his suit. She had seen him around town with a number of different women. Some of them were married. Ostensibly it was for business, but Molly wondered—not that it was any of her concern. "He's a dandy," she often thought to herself with a half smile. The kind of guys who had always attracted her were more rough and tumble, men who were a bit on the outs with society. Like her ex.

Now the office was empty, silent except for the sound of Larry's voice. He was still on the phone. Molly was about to call Kute Kids to let them know she'd be a little late, but an important fax came in and she got distracted. Then the other lines started ringing. A writer in Vermont hadn't received his check. An artist was still missing two photos that he needed to retouch. Panic. Panic.

Once it passed 5:30, Molly started getting anxious. She really needed to pick up Danny by six when they closed Kute Kids. If parents came late, they were fined. And the fines were hefty—$15 for the first fifteen minutes, $25 for every ten minutes thereafter. Mrs. Oltz, the director, was usually pretty pissed about it, too, thought Molly with a rising sense of panic.

Molly finally stuck her head into Larry's office and raised a finger. He covered the mouthpiece and mouthed, "Five more minutes."

Molly busied herself, though her eyes kept darting to the clock. Quarter to six. If she drove at breakneck speed, she could still make it—if traffic wasn't bad. When Larry got off the line, she sneaked a peek into his office, hoping to find him packing up his briefcase. He was reaching again for the phone—didn't even notice her.

While Molly waited for her chance to finally leave the office, she kept thinking about Danny, about bedtime, the way he always wanted her to crawl under the covers with him, cuddle him and tell him stories. Sitting at her desk, Molly closed her eyes and summoned his image; now she could feel him, smell the scent of his hair, sweet and clean, hear his voice, high and excited, his words tumbling into each other. Danny.

Molly made good time down the highway. Curving down from the eastern heights, she skimmed the edge of the lake, on her right Stewart Park with its tall willows arching gracefully over the shore.

She'd be late for Danny's pickup—but not *that* late. Once she reached the edge of town, however, it seemed every stoplight and intersection conspired against her. Then she hit the construction on Route 13. The downtown traffic was snarled. The air was rife with choking dust as commuters heading home through the hub of town were slowed to a crawl. Then Molly's lane came to a complete stop as men with red flags waved the oncoming traffic around a swirl of dump trucks and graders.

"Come on. Come on," she said, banging her hands futilely on the steering wheel.

She switched on the radio. It was already well into the local news. She listened to some mindless babble about sports, then the recap: something about a Conrail tanker car derailing alongside a trout stream just south of town. Seven thousand gallons of diesel fuel had spilled out. The plume was now in the fast-flowing waters of the inlet and heading toward the lake, killing all the fish and aquatic life in its path. There was mention of development plans for the Westend. Sales figures for new and existing homes. Though the economy in the rest of the country was vibrant, the sales figures for last month were still sharply down. Molly listened but couldn't quite concentrate. She put on an easy listening station, but it just irritated her. She peered up at the distant sky; in the waning light she could see a fresh line of dark, menacing clouds moving in from the west.

Traffic started to move again. She checked her watch. Twenty after six! There goes a chunk of today's pay to fines, thought Molly, and could feel her stomach wrench into knots. By now all the other children were certainly picked up and Molly could envision Danny waiting just inside the door, his jacket on, his little lunch box clutched in his hand. He always looked so desperate when she was late—though he never uttered a complaint; he just looked at her with that hurt look.

Molly took a quick left on Green Street, passing the dilapidated houses caught between the commercial and residential, up past the fire station where they were hosing down an engine, another left on Albany Street to West State.

The daycare was housed in an austere building, built of concrete block with big plate glass windows looking out on the busy street. It had gone through many incarnations. Molly could remember when it had been an auto body shop, then a human body shop where college kids and yuppies pedaled bicycles that didn't go anywhere. She thought about the incongruity of people trying to burn up calories while other folks downtown or in their shacks out in the hills were going hungry; subsistence farmers eking out an existence on their hard scrabble land.

As Molly pulled up to the curb, she saw one of the new women from Kute Kids at the front door. Her back was to the street and it looked like she was locking up.

"Hello!" Molly called out as she trotted up the walk in her heels.

The woman started, then turned, her wide flat face turning puzzled as she recognized Molly. Molly had seen her only two or three times before, and ruefully noted that she looked barely out of high school. Only the wire-rimmed glasses over her unlined face gave any suggestion of age.

"Whew! I'm sorry to be late," Molly could feel a rivulet of sweat trickling down her side. "Where's—?"

"Huh?" said the girl. Her dark hair was clipped as short as a boy's, and she had a big gold stud in her nose. Her coat was open revealing a peasant blouse with embroidered border.

"My son," explained Molly, catching her breath. "Danny. Danny Driscoll." Molly's smile suddenly felt pasted on her face.

"Danny," echoed the girl. She look confused.

"Yes! Where's—?"

"I'm sorry, they've all been picked up," she said flatly.

"What are you talking about?" Molly's hands were trembling and suddenly her knees felt weak. "I just came to get my—"

"Maybe your husband picked him up?"

"I don't have one! What the *hell* are you talking about?"

"But your boy's not here," she said plaintively.

"Did Danny go home with another child?" she asked with strained voice. Molly's throat felt like it was closing, choking her. "Is that it?"

The girl didn't answer.

"Where's Mrs. Oltz?" Molly pushed her aside and opened the door. "Mrs. Oltz?" She called out as she stepped in.

The place was dark. Empty. In the faint light from the street Molly could see the little chairs upside down on the children's tables. Toys had been cleared away and floors were still wet from being mopped. Under the odor of cleanser lingered the smell of urine and mold. Molly fought the swell of panic threatening to overtake her.

"Mrs. Oltz!" Her voice echoed through the empty rooms. The only returning sound was a refrigerator. It came on with a clank and then whirred. Maybe Mrs. Oltz was in the kitchen? Certainly she would know where Danny was. "Mrs. Oltz!"

"Mrs. Oltz left," came the voice of the girl from the dimness behind her. "She had to go to the dentist. She had to get a tooth pulled and—"

"So where's my child?" Molly spun around to confront the girl. "You know, my boy? Danny! The little guy with blond curly hair? Hey, get some lights on here!"

The lights came on and Molly squinted in the sudden brightness. Illuminated, the room seemed even more deserted. The girl looked pale and frightened.

"I'm new and…" she tried to explain, but Molly didn't want to hear it.

"He had bib jeans on and a red plaid shirt," Molly said, prowling around the room. "You remember?"

The girl looked at her dumbly and Molly's mind felt like it was spinning out of control. Desperately she fought to calm herself. Maybe they had sent him home with someone else? They weren't supposed to do that, but...if she could just get hold of Mrs. Oltz. She'd know. Of course!

Molly turned on the girl. "When did Mrs. Oltz leave?"

"Around two."

"Where's Sylvia?"

"She was sick and didn't come in today."

"And Louella?" Molly eyes kept darting around, instinctively checking the doors and windows.

"She just comes in mornings and stays till lunch."

"You mean you've been *alone* here with all the kids since *two?*"

"Yes, but..."

"Okay. Fine. Then you were here when the parents came to get them, right?"

"Yeah. I think so."

"What the hell do you mean *think so?*"

"You're confusing me." The girl looked as if she were going to cry. Molly was herself already crying and couldn't help it.

"Please try to think," she pleaded. "You were here, right?"

"Yes."

"And saw Danny today—you *do* know the boy I'm talking about, don't you?" Molly was now moving through the building, flipping on lights as she went.

"Yes, yes," said the girl in the tiniest of voices. Her eyes were now flooded with tears and her nose was running.

Molly did a quick check of the kitchen. Then two bathrooms, the kids' and the employees'. Nothing. The girl trailing in her wake kept sniffling. Molly reversed course abruptly, bumping into her.

"Did one of the parents take Danny home?" The refrigerator had stopped and Molly could hear the blood pounding in her ears.

"I don't think so."

"Think? Either someone did or they didn't. Come on!"

"No," she shook her head. "No one!"

The exit leading to the play area in the rear was closed. She unlocked it and swung open the door. A blast of cold air rushed in. Outside, the line of deserted swings rocked in the wind. The slides and sandbox were empty. The fence was high. Taller than any adult. "Did you have them outside today?"

"Only a little in the morning. Then we had lunch. And I know he was here then." It was the first time that the girl had said that she had actually seen him.

Molly shut the door. "If no one took him, then he's *got* to be here."

"But he couldn't be, because they're all gone. I'm sure…"

Molly was already in the small alcove off the hall where they put the kids' coats and boots when the weather was inclement. As soon as she flipped on the light she spotted Danny's red jacket hanging from a hook. Her chest constricted and she began breathing rapidly, shallowly. It felt like the air had suddenly been sucked out of the building.

"Oh my God!" Molly gasped, clutching it tightly to her face. The silky jacket with letters "Big Red" emblazoned on it was the one Mr. Greenhut had given him when his own boy had outgrown it. Danny treasured it. Would never go anywhere without it. "A big boy's jacket," he had called it and had refused to take it off—even in bed. He would never have willingly left without it.

Then she spotted Danny's dinosaur-stickered lunch box tucked in the corner. Molly yanked it open. The thermos tumbled out and rolled across the floor. The box dangling from the handle was empty except for a nibbled core of an apple and some crumbs of bread.

The girl stood framed in the doorway of the alcove watching her.

Molly bolted right past her and raced back to the kitchen. "Danny!" she called out, her voice shaking, "Honey, are you here?" She went straight to the stove and pulled open the oven door. Except for layers of burnt-on crud, it was bare. She raced from one end of the room to the other; down on her knees she yanked open the deep floor cabinets, tugging out things to get an unobstructed view, pots and pans, packages of Pampers and paper toweling, blankets and towels flying across the floor. "Danny? Danny?" He could be hiding anywhere, she realized. He liked to play games, concealing himself in tight places and then jumping out and startling her with a loud Boo! It was a game that always frightened her—yet he kept doing it no matter how much she pleaded.

Her eyes went to the massive refrigerator/freezer. "Oh Jesus!" she uttered and lurched for the handles. In her mind's eye she saw a child's body curled up in a frozen, fetal pose. She jerked the heavy door open with such violence that containers of juice and milk tumbled out and sloshed across the linoleum floor. Except for some yogurts and bruised fruit, it was empty. The freezer had nothing but a box of ice pops.

The girl was standing lamely in the kitchen watching her. Her inaction infuriated Molly.

"Don't just stand there!" she ordered, tracking the milk and juice out into the main room. "At least help me look. Check the other rooms. If his jacket's here, he's got to be here! Somewhere! And what the hell's in here?" she asked rattling the padlocked door to a closet.

"It's just for storage."

"Well get it open!"

The girl started to fumble with the keys. Molly grabbed them and popped open the lock. In an instant she was digging her way through the closet, flinging aside brooms and mops as she waded into the darkness. "Danny! Danny!" Now she was screaming, she realized, and didn't care anymore.

A moment later she was at the door leading to the basement. There was no light switch and she started down the rickety stairs. The cellar smelled of rot. "Danny? Can you hear me, love?"

From above she could make out the sound of the girl moving around the other rooms. Then her muffled voice. She was on the phone. Talking, Molly guessed, to Mrs. Oltz.

"Hey, where the hell's the light switch?" Molly shouted.

"I think the bulb went out," the girl called back, coming to the head of the dark stairs.

"You mean you don't have a goddamn light down here?" Molly's terror was turning to fury.

"Here," said the girl, returning with a flashlight.

Molly swept the beam around the basement. There were piles of trash on the floor, heaps of soggy newspapers and crumpled milk cartons, a discarded sofa black with mildew and embroidered in networks of spider webs. Had she known this place was such a pigsty, that the workers were so *stupid,* she would never have sent Danny here, she thought in a fit of guilt.

"Anybody ever come down here?"

"Yeah. To do the diapers," explained the girl. "But he can't be down here. I'm sure of that."

"How can you be so…Oh, shit," mumbled Molly, fear gripping her. Up against a wall at the far end of the cellar near the furnace was a commercial washer and next to it a bulky gas dryer. When she got closer, she discovered that there was just enough space between the dryer and the wall for a kid Danny's size to squirm his way in. She poked the flashlight into the gap and forced her head into the opening to take a look. From what she could see, there appeared to be some kind of compartment at the bottom of the housing. It was where the burner or motor—or whatever the hell it was—sat. Just large enough to accommodate a small body. If a boy were hiding there and someone turned it on, she thought, her imagination reeling free, he'd be burnt or mangled in the belts.

She tried to slide the big steel casing away from the wall, but it wouldn't budge.

"Here. I'll help you," said the girl, and together they pushed and heaved. Inch by precious inch they wedged the dryer further away from the wall.

"Little more," Molly huffed. Then she was down on the floor, the rough concrete fraying the knees of her stockings, the white dust caking her navy skirt. There was a substantial space below the tumbler but, except for the burner, it was empty.

"He's not down here," the girl said. "I'm sure. You've got to believe me."

"Are there any other doors?"

"There's a side door. But it's boarded up."

"Let me see it."

Molly raced back up the stairs. The doorway was covered with a sheet of plywood. She pounded her fists against it. Nailed shut.

A wave of nausea and dizziness swept over Molly. The room began to turn and Molly had to sink down on one of the low tables just to keep from keeling over. She sat with her head lowered into her hands and could slowly feel the blood draining back. There was no way Danny was still here. "What's your name?" Molly asked, trying to get a grip on herself.

"Cheryl."

"Cheryl," she repeated. "I need you to think. Think real hard."

"I've thought. I've thought of everything, don't you know!" She was now bawling openly. "I remember him, of course I do! He's that nice little boy with the blond hair. With those curls. Big brown eyes. Always jumping around," she blubbered.

Molly got her pocketbook which lay by the door where she had first dropped it. She rummaged through it and found some crumpled tissue. She wiped her eyes and then held one out to Cheryl. "Here,"

The girl loudly blew her nose. She kept her gaze lowered, studying the damp tissue, afraid to meet Molly's eyes.

"Look, either someone took him or he got out on his own, right?" Molly tried to reason with the girl.

"No one took him."

"You're sure?"

"I'm *positive!* We keep the front door locked. We always do. That's the rule. Nobody could get past me."

"So how did he get out?" she asked, as much for her own benefit as the girl's.

"I don't know. I just don't know!"

"Where exactly is Mrs. Oltz?"

"I called her. She said not to do anything. That she'd be right over."

"Well, I'm calling the police," said Molly. "Where's the phone?"

Molly was just hanging up when Mrs. Oltz came storming through the front door. She was holding an icepack to the side of her face that was swollen like a balloon. Her eyes were tiny, angry slits cut into the white sea of her fleshy face. Her gray hair stood in wiry knots.

"What's going on here?" thundered Mrs. Oltz, her words garbled through her twisted mouth wadded with cotton. "What the…?" She took in the scene of the littered floors.

"That's just what I'd like to know!" said Molly advancing on her. "Where's my boy?"

"You didn't pick him up?"

"What the hell do you think I'm doing here?"

"Well then somebody else must have picked him up."

"Who?" asked Molly.

Mrs. Oltz turned on Cheryl. "Well, who?"

The girl shook her head and started to cry again.

"I leave you for a few minutes," said Mrs. Oltz, "and look what happens! And look at this mess!"

The girl was now sobbing uncontrollably.

"Please!" Molly tried to inject.

"Just let me handle this," Mrs. Oltz threw up a hand to silence Molly. "I'll get to the bottom of this." She turned back to Cheryl. "Now stop your sniveling, girl."

Cheryl cried louder and Mrs. Oltz grabbed her and shook her. Molly was dumbfounded. She thought Mrs. Oltz was going to slap her. Why did I leave Danny here, thought Molly, why?

"When did Danny Driscoll leave?" she demanded.

"But he didn't! Let go of me!" Cheryl tried to struggle free.

"Well, he couldn't just disappear," said Mrs. Oltz, releasing her grip. "You kept the door locked, like you were supposed to, right?"

Cheryl nodded.

"I want to call the other parents," Molly said. "The police are on their way."

"The police? The police?" Mrs. Oltz looked daggers at Molly, then turned on Cheryl.

"I called them," said Molly defiantly. Just then a patrol car screeched up in front.

"Come on, let's just *all* calm down." Officer Richie Pellegrino held up his hands. All three women were shouting at once and he couldn't understand a word. "There's probably a real simple explanation." He was a short, barrel-chested man with a belly that arched over the wide belt holding his equipment. The cop looked vaguely familiar to Molly. She had met him somewhere, somehow in the past, but for the moment couldn't place him.

"Okay," said the cop, "Who was on duty here?"

"I was," said Cheryl. "And I saw every parent who came in."

"Then he should still be here!" Molly jumped in. "His jacket and lunch box are still here. Look!" She held them up. "But he's not!"

"What about the father?" asked Pellegrino.

"There is none," said Molly not missing a beat.

"Grandparents. Other relatives who might—"

"No, no."

"Or a—"

"No! I'm the only one." Molly jabbed a finger deeply into her chest until it ached.

"I'm gonna need a good description of the boy." Pellegrino took out his pad and started jotting notes. "You got a picture on you?"

Molly fumbled through her wallet. "This is old. He was only a baby here. I got a better one—"

"This'll do the for the moment."

"Look, we're losing time just standing here." Molly pleaded, "If someone kidnapped Danny, he could already be miles away."

"*Kidnapped?*" echoed Mrs. Oltz indignantly. "No one's kidnapped anyone!"

"But I was watching—" Cheryl tried to chime in.

"Whoa! Hold on everybody," Pellegrino said. "Let's just do this one step at a time." His radio squawked and he mumbled something into the mike clipped to his collar. "Give me a description."

Molly raced through it. Every last detail. From his curly blond hair to the sneakers he was wearing—those expensive Nikes that she had finally broken down and bought for Danny, the ones with the green *whoosh* on the side that he called "wings."

Pellegrino, scribbling, could hardly keep up with her.

"*Please,*" Molly begged. "Do something. *Fast!*"

"Don't worry. All the units picked up this call. Hang on," he said, and turned back to his mike. "Blond four-year-old. 'Bout forty-five pounds. Last seen wearing denim overalls. Red flannel shirt. White and green sneakers…"

When he finished, he turned to Molly. "Look, I know you're worried. My boys were little once, too, you know," he said gently. "But kids have a way of getting into things. It usually isn't as bad as it first looks. We'll get everything ironed out. You'll see."

Molly had never liked cops. As a kid growing up in Ithaca, she had been dragged in a couple of times. Once for shoplifting some lipstick up at the mall, and once for drinking beer at the falls near the high school. The kids she was hanging out with were always getting hassled, too. The cops in town had always struck her as cold and robot-like. They got their kicks out of busting you. This guy, with his soft blue eyes and silvery temples, however, actually seemed to care and she desperately wanted to trust him.

"When was the last time anyone saw him and where?" he inquired as he pulled out his notepad.

"I left at two o'clock, and he was right there," said Mrs. Oltz pointing emphatically. "On the floor. By that toy box. Playing with two other kids. It was the Ruzicka boy and Patty Bruce. They built a fort out of blocks. And they had a fire truck. They were playing war, and they were getting wild. So I had to get them to pipe down."

Molly found herself wondering if Mrs. Oltz was in the habit of bullying the children as she had just done with Cheryl.

"I remember them playing, too," agreed Cheryl. Holding her breath, Molly turned to look at her. "And then, about an hour later," she went on, "I had them clean up so we could have story time."

"We always try to get the kids to calm down before the parents start arriving," added Mrs. Oltz.

"Was he there—with the other kids?" asked Molly.

"Yeah," said Cheryl, "I remember him sitting there. He was joking with the Lifsey boy. Stevie. They kept poking each other and I had to ask them to be quiet so the other kids could hear."

"And then?" urged Molly.

"And then the parents came. And, well…" Cheryl became agitated and her eyes started to well with tears again. "And then…then…he just wasn't there!"

Molly stared at her and felt empty.

"Let me take a look around," said Pellegrino, pulling a long, black flashlight from his leather belt and heading toward the kitchen. Molly followed. The thing in his hand looked more like a club than a light. "Sometimes a kid'll just curl up and go to sleep somewhere. You find them and they're perfectly okay."

"But I just searched the place. *Everywhere.*" Molly was trying to keep up with him as he strode through the debris cluttering the sticky floor.

Pellegrino kicked aside some pots, opened a cabinet and checked it with his light. "Okay, but I gotta do it, too. Follow procedures," he explained as he moved from cabinet to cabinet. Down on his knees, he shined his light behind the fridge. Then he was back into the hallway.

"Are they really out looking for Danny?"

"Yeah. Of course." He climbed over the tangle of brooms and mops and overturned buckets as he waded into the storage closet. "We take missing kids very seriously." He moved past her as if remembering something and went back into the kitchen and stared up at the ceiling. With a grunt he heaved himself up on one of the counters, pulling up one leg at a time until he was standing, his head touching the ceiling. He played the beam across the top of the cabinets. "Hey, anybody check up in here?" he asked, poking the trap door near his head.

Molly shook her head. He pushed open the portal and hoisted himself into the attic. Molly could hear his radio crackling as he rummaged around overhead, moving and sliding what sounded like boxes.

When he came down, the dark blue of his uniform was littered with tufts of dust and strands of pink insulation. Coughing, he haphazardly brushed himself off and went systematically again from room to room. "Hey, what's this door?" he asked finding the basement. "Anybody check down here?"

As he emerged from the cellar, Molly was waiting at the top of the stairs. "Okay," she inquired, hands on her hips. "Now what?"

Pellegrino was sweating. He took off his hat and wiped his forehead. His gray hair was clipped in a brush cut, like Molly's father used to have. She thought about her father, a man she could only remember as unsmiling, depressed, eyes vacant except when he was drunk and angry—which was often; her mother who had died without ever seeing Danny. Danny, oh God! The evocation of his name caused something to seize up in her breast.

"I just called in," said Pellegrino, seeing the look on her face. "We got three units out there now just searching for your boy."

"I'm calling the other parents," said Molly.

"Yeah, yeah, good idea," said Pellegrino.

"Let me call them," said Mrs. Oltz, trying to take charge. "I don't want to start getting people all riled up."

"Give me the fucking numbers," demanded Molly, holding out her hand.

Mrs. Oltz meekly handed over the school directory.

The route up South Hill past the old Morse Chain factory is steep, an unrelenting incline as the narrowness of Aurora Street spreads into the four-lane highway that is Route 96B. It's a demanding climb for the little boy whose face has been whipped red by the cold wind coming off the lake. The sun, obscured at times by billowing clouds, hovers low above the horizon; the air is damp and smells pungently of vegetative decay and vehicle exhaust.

The afternoon shift at Therm, where they machine the blades

for aircraft turbines, has just let out and the highway is jammed with the cars of workers anxious to get home. Delivery vans and tanker trucks headed through town are interspersed with the Sport Utes of Ithaca College kids on their way down to the Commons or out to the mall.

The boy stops momentarily as if attempting to gain his bearings. He turns to gaze down at the rooftops of the city nestled in the valley below. Shivering with cold, he wrinkles his brow in thought, then pushes on up the highway. Vehicles continue to whisk past, whipping up clouds of blinding dust and sand.

Further on, the boy cuts diagonally across the highway, prompting the sleepy driver of a large tractor trailer to slam on his air brakes. The line of traffic behind him jerks to a reflexive halt. No one seems to notice the boy, except as an obstacle to be avoided. No one gets out to confront him or question him. It is as if he were invisible.

Once across the highway, the boy slides down the embankment and pushes through the shrubbery. Now he is moving through the backyards of neatly kept Tudors and gingerbread Victorians, his feet shuffling through lawns deep in crisp fallen leaves. Here the air smells clean, the surroundings feel less frenzied. The boy's features become more relaxed. But he continues to climb the hill, moving ever upward.

"Mrs. Lifsey? Dianne? This is Molly Driscoll. You may not know me. My boy Danny goes to Kute Kids?" Molly fought to keep her voice from wavering as she talked into the phone in the hallway, the roster of names quivering in her hands. Cheryl and Mrs. Oltz, positioned on either side, listened anxiously. Through the plate glass window, Molly watched Pellegrino outside leaning into a squad car that just pulled up onto the sidewalk. Please dear God, she silently prayed, let him be with one of the other kids.

"Is Danny with you?"

"With *me?*" exclaimed Mrs. Lifsey, her voice leaping an octave. "Why in the world would Danny be with me? What's wrong?"

"I'm at Kute Kids. I came to pick him up and he's not—"

"Oh my!" gasped Mrs. Lifsey, then caught herself. "Maybe he just went…"

"Did you see Danny when you came to pick up Stevie? You know, he's…"

"Sure I know Danny. Stevie plays with him and—"

"Look, just tell me if you…"

There was a momentary silence.

"Mrs. Lifsey? Dianne?"

"I'm trying to think. I'm trying…I remember seeing him in the morning. He was there when I brought Stevie. He was wearing a…a red plaid kind of shirt?"

"Yes. Yes. That's right."

"And when I picked up Stevie…"

"Yeah?"

"I didn't see him."

"When did you pick him up?"

"She was here about five," whispered Cheryl. "There were still others here."

"Sometime just after five," confirmed Mrs. Lifsey.

Molly called Tanya Dawson. Molly knew her from her days waitressing at the Ramada. Tanya, who worked in the kitchen, had twin girls in Kute Kids. Their father was the assistant manager at Midas Muffler. The girls were coffee-colored and wore their hair in cornrows. Tanya always dressed them like little dolls.

"Oh, yeah, sure Molly, I 'member you. Howya doin'? Where you workin' now?"

"Look, Tanya, I got a serious problem. My little boy vanished from Kute Kids."

Mrs. Oltz rolled her eyes in silent protest while Cheryl chewed her nails.

Molly quickly filled Tanya in. "Did you see him today when you came by?"

"Sure. In the morning. When I dropped off Keisha and Aisha. Hey, haul' on a secon.' Wait! Gordy had to go back and bring 'em lunch. Gordy! You know Molly? Tha' girl that used…Yeah. Yeah. Her little boy is missin' from—"

She could hear Gordy in the background saying, "No shit. *Missing?*" Molly had seen him over at Midas a couple of times.

Gordy came on the phone. "Yeah, I know your boy. Little wild guy with that big mop of curly hair. The kids call him Salad Head."

"That's him," Molly choked a laugh.

"Sure, I saw him at lunch. He was eating a sandwich."

"Then?"

"I left the girls their lunch. You know, lunch is expensive there, and me and Tanya…"

"Sure. Sure."

"That's all I know. Geez, we hope you find him."

Molly kept moving down the list. She called Bea Bruce's number. Bea was a single mother who worked the production line at Borg-Warner. Molly knew her from high school.

A strange man answered. "Whatta you selling?" he asked gruffly.

"I'm not selling anything. I just want to talk to—"

"Well, she's not in," he said and hung up.

Molly called right back.

"Hey, I told you already. We don' wan' any!"

"Oh, God," said Molly, holding the phone aloft in despair. "He just hung up on me again!"

Pellegrino was just coming back in the door. "Hey, if you can't get through just give us the name and we'll take care of it."

Molly kept calling. People remembered Danny, or couldn't quite place him. Saw him that morning, or didn't. The further down the list she got, the more her anxiety grew. A couple of parents were out and she left her number on their machines.

"Now what?" she asked, as much for her own benefit as the room's.

Mrs. Oltz was uncharacteristically subdued.

"I'm so sorry," said Cheryl. "I don't know how this could have happened."

"Every unit's got a description of him," said Pellegrino, handing her a missing persons form to sign. "We're checking the neighborhood. We're talking to anyone who might have noticed anything."

Looking out the window, Molly could see that there was yet another squad car on the opposite side of State Street. It stood in front of the bar. A young policeman was talking to a squat middle-aged man she recognized as the owner of the tavern. The cop was consulting his pad while the other man stood with his hands on his hips.

"Why don't you go home," said Pellegrino, taking her gently by the arm and leading her toward the door. "If you're near the phone, at least we can get you when he turns up."

She noticed that he said *when* not *if,* and, although she was thankful for the kindness, she started to cry.

"Hey, come on, Mrs. Driscoll," he said, and she could feel his beefy arm around her shoulders. When she turned, she saw how Pellegrino was watching her, his lips drawn in a tight, worried line. "We're on top of this. It'll all be fine. You'll see."

chapter two

Molly got into her car and pulled slowly up the street. Could Danny have just slipped out? she wondered. Maybe he tried to make it home on his own?

Molly drove a half-dozen blocks east, heading up State Street, and then realized he would never have gone this way, a little boy tackling a steep hill like this. She yanked a sharp U-turn and plunged down back into the valley and toward Route 13.

It was getting darker and harder to see. A few snowflakes hit her windshield. Snow in October? she thought. How bizarre. And Danny without even a jacket. As Molly merged into traffic, she tried to imagine Danny walking along the edge of the busy highway. She slowed down, trailing along the right shoulder, her eyes constantly flipping to the far side of the road.

Her trailer was dark and empty and there was no sign of Danny anywhere in the park. She turned her car around and headed back into town, tracing yet another path to the daycare.

For the better part of an hour, Molly kept driving compulsively back and forth, weaving through the city streets now turning vacant, a fine snow powdering the sidewalks and streets. She kept thinking of Danny, their last minutes together in the morning.

"Are you sure you're okay?" she had asked as they hurried up the sidewalk leading to Kute Kids. Daylight was struggling to break through the thick overcast and the air had a bone-chilling dampness which she knew would linger until spring.

Danny had yawned sleepily. His hands were ice cold and she detected a shiver. When Molly touched his forehead, he felt hot. "We could stay home," she had ventured tentatively, checking her watch. God, she was really late. Again.

"And go fishing?" He peered up at her with his big eyes, dark and almond shaped. It caused her to pause, almost forget time. For an instant he brightened, a smile beginning to play on his beautiful lips, his baby teeth so even and small. "And we could get some pizza, too. 'Stead of this." He lifted his lunch box that he had spent hours carefully decorating. Already the stickers were coming loose in the corners. "I told you a hunnerd times. I don't like peanut butter."

"Sweetie, are you feeling sick? I don't have a lot of time. We've got to make a quick decision. Should I take you home? Or do you just want pizza?"

"I'm sick *and* I want pizza," he said emphatically, but his head drooped as if he were suddenly embarrassed to have made a demand on her. "Anyhow, you can't stay home. You could lose your job." And then what would we do? thought Molly.

When Molly had stooped down to come close, Danny had surprised her by throwing his arms around her neck and giving her a wet kiss. "I have the prettiest Mommy of any of the kids here," he had whispered in her ear.

"I have the smartest, best-looking boy of all the kids in the world—but that's our secret," she said, nuzzling her apple-cheeked boy.

Molly had given him a quick kiss and then, taking him by the hand, hurried with him up the last yards to the daycare. There never seemed to be enough time in a day for him no matter how much she rushed or how little she slept. And now he was missing and Molly was beginning to wonder if she would ever have the chance to make it up to him. Damn it! she kept cursing herself, why didn't

I just let him sleep in, keep him home this morning? Did I have to drag him off sick to daycare?

As the darkness settled in, Molly slowly filled with a sense of nauseous dread. She kept darting from the telephone to the window, waiting for the call that didn't come, then peering out into the approaching night.

She tried to reach her friend Rosie, but no one was home. And they still didn't have an answering machine. How many times had she told Rosie to get a lousy machine? At last the mercury vapor lights came on in the trailer park, flooding the neighboring mobile homes in a white, sepulchral light. What if someone had taken Danny? One of those real sickies? At this very moment he could be abusing him, torturing him. Or worse. There was that little boy whose father started that television program, *America's Most Wanted*. They found his severed head in a canal. "Oh, God!" she caught herself. Danny had to be all right. There had to be a simple, obvious explanation! Damn! Where the hell were the police when you really needed them? Probably out giving parking tickets. People were getting raped and murdered while those idiots worried about alternate side of the street parking! Then Molly thought of that nice cop, Pellegrino, and her anger ebbed away, leaving her empty inside.

She paced the length of the little trailer, back and forth, the floor reverberating with each footfall. Outside, the wind was blowing hard and she could hear it whistling through the cracks in the window. The sink was dripping, both the hot and cold side—and the shower. The landlord wouldn't allow Danny to have a kitten because it might mess up his precious dump! A tin box so small, so narrow, you could stand in the living room and just about touch either wall. It smelled of rot. She felt her face flush as she surveyed her cramped little home.

In the bedroom she shared with Danny, some of his toys were still scattered on the floor from the previous night—his beloved Nerf gun, his assorted Hot Wheels, a pile of stray Legos near a windmill he had built. Danny's picture—the one she had gotten on special at Penney's last Christmas—sat on top of the dresser. She reached for the photo and suddenly burst into tears.

Molly's mouth was sore from chewing on the inside of her lips. She didn't know how much more of this she could tolerate. The police had told her to sit tight. Sit tight and *what?*

At least, if Gordy Dawson was right, Danny had eaten lunch. But by now he was probably famished. Peanut butter. He didn't even like his last sandwich, she thought, wretchedly. Couldn't she have at least taken the time to have done something better? A BLT, which he loved. On toast. It was now more than seven hours since he…Hell, a kid didn't starve by just missing a meal! she reminded herself.

Molly picked up the phone and called Bea Bruce again. This time she got her machine.

"Hi, you've reached the home of Bea and Patty Bruce," announced a little girl. "We're not here to take your call right now, but if you leave your…" The message went on and on. She waited for the beep.

"Hello, this is Molly Driscoll calling. This is an emergency. Please call me as soon as you get in. My boy Danny is missing from Kute Kids. It's now 7:30, and there's still no sign of him."

Please, dear God, prayed Molly—who no more believed in God than in the tooth fairy—if there's any justice in this miserable world, please bring him back to me. I'll do anything, anything. Just let him be safe. Let him be out with Bea Bruce having a hamburger at Wendy's. Or with the Ruzickas.

She tried the Ruzickas again. They didn't have an answering machine. She hoped the cops were out there ringing doorbells and beating the pavement. She hoped to God that they knew what they were doing. She dialed the city police.

"Ithaca Police Department, Officer Sisler speaking."

"It's me," she said, gripping the phone so tightly her knuckles felt they might pop. "I just wanna know what you turned up—"

"Look, Mrs. Driscoll, we talked just ten minutes ago. Nothing's—"

"Well, it feels like ten years—"

"Could you hold on?" She could hear the other line beeping.

"Don't leave!" she cried. "Please!"

"Hang on, it could be about your boy."

Silence weighed heavily.

"Well?" she asked when he came back on.

"Naw. Somebody complaining about a dog barking."

"*What*," she screamed. "You're worried about a dog when a little boy—"

"Hey, lady, just hold on—"

Molly caught herself. Here she was attacking the only people who could possibly help her. "I'm sorry," she murmured, suppressing a sob. "I didn't really mean…I'm just…"

"I understand," Sisler said softly.

No you don't, thought Molly bitterly. Not really. No one can, unless it happens to them. Something is terribly wrong, and nobody's doing anything. "I'm at my wits end," she said quietly.

"We're doing our best. It may seem to you like nothing's going on, but we're all over it."

"What's your name?"

"Officer Sisler."

"No, your *name*."

"Jerry."

"Jerry," she repeated. "You got kids?"

"Not yet. Just got married. But my brother has three. Look, I can imagine."

"Okay, then why haven't you pulled the State Police in? And the F.B.I.?"

"Because it's in our jurisdiction. Look, we've got a top-notch investigative unit. They know what they're doing. And anyway, the troopers monitor us. They know we're looking for your boy. They've got the full description. Just hang in there. Please. Something will turn up."

Something will turn up. It sounded like a body surfacing in the lake. Canal. Body. Danny. Oh, Lord!

The phone book lay on the table next to the telephone open to the first page, where all the emergency numbers were listed. She depressed the button on the phone just long enough to get a new dial tone. What the hell, Molly thought, so I step on a few toes. She called the nearby State Police barracks. Molly had never been crazy about them either. With their gray uniforms and tall shiny boots, they reminded her of those storm troopers in old movies.

"State Police."

"This is Molly Driscoll. My boy's the one that disappeared from the daycare in Ithaca?"

"Yeah?" said the trooper on the other end of the line. His tone did little to reassure her.

"You know about him, right?"

"Let me see, I just got on duty about an hour ago." He was shuffling papers.

An hour ago and he obviously didn't know. Molly could feel her anger rising again. "The Ithaca Police told me that they were in direct contact with you. That you monitor their calls."

"Yeah. We do." A radio squawked. "One second," he said. Molly could hear him talking in the background. Then he was back.

"So?" she asked.

"I'm sorry," he apologized. "We were talking about—?"

"We're talking about my boy! Danny Driscoll. It looks like he's been kidnapped!"

"And the Ithaca Police are covering it?"

"Covering *it?* I wouldn't go that far. I don't know what they're covering."

"Happened in the city?"

"Yes, but—"

"Well, that's the agency that has the case. It's their jurisdiction. But we'll gladly assist them if they need additional help—if they request it."

Molly took a deep breath and let it out in a noisy, frustrated exhalation.

"Why don't you fill me in and—Wait! Here it is. Yeah. Blond curly hair. Blue eyes. Five years old. About sixty pounds.

"*No!* Brown eyes. Brown! And he's *almost* five and weighs forty-five—not sixty!"

"Why don't you just give me the description again, and I'll call all my units. All right?"

"Sure," she said, sinking down on the sofa. As a young girl she had had a recurrent dream in which she was standing chest deep in a lake and there was a snake pursuing her. She was always pushing through the water, trying to make it to shore, but knew that the snake could swim faster. Somehow this felt just like that.

Molly began from scratch. Eye color. Height. Clothes. All the salient details. But how could you convey the feel of his body touching hers when he crawled into her bed and slept pressed tight to her. His skin silky smooth. His sleeping face serene, angelic, even his smell, clean and milky. The way his eyebrows wrinkled in dreams as he sucked his thumb.

"I'll get this right out."

"How about your getting it out while I stay on the phone—not that I don't trust you or anything."

"If it makes you feel better."

"It does. Please."

Molly stayed on the line and listened. She picked up bits and pieces. Five-year-old. Last seen in Ithaca…wearing…

"Thanks," she said when the trooper was finished. "Listen, take my number. You find out anything, call *me* right away."

"I will."

"I mean like anything. *Anything.* I don't care what it is."

She went to the window and peered out again. It was dark. A light snow had just started falling; she could see the flakes drifting down under the bright arc lamps. The rutted road through the trailer park was wet, but the snow was sticking on the little patch of dirt and grass in front of the Potters' trailer where their kids used to play—before the parents were arrested for dealing dope and Social Services seized both kids. Potter and his wife were out on bail, she knew from the *Journal,* but the two boys were still in some foster home. Their bicycles and toys lay abandoned in the yard, slowly disappearing under wet snow. It was cold outside, real cold, and Danny didn't even have his jacket. Just a flimsy flannel shirt.

Molly looked out the window on the opposite wall. In another trailer a big, heavy woman who she didn't know was washing dishes, a cigarette dangling from her lips. She was wearing a leotard top, and her pendulous breasts swung over the sink as she scrubbed a pot. A motorcycle sat parked in front, the snow building up on the seat. Through the closed window, Molly could hear the dull thud of a stereo, the monotonous beat of hard rock, each beat counting off the seconds. Every minute that Danny was gone seemed to diminish his chance of return.

Molly's thoughts swirled back in time to other crises. Chuck packing his bags just as they were prepping her for her C-section. That irresponsible bastard!

Disasters always seemed to come in clusters. She had developed complications, a post-operative infection. They had cut her open a second time. Two weeks later, Molly had emerged from the hospital wobbly and weak. They had packed her into a cab she had barely enough money to pay for. Forget the doctor and hospital bills. Forget the truck, too—Chuck had taken that. She came home to discover that he hadn't paid the mortgage in months—though he said he had—nor the utility bills.

She had strung out the creditors, but three weeks after she was home and before she could get back on her feet or land a job, the bank took their little house. Chuck had forgotten to mention the eviction notice. The sheriff's people carried her furniture out of the house and plopped it on the front lawn for the entire neighborhood to see. As it sat there swelling in the rain, she picked up Danny, a few clothes, and marched away. Screw the furniture. It was all beaver board from Sears and she had never really liked it anyhow.

That very afternoon, with the help of a storefront lawyer, she started divorce proceedings against Chuck and declared bankruptcy. He was still running up bills—in *their* names! She had married him because she thought he was a romantic. He would unexpectedly bring flowers. Take her nights dancing—and boy could he move, swiveling his tightly muscled body as if he had been given extra joints. In the slow numbers, she would cling to him as he crooned softly in her ear. He knew all the country lyrics about jilted lovers and being a one woman man. By the end of the evening she was so hot and bothered Molly couldn't wait to get home and lunge into bed with him. Some romantic he turned out to be.

"Look, there's not much we can do about the house," Alex Greenhut, her young lawyer, had said stroking his wispy beard. "And we can't worry about that now. First thing we've got to do is get a roof over your head. Your heads," he added, looking at the baby cradled in her lap. Her dripping suitcase was standing in a corner. "You obviously qualify for—"

Molly knew what he was going to suggest. "No way," she snapped back, looking him fiercely in the eye. "I may be in a bad way right now, but I've got some pride."

"Sure," he said quietly, never missing a beat, "but sometimes a person's got to swallow that and deal with the realities."

Without another word, he picked up the phone and called Social Services. "Hey," he said afterwards, seeing the look on her face. "If you feel guilty, you can always send them a check when you're back on your feet. And me, too, while you're at it," he added with a compassionate smile. He was a godsend and for a short time Molly thought she was in love with young Alex Greenhut.

They found her a place to live, a trailer in a park north of town. It was rundown and filthy from the previous tenants, but she cleaned it up, grateful to have a warm place for herself and the baby. They put her on Medicaid and gave her food stamps, which she hated and never got used to. Every time she bought groceries and had to pull out that book of stamps, Molly could feel her face flushing and her hands trembling. But, like Alex used to say, you do what you gotta do. But she didn't do it for herself. She did it for Danny.

She took up the phone.

"Ithaca Police, Officer—" a voice started at the far end of the line.

"Jerry," she said, cutting him off.

"You? We talked just—"

"Look, I can't just sit here."

"But—"

"But nothing. I'm going to see what I can do. If you find him, or find out anything, call me here and leave a message. I'm going to keep checking in with you, too."

"Listen—"

"Listen nothing. The State Police didn't know diddly about him."

"How—"

"I called them. Look, I'm not blaming anyone. I just gotta do what I can. And you guys have got to keep looking. Okay?"

"Okay."

Molly hung up. She took Danny's picture from the dresser, stripped off the backing, and slipped the photo out of its frame. She snatched up her coat where it lay by the door and headed out into the snowy night. It was wet and heavy and kept coming down. Snow? It was not even November yet! Chrissake, the leaves were still on the trees! What the hell was this world coming to?

Molly hurried back down the hill towards town, driving as fast as she dared on the slick roads. Restaurants, she thought. Or shopping. Of course. It was just a hunch, but if people weren't home, where else could they be? Either up at the mall or eating—or both. There wasn't much else to do in town on a weeknight. She had bumped into the Ruzickas a number of times, and they had never struck her as particularly prosperous. The husband had a beer belly and grease under his fingernails. His wife, Molly knew, worked up at the University doing something in maintenance or cleaning—not a professor or anything. People who sent their little ones to Kute Kids weren't exactly the crème de la crème of Ithaca. Which meant that she could eliminate the fancy eating places with linen table cloths and waiters.

Since the Ruzickas lived downtown, Molly headed first to the shopping strip on Elmira Road. The snow was now coming down in globs, and her worn wipers made a streaky mess of the windshield. The outside world took on a surrealistic look, lights and glistening pavement fractured and smeared by the melting snow, the images refracted through her tears. It was hard following the street, but the fast food places were so brightly lit that you'd have to be blind not to see them.

She pulled right into Pizza Hut, abandoning her car with the engine still going, blocking a line of neatly parked cars. Pushing through the glass door, she dashed among the maze of tables. People looked up in surprise as she skidded on the slippery floor from one end of the restaurant to the other. The teenagers behind the counter looked stunned. She even checked out the bathrooms, both the women's and the men's.

Before anyone could react, she was back in the car, driving down the strip to Wendy's. When it was all over with Danny safely back home, she knew she would laugh about her escapades. She'd tell the story to Rosie about how people had gawked at her with her wet hair plastered to her face, as if she were going to pull out a sawed-off shotgun.

It was a lousy night and Wendy's was nearly empty. So was Burger King and McDonald's and Taco Bell. Arby's was deserted, too. In fact, it was closed: "Bankrupt" said a sign on the door. She checked the supermarkets. Ran up and down the long aisles of Tops and then Wegman's—both upstairs and down. Molly backtracked into town and drove up the steep incline of Buffalo Street towards Collegetown, her car fishtailing in the snow. Not a chance that the Ruzickas would eat there with all those college kids, but Molly had an idea.

College Avenue was crowded with sports cars, stereos thundering, willowy girls with their hats on backward driving chunky utility vehicles. There wasn't a single parking slot near Kinko's. Molly double-parked, blocking in a new BMW.

In the copy shop, a bunch of students waited for service. She skirted them all and marched to the head of the line. Pressing herself against the counter, she called out to a pimply kid with glasses who was working three clattering copiers at once. "Hey!"

The students behind grumbled.

The guy at the machines gave a dismissive toss of his head. "I'll be there in a—"

"Now!" she shouted. "Now! This is an emergency."

The kid's head swung around, startled.

"Hurry!" said Molly.

"Geez," he said coming to the counter. "What's the big—?"

"I need copies of this," She held out Danny's picture. "And right away."

The guy took the photo and looked at it. The shop had fallen silent and everyone was watching Molly. "Copies. Lots of them," she repeated. "My little boy's been kidnapped!"

Behind her she could hear the patrons buzzing as the word "kidnapped" made the rounds of the shop.

"Sure," he said. "You wan' color or black and white?"

"Whatever. Black and—no, color. Wait, what do they cost?" She rummaged through her purse. By the time she figured out how much she had, the guy was already at a machine. He hit a button and the thing started spewing out perfect color copies, layer upon layer of smiling Dannys.

"I don't have that much money with me," she explained when he rushed back with the pile. There must have been a hundred pictures in his hand. It was at times like this that she wished the bank hadn't revoked her credit cards. "But I can—"

"Forget it," he said with a wave, surprising her. "I just hope you find your kid."

The students were all craning toward the pile in Molly's hand, muttering and shaking their heads.

Molly held up the picture for all to view. "If any of you see this boy, please call the Ithaca police right away. Okay?"

The store turned utterly somber. A young woman nodded. Then everybody followed suit, nodding and mumbling a yeah, yes, sure, of course.

Incredibly, she found the Ruzickas. They were in the mall, up in the food court eating quickie Chinese. Spotting them from across the central arcade, Molly's heart started pounding. Her eyes swept the immediate vicinity. There sat the parents with their little boy and their school-age daughter, the four of them hunched over their Styrofoam containers, shoveling in some stringy green mess with noodles. Just the four of them. No sign of Danny.

Wading obliviously through crisscrossing lines of people, Molly took a deep breath as she approached them.

"Hi," she called out as she neared their table.

The whole family looked up blankly.

"I'm Molly Driscoll. You know, Danny Driscoll's mother?" She shifted her attention from mother to father and finally to the little boy. None of them seemed to register this. It was as if everything were moving in slow motion. "My boy goes to Kute Kids."

"Oh, yeah," said Bonnie Ruzicka finally. She was a big-hipped woman with round face and oversized glasses. "Kevin goes there, too, don't you?"

"Huh?" said the little kid.

"My boy's missing."

"*Missing?*" echoed Bonnie.

"Might have been kidnapped," said Molly, finally getting their attention.

"No shit!" said the husband.

"*George!*" said the woman, admonishing him.

"Sorry about the French," George apologized.

"I'm trying to find out if anybody has any ideas about where Danny might be, who he went with, or who took him or…" she pulled out one of the pictures from her open purse.

"That's Danny," piped the boy, pointing with his bony little finger.

"Yes, that's right, Honey," said Molly eagerly. She remembered what Mrs. Oltz had said about their playing together after lunch. Molly moved closer to him and stooped down, bringing herself to eye level with him. "Is Danny your friend?"

He picked up his Coke, drew on the straw, and nodded, his mouth still sucking.

"Did you play with him today?"

The boy nodded again, his mouth still on the straw. Now he was both drinking and blowing bubbles into his soda.

"And what did you play?"

The boy, still attached to the straw, shrugged.

"Talk to the lady, Kevin," warned George. He pulled the boy's soda away.

"I dunno," mumbled Kevin, looking like a whipped puppy. He kept his eyes lowered, his legs rhythmically swinging against the table supports.

"Mrs. Driscoll is worried about her little boy," said Bonnie. "Howdya think I'd feel if you was disappeared?"

"I dunno," said Kevin, his knees still striking the table.

"Stop whacking the table and look at the lady when she talks to you!"

"Let me," urged Molly. "Kevin," Molly addressed him, gently placing her hand on his leg in an effort to quiet the agitated banging. He felt thin and his knees were all sharp angles. His jeans were frayed and torn and his shirt was two sizes too big. "You were playing with Danny on the floor today, weren't you? And you were having a good time, right?" Molly smiled and held his eye.

"Yup," he answered and grinned tentatively back at her, his glance then shifting towards his parents as if checking for approval. He stopped wiggling his legs.

"And were you playing war?"

"Nope. Fire and amulance."

"I'll bet it was real exciting. I know Danny loves to make accidents and have the police and fire trucks come—"

"And amulances, too."

"And ambulances."

The whole family was smiling now.

"But Cheryl, she made us clean up."

"Because it was story time?"

"A dumb baby story about some stupid, fat elephant."

"And Danny was there?"

"Yes. And Stevie. And them two kept laughing. And then Cheryl sent Danny to stand in the kitchen by hisself. But he wasn't bad. He was just having fun. It was really Stevie was the bad one."

"In the kitchen," reiterated Molly as much for her own benefit.

"Kitchen," Kevin repeated and then turned his attention to the chow mein which had congealed into a gelatinous gob. With his plastic fork he played with it, mounding it high and watching the glop ooze down the slopes of the hill.

"And then?"

"He kept sticking his head out. And making these faces. And doing funny things. Like this," Kevin put his index fingers into his mouth and spread the corners of his lips while extending his tongue. "And everybody was laughing!" Kevin giggled.

"And what did Cheryl do?"

"She told him to stop."

"And?"

"He did. But then he started being silly again."

"So?"

"She put him in the basement."

"*The basement?*" gasped Bonny.

"What the fuck kind of place is that?" demanded George.

"Daddy," said the girl, speaking for the first time. "You're not—"

Molly tried to stay calm, though her immediate urge was to find Cheryl and wrap her fingers around the girl's throat. No wonder she hadn't given straight answers. "Kevin," Molly went on, struggling to keep her voice level. "Did she let him up? Out of the basement?"

He looked at her. Shrugged.

"Did he come up? Try and remember, it's important."

The boy wrinkled his forehead. "I dunno."

"Come on Kevin," said his father gruffly. "Out with it. Did he come up or didn't he?"

"I dunno. I dunno," the boy looked as if he was going to cry.

"That's okay," said Molly getting to her feet and ruffling the boy's hair. Even his head was bony. "You've been a big help." She turned to the rest of the family. "Who picked Kevin up today?"

"Me and Amy," said Bonnie Ruzicka motioning to her taciturn daughter with the stringy hair. "It was 'bout five. George waited in the truck."

"I was listening to the news," George chimed in.

"Was Danny there then?"

"I didn't see him. No...I'm sure of that. I've got a good memory. I did see him in the morning, though. There were maybe six or seven other kids there when I dropped Kevin off. He had on this red shirt." She turned to her daughter. "You see her little boy when we picked up Kevin?"

The girl shrugged. "I dunno," she said, sounding remarkably like her brother.

chapter three

By nine o'clock, Detective Lou Tripoli had taken on the case. He had been monitoring the radio since the call about the Driscoll kid had first come in at dinnertime. Richie Pellegrino was in the State Diner on a coffee break and Tripoli swung over across town to meet him.

Shaking the snow off his coat, he headed for the grill where Pellegrino sat hunched over the counter.

"What a weird night," said Lois Cassaniti, one of the regulars, as Tripoli passed her stool. Lois took a puff of her cigarette and let the smoke trail skyward.

"Yeah, I'm not ready for this."

"We've had early snows, but never like this. This early."

"Hey," said Tripoli with a lopsided grin as he slid into the vacant seat next to Pellegrino. "I don't believe this. You're actually eating doughnuts?"

"They're good, Trip. Fresh," Pellegrino talked with a full mouth. "Hey, Kesh, another coffee here," he called over to Sam Keshishoglou, who was busy working the grill. "And a couple more of these things," he held up a doughnut powdered with sugar. The front of his uniform was coated with a fine layer of its dust.

"What's going on?" asked Lou.

"I'm not sure," said Pellegrino. "You never know in these things. But it's getting to be a long time now. That's not a good sign. Mother's freaking out. Calling the switchboard every ten minutes."

"What would you do?"

"Same, probably," agreed Pellegrino. "Probably more."

"The mother?"

"Driscoll. Molly Driscoll."

"Driscoll?" Tripoli scratched his head. Then he made the connection. "That's the girl who…?"

"Hell-raiser when she was younger. I knew her ever since she was that high," Pellegrino held his hand out to the level of his stool. "She'd be out on the streets at all hours of the night. Her old lady never gave a shit. I got called to Andrew's candy store a couple of times—you remember that old place?" Pellegrino smiled to himself. "Somehow she had snaked her hand around the counter and into one of the cases. She must have swiped a full pound of these chocolate-covered walnuts. But by the time I got there she had already consumed all the evidence. Couldn't see taking her in just because she had chocolate on her breath." He laughed. "Probably was just plain hungry. So I punished her for stealing."

"Huh?" said Tripoli, turning.

"Yeah, I bought her a hamburger and a Coke." The corners of Pellegrino's eyes wrinkled when he smiled. "She was a hell of a smart little girl as I recall. Kind of cute. Maybe a bit of a wiseass, too. Used to throw stuff and then duck behind a tree every time she spotted my car—though I don't know if she remembered me today."

Tripoli tried to conjure up her image. He had seen her around town as a teenager, then as a young woman. "I thought she got married or something?"

"Did. The guy took off on her and she took back her old name, I guess."

"Molly Driscoll. Sure. Yeah, yeah. I remember her." Long dark hair and dark eyes. Bright looking woman with an interesting sort of edge to her. She was petite, but well proportioned; a bit shorter than he was, which didn't exactly make her tall. As he recalled, she was a touch on the muscular side, but just enough to make her shapely. A bit of a firecracker, she was. "Molly went to high school with my little brother, Freddy. Real good looking. And sharp, you're right. Hell, if she had been born up on the hill to one of those professors she'd be a lawyer or something."

"I remember when the father took off—a real number one scumbag. Mother was a drinker. Remember how we used to have to pick the old lady up at the Chanticleer Bar and cart her home?"

Tripoli laughed. "Christ, that woman had a mouth on her. Good looker, too. Until the sauce caught up with her."

Kesh brought the coffee and more doughnuts.

Tripoli picked up a jelly doughnut and held it up. "You make these?"

"You kidding?" Kesh wiped his hands on his apron.

"That explains why they're so good," said Pellegrino with a wide grin.

Kesh laughed and went on to another customer.

"Molly Driscoll. Molly," Tripoli searched his memory. "Used to hide out in the gorge near the Ithaca Falls with that wild bunch. Joel English. Buddy Saul. Junior Elmo. Used to cut school to drink six packs and smoke joints."

"She was probably sleeping with all those guys."

"I doubt it," he said. "Anyway, now they're all sleeping in Attica."

"Auburn and Attica," Pellegrino corrected. "Buddy Saul just got out."

"So what's the story on her little boy?"

"I'm still hoping that he'll turn up okay. You know how these things go. I figure he's not out there wandering around and having a good time in this weather."

"Colder than a witch's tit," said Tripoli, taking careful sips of his hot coffee.

Pellegrino opened his pad. "We're still trying to get ahold of two sets of the parents who also had kids there at the daycare. And we're still trying to get a line on that Ford pickup."

"What's the story?"

"Sonny Makarainen who runs the bar across the street saw this skinny guy, about forty, with a ponytail, sitting in a pickup right at the side of the daycare, smoking and staring at everyone coming and going with their kids. Guy's there somewhere between four and five. An '86 or '87 F-150, four-wheel drive. Rusty wheel wells."

"Shitload of those in town."

"Got a big ding right in the middle of the driver's door. It was covered with white primer."

"That's better," said Tripoli.

"Sonny's pretty reliable." He took a last bite of doughnut and wiped his hands together, shaking loose the powdered sugar. "And some guy who works the pump at Chuck's Texaco station and has a scanner called in. Said he saw a little blond kid riding in an old Chevy that came in for gas."

"And? The kid struggling?"

"Naw. And the description doesn't really match."

"Molly," muttered Tripoli thoughtfully. "Molly Driscoll. That poor girl didn't exactly have a lot of breaks in life. Kind of rough around the edges, but I always liked her. Damn! I hope this turns out okay." Tripoli was thinking about those two teenage girls in Dryden who had been abducted from their home and then hacked into pieces. The State Troopers had to gather up remains that were scattered over a five-acre area of woods. And that mother up in Lansing who had reported her two-year-old missing. It took her a month to finally confess that the little girl was dead and she had buried her in a Hefty bag. She kept claiming right until she went to jail that the kid had stopped breathing and that she had panicked. Tripoli didn't know what to believe about that one, though the coroner seemed pretty certain.

"You thinking about that Lansing girl, huh?" asked Pellegrino, reading Tripoli's mind.

"Always a possibility."

"You remember, Trip, that woman out near Richford? Five of her little kids die. One after another. Period of eight years. Sudden crib death—or whatever the hell they call it. Then, last year, fifteen years later, they nail her for suffocating her babies."

"'Munchausen's syndrome by proxy,'" intoned Tripoli, still lost in thought.

"Huh?"

"That's what they called it."

"Never had these kind of bizarre cases when I joined the force. Gets you to wondering what's happening to this place."

Kesh came over and refilled their cups. "Or what's happening to the human race," he added. Kesh put the pot back on the burner and, wiping his hands on his greasy apron went back to turn the liver and onions that were starting to smoke. "Hey, you guys want anything else?" he called out.

They shook their heads.

"Molly Driscoll," mumbled Tripoli.

"Yeah," said Pellegrino.

Both their radios squawked in unison. Somebody on Third Street was waving a gun under his wife's nose.

"Gotta go," said Pellegrino, getting up in a hurry and leaving Tripoli to cover the check.

Though there are still hints of daylight in the fields, the sun has long been hidden by thickening, billowy clouds. As the boy enters the woods, the darkness closes in around him. Gusts of wind shake the branches high above his head, and the towering trees, casting off their last leaves, sway back and forth in anticipation of the coming storm.

There are no trails, the brush is dense, and the child's progress is slow as he gropes his way through the ever denser undergrowth. A pair of deer, startled by his presence, leap up and flee, crashing loudly through the brush. Numbed by the penetrating cold, the child is slow to react. He mutely turns to watch the white tails disappearing into the darkness, then pushes on once more.

Again the land begins to rise, now so steeply that the boy is at times on all fours, clambering like an animal, his sneakers slipping and sliding in the dead leaves, his numbed hands clutching ineffectually at the protruding roots of the ancient trees.

The snow at last has begun to fall. Heavy and wet, it pelts the carpet of leaves blanketing the forest floor, sending up a crackling noise like the sputtering of a campfire. The woods have become ever darker, and the damp cold has settled like a shroud over the small, struggling figure. And yet the child presses on, moving now more by feel than sight through the indifferent forest.

Molly got a handful of quarters in change from Sterling Optical and called the Ithaca Police from the mall. Nothing new. She found the number for Joe and Mildred Oltz in the phone book. They lived on Floral Avenue, just on the other side of the Cayuga Lake inlet.

"I was just trying to call you," said Mrs. Oltz. "I left a message on your machine. He still hasn't turned up? Well, Joe and I are just as worried as you are. We're absolutely—"

"Mrs. Oltz," Molly cut her short.

"You can call me Mildred."

"I need to get ahold of Cheryl."

"Cheryl?"

"I don't have time to explain. I just need her address and number."

"Cheryl's address?" she repeated as if stalling for time.

A man's voice grumbled something in the background.

"Oh, of course," said Mrs. Oltz abruptly. "I got it right here. Let me see. Cheryl Goldner."

The roads were terrible, cars stuck left and right, and Molly had a hard time getting to Cheryl's apartment. The street was dark, and many of the buildings on Stewart Avenue didn't seem to have numbers. She had to keep walking back and forth on the block until she found the right place. Cheryl's was one of two apartments on the second floor, known by real estate people as low-end student housing.

When she knocked, there was no answer. Molly then heard a floor creak behind the door. Someone was there. She knocked again. Still no answer.

"Cheryl? Cheryl?" she kept repeating as she continued to knock.

"Who is it?" inquired a timid voice from behind the closed door.

"Let me in," ordered Molly.

Finally the door inched open. Molly shoved it aside and marched right in. Her hair was wet and plastered to her head, her cheeks red with cold. Her eyes were filled with a fierceness that terrified Cheryl.

Molly looked around the room. The place was seedy, student living at its most debased, empty cartons, dirty dishes in the sink, bricks and sagging boards creating a bookshelf that held a lot of science books. A shabby double futon on the floor. Lots of soiled cushions. Cheap wall hangings from India by way of the House of Shalimar on the Ithaca Commons imperfectly covered the cracks in the plaster.

"Look, I know what happened," said Molly not mincing words. "I know all about the basement."

"Ooh," uttered Cheryl. Her jaw was trembling.

"It was stupid and cruel…" Molly let it sink in. The girl seemed to shrivel into the corner. "But I'm not going to tell anyone if you at least come clean with me."

"He kept acting up, making all the other kids misbehave."

"I'm not interested in *why*. I want to know *what* happened and *when*."

"But it's like I told you."

"So far you've told me nothing."

"He started carrying on with that Lifsey boy. Stevie. The two of them just kept going at it."

"So?"

"So I made him stand in the kitchen. We do that."

"And?"

"He kept being disruptive…"

"So?"

"So…"

"You stuck him in the basement," said Molly, biting her lip. Danny was so afraid of the dark that not only did she have to leave a night light on in their room, but also the overhead light in the hall-way—just in case. "A *dark* basement."

Cheryl started whimpering.

"Did you let him out?"

"Of course!" she sobbed. "He was kicking the door and crying."

"Oh, God." Molly gritted her teeth.

"I didn't mean to scare him, but I just couldn't—"

"And then?"

"And then he was finally quiet. He sat down with the other kids and listened to the story."

"Go on."

"He was quiet then…very quiet…Then—I don't know," Cheryl shivered. She went to the bathroom and pulled a line of toilet paper off the roll and loudly blew her nose. When she turned around, Molly was standing in the doorway, blocking her exit. Her fists were balled up and she looked as if she could barely control herself, that at one wrong word she'd haul off and smash her in the face.

"What does that mean?"

"One minute he was there. I thought he was there. And then—"

"Come on. You're punishing this boy—and then suddenly you forget him?"

"The early parents started arriving. There were a lot of kids there! Too many! You don't know what it's like working at that place. And I was alone. I wasn't supposed to be alone. And everything's happening at once. One of the little girls wet her pants, and then another kid fell down and cut his knees and was *bleeding*. And the parents are coming and two other little boys are hitting each other with shovels and…" she shook her head as the tears ran free. "I'm so sorry," she said. "Terribly sorry."

"What good is sorry?" said Molly. "I gotta find my boy. And I hope to God he's alive—for your sake, too." She started to leave, then turned abruptly. "Could a kid reach the lock?"

"What lock?"

"On the front door."

"No way," said Cheryl.

"What about standing on a chair?"

"He couldn't have done it without my seeing him."

"Sounds to me like you weren't exactly on top of things." Somehow Danny got out. He didn't walk through walls.

"I know I was careful with the door. I'm sure."

"Did you ever go to it and find it open?"

"'Course not. I'd have noticed *that!* Every time I went to the door I had to unlock it."

"Could someone open it from the outside?"

"Not without a key."

Molly went to the apartment door. "I'll be back," she said, turning. "Don't plan on leaving town or anything."

Molly started down the stairs.

Cheryl was already at the top of the landing, leaning over the railing. "You aren't going to tell, are you?" she called down plaintively.

"Has Pellegrino called in?" she asked when Officer Sisler picked up the line. Molly was back downtown, standing at an outside phone on the west end of the Commons, her feet and coat soaked.

"Huh?"

"This is Molly," she said, trying to suppress her shivering.

It took him a beat. "Yeah. Right."

"He promised he would keep me posted."

"He's out on patrol. He'd let us know if he had something. And we'd get you."

"Yeah, but I'm not home."

"Don't worry, we'll find you. And you've got an answering machine, right?"

She hung up, crossed Cayuga Street, and went up to the *Ithaca Journal*.

The main entrance to the two-story brick building was closed; but when Molly went down the side alley, she found the rear door leading to the printing plant unlocked. The big presses were open and a couple of the pressmen were cleaning the machines. The thick, cloying smell of ink and paper was oppressive.

"Where's the office?" she asked one of the workers. He wore a baseball cap that said NAPA AUTO PARTS, and one side of his shirt was stained with red ink. He looked as if he had been shot. "You know, the one with the reporters."

"Up those stairs at the end, but…Hey, lady, you can't go up there!"

The editorial office smelled of smoke. There must have been a dozen computer terminals, but only a couple of people. The room was absolutely silent except for the click of keys.

"Excuse me," said Molly, leaning over a young guy with a pony tail who was squinting at a terminal.

He started with a comical grimace, then looked up.

"I didn't mean to scare you, but my boy's missing," she said. "Missing from the daycare on State Street." She took out the picture of Danny and handed it to him. "I want you to put this in the paper. On the front page."

"Hmmm," was all he said. He looked confused. He stared at the picture and then Molly.

"You're a reporter, aren't you?"

"I do the sports," he said. "Wait a second."

He got up and walked to a young, blond woman who was typing at another terminal in the rear. "Have you seen Wally?" he asked her.

"I thought he was over at the city desk." Her fingers continued to fly over the keyboard as she spoke.

"Naw."

"Maybe he went to the men's room. You try him there?"

After a brief absence, during which Molly thought she was going to kill the placid young blonde who kept obliviously typing at her terminal, the sportswriter returned. "Wally's the city editor and—oh, wait, there he is!"

A pudgy-faced man with a bald dome and reddish-hued goatee came down the hall toward them. He had a cup of coffee and a Danish balanced in one hand, a sheaf of papers in the other. They intercepted him at the door to his office.

"What's up?" he asked. Molly quickly took his measure. He looked like a decent guy to her. But who the hell knows, she thought.

"This is Wally Schuman," the sports guy said by way of introduction. "This is—"

She shoved the picture at him. "My boy's been kidnapped. You've got to put his picture in the paper. Fast."

"Whoa," said Wally, parking his coffee and Danish on the water cooler. He took a long look at Danny's photo, then stared at the mother. She looked like a drowned rat, but a good-looking one with a pretty, open face. High, broad cheeks. Something of a mildly prominent, almost aristocratic nose. Definitely a townie, he pegged her. Working class. And maybe not working. Intelligent. Scared. "How do you know he's kidnapped?"

Molly tried to fill him in, her explanation emerging in disjointed bits and pieces. "…It was already being locked. I mean when I got there. To Kute Kids. Like he vanished in thin air! Which is why you've got to…" Even to her own ears it sounded jumbled and ridiculous.

"You want a cup of coffee?"

"I don't have time. I mean thanks, but I just want you to promise to get his picture in the next paper. That's all."

"Look, it's already," he checked his watch, "past 9:30. The morning paper's been locked in."

"Oh, yeah?" she said half-defiantly, "Supposing half the fucking town burned down or there was an earthquake. You don't think you could manage to sneak that in?" As Molly spoke, her voice sounded far away to her, and she noticed it was strained and high pitched.

Schuman was careful not to smile. He had a couple of kids—not that young—and considering what had happened in the past in Tompkins county, he knew it was no joking matter. "It's only been a few hours so far, right?"

"I know my boy," she said. "I know him like a book. He's always dying to get home. I'm the only one in the world he's got," she said touching her chest. "He's always been afraid of losing me. When I sent him off to daycare in the beginning, he wouldn't even let me go. I always have to promise to be there on time. And today…" she started choking up, though she swore she wouldn't any more in front of people, "...today I was late!"

The two men exchanged looks. The woman who had been sitting in the back had left her terminal and migrated towards them.

"Put it in," she said.

All three turned to her.

"Just put it in," she repeated as Molly looked on with new respect. "We can fit it in. Move that story on global warming to page two. Or put it on hold if you don't have the space. There's no urgency with it, right?"

Schuman hesitated. Rubbed his chin.

"Oh, please," pleaded Molly. "*Please.*"

"Yeah, why not," agreed the city editor. "We'll do it as missing, not kidnapped," he explained to Molly. "It's just a little early and you really don't know. And we've got to touch bases with the police. Debbie?" he turned and nodded to the woman.

"I'll take care of it," she said.

"You know," said Schuman, "television is a lot faster than we are."

"Damn! I never thought of that," said Molly slapping her own forehead. "I've been so confused and—Hey, how do I get them?" she asked.

"The main stations are up in Syracuse. Let me get on the horn and see if I can rattle a few cages."

Fifteen minutes later, Molly was back home. There were a half-dozen messages on her machine—the parents she had talked to checking to see if Danny had turned up. Some sounded genuinely worried. Others seemed motivated more out of curiosity than concern. Nothing from the police. The trailer suddenly felt cold and empty. Molly turned up the furnace, but it seemed too weak to drive out the chill. She thought about Danny out in the cold without a jacket.

Still dressed in her coat, she moved over to the front window and pressed her face against the cold glass. In the neighboring trailers, the light of television screens flickered and shadows danced. The snow had stopped. She could make out the line of hemlock along the drive into the park, their branches bowed under the load of snow. The lower limbs were almost touching the ground and looked ready to snap.

The night seemed so dark, so cold, so vast. Molly tried not to imagine a little boy lost. Next door, outside the Dolph's trailer, a beefy, thick-necked black dog tied to a chain was barking, standing on its hind legs and yanking its line taut.

Deep. Icy. Saturday. Sunday. Fishing. The words kept circling in Molly's mind, as if recorded on a continuous loop of tape…

"Are we going fishing like you promised?" Danny had asked in the morning, holding Molly in the hallway of Kute Kids when she tried to leave. Mrs. Oltz was waiting there to take him.

"If I promised, then I promised. Right?" she said, hectically.

"Yeah, but when?"

"Saturday. If I don't have to work."

"But…?"

"Then Sunday. But Sweetheart, I've really *got* to get…" Mrs. Oltz stood looking on impatiently. God, how Molly hated leaving him.

"And I want to go to the lake. Not that *baby* reservoir."

"Okay, the lake it is." She thought of the reservoir, with its dizzyingly high hundred-foot dam, the rapids below rushing through deep gorges when the fall rains came, trees perched precariously on the lip of the ravines, their roots clinging tenuously to the crumbling shale. The lake was better. Yes. Felt safer.

"Because that's where the *really* big fish are! In the deep lake."

Deep. Icy. Saturday. Sunday. Fishing. The last thing in the world she wanted to do was stand on the wind-whipped shore and impale a worm on a hook. But then other parents were arriving with their children, jamming the narrow entranceway.

"And then we need to get Billy and go over to the farm to feed his uncle's lambs. He said that we could ride a horse. But we gotta be there on Saturday 'cause his Uncle goes away Sunday. What day is today?"

"Wednesday," she said, pulling him aside so the others could squeeze past.

"When's Saturday?"

"Tomorrow's Thursday. Then comes Friday. And then—"

"Yeah, I 'member. Saturday," he had smiled happily.

She had finally pulled loose and kissed him good-bye. A last kiss.

Deep. Icy. Saturday. Sunday. Fishing. He wanted so much, and she worried that she gave him too little.

A little before midnight there was a knock on her door. Molly, who had been sitting on the couch staring blankly into space, jumped to her feet. At the door stood a man, stocky and dark, a solidly built guy with eyes that appeared a bright green in the light spilling through the doorway. It took her a moment to recognize him. It was Freddy Tripoli's older brother. She hadn't seen him in years, and now he had a dark mustache. The last time he was in uniform, driving a squad car. He had brought Molly's mother home early one morning after one of her binges.

"I'm—" he started.

"Yes, I know. Freddy's big brother."

"I'm a detective now." He started to take out his badge, but Molly had already stepped back from the door to let him enter.

"Have you heard anything?"

He shook his head, and she went back to the couch and flopped down exhausted, leaving Tripoli framed in the doorway. He noticed the pile of photos on the floor next to her. Nice-looking little kid.

Molly had cut her hair since he had last seen her, but it looked good on her, framed her face nicely, and maturity had served her well. She still had that good bone structure. Heart-shaped face. Sensuous bow-shaped mouth. Her two front teeth were canted inward just ever so slightly. Just now she looked disheveled. Obviously she had been out, walking in this lousy weather.

Tripoli glanced around the trailer. It was clean and neat, but it was hardly more than a notch above a dive. He knew Freeman's Floral Estates well, having spent a disproportionate amount of time here responding to domestics and drugs, harrassments and thefts. He could stand in the center of the fifty-unit park and identify the residents, home after home, citing each case and its disposition. Molly's trailer sat in the rear where the smaller, more rundown trailers were tucked away. Unlike the once lavish doublewides at the entrance, these were cramped, usually overcrowded, and their occupants tended to tack on extra rooms and storage sheds. More often than not they were usually cobbled-up structures that sagged and soon rotted, leaving them looking more like ramshackle shanties than homes.

Tripoli remained at the open door for a moment, trying to match this woman with the hell-raising high school kid he had known.

"I can remember you and Freddy, but I can't remember your name," Molly admitted.

"I'm Lou."

"Right. Louie Tripoli," Molly repeated to herself with a nod. The Tripolis were a big, extended Ithaca family. There were Tripolis that owned the dry cleaners on Seneca Street, the Tripoli Paving company, the Sunoco station, the Busy Bee luncheonette on Cayuga Street, and that new Italian restaurant—whatever its name was—up in the Cayuga Mall.

She remembered how Tripoli would pick up Freddy at the high school. He was a cop already then—which made him seem so much older—and his shiny patrol car would be waiting in front every afternoon when the kids were let out. The car with its red lights always caught her eye. It made her a little nervous and she would observe it through the corner of her eye as she sidled off with her friends, watching how Tripoli would grab Freddy and affectionately hug him in a way that men usually didn't do—not the men she knew. Seeing that, Molly used to wonder what it was like having a brother. An older brother to look out for you.

"I'd like to ask you some questions if I could," he said.

"You want to stand there in the door or do you want to come in?"

"Well, if you don't mind," he said politely.

"Help yourself," she said. "And you might as well close the door while you're at it."

"Oh, yeah, sorry." Tripoli wiped his feet free of the clinging snow, then stepped in and closed the door. Instinctively, his eyes swept the place, taking in everything in a near-single glance. On a bookshelf there were dog-eared textbooks, children's books, and on the bottom shelf he recognized a set of that *Great Books* series that Time/Life was always trying to sell through the mail. "Mind if I take off my coat?" he asked.

"Suit yourself."

When he had taken off his overcoat, Molly saw that he had a sport jacket and tie on. He had an easy way about him. A lot more polished than his brother Freddy. For a cop he even seemed gentle.

"I'm sorry if I sound such a—" She shook her head.

"Hey," he held up his hands, "No apologies necessary. I understand. Don't worry. We just want to get your boy back."

She showed him a chair, and he took it and pulled it up close to where she sat on the sofa. There was something about his eyes, perhaps their clarity and brilliance of their light green color, that held her gaze. They looked like jewels. "Do you have any ideas?" she inquired. "Anything at all? Some leads maybe? Some—"

"Truthfully? No. But we're starting to focus in on this thing." He held his hands out and slowly brought them together as though narrowing a gap.

"What exactly does that mean?"

"I got ahold of Bea Bruce—"

Molly perked up. "And?"

Tripoli shook his head. "She didn't know anything. Neither did her girl. I got ahold of the Ruzickas. But you already talked to them, so I hear."

"Okay, so what do we do now?"

"Sit tight."

"That's what everybody keeps saying. Sit tight. Hang in there. Wait." She could feel herself getting angry, and fought to stifle the bitterness.

"I've got three investigators out canvassing the whole town and questioning everybody—including the other kids from the daycare," he said. Then he turned quietly thoughtful. "Look, do you have any idea of where your boy might go if he wanted to leave home?"

"*Danny?* Hell, you couldn't pry him away from me."

"Is there some place he might have talked about wanting to go—you know, kids get all kinds of ideas."

"He kept going on about fishing this morning. But he'd never…"

"Fishing where?"

"We always go to the reservoir."

Tripoli lifted an eyebrow. "Reservoir?"

"Not a chance. Anyway, he was tired of that and wanted to go fishing in the lake." For an instant she was assaulted by the vivid image of Danny in a row boat drifting out on the dark, snowy lake. "Come on, there's no way he could get down to the lake. He's just a little boy." She could hear the element of uncertainty creeping into her own voice. Tripoli said nothing for a few moments.

"The boy's father—" he began.

"Chuck? *Chuck?*" She gave a loud laugh. "My ex-husband? You think he took Danny?"

"I don't know," said Tripoli.

"Let me tell you about Chuck. He took off the day Danny was born. We're talking almost five years now, and I've never heard from him since—that's how much he cared about Danny! I couldn't even find him to serve the papers for a divorce. Do you *really* think he's going to come back to claim a kid he's never even seen?"

"Anything's possible. I've got to explore every lead."

"You got a cigarette?" she asked.

He reached into his breast pocket, then caught himself. "No. I don't smoke anymore. If you want, I could get—"

"Naw. Forget it. Gave it up myself. I just don't know what to do with my hands." She threw them up in the air and let them fall back into her lap.

"Do you at least have any idea where Chuck might have gone?"

"Not a clue."

He took out his pad. "What's his last name?"

"Halliday. I used to be Halliday, too, but…well…"

"Chuck Halliday. Hey, I know who that is," said Tripoli. "He used to run that contracting business—"

"Out of the back of his truck. Yup, that's the winner."

"Just took off, huh?"

"Disappeared. Didn't even leave a note. It was like aliens came in and plucked him up into outer space."

"Did you report him missing?"

"Missing? Nobody was missing him! That jerk was still stretching rubber on our checking account and running up charges on our plastic."

"Any relatives?"

"A mother in Cleveland. I tried calling her when I realized that he had taken off, but she didn't know where he was—they hadn't been talking for years. Nor had his uncle in Dallas. Or his cousin in Milwaukee. I'm telling you, the guy simply vanished into thin air."

Tripoli was hastily jotting notes. He looked up from his pad. "Left you high and dry?"

"But not exactly empty handed."

A lot of guys could give you a baby, thought Tripoli, though he didn't say anything.

"And Danny's no ordinary kid. He's smart as a whip. He knows what he wants and he can wait for it. Plan for it." She picked up his photo. Whenever she gazed at Danny's face, she couldn't help seeing Chuck—whether she wanted to or not. Those dreamy eyes and long, long lashes—bedroom eyes, she used to call them when she still loved him.

Tripoli nodded.

"You know, Louie—I mean, hey, what am I supposed to call you?"

"Lou's fine," he smiled. "Louie, well that's my Uncle Louie. I was Louie when I was a kid."

"Lou," she repeated absently. She was thinking about Chuck. And her father. How when it came to the crunch, you just couldn't rely on a man.

Tripoli was saying something to her. "Huh?" she said, waking from her reverie.

"I was asking about your work? The people you work with?"

"You mean Larry Pierce?"

"Well everybody," he said and she gave him a quick rundown of the magazine, about Sandy and Ben and Doreen. He kept probing, asking about the company's finances, its backers, the people who came and went at the office—which seemed odd. All the while he kept taking notes.

Tripoli lifted Danny's photo from the pile that lay strewn on the coffee table. "We have your description of Danny, but I just want to go over it with you again." He replaced the photo and picked up his notepad. "Sometimes people miss things."

Molly went through her litany, the plaid shirt, the bib overalls, the sneakers.

"Any identifying marks, that might help us? You know, a chipped tooth or a..."

Molly though about it.

"He has a small scar on his forehead, on his right side just above his eyebrow. Got it when he fell off the monkey bars."

Tripoli noted it down.

"He chipped a tooth. But just a little bit. You can hardly see it."

"Anything else?"

Molly thought for a moment. "Well, he has this small birthmark on the back of his neck."

"What color?"

"Sort of wine red. The kids at daycare used to tease him about it, but he never let it bother him. He told them it was his star for being good." A tear dropped into Molly's lap. "It almost did look like a star with points."

"Anything else?

"No, I think that's all."

When he was satisfied, Tripoli closed his notebook and sat thoughtfully for a moment. "Do you think I could see where Danny sleeps."

Molly looked at him surprised. "Why would you want to do that?"

"Sometimes you can pick up—well, not a clue but an idea."

"You're not into that psychic stuff, are you?"

He smiled and shook his head. "No way."

"Last thing in the world I want," she said, leading the way to the rear of the trailer, "is a cop who thinks he can get my kid back with some mumbo jumbo."

Tripoli could feel the trailer sway under his feet as they walked, as if it were a boat loosely moored to its pier.

"We share this room." Molly sounded apologetic. "It's just till I can get a bigger place, a nicer one. We've been saving," she said. "Danny and me. We have this plan."

She watched Tripoli as his eyes searched the room in which there was barely enough space to accommodate the beds that met head to head in the far corner. The small area in the center was littered with toys. There was a fort made of blocks peppered with little plastic soldiers. Military men with bazookas and automatic weapons.

"Oh? What plan is that?" He was kneeling down in front of the toy shelf, examining the boy's toys. A Mutant Marauder Mobile Command Unit. Nerf soccer ball. Puzzles. Two cowboy hats. Spurs. A sheriff's badge. And guns, lots of guns. A pair of western six shooters in a holster. A Supersoaker. Three different light sabers.

"We were…are…going to buy a little place in the country. Danny loves being outdoors. And he wants a puppy so bad. I promised him we'd do it. When he wouldn't let me leave him at daycare in the beginning, I told him I was working to…" Molly felt her throat close and tears start to come, but she caught herself. "I was working so that we could get the money to buy a little farm. Not a real farm, you know, but a…" she blinked to clear her eyes. "Which is why every morning he'd let me…" She couldn't go on. Why was she running at the mouth, telling Tripoli all this? What difference could it make?

Tripoli picked up the Supersoaker and hefted it in his hands. It still had water in it.

"This whole arsenal," said Molly reading his thoughts. "Believe me, it was not my idea. Danny's fascinated by guns and swords. Lord only knows why. I suppose it's just little boys."

"I wouldn't know," he said. "I don't have any. Kids, that is." He wondered why he said it. He thought with a touch of emptiness about his ex-wife, Kim, who never really wanted children.

She looked at him for a moment. Wondered why he had mentioned it. Wondered how it would affect the search for Danny. Could he really understand what she was going through?

He bent down and picked up the Lego windmill that lay on the floor. "Your boy make this himself?"

"Certainly wasn't me." Molly swallowed the lump in her throat and tried to smile.

"Pretty neat for a four-year-old," he said spinning the blades.

"The only thing I was worried about was that he might go into contracting," she said with a sad smile as she picked up his Nerf gun. She loaded it and shot it against the wall and watched as the Nerf bounced to the floor. "This was his favorite toy. He was always going around shooting everybody with it. Kept shooting me in the butt while I was trying to do the dishes," she laughed and cried at the same time. "He played with the Pakkala kids in the other trailer. They have them, too. They'd have these Nerf wars."

Molly dropped the gun and walked over to the dresser to pick up the empty picture frame. She held it as if the picture were still there. "He had such beautiful eyes. The longest lashes—" She finally realized what she had been saying. "I mean *has*…Has! He *has* beautiful eyes. He *plays* with the kids. Not played!" Then she broke down and wept. She cried and cried and couldn't stop. Lou Tripoli put his arm around her and held her convulsing shoulders.

Molly was so tired she was numb. She put water on the stove to boil and sat staring into space, telling herself that as long as it was night there still remained a reasonable chance Danny would pop up. In her mind, daylight became the enemy. It represented a new phase, a new page. She thought back on Tripoli…

"You gonna be all right?" he had asked when she had finally calmed down.

She wiped her eyes and nodded her head. "You want coffee or something? I can make some fast."

"No, I've got to get moving," he had explained.

"To where?"

"I've still got some ideas. Hey, mind if I take one of these?" he asked picking up one of the photos of Danny.

"Take a bunch. Take them all."

"All I need is one. We'll copy it into a report and every officer will have one in his hand."

She took a piece of paper toweling from the kitchen and blew her nose. "You said you had ideas. Like what?"

Tripoli didn't dare mention the red pickup, didn't want to needlessly alarm her. He just shrugged and smiled encouragingly.

"You'll find him, won't you," she said when he didn't reply.

"I'm going to stay on top of it," he responded, sidestepping the question. The answer, of course, was probably yes. Ultimately, the whereabouts of missing kids always became evident—in one form or another. Given the time that had already passed, unless an ex-husband or someone who had an insatiable longing for a child had abducted Danny, the probability of a happy resolution was rapidly diminishing. It was best she somehow prepare herself for the unthinkable, perhaps even get ready to bear the unbearable. But he didn't say any of this.

He had put his hand on her arm. She had looked down at where he touched her. His hand was big and broad and there were little tufts of dark hair on the backs of his fingers. Then he had left…

The pot of water on the stove was boiling over, and it brought her back to the present. She stared at the dead screen of the television. Danny loved to watch cartoons—especially the old ones like

Bugs Bunny and Wile E. Coyote. He would roar with laughter at Road Runner, then run in dizzying circles around the trailer making beep-beep noises and bumping into everything. Oh God, she moaned, he's still such a baby. If there has to be something bad, let it happen to me, not him.

Later, when she looked out the front window, there was still no hint of light. Good, she told herself, good, there's still time.

About five in the morning she dozed off, still sitting on the couch. The sound of a noisy truck starting its engine insinuated itself into her trailer. It probably was Rick Dolph going off to his job as a custodian, she reasoned somewhere in sleep. Then she dreamed. Disjointed, confused dreams. Dreams about a phone urgently ringing…

But the phone really was ringing. Molly popped open her eyes, trying to orient herself. She was sprawled half off the sofa, and the trailer park was humming with activity, radios and TVs blaring, babies crying, motors running. She could smell bacon frying. The sky had already lightened in the east. Morning. And Danny. He was still gone. The ringing kept going. Danny. *Danny!* Molly lunged for the phone.

"Molly!" cried a familiar voice. It was Rosie Green. They had been friends since junior high when she was Rosie Lopez.

"I just got to work," exclaimed Rosie, "and I saw the morning paper. And my God —there's Danny's picture!"

"He's—" Molly started to cry.

"Why didn't you call me?"

"I did. I did! I kept trying, but no one was—"

"I was overnight at my cousin's, remember?"

"Oh!" exclaimed Molly. "Damn! I forgot. I wasn't thinking."

"And Ed, he was—"

"Oh, Jesus!"

"I'm coming right over," she said and hung up.

Ten minutes later she came rushing into the trailer. Molly threw herself into Rosie's arms and wept.

"What happened?" asked Rosie, stroking her.

Molly pulled her hands through her hair and shook her head.

"Did someone take Danny?" asked Rosie.

"I don't know," she sobbed. "I just don't know. Nobody knows."

Rosie sat Molly down and clutched her tightly. Simply waited for her to speak. Haltingly, Molly related how she had gone to Kute Kids to pick up Danny. "I was late!"

"That has nothing to do with anything. They're supposed to be watching the kids, right? And the cops, what the hell are they doing?"

"They're looking," said Molly.

"What's that supposed to mean?" Rosie was now crying, too.

"Yesterday was a complete nightmare. Nobody's talking to anybody. The State Police didn't even have a clue. And—"

"That's the police for you. When you don't need them, they're all over you, hassling the shit out of people. Then, when you *really* need them—"

"But Freddy's brother was here. He on the case."

"Who?"

"You remember Freddy Tripoli."

"Sure."

"Well his brother Lou is a cop. A detective now."

"Oh, yeah. That's right…that's the guy who kept harassing my brother."

"Well, he's in charge."

"And we're supposed to feel good about that?" asked Rosie.

"He seems like a smart guy. And he's really on top of it."

"Well, maybe," said Rosie grudgingly, "but I wouldn't screw around. I'd get myself a private detective. Ed's got a cousin who's married to a…"

Molly weighed the idea. Thought about Lou Tripoli's visit. "No," she said finally. "Not yet. We've got to give the cops a chance. I think they're on top of it now. They're going to find him. You'll see." And she tried to smile. Obviously Rosie didn't really know what to do either. She kept pacing the trailer, wringing her hands and trying to come up with schemes. She'd get all her friends and relatives together and they'd form a search party. And they should call the F.B.I., of course! It was a kidnapping, right? And that was a federal offense.

"And how did Danny get out? Little boys don't just evaporate."

"I don't know." Molly tossed her hands. "That's the mystery."

"Who the hell was watching him? Hey, wait! Did Danny do anything different that day? Say anything? Like maybe he wanted to go somewhere?"

Rosie kept going, searching for clues, but Molly realized that she was running through the same maze of questions that had plagued her all night. Yet, there was comfort in having Rosie here, tracking back and forth, racking her brain. At least she wasn't alone. She thought back about Rosie. How they'd been going to the same schools since the third grade. Most of the kids Molly had grown up with had left town in search of jobs and better lives—and some had ended up bouncing in and out of jail. Rosie had been one of the few to stick with her family in Ithaca. One of the few old and trusted friends she had left.

"I don't believe this," uttered Rosie, slumping back down on the couch next to Molly and taking her hand. "Oh, God, little Danny." Her voice cracked. "He's like my own little boy."

It was true. Rosie had helped take care of Danny since he was a toddler. It was little more than a month after Rosie had lost her own baby that she and Ed had taken Danny into their home so that Molly could commute to classes in Cortland. Without them, she would never have made it through the community college. And they had refused to accept a penny. If that wasn't friendship, then…

"Listen," said Molly finally. "You'd better go back to work. I don't want you getting in trouble."

"I'm not leaving you," said Rosie fiercely.

"I need to be alone a little," she lied. "I haven't slept and…"

Rosie looked askance at her.

"I'll be okay. You'll come back, right?"

"Of course!"

After Rosie left, Molly felt even more alone than before and regretted sending her off. She kept thinking about Rosie, whose newborn baby had died in her arms after four agonizing and uninsured days in the hospital. At the time, Rosie had been working at the auto body shop out on the Elmira road, keeping the books and inventory. Molly had once gone out to the shop to deliver something to Rosie. The building was enveloped in a fog of wretched-smelling solvents and paint, and Molly couldn't guess how she could stand it. When Rosie had lost her baby, she was convinced it was because of the chemicals and swore she would never again expose her body to those kinds of poisons.

Now Rosie stood anchored to a cash register at the East Hill P&C, still working off the medical bills. Laid out end to end, the groceries she had checked through her line would probably reach another solar system. Her husband Ed, a black guy who was a union mason, earned a decent hourly wage when he worked. The trouble was that the building trades had come to a virtual stop. The last thing Rosie needed was to lose a day's precious wage.

chapter four

Tripoli had trouble finding the magazine office. It shared the rear quarters of a low-slung, brick structure that sat on the edge of the industrial park by the airport, a drab affair in which someone had planted some young maples in the rear to break up the institutional bleakness. The building had been chopped up into a myriad of sections. Inside were a number of tiny biotech labs and a couple of startup electronic and software companies. The place smelled of chemicals and human sweat. The signs were confusing and, when he finally found it, there was no one at the front desk. Tripoli walked past the receptionist's desk and directly into the publisher's office.

Larry Pierce, who was on the phone, looked up, annoyed. "I'm busy," he said covering the mouthpiece, "and my assistant's out. If you could—"

"I can wait," said Tripoli calmly and seated himself, Larry letting out an impatient sigh and making no attempt to hide his annoyance. He watched Larry in amazement as he banged out an email, checked his Palm Pilot, fished through a drawer for a file, and checked the Caller I.D. readout on his cell phone clipped to his belt, all the while keeping rapid-fire conversation going. The man seemed to give multitasking a new dimension.

Tripoli took in Larry's side of the discussion. Something about money, rate of returns, investing in the magazine. Clearly he was hustling someone, trying to be smooth, but Tripoli could feel the waves of energy coming off the guy. Maybe this was the speed of the city, but he certainly was out of place in Ithaca.

From what Tripoli had managed to learn, Pierce had been a top editor at a New York magazine, the kind of bigshot for whom people would drop everything—cancel their appointments and divorce their wives. Yet here he was in a kind of self-imposed exile which Tripoli found a little hard to comprehend.

Tripoli was still waiting. In his sport jacket and tie, he figured Pierce had him pegged as a paper salesman or jobber. Everything fit except the five-o'clock shadow. He ran his hands across his jaw. God, he needed a shave. And a nice hot shower, too.

Larry drummed his fingers on his desk.

"Look," he said impatiently into the phone, "why don't you let me talk to your partner. A couple of quick minutes. That's all I'll need…Okay. Okay. Look, I got somebody in the office now. Yeah. Right. Great!" Then he slammed down the phone.

"Okay," he said at last, turning to the visitor. "I don't have a lot of time today."

"I'm Detective Tripoli." He brought out his badge and took a perverse delight in Pierce's surprise, which made him realize that for some reason he didn't really like the guy. Too full of himself. Pompous. A touch arrogant. "Ithaca Police."

"*Huh?*"

"I understand Molly Driscoll works for you?"

"Molly's my editorial assistant, but…" His face turned florid. "What's the matter?"

"Was she here yesterday?"

"Yes. Yes. Of course."

"The whole day?"

"Yeah. Well…"

"You were here all day yourself?"

"Except for a lunchtime meeting. Hey, what's up? What's this all about?" Apparently he hadn't seen the paper. "Molly left a message this morning that there was some kind of family emergency and—"

"What time were you out for lunch?"

"I don't know exactly. Well, maybe between quarter of twelve and two." Pierce took off his glasses and rubbed the indentations on the bridge of his nose. Without his glasses he looked owl-eyed. "What gives, anyway?"

Tripoli kept going. "Was anybody else in the office then?"

"Sure. Molly was here. And Doreen, too. She's one of our senior editors."

"Can I talk to her?"

"Of course." He buzzed Doreen to come in. "Why don't you at least tell me what's going on?"

"Her boy's missing. Disappeared out of daycare."

"You mean *Danny?*"

"You know him, then?"

"Yeah. Sure. Of course. Cute little kid. A bit on the wild side. She brought him here once and he turned the place upside down." Pierce laughed nervously and then caught himself. "Oh my God, you mean somebody took him?"

Tripoli nodded.

"When did this happen?"

"Larry?" said Doreen sticking her head in the door.

"I want to see Lou Tripoli," said Molly when the officer at the switchboard slid open the glass partition.

"He's out in the field on an investigation." He checked the board. "I don't know when he's going to be back."

"I'm Molly Driscoll. Are you Jerry?" she asked.

"No. I'm Officer Barber."

"You got any word on my boy?"

"You better talk to Lou Tripoli."

Molly looked alarmed. "What does that mean?"

"Nothing. It's just that he's in charge of the investigation."

"Okay, then I want to talk to him. How do I get ahold of him?"

"I'll try to get a message to him. Where are you going to be?"

Molly drove back from the downtown police station to the trailer park. Her head was throbbing and she felt as if she'd been drugged. The snow had stopped, most of it had already melted, but the clouds were still low and heavy.

She noticed people with television cameras milling around her trailer. Her neighbors stood watching from the safety of their front doors. There were two vans with dish antennas mounted on top. Judging from the bright logos, one crew was from WELM in Elmira, the other from WSTM in Syracuse. Cameras were trained on Molly as she pulled up.

As she got out of her car, someone shouted, "We understand your boy is missing."

She turned to face two lenses. "Kidnapped," she answered bluntly. "I've got a picture of him, here," she said, holding it squarely in front of her. She tried to keep her hand from trembling so they could get a good, steady shot of Danny.

Neighbors started crowding around as the television people interviewed her, asking her what had happened. She tried to explain about driving down to Kute Kids and finding the place in the process of being locked up. "I went in and found Danny's jacket still on the hook." Her throat kept closing down, she felt on the verge of crying. But she was determined not to become one of those weepy types that television was always exploiting. "I want to ask whoever took my son to *please* bring him back safely. And to do it *now*. I wish they would ask themselves what it would feel like if it were them—imagine that it was their child."

They found the owner of the F-150 pickup with the ding in the door and pulled him in for questioning. His name was Charley Paul and he had a record.

An improvised command post was set up in the fire house on Green Street, not a block from Kute Kids. Already a dozen cops were out canvassing the immediate area and chasing down leads. The Tompkins County Sheriff's office had given Tripoli three of its principal investigators, and the State Police had offered further assistance. The firehouse was busy with uniformed and plainclothes cops coming and going, phones ringing and radios crackling. They had just gotten the computer system set up and wired into their net when they brought Charley Paul in. They took him straight to the kitchen in the rear of the firehouse where it was quiet and kept him waiting until Tripoli returned.

Tripoli recognized him right away. Paul worked at the Tompkins County Solid Waste facility, and Tripoli had seen him on a number of occasions when he had gone to the dump with stuff for recycling. Besides the usual glass and newspapers, Tripoli was always dragging in corroded plumbing fixtures and odd bits of metal left over from the days when he was still remodeling his Greek Revival in Newfield. But since his wife, Kim, had left him three years ago, he had done little to the house, nothing more than carry away the detritus from those days of optimism. Charley Paul was always there at the recycling center, half sober, making sure you put things in the right bin.

Charley Paul was a scruffy figure with a pony tail and bushy sideburns. He wore a red bandanna around his forehead. Yet he was the kind of guy who in former years would jump hippies and hack at their long hair. Funny, thought Tripoli, here they were, guys like

Charley, years later adopting the very styles which they had held in such contempt.

"Whatta you wan' wit' me?" said Charley, hardly cowed. He sat at the mess table and stared defiantly up at Tripoli, who stood leaning over him. Tripoli had his hands on his hips, his sport jacket pulled aside enough to reveal a glimpse of the 9mm Glock parked on his belt. Charley Paul had a long record of drunk and disorderlies as well as a couple of assault charges and an order of protection keeping him away from his third ex-wife. He looked like a genuine scumbag and Tripoli pondered if he could also be into little boys.

"You were parked yesterday for a couple of hours by Kute Kids?"

"Huh?" Charley was playing with a pile of crumbs left on the table, making little lines with them.

"The daycare place up the street."

"Daycare?"

"You going to answer every question with a fucking question? Come on, you know exactly what I'm talking about."

Charley shrugged.

"You were seen there by reliable witnesses."

"Free country, ain't it?"

"What were you doing there?"

"Nothin'" said Charley. "Hey, don't I get a lawyer?"

"I haven't arrested you…yet."

"Then I don't have to answer any of your fucking questions, do I?" said Charley, smiling to reveal the missing teeth in front.

While the crews were loading their gear back into the vans, a shiny BMW that looked decidedly out of place was circling around the trailer park, bouncing along the potholed and puddle-filled road, mud splattering its fenders and doors. The driver seemed to be unsure about where he was headed as he wound through the thicket of rust-stained trailers. Finally, he noticed the small crowd near an old trailer in the rear of the park, spotted Molly, and drove over as close as he could to the television vans. He got out and stood for a moment as if trying to orient himself. Within earshot a dozen stereos thumped, dogs barked, and children yelled. From a nearby trailer there was a sudden flurry of angry shouts, a series of doors slamming. A woman's voice viciously cursing.

Molly saw that it was Larry, her boss. He looked a bit lost. It struck her that he had probably never been in a trailer park before.

"Molly," he said coming up to her and awkwardly grasping her hand in both of his in a way that took her by surprise. "I just heard..."

Molly's eyes flooded with tears, and Larry gave a constricted smile, unnerved by her emotion

"I'm...I'm...I'm..." She didn't quite know what she was, other than speechless at the prospect of her new boss coming all that way to see her.

"You want to come in?" she finally ventured as the television people started their engines and began to leave.

"If you'd like," he said gently. Molly looked a sight. Her swollen eyes were highlighted with dark circles, and her skin was a ghostly ashen.

He followed her in. The interior was musty and cramped. It was obvious in a glance that Molly had tried to make the best of it, everything neat and in its place. The scant rugs, though threadbare, appeared clean. A colorful blanket was draped over an old sofa which leaked stuffing. The kitchen was orderly, though the linoleum was cracked and stained, and the cabinets looked worn and chipped. He had never really given much thought to how she lived, never realized that she was existing in such marginal conditions.

"I...I... blame myself for this," he said, stammering for the first time that Molly could recall. "If I hadn't kept you so late...Oh God,

I feel awful. Really awful. I keep thinking if only…" But he couldn't finish the sentence.

"If I had come earlier," she said, "Danny would have been gone already. Anyway, it was my decision to stay." Molly knew where the blame lay: she had been just too absorbed with her job, doing it, keeping it, to think of much else. "Look," she said struggling, "would you like maybe a cup of coffee or something?"

"What about *you?* Have you eaten anything?" he hunched over to bring his face close to hers. She shrugged. "I figured as much. Let me get you some food, okay?"

"I think I've got stuff in the fridge."

"I'll get you something to eat. But maybe you need to be here by the phone? I'll bring some takeout?" It was obvious he both wanted and needed to do something.

"When I sit here," she said glumly, "nothing happens anyhow. I just sit and see Danny. Maybe I'm almost better off outside for a while."

"Come on then," he said. "That's decided."

Tripoli found Rosie Green working a checkout line at the P&C off Judd Falls Road.

"I'd like to talk to you for a moment," he said, leaning over the counter.

"About what?" she asked, hardly looking up as she continued zipping items across the scanner. She plopped a bunch of grapes on the scale, then a few pounds of bananas, her fingers nimbly keying in the digits. He noticed that her jaw was clenched; her mascara was slightly smeared and her eyes were rimmed in red. A compact, busty woman with sleek dark hair tied at the back, her skin was a flawless shade of olive, and her eyes seemed dark and serious.

"Do you think maybe we could step aside somewhere?"

Rosie stopped, looked up—a jar of mayonnaise suspended in her hand. "Who are you?" she asked.

The people waiting in the long line were impatiently watching the exchange.

Tripoli didn't want to pull his badge. "I'm Lou Tripoli. I'm with the Ithaca—"

"Oh…" she uttered, finally making the connection. "It's you! I didn't recognize…"

Tripoli nodded in acknowledgment.

"Miss!" said the middle-aged woman motioning towards her groceries. "Could you please…?"

"Sorry." Rosie looked distractedly at the woman. "Hang on," she said turning to Tripoli and got the belt moving again. Amidst customer groans, she popped the "CLOSED" sign behind the woman's groceries.

Tripoli watched Rosie as she hurried through the remains of the purchase and started bagging it. Though she had changed a lot in the intervening years, he could still connect her with the skinny girl who used to play on Titus Avenue. Rosie Lopez. When they had tried to arrest her older brother on a possession charge, the whole family had turned out to raise a ruckus. Rosie, a teenager, had gotten so angry and protective that she ended up jumping on Richie Pellegrino's back. Well, that was a small town for you, Tripoli thought. It's what kept him bumping into his ex-wife and her latest boyfriend more often than he cared to recall.

In less than a minute, Rosie had completed the transaction and together they walked over to the privacy of the dairy case.

"So what's going on? Have you got any leads?"

"We're working on it," said Tripoli.

"So what are you doing here then?" she asked, hands on her hips.

"I need to ask you some questions. About Molly."

"I don't get it."

"You're her friend. And you knew the boy."

"That right. I know Danny."

"When did you last see him?"

"On the weekend. Last weekend."

"And Molly?"

"Same time."

"So you didn't pick up the boy?"

"Of course not!"

"Or your husband?"

"No!"

"Do you know anyone who might have?"

"You can't just march into daycare and pick up somebody else's kid—you should know that!"

"What was Molly's relationship with the boy?"

"*Relationship?*"

"You know…" He waved his hands.

"You must be joking. And asking a question like that! Obviously you don't have the slightest fucking idea what that girl has gone through to raise that boy, do you?"

"Well, maybe because of that. You know, sometimes people—"

Rosie's complexion turned an ominous shade darker. "If you think for one second…" she brought her face so close that Tripoli could feel her breath. It smelled of mint.

He didn't flinch. "I'm not thinking anything. I'm just trying to get some—"

"You're thinking it was like that woman in Lansing who buried her baby and then claimed she was kidnapped."

Tripoli fixed her with his eyes and leveled a finger. "Now I didn't say anything like that."

"Well let me tell you, every single day of Molly's life's been a fight for her. She keeps getting kicked in the teeth, but she just shakes it off, picks herself up, and gets going again. And why?

Because of Danny. Hurt a hair on his head? She worships that boy. She'd fucking die for him!"

Tripoli let Rosie go on, watching her anger play itself out.

"That girl pulled herself up…hey, you know where she came from?"

Tripoli nodded.

"The gutter is where. A little girl and she was already taking care of her fucked-up mother. Cooking. Cleaning the house. You know when Danny was born, her life was all messed up, but she kept her head together. Got a job. Went back to school. Stayed up half the night studying her books—taught herself *everything*. Had somebody'd just given her a running start, she could have been president of the whole United States!"

Tripoli, touched by Rosie's passion, couldn't help but smile.

"That boy is all she lives for. And now this. After all she's been through! Why *her?*"

Tripoli just stood there by the yogurts and sour cream listening.

Rosie bent down to pick up a pack of unsalted butter that someone had knocked to the floor. She placed the butter back in the cooler, straightening the pile.

"Okay," she said taking a deep breath and turning back. "What else did you want to ask me?"

"I think you may already have answered my questions," said Tripoli quietly.

The Gables was once a stately old Victorian home. Now it was a restaurant tucked close to the busy highway that led out from the line of strip malls. All red velvet and polished brass, plush carpeting and Tiffany lamps, it was an attempt to harken back to quieter, more solid times.

Molly was baffled. Why is he taking me here? thought Molly, as the hostess led them to their table. Larry caught a glimpse of himself in the mirror and straightened his tie. For him, diners and fast food places apparently didn't exist.

"Give us that table in the corner," ordered Larry, who seemed to know the woman.

Molly sank down into the chair that he held for her. She could feel the heavy trucks roaring past, setting the crystal and mirrors to rattling. She had once thought this place the height of elegance and sophistication. Yet now all this glitter meant nothing. Everything felt off kilter. Even the smile of the approaching waitress felt patently false.

Molly had not been here in years. In fact, the last time was before Danny was born. Chuck was about to get a contract for a huge renovation job, and they were celebrating with a champagne dinner. Nothing was too good for Chuck. "Money was meant to be spent!" he used to say, and to the very end he had remained true to his word. Of course, the contract had fallen through—some minor contingency about city approval he had overlooked. But dinner had been fun. They had gone out dancing afterwards and made passionate love that night. That, in fact, was the night that Danny had been conceived.

It was odd to be here now, coming full circle. Molly picked up the menu, but couldn't seem to focus on what was there.

"Could you order, please. I'm a wreck. I just can't concentrate."

"Of course," he said and called back the smiling waitress. "We're in a rush," he uttered, and started ordering as Molly's mind drifted.

"Tell me about my Daddy," Danny used to ask. She let her mind play over these exchanges that were always the same.

"Well, he was a very big and strong man," she would say.

"And what did he do?"

"He built houses."

"Big houses?"

"Yes. Very big."

"How big?"

"Big as you can imagine."

"Like to the sky?"

"Almost. When you get older, I'll show you some he built."

"Why did he leave?"

"I think maybe things were too much for him."

"Too much building?"

"Yeah. Among other things. I think maybe he just got tired of working. And scared of having a family to worry about."

"You mean *me?*" He looked at her wide-eyed and suddenly she had felt so sorry for him.

"No, no. It was me. He never knew you, Sweetie. If he had, he *never* would have left."

When the soup arrived, Molly lingered over it, still lost in her reverie. Larry took a taste. "Hmmm, it's good," he said, "Go on, give it a try."

Molly took a spoonful and put it to her lips. And then she started crying. She used the napkin to muffle her sobs, but they kept coming.

People began staring at her.

"I'm sorry," she gasped. "So sorry."

"You don't need to apologize," he whispered. "I think you're very brave and...and...and the way you're standing up to this, why..." Larry reached across the table and took hold of her hand.

"Soup reminds me...of Danny," and again she dissolved into tears. "He likes soup so much, and when he went off to Kute Kids I had to pack his lunch and it was lousy peanut butter and..." the sobs convulsed her. "I'm so sorry..."

"Come on, try to eat," he urged. "You need strength."

Between sniffles, Molly took a few spoonfuls. The liquid, though warm, seemed to have little taste. Her stomach started to churn. Through the veil of tears, she kept staring around the ornate room.

"I can't!" she said finally. "This is all wrong. I really appreciate your bringing me here, but…I've got to go back." Molly pushed back her chair and stumbled to her feet.

Larry was already up when the waitress came rushing over. "Is something—"

"Just let me pay for the lunch," said Larry handing her the magazine's AmEx card. "Please hurry."

Molly was already out the door. By the time Larry reached her, she was hanging on to the fender of his car, doubled over and retching. He took hold of Molly and held her by the waist as her body convulsed.

"Oh, God," she uttered, wiping her lips with a tissue. Her knees were trembling, and she was too weak and embarrassed to even offer an apology. Larry got her into the car and drove her quickly back towards town.

"Better now?" he inquired solicitously.

"Much. Sorry to waste the soup," she said with a wan smile.

"I'm sorry. I shouldn't have taken you there. I don't know what I was thinking."

They drove further in silence, ascending the highway that overlooked the lake. Molly kept staring down at the water, it looked cold and deep and foreboding. When they neared the trailer park, Larry broke the silence. "I want you to know that the last thing you have to worry about is your job. It's waiting for you. Whatever it takes."

Molly started to cry again.

"And your salary keeps coming, too."

Molly shook her head, though not very strenuously.

"Come on, the people in the office wouldn't have it any other way. And they're the ones who really run the show. They wanted me to tell you that you can call *any* of us—me, Doreen, Sally, or Ben—day or night."

The road curved around the first doublewides which hid the

smaller trailers in the rear.

"Danny'll turn up safe," she said, hunting for a fresh tissue. "I just know it."

"Of course."

"They've got his picture in the newspaper," she said as he pulled up. "And someone will see it and—"

"Good idea," he turned off the engine and sat there. "I was just thinking of that."

"*What?*" Molly turned to him in surprise.

"I mean aside from the police, that would be the logical—"

"I figured that's how you knew?"

Larry look to her baffled. "Oh no, I didn't see that."

"Then how did you find out?"

Larry hesitated.

Molly wiped the tears from her eyes and blew her nose. The color was back in her face, this time beet red. "Well?" she persisted.

"This detective came around."

"Detective?" Molly's jaw tightened. "You mean Tripoli?"

The police were canvassing the trailer park, too. As Larry drove off, Molly spotted a uniform at the Dolph's trailer. Old lady Dolph, in frayed pink bathrobe with matching curlers, opened the door a crack. Her mongrel squeezed out, growling and baring his teeth.

The cop had a hand on his can of mace. "You wanna put that dog back inside?"

By the time the dog was locked away, Molly was already in her car.

"Just want to ask you a few questions," Molly heard before she started the engine. She could guess what the questions were. Tripoli, that two-faced bastard of a cop, suspected *her.*

At the police station on Clinton Street, she was directed to the command post on Green. When she got to the firehouse, she finally found the right door and stormed in, brushing past a guy with pony tail and puffy sideburns. A real dirt bag, she thought.

"Well, excuse me," he chimed, smiling a snaggled, missing-toothed smile as he looked her up and down. "Hmmmm," said Charley Paul admiringly; Molly could feel her skin crawl.

There were cops and troopers milling about, men and women sitting at phones set up on a long table. She recognized Dianne Lifsey off to one side. Her boy Stevie was in an adjacent room, sitting with a police woman. There were maps of the downtown city blocks taped up on the walls, marked block by block with different colors and pins. A uniformed cop was sitting in front of a television screen watching what looked like a tape from a surveillance camera. Molly recognized the view of the area around the Green Street Mini Mart.

"Where's Tripoli?" she demanded of one of the female officers.

"He's probably over in…" she began to motion, but Molly was already off.

She found him in the kitchen. His back was turned to her and he was pouring a cup of coffee.

"You sonofabitch!" she shouted.

Tripoli whirled around on his feet, nearly knocking over his cup. His hand was already instinctively reaching for his gun.

When he spotted her, he looked almost relieved. "Oh…" was all he said.

"I may not be the world's brightest individual, but I certainly know what you're up to. You think *I* did something to Danny."

"Look—"

"Look my ass!"

"It's my job to follow every—"

"If you guys had been doing your job, this might never have happened. Instead, you're out giving parking tickets and chasing people with missing taillights when you've got all these crazies roaming town!"

"Calm down!" he said.

"If you think for one instant I'd do anything to my baby—well, then…" and she turned on her heels and marched out of the fire-house without finishing her sentence because she knew she would start crying again.

Tripoli started to pursue her, but she jumped into her car, slammed the door, and drove off.

The phone was ringing when she got back to the trailer. She fumbled with her keys, and by the time she got the door open her machine was already squawking the taped announcement.

She leaped for the phone and shouted "Wait!" into the mouthpiece while she groped for the button to kill the machine.

"Okay," she said breathlessly when it stopped. "Are you still there? Hello?"

"I saw your little boy," said a creaky old woman's voice.

"*What?*"

"I saw Danny."

"What?" Her heart felt as if it had stopped. "Who is this?"

"My name is…" the woman paused as if having to recall. "My name…is…Edna."

"Edna who?"

"Poyer."

"Edna Poyer," repeated Molly. Her heart had now kicked in full speed.

"Yup."

"You said you saw Danny?"

"Yup! Yesterday."

"Where?"

There was a voice in the background.

"Can't you see, I'm having a conversation?" said Mrs. Poyer indignantly.

"Mrs. Poyer? Edna?" said Molly.

"Give me that phone back!" demanded Mrs. Poyer.

And then the phone was hung up, the connection severed.

"Hello?" cried Molly into the silence. "Hello?"

Molly hung up and ran for the phone book. There was not a single Poyer in the Ithaca directory. She called Syracuse information. Then Elmira and Binghamton.

She called the Ithaca City Police and was switched over to the command post.

After a long wait, she got Tripoli on the phone.

"Oh, you," was all he said.

"I'm sorry. I know you're trying to help," said Molly without a hint of apology in her voice.

"I'm glad you realize that." He sounded a little offended.

"I just got a call. Some old lady says she saw Danny."

"When?"

"Yesterday."

"Where?"

"That's just it. The connection got broken. Someone took the phone away from her."

"Got any idea who it was?"

"She said her name was Edna. Edna Poyer."

"Oh, her," said Tripoli. "Wait, hang on a sec." He covered the mouth piece and she could hear him talking to someone. "Oh, yeah. Sorry," said Tripoli, coming back. "Where were we?"

Molly tried to control her rising anger. "Edna Poyer. You said you know her?"

"Edna? Sure, she's one of our regulars."

"What does *that* mean?"

"She's up at Oak Hill Manor."

"Oak Hill? You mean the nursing home?"

"Edna's got a tendency to take unauthorized walks. Also, she likes to call us. She sees a lot of things. Suspicious people. Her dead husband. President Truman."

Molly thought for a moment. "Okay. So maybe she's a little nuts. But maybe she did see something."

"Sure. Always a possibility."

"You gonna check it out?"

"We're covering every single base—as you've discovered."

"Yeah…Look, I'm sorry. I didn't mean to blow up like that," said Molly finally.

Tripoli didn't say anything.

"But I don't give a damn about your feelings," she said softly. "I just need to find my boy."

Tripoli hung up the phone, wrote down the name Edna Poyer, and then went over to Jerry Sisler, who had asked to join the Driscoll team. Sisler was at one of the computers doing background checks on the daycare staff as well as running criminal histories on likely suspects. Among other leads, he was compiling a preliminary list of men who had a predilection for very young boys. Sisler had joined the force only three years ago. He was young and still bright-eyed, a fair-haired, pug-nosed kid whose father had been a cop, too. The older Sisler had been killed in a freakish accident. A tanker carrying septic waste had jack-knifed on the highway near Dryden, swinging around and crushing Cliff Sisler's cruiser. Tripoli had taken the young Jerry under his wing, and to the rest of the department it was clear that he was grooming him to be a detective.

"There are a lot of nuts here in Tompkins County," said Sisler, punching the Enter key. The printer spewed out the file of known offenders. "Flashers. Pedophiles and perverts. Rapists. Kiddy diddlers," Sisler scanned his list. "Run-of-the-mill sexual offenders. Guys accused of molesting their little stepsons and nephews. This should be pretty complete, I think."

"We'll get Jack Knuutila and his troopers to run them down and establish their whereabouts for yesterday afternoon. And what about Oltz?"

"She's clean, but her husband was up on tax evasion charges a couple of years back. Louella, one of their help, had her license pulled for DWI and her husband did a little time for B&E."

"Oh?"

"Small time shit. The asshole broke into someone's garage and stole a VCR that didn't even work."

"And Sylvia?"

"Sweet old grandmotherly type. Not even a parking violation."

"What about Cheryl?"

"Nothing much. She got snagged for shoplifting over at Kmart two years ago. Some cosmetics and crap. Her father flew in with a bigshot lawyer from New York, and the case was dismissed."

"What's the story on Charley Paul?"

"He's a wife beater, but other than that not much. His ex just got a protection order."

"Who's the ex?"

Sisler pulled a file and shuffled through it. "Austin. Sheila Austin."

"Didn't we—"

"Yeah, we had her a couple of times for drunk and disorderly."

"Where does she work?" asked Tripoli with a half smile. He had already made the connection and took pleasure in watching Sisler play catch up.

"In that convenience store…Oh!" he said, slapping his forehead. "Up the block from Kute Kids. He's been stalking his old lady?"

"What do you think?

"Sure. That's why he doesn't want to talk."

"You're a little slow," said Tripoli with exaggerated indulgence, "but eventually you get it."

Sisler reddened. "Okay, what else?"

Tripoli thought for a moment. "Why don't you see if you can get us a list of women who had a child die in the last five years—six—no, wait, make it seven. I want it with male children first.

"How do I do that, Trip?"

Tripoli liked Sisler. And he knew he would be a good detective one day. But sometimes he seemed as bright as a small appliance bulb.

"I don't know," said Tripoli. "That's your problem. Talk to Lynn Spino." He motioned in her direction where she stood off to the side talking to a trooper. "Lynn's done it before. And—while you're at it—I want a list of recent miscarriages. Check with the doctors over at Fifty Fingers on Buffalo Street," he said, referring to the five gynecologists who handled almost all the obstetrics in town. "And get a list of people who lost custody of their kids—flag those around the Driscoll boy's age. You can probably get that through Social Services. And get ahold of the parole office. I want to know who's out on the street that we need to be worried about."

Tripoli left Sisler and walked to the wall where the street maps hung. He stared blankly at the big county map, the highways radiating out from the base of the lake where Ithaca sat nestled in the valley; stared at the flat projection of hills and streams as if it contained the secret to Danny Driscoll's whereabouts. And he thought about Molly, the sheer hell she was going through.

The Oak Hill Manor Home was just above town on South Hill. It sat on Hudson street discretely tucked away in a neighborhood of elegant old houses that Molly had always admired.

Molly parked at the side of the building and took the first door she could find, which brought her into the lobby. She stood there for a moment trying to get her bearings. Down one of the corridors she could see old folks sitting in chairs and an ancient man shuffling down a hallway hunched over a walker. Somewhere a person was persistently coughing, trying to clear his chest of phlegm. Two televisions were running, competing with the piped-in music oozing in from overhead. The air was filled with the powerful scent of disinfectant which failed to mask the odor of age and human decay.

A portly woman in uniform whites approached Molly, her head so massive and doughy that her eyes seemed little more than sunken raisins. She wore a nameplate that identified her as Daphne.

"Oh, you're the woman on television with the missing boy. I recognize you."

"They've got it on already?"

"Oh, yes. Definitely. They had you on the news at noon. And in the paper, too—which is why Edna called you."

Daphne seemed to know everything.

"I was the one who took the phone from her. I'm sorry she called you," she smiled sympathetically. "You certainly don't need more upset."

"Then she didn't see my boy?" asked Molly, the disappointment swelling in her voice.

"Honey, that woman's been seeing a lot of people in the last years—JFK and Elvis included," she shook her head and laughed. "Mostly it's politicians, though. She was one of those political science professors up at the University, I hear. Smart as a whip in her day. But, well, you get close to ninety and things up here," she touched her temple, "just go downhill."

"Could I talk to her?"

"Why of course," Daphne said. "She's always happy to have company. But I wouldn't take anything she says too seriously." And she led the way.

They walked down a long hallway, skirting a man in a wheelchair who was chanting to himself as he rocked back and forth. In one of the rooms, a woman with crumpled features lay in a bed, her tiny head nestled in a large white pillow, her eyes closed, her mouth gaping wide. In the next room, a man with an oxygen tank feeding a gizmo hooked into his nose sat upright in a chair, staring blankly out a window. It struck Molly as bizarre that she was here, of all places, looking for her little boy.

Edna Poyer had a room to herself. She was a remarkably sprightly little woman who apparently liked makeup, though no longer had quite the knack for applying it. Her lips had been painted with a shaky hand and her face was garishly rouged. She was sitting on the edge of her bed when Molly came in, and she immediately got to her feet.

"Mrs. Poyer, you got yourself a visitor," said Daphne loudly. "Though what you did was not very nice."

"Please," Molly said, silencing Daphne with a hand.

"Well, I'll leave you two," Daphne said with raised voice. Turning to Molly, she added sotto voce, "She doesn't hear none too good, so you gotta talk loud."

"I heard that," Edna said when Daphne was out of the door. "That woman's always patronizing me!"

Molly was taken aback. So, she *was* alert.

"Now," Edna said, "we've got to get ready for our meeting." With a delicately boned hand, she fussed with her hair which was snow white and so sparse you could see the pink of her scalp.

"Meeting?"

"National Security Council, right? That's why you're here, isn't it?"

Molly's hopes nosedived.

"They need us to advise them. We want to be primed and ready to go. Did you bring the briefing papers?"

"That's not why I came."

"Oh?" said Edna, looking askance.

"I came because of my boy. Danny. Danny Driscoll."

Edna looked thoroughly puzzled.

"Is he one of my grad students?"

"No, he's just a little boy."

"Well, you certainly look too young to have a son who's a grad student. To me, though, everyone looks so young!" she giggled. Her skin was paper thin; lines of blue veins coursed their way up the sides of her neck and temples.

Molly tried to control her impatience. "You called me about a half an hour ago."

"Oh, you're the one working for the Warren Commission?"

"I'm the mother of the missing boy."

"Oh, the missing boy," said Edna as if it were the most obvious thing in the world.

"You saw him?"

"Couldn't miss the little tyke. Cute little boy."

"Where'd you see him?"

"Out in front of Woolworth's," responded Edna immediately.

"What were you doing there?"

"Where?"

"In front of Woolworth's."

"If I was there, I was probably shopping."

"So you were standing where?"

"You know…what's your name?"

"Molly."

"You know, Molly, I knew that McCarthy was going to fall under the weight of his own arrogance. I remember—"

"Mrs. Poyer—"

"Professor Poyer," Edna corrected.

"You said you saw my little boy."

"Yes. I saw him. In front of Woolworth's."

"When?"

"When I was there!" she shook her head. "Heavens, you keep

asking the same questions all the time."

Molly tried to keep in check her mounting frustration. She took a deep breath and slowly exhaled. She was beginning to suspect that Lou Tripoli might have been right.

"What did you see?"

"I saw your little boy. You could hardly help noticing a little guy like that crossing streets on his own. I would *never* have allowed any of my children to be out on their own, what with traffic and all."

"So?"

"So naturally, I asked him, 'Are you allowed to be out alone?'"

"And?"

"And he said it was okay, and just marched on."

"To where?"

"Last thing I saw he was heading to those stairs that lead to South Hill." Edna turned to gaze out the window. A flurry of yellow and brown drifted down from a nearby tree whose base was already encircled with a carpet of leaves matted from the early snow. In the protected shadows there were still hidden patches of snow.

When Edna turned back she said, "I think I'm going to be offered that ambassadorship to Czechoslovakia—and it won't cost anyone a plugged nickel. How's that?"

"What did the boy look like?" asked Molly, quickly adding, "The one in front of Woolworth's."

"Of course, this administration owes me a few favors."

"Professor Poyer—"

"Heavens, call me Edna."

"Edna. The little boy you saw at Woolworth's? What did he look like?" Molly insisted.

"Him? The little guy?"

"Yes. Yes!"

"Maybe four. Five. Not six. Big head of blond curly hair. That the one?"

"Yes," said Molly hoarsely. "What was he wearing?"

Edna wrinkled her forehead in thought. "Hmmm," was all she said.

"Thanks," said Molly, getting up to go. Edna had obviously studied the picture in the paper.

Molly had reached the doorway when she heard Edna voice. "Had on a little flannel shirt."

Molly froze.

"One of those red ones with crisscrossing lines. Blue and yellow."

Molly's breath caught. Her heart started to pound and her thoughts raced.

"I remember he had sneakers on. White sneakers with markings or something?"

Molly slowly turned, afraid to startle Edna. She looked searchingly into the milkiness of Edna's eyes.

"My memory just isn't what it used to be," admitted Edna.

"Wait," said Molly, trying to recall precisely the description she had given Wally Schuman and his reporters, "you read that in the paper, didn't you?"

"There's been absolutely no mention in the papers yet about my appointment. Everything's still hush-hush," said Edna, putting a gnarled finger to her painted lips. "And I hope I can rely on your discretion."

Molly found Daphne in a resident's room nearby. She was hoisting another frail man from his bed to a chair.

"Was Edna out yesterday?"

Daphne nodded.

"About what time?"

"The police brought her back around four in the afternoon."

Molly's heart was now racing so hard she felt light-headed.

"Do you have today's *Ithaca Journal* here?"

"Sure. One second." She lifted the emaciated man seemingly without any effort and slipped him into a contraption with wheels that reminded Molly of Danny's old highchair. "There you go, Mr. Cantrell."

Mr. Cantrell's hands were shaking and he mumbled something inaudible. Daphne slid a tray into the chair, locking the man tightly in place.

In the office, Daphne found the morning's newspaper. Sure enough, on the front page was Danny's picture. And in color. Molly scanned the story feverishly. It gave his age, his height, but nowhere did it mention that the shirt was flannel. Just that it was red. She grabbed the phone in the nurse's office and called the police hotline listed in the paper.

"Let me talk to Lou Tripoli," she said when an officer answered.

"Who's this?"

"Molly Driscoll."

"He's in a meeting."

"Well get him out. It's important."

She waited.

"Okay, what's up?" asked Tripoli when he finally came on.

"I'm up at Oak Hill Manor."

"Oh, shit," he mumbled.

"No you hear me out. That woman may be out of her skull some of the time, but she's not totally bonkers."

"You can't rely on anything she says."

"She was out yesterday on the streets."

"We know that. We were the ones who brought her back."

"She says she saw Danny in front of Woolworth's. By himself. Walking."

"That doesn't—"

"Hold on. She described what he was wearing. A red flannel shirt. Sneakers."

"Well, that description was out to every agency in the county. She could have—"

"Not the flannel part. That wasn't in the papers. And don't tell me that she has a scanner and monitors the police frequencies."

"So she got it from the TV."

"Wait. There's more. She described his shirt as red with blue and yellow crisscrossing lines—which is exactly right except for some black lines—and *no one* knew that. Not even you guys."

"I'll send up someone to talk to her—if you insist."

"I insist."

"But I just can't drop everything this instant. I just don't want to waste precious time checking out red herrings when we could be following better leads. We've got tons of possibilities we've got to exhaust. Come on, please, Molly, trust me on this a little. Okay?"

It's odd, thought Tripoli the next morning as he stared out his window at the passing traffic. People act like a school of fish. All of a sudden they all turn left. Or right. No telling. Now they were all terrified. They were keeping their little kids home from school, locking doors usually left unlocked, eyeing one another suspiciously. Somewhere in town there was a maniac loose who was abducting little children. Tripoli knew you couldn't reason with rampant fear, yet he could feel the pressure building. Maybe he was causing some of it, too. They were pulling in and grilling anyone within a fifty-mile radius who had a record which might indicate an abduction or kidnapping—and getting absolutely nowhere. Canvassing the neighborhoods was yielding nothing. They had gotten calls from people who claimed to have seen Danny. He had been spotted in the Pizza Hut out on Route 13, up by the roller rink in the Northeast, down at Cass Park on a baseball field. Every little blond kid seemed to be a sighting, yet they had no choice but to check out every possibility, no matter how improbable.

Richie Pellegrino came by in the early afternoon after his shift. "How's it going, Trip?" he asked, dropping into one of the metal folding chairs next to Tripoli. It creaked under his weight.

"I don't know," Tripoli shook his head. The people on his team were still working the phones, but turning up nothing you could really dig your claws into. "This looks worse and worse with time. The troopers are helping us put together a search party. In another hour, they'll be ready to roll."

"Yeah, but search where?"

"That's the question. Suppose he wasn't abducted. Suppose he walked on his own. How far do you think a little kid could get?"

"Depends on the kid…" Pellegrino scratched his head. "A couple miles maybe."

"Yeah, I was thinking along the lines of a three-mile perimeter for starters. Check out all the gorges. Maybe use dogs…You know, I would have done it earlier, but she—the mother—had me convinced that the kid was swiped. Now I'm not so sure. I keep worrying. We got dozens of sightings, but none of them seems legit. There's always something off. But what if I make a mistake and…"

Pellegrino couldn't help but detect the note of guilt in Tripoli's voice—which wasn't very characteristic of the man. "Hey, you want me to do something?"

"Appreciate the offer."

"I feel sorry for the girl."

"Well, in that case…Molly called from up at old Edna's."

Pellegrino rolled his eyes. "Geez, Edna."

"Says that Edna saw the boy that same day he disappeared in front of Woolworth's."

"Well, she certainly was out roaming then. Stevenson brought her back."

"Yeah…"

"Remember when that guy with the ski mask tried to rob the

Trust Company?"

Tripoli smiled at the memory. "Yeah, and Edna saw him ripping off his ski mask on Aurora Street while he was fleeing."

"Said the guy looked exactly like Sidney Poitier."

"Except it turned out to be Joe Fitchen, who's about as black as an albino. Just one little thing here, Richie. Keeps nagging me."

"Like?"

"Molly says old Edna can describe the kid's shirt."

"That's no secret."

"But apparently she told Molly that the shirt had crisscrossing stripes of yellow and blue."

"And how reliable is Molly?"

"You want to go up to Oak Hill for me?"

"Visit my old friend Edna?"

"It'd be a help."

"Don't hold your breath." Pellegrino heaved himself up from the chair. The seat was so hard one of his legs had gone to sleep. He worked it, trying to bring it back to life.

"You know, it's very simple," said Tripoli, thinking out loud. "The kid either walked or was taken. There's no other choice, right?"

"The father," said Pellegrino. "Did you get a line on him?"

"Nothing. Zip. Relatives don't have a clue. His mother hasn't seen him in eight years—you might say they were estranged. You know, Chuck must have dumped his social security number and driver's license and started from scratch. Sisler found an old set of prints on file at the courthouse from when he got a gun permit; but I ran it through the F.B.I.; he's not gotten in trouble, not popped up as an unidentified body somewhere, and not applied for a new pistol permit."

"I'll go say hello to Edna."

Molly couldn't sit still. She kept driving around town, starting in the Green Street neighborhood and moving in an ever-widening circle.

Every time she saw a cop car, she would flash her lights, come abreast of them, and roll down her window.

"Any news?"

By now all the cops knew who she was. Sometimes she didn't have to flag them down; sometimes they just pulled over when they saw her and got out of their car.

"Trip is doing just about everything he can," said Officer Harry Beaner, taking off his dark glasses and squinting in the low sun. Molly could see Danny's picture attached to the clipboard on the front seat of his patrol car. "And Trip's the best."

"Trip?" she repeated.

"Yeah, that's what we call him. His friends and people."

"Trip...hmmm." She liked the sound of it. It fit him.

"He's good people," Harry continued. "Believe me. He'd give you the shirt right off his back—if you needed it."

When she swung by her trailer, there was an unmarked radio car parked in front. Tripoli was sitting inside eating a sandwich. There were puffy bags under his eyes, and he needed a shave.

He stepped out of his car as she pulled up.

"How're you holding up?" he asked, chewing and hurriedly swallowing the mouthful.

"Good as can be expected under the circumstances."

There was mustard smeared on the left side of his mouth. She laughed despite herself and pointed to her lips.

"Oh," he said and leaned into his car to hunt for a napkin.

"Here," she said, opening her purse and pulling out a tissue. "I think this is clean."

"Thanks," he said.

"No, the other side."

He briskly rubbed around his lips.

"Here, give me that," she said impatiently, took the tissue and wiped his chin.

He seemed embarrassed by the gesture.

"You look tired," he said.

"Looks like you didn't get too much sleep either, huh?"

"Sleep?" He smiled wearily. "What's that?"

"You want to come in?"

"No. I just came by to get something."

"Like?"

"A piece of Danny's clothing."

Molly felt her stomach sink.

He raised a hand. "Now just hold on before you start to panic."

"Who's panicked? I just—"

"We've organized a search party. We've got over a hundred people. And I got some dogs lined up."

"Good!" she said emphatically.

She went into the trailer and came back in less than a minute with a handful of Danny's clothes.

"None of this has been washed. Come on, let's go," she said, leaving no doubt about her intentions.

When they got to Woolworth's, there was already a group searching the stream bed behind the store. The men were in high waders, working both ends of the creek, which was flowing briskly. The late afternoon sun was low, casting long shadows across the cold water, magnifying the size of every boulder and tree.

While they sat in his car watching the operation, Tripoli told Molly they were also checking the inlet and the near end of the lake.

"What does *checking* mean?"

Tripoli hesitated.

"You mean like dragging?"

He nodded.

"Do me a favor?"

"Hmm?"

"I can't stomach bullshit. Just give it to me straight from now on, no matter what it is, no matter how bad. Okay?"

He nodded.

They were also searching up at the reservoir, he told her quietly, and Six Mile Creek near Giles Street.

"You're thinking maybe he went *fishing?*"

"I'm beginning to think that maybe he got out somehow. He was probably pissed off after they punished him."

Molly looked at him long and hard.

"The girl who was working at Kute Kids…" he swallowed. "Cheryl? Turns out she wasn't such an angel with kids."

Molly kept quiet.

"She had locked Danny in the basement as punishment for a little while."

Tripoli watched her face expecting a reaction. When he got none, he said, "So you knew, huh?"

"Yeah. I knew."

"So who's bullshitting who?"

"That's different."

"Like hell it is!"

"I got Cheryl to admit to it by promising not to tell."

"Well, from now on I'd appreciate it if you don't cut any deals with my witnesses, all right?"

"Hey, I'll be straight with you. Just you be straight with me. Okay?" Molly held out her hand.

"Okay." Tripoli took her hand. "A deal," he said, shaking her hand and holding it tight.

Molly looked down to see her fingers enfolded in his large grip, looked up at him, and felt his hand slip shyly away.

He looked at her for a long moment, then shifted his eyes away. Later, when he wasn't aware, she ventured a look at him, studying his face in profile. His features were strong, cleft chin, prominent nose and brow—all clearly delineated, like his character. He had a strong sense of self, of right and wrong, knew who he was. Molly liked that about him. It gave her comfort and made her comfortable in his presence. She knew she was lucky to have him looking for her boy. She could hardly have found a better man for the job.

The door to the trailer was unlocked and Rosie walked right in. She caught Molly sitting at the kitchen table staring blankly into space.

"Oh, Rosie," she gasped, and the tears sprung to her eyes. Her hands were balled into tight fists. "I'm scared. Really scared now. It's too long already."

"I kept trying to call you all day, and either the line is busy or you're out," she put her arms around Molly and brought her face close. "What's going on?"

"Nothing's going on!" Both of them were crying.

"I tried to work, but couldn't keep my mind on anything but Danny."

"It's so damn cold outside and he doesn't even have his jacket. He hasn't eaten." Molly trembled. "He's lost. Someone's taken him. He's dead already. I don't know what to think."

The icy air was pouring into the trailer and Rosie went back and closed the front door.

"Oh, I'm so tired." Molly put her head down on the table and wept. "None of this feels real anymore."

"You need some food," said Rosie in her usual take-charge way and set to work, rummaging through the cabinets and fridge. She found some eggs, some mushrooms, and cheese. "Louie Tripoli came by to see me at work," she said as she beat the eggs with milk and then slipped the mixture into a hot frying pan that sizzled.

"He saw my boss, too. I'm worried that he's wasting his time—that maybe he suspects me in some way."

"Well if he did, he doesn't anymore," Rosie laughed. "Not after the earful of shit I gave him!" She layered the mushrooms and cheese on the congealing omelet.

"He's not a bad guy, really." Molly pressed her fingers against her head and rubbed her temples, trying to drive away the dull throbbing that had started in the late afternoon. "He even gave me the number to his cell phone—said I could call him day or night."

Rosie slipped the omelet onto a plate. "Yeah. Sure." She brought the plate to the table. "I'm sure they want to find Danny as much as we do—whatta you want to drink with this?"

Suddenly, the phone rang and Molly lunged for it.

"Hi, this is Wally Schuman," said a man's voice.

It took Molly a second. "Oh, right, the newspaper man. Thanks for the picture. And all the help."

"Don't even mention it. Reason I called is that we're running another story."

"And Danny's picture, too?"

"Sure. Of course. It's on the wire now, too. It looks like a lot of other papers around the state have picked up the story. Our Gannett wire service has it, too."

"Good. Ask people to call the police if they've seen anything, anything at all. Somebody spotted Danny that afternoon, you know."

"*Really?*"

Molly told him about Edna Poyer. He, too, knew Edna. Everybody in town seemed to know Edna. "But she described his shirt perfectly. There was no way…Look, somebody else must have seen him, too."

"Well, we'll run it in the story. See what pops up."

"And maybe just say something like…well, if anybody took Danny, I'm begging them to let him go. I'd do anything to get him back. *Anything!*"

Despite herself, Molly was crying again. "Damn it!" she said, banging down the phone. "I can't even talk anymore. I don't know what to say. What to do."

"You gotta trust in God," said Rosie. She got Molly to sit down, then slid in next to her and tried coaxing her into eating as if she were a child.

"Well, maybe that's okay for you," said Molly blowing her nose loudly. "My mom believed in all that Jesus and church crap, and just look where it got her."

They ate in silence. Rosie kept wanting to turn on the television to see if anything was going on, but Molly couldn't bear it. Rosie wanted to sleep over, but Molly was afraid that having her stay the night would lend an air of permanence to Danny's absence. The thought of Rosie sleeping in Danny's bed—or even out on the couch—somehow seemed more of threat than a consolation.

"Go home and sleep," she insisted around midnight. "Ed needs you, too."

"But…"

"I'm going to take a sleeping pill and knock myself out."

chapter five

The days started to flow into each other. Time became elastic; Molly was no longer sure if it was being compressed or stretched. She kept checking her calendar. How long had Danny been missing? What could be measured before in hours now became days. First three days. Then a week. Then almost two weeks. It was all a nightmarish blur.

Somewhere in that dream-like continuum, Doreen came over from the office with bread she had baked. "It's nothing," she said, looking a bit embarrassed. "It's the only thing that came to mind. That I could..."

Days later, Ben, the editor Larry had hired just before she joined the crew, came by with flowers. "I just wanted to let you know we're all thinking of you," he said.

Molly opened the paper wrapping to inhale their fragrance. "Oh, they're lovely," she uttered and, before she even realized it, her tears were wetting the petals.

Ben awkwardly put his arm around her shoulder. "Come back soon. We miss you," he whispered, and then fled before getting emotional himself.

Dianne Lifsey, little Stevie's mother, called to commiserate and find out what was going on. "We still can't get over what's happened," said Mrs. Lifsey. "It's terrible. Really terrible." In her voice Molly thought she detected an undercurrent of better-your-Danny-than-my Stevie, but she could hardly blame her.

"The state authorities have shut the place down," said Stevie's mother. "My husband says that Kute Kids probably had extensive liability coverage. You might want to look into it. He's a lawyer, you know."

One morning, there was yet another TV crew outside waiting for her. They were from one of the major networks, and reluctantly she let them in. With their lights and equipment squeezed into the trailer, there was hardly room to turn around.

The producer was a young man who, despite his beard and mustache, looked almost like a teenager. He kept asking inane questions like, "How does it feel to have your boy missing and not know where he is?"

Molly refused to be provoked to tears or give a flippant reply. She tried to respond calmly. She appealed to the kidnapper to not harm her son and asked viewers to be on the lookout for Danny.

"Did you investigate that daycare center before sending your boy there?"

Molly didn't even tackle that one.

While the crew was packing, the producer turned to her and said, "This is going to get you national attention."

"Great," said Molly, finally yielding to her impulses. "Now my kid can be a star on milk cartons."

At least two or three times a day, Molly talked to Tripoli. "We're still working on it," he said, but she could detect in his voice, even see in his face when he came by, that they were losing hope. Molly clung to her hope, although with each passing day it grew progressively harder. She spent every single day searching the town and surrounding areas, handing out pictures of Danny, tacking up posters. She checked in with the police constantly, hounding them for any leads and racing off to investigate them on her own. A farmer had found a boy's sneaker in a pasture, size one. One of the little girls from Kute Kids just remembered Danny saying something about going on a trip. Sometimes she worked alongside Tripoli, and was surprised and grateful that he never made her feel like she was in the way. At nights, although she was exhausted, sleep did not come easy as her mind raced, trying to find an answer.

Late one night, two weeks after Danny went missing, she lay in bed, staring at the ceiling. Outside the wind had picked up again. She could hear the dry leaves being tossed and scattered around the trailer, the rumble of a distant truck on the nearby highway. Around one in the morning, the Dolph's dog started its compulsive barking at the night.

Molly took a hot shower, washed her hair, and got into a fresh nightgown. Sleep would never come, she told herself as she crawled back into bed. But when she closed her eyes, she immediately fell into a deep and dreamless oblivion.

Then, out of the blackness, came the jarring ring of her phone. In the stillness of the night, it seemed unusually loud and harsh.

"Oh!" she groaned aloud, bolting upright in her bed. It took her a couple of extra rings to figure out where she was and what was happening.

Barefoot, she dashed for the phone in the living room, her mind struggling to break out of its haze. The phone was not in the living room, but had been left on the kitchen counter. Groping her way around in the darkness, she finally took the receiver into her hands.

"We've got your boy," said a gritty male voice.

"*What?*"

"You heard me."

Standing in the unlit trailer, feet bare on the cold linoleum, Molly's senses were suddenly alert. "Who is—"

"If you wan' him back, it's gonna cost you."

Molly's chest tightened.

"What do you want?"

"First, don't talk to the police."

"Okay by me. That's no problem." Something about the voice bothered her. "Just tell me what you want?"

"Money."

"Fine. How much? Where?"

There was a brief pause, as if the man seemed to be taken aback by Molly's quick agreement.

"A hun'red thousand," he said. There was the whoosh of a passing car in the background, then silence. He was probably standing outside in a phone booth.

"No problem," said Molly without a flinch in her voice. Now she knew what it was about the guy that struck her. "Tell me where you want it delivered and it's all yours, mister."

Silence. "Okay…" he said, stalling.

"Just one thing," Molly added. "Tell me what he's got on."

"Huh?"

"Describe what he's wearing. You want to make an exchange. No problem. I got your money. And you got my kid, right?"

"Not right here."

"But you've seen him, right?"

"My partner—"

"Your partner nothing. What's Danny wearing?"

"Clothes," said the guy.

"Mister, either you're full of shit or your memory's shot. Which is it?" Molly was now getting angry.

"You want the kid, don't you? You give me a lot of bullshit, and—"

"You want the money, don't you?"

"What the fuck is this?" shouted the guy. "I'm gonna hang up if you keep giving me any more of this crap."

"Hey, be my guest," said Molly, "But the next time you call, you'd better have a better description." And *she* hung up.

Molly turned on the lights. She found her pocketbook, rifled through the jumble of Kleenex and keys and stray lipstick, and pulled out a yellow slip of paper. On it, in Tripoli's awkward scrawl, was the number to his cellular phone.

He answered almost immediately. "Oh, Molly. Yeah...listen, hang on a second, can you?"

She could hear him talking in the background. It sounded like a one-sided conversation. Apparently, he was on another phone.

Then, a minute later, he was back. "Okay, sorry about that," he said yawning loudly.

"I just got a call from some creep who says he has Danny."

"Yeah, I know."

"*Know?*"

"We've got a tap on your line. I'm glad you kept him talking."

"You got him?"

"Got the asshole. Soon he'll be sitting and staring at a wall of steel bars."

"So who was it?"

"Just your run-of-the-mill lowlife. Don't worry about it."

Molly was thinking about the phone tap. "That means you *knew* Edna called me."

Silence.

"Well, did you or didn't you?"

Silence.

"Well, yeah, I knew. Sure."

"And you—"

"Give me a break, Molly, will you?"

"You've got to stop bullshitting me."

"And you've got to trust me a little bit, too. I'm running an investigation. I can't tell you every little thing that I'm doing."

"Well I'm glad you had a tap on the line," Molly confessed. "I was thinking, damn, maybe that jerk really did have Danny and here I was blowing him off."

"Is that an apology?"

"Don't get carried away, Trip," she said.

"*Trip?*" he echoed.

"I'm running my own investigation on you."

Molly wanted to continue, say something witty, but the only things that kept coming to mind were ragged images: the narrow little suspension bridge dangling over the deep gorge where every year a couple of University students leapt to their deaths. The thundering falls down at the high school, its drenching spray coating the slimy sidewalls of the ravine with ice. The crevasses and fissures of the Ithaca landscape that could swallow a child whole. There was comfort in Tripoli's voice, a confident, reassuring tone; as long as they were talking, the horrors seemed held at bay. She knew he was tired, but selfishly craved to keep him on the line.

"Hey, Trip—all right if I call you that?"

"You can call me whatever you want—as long as it's clean." He tried to joke.

"I'm sorry to ruin your sleep."

"Nah, no problem. I gotta get up anyhow. What time is it?"

Molly went over to the clock. "4:30."

"Oh," he groaned, "I thought it was like six or something. Well, doesn't much matter. Once I'm up, I'm up."

"You don't sleep much, do you?"

"I do. But I'm like a camel. I've learned how to store it. Goes with the territory."

From what Molly could hear, he was now apparently in the kitchen rummaging around dishes, she judged, making coffee.

"What kind of place do you live in?"

"It's an old Greek Revival."

"Sounds nice.

"It was Kim's idea. My ex. Trouble is, I never got it quite revived."

Molly laughed softly.

"I redid the kitchen but, well, it's a little rough to say the least. It was this romantic idea we had. You know. Find a nice old house in the country with some land and a barn and fix it up. Trouble is, when the romance went out of the marriage it also deserted the project. And here I am, alone with my insulation and wallboard."

"You want to come over here?" asked Molly, surprising herself with the audacity of her suggestion.

Silence.

"I'm up for the duration, too," she quickly added. "I just thought…" Molly was so tired, she didn't know what she thought. Just knew that if he was near, she'd somehow feel more secure. "You might as well have coffee over here—hey, where do you live, anyhow?"

"Newfield…"

He was clearly debating with himself.

"Okay," he said finally. "I can come over for a little. But let me just check in at the command post first, okay?"

"Whatever," she said. "I don't think I'm going anywhere right now."

Tripoli got to Molly's place more than an hour later. Camel or not, he looked thoroughly washed out.

"We questioned the idiot who called you. A real A-number-one dirtball," he said crossing the threshold to her door. "He didn't know anything."

"Coffee?" she asked. Molly was dressed in a robe over a pinkish nightgown whose frills peeked out at the neck. Her hair was tousled.

"Huh? Yeah. Sure." He was so tired he couldn't think.

She brought him a cup.

"I gotta sit down. I'm a little more blitzed than I thought," he admitted.

"You want to put your feet up?"

"Well…" he looked at her dubiously. "Yeah. Okay. Mind if I borrow your couch for a minute?"

"Sure."

Tripoli kicked off his shoes and lay back, the cup balanced on his chest. "Yeah, now this is an improvement," he sighed. He took a sip of coffee and felt a lot better. "You can't sleep, either, huh?"

"Sleep? I'm afraid to even close my eyes."

"I can certainly understand how you feel."

"Do you really think so?"

"Hey, it doesn't take much imagination."

"It's like there's a piece of me that's missing. And not just an arm or leg. More like a chunk carved right out of my insides," she grasped her chest. "Something vital. I keep thinking…well, what if we don't *ever* find Danny. One way or another. If you never know, if—"

"You're getting ahead of yourself. I think maybe we should take things as they happen."

There were tears in her eyes.

Tripoli's face contorted.

"Hey, I'm not going to cry again, don't worry."

He motioned for her, and she came over to the sofa and sat down on the floor beside him.

Without thinking, he reached out and took her hand.

She placed her other hand on top of his and let it rest there for a moment.

"A cop's hand," she muttered, taking it and turning it over to study the inside. It was massive and muscular, the fingers stubby. "They say you can tell a lot about a man by his hands."

He didn't say anything, just turned to watch her with his green eyes.

Molly looked at him. "You ever kill anybody, Mr. Cop?"

"No," he smiled, "though there are some real lowlifes I'd love to see moved to another planet."

"Ever shoot anybody?"

"Yeah, once. Some idiot who came at me with a knife. I got him in the leg. I'm not particularly proud of it."

She moved nearer to him. He reached out and tentatively stroked her hair. Tripoli could feel himself losing control. It was nuts, he told himself, but he couldn't help it. She seemed to be melting under his touch, and his exhausted brain was split in two, the hemispheres debating loudly. The rational half was being drowned out by the thumping and churning on the other side. "Hmmm," he said with muffled voice, bringing his nose close, "I love the smell of a woman's hair."

Molly turned her face up to his in an unmistakable offer.

He bolted upright, spilling the last dregs of coffee on his shirt. "Shit!" he said, wiping it off as best he could. "Hey, look," he said, gathering himself, "This is totally crazy."

"Sure," she said. "But I'm crazy already, so what the hell's the difference."

"I don't want to take advantage of you." His hands were shaking. "You're vulnerable."

She looked at him.

"And, yeah," he admitted, "I happen to be kind of vulnerable right now myself."

He kept talking. She let him talk. Didn't quite hear his words. Just looked at his face, open and exposed. There was pain written all over it. In that instant, she saw that he needed her almost as much as she needed him.

"Oh…" he uttered when he ran out of words. Molly's cheeks were flushed, her lips parted, and she was breathing heavily. The look on her face ignited him, silencing all the competing voices.

Their eyes were locked. Tripoli's face was florid, and she could feel his excitement under her touch. A vein on the side of his neck was throbbing.

Molly felt giddy, drunk with exhaustion as he took her face in his hands. She could feel his breath on her cheek. Then their lips met and Molly was surprised. Not by the kiss, but by its gentleness. She closed her eyes and kissed him, then moved her cheek against the coarseness of his stubble; the hint of a weary sigh bubbling up from deep within him.

They clung to one another, held each other tight.

"This way," she uttered hoarsely, took him by the hand and led him towards the rear of the trailer, the two of them moving in a trance.

He was disturbed to see the little boy's cot there in the bedroom and his toys just as he had seen them earlier. She took off her robe, pulled back the covers, and then everything was swept away by the wonder of her. Her nightgown was sheer and he could make out her breasts, the darkness of her nipples, the shape of her hips and legs.

"You going to just stand there?" she whispered.

"'Course not." he said, feeling clumsy, then slipped off his shirt and pants, and slid in next to her.

Molly pressed her face into his chest and clung to him, her grasp so tight it hurt. He could feel his bare chest becoming wet. She was crying, silently weeping.

He moved her slightly away and wiped her tears with his fingers.

"Come," she said, lifted her nightgown and offered herself to him.

She felt smooth and slippery, and in an instant all his thoughts were banished. He began moving with a tenderness and grace that Molly had never expected from him. She pressed herself upwards, towards him, wishing that she could absorb him completely, deeply, have him enter her and fill the agonizing void. Then she thought about Danny—couldn't stop herself—and burst into sobs.

He stopped abruptly, pulling back with his arms extended and looked worriedly down at her.

"No, don't stop," she pleaded in an urgent whisper. "Go. Go!" she cried, feeling herself being catapulted away. And a moment later, every worry and thought, every pang of guilt and anger and fear fell by the wayside as Molly felt herself being flung ever higher, the focus of her mind narrowing to a tight beam concentrated at her core. She cried in his ear, mutterings that made no earthly sense but spoke to levels deep within his mind. Now he was gasping for breath, and she could feel his whole body throbbing. If only I could stay here forever, she thought in the recesses of her mind, but then felt herself leveling off.

He came, quickly, a series of rigid jolts, his voice calling out in a low and lonely sounding sigh. Then he lay still and Molly could feel the world returning, the painful, cruel, sometimes joyous world. She gripped him tightly, her hands wrapped around his back, so fixedly he couldn't move. He was sweating and she freed a hand and lovingly wiped his brow.

"I'm sorry," he whispered finally.

"Shhh," she shushed him.

"I shouldn't have done this."

"Ssssh," she said, pressing her fingers against his lips. "Just stay here. Don't move. I want you here."

"Everybody's isolated," he said, lying in the darkness, his fingers tracing a circle around the crispness of her erect nipple. "Lonely. You see it as a cop all the time. It seems so rare that people touch each other's lives. Maybe it's always been that way. Maybe that's humanity's condition. I don't know."

Molly's eyes were closed.

"You sleeping?" he whispered, getting up on an elbow.

"No. Just listening. I like to listen to you talk." She moved closer, kissed him and then snuggled tightly between his arm and chest.

"What troubles me about life," he went on, "is that everything is so temporary. Not that I want to live forever, mind you. It's that even love seems to just come and go."

"Tell me about it," uttered Molly with a sad little sigh.

"I suppose you've got to take the good things when they come, as they come."

Silence.

"I'm feeling a little like a heel," he confessed later, sitting up in her bed. "We shouldn't have—"

"But I wanted to," she insisted. "You know, for a cop, you've got a heavy load of guilt."

"I'm just worried about the appropriateness of this is all."

"I don't think like that."

"Well, that's one of the things that I admire about you. You seem to do what has to be done or what you want to do, and you don't agonize about it."

"It's a waste of energy," she said. "I don't believe in spinning my wheels. Right now, the only thing I want to do is find my boy. I'll do anything I have to do to get him."

"Is that why you slept with me?" he asked pointedly.

"Don't be stupid. I slept with you out of pure selfishness. Out of need. And what's more, I like you. It wasn't just sex, don't you see that?"

He thought about it, then smiled. "Okay...Yeah."

When Molly awoke, Tripoli had already gone. It was almost nine and there was a note sitting on the counter.

> Sorry, I had to run off.
> Didn't want to wake you.
> Trip

A minute later, Rosie called.

"Did you get any sleep?"

Molly was tempted to tell her about Tripoli. After all, they rarely kept secrets from one another. In the end she decided against it— not that Rosie would be judgmental. It was just that she harbored this inherent distrust of cops and would probably put the wrong spin on it.

In the afternoon the phone stopped ringing and people ceased knocking on her door. Is this what it's going to come down to? she wondered. Me sitting alone, waiting for some word that will never come?

The F.B.I. had been called in because of the proximity to the Pennsylvania border. Danny's picture and description had been shared with law enforcement agencies around the country and posted with the National Center for Missing Children. There was a toll-free number leading to the command center and a reward offered for information. Yet nothing had turned up. Not a solitary trace of the boy. And all the media attention so far hadn't helped either. The only result was that her mailbox continued to be stuffed with cards and letters of concern. Some of them contained checks, even if mostly small ones, fives and tens. They were from people all over the country. Old, retired folks. School kids. Mostly working people, she surmised from the handwritten notes.

"Look at this," she said when Tripoli came over one evening. She lifted the stack of checks and let them flutter to the ground.

The police had been screening her mail at the post office and Tripoli was already aware of the contents.

"What are they thinking?" Molly asked. "That I can just go out and buy another kid?"

"I think they don't know what to do and want to help in some way."

"Sure," said Molly. "I understand. I'm just becoming bitter."

"Don't, please."

"You think I can control what I feel? And what am I supposed to do with this money? Should I send it back? Send a thank you note?"

"Why don't you hang on to it. You may need it."

"For what?"

Tripoli didn't want to say. He thought about telling her to keep it for when Danny came home, but he was really thinking about the expense of a funeral.

The beeper on his belt vibrated, and he looked down, trying to decipher the readout.

"I'll try to be back," he called over his shoulder as he hurried off to his car.

Molly waited up but, when he didn't return, she finally went to bed around midnight. First she was too hot and threw off the covers. Then she was too cold. She could hear the neighbor's mufflerless pickup cruising past. A cat in heat mewling. Somebody closing a door. Even her furnace seemed louder than usual. It was as though someone had captured the knob controlling the volume in her brain and just kept ratcheting it higher and higher.

Then, just as the sky was beginning to lighten, she finally lapsed into a deep sleep and began to dream. She was floating in billowing clouds of the most beautiful colors, pinks and purples and golds in profusion, their swirling shapes constantly changing. Everything was in turbulent motion, yet she felt oddly reassured and peaceful. She could hear the beat of a drum, and then the lush warm air became filled with beautiful music. Someone in the distance was singing in a high, reedy voice and, as the sound drew near, she suddenly realized it was Danny—Danny singing to her.

Then she saw animals—a huddled flock of sheep and goats, bleating and baahing. And there again was Danny standing in their midst, smiling at her. The vision was so crisp that she could make out the individual strands of Danny's hair, the lines inscribed on the irises of his eyes. Even within the depth of sleep it was apparent to Molly that she had never had a dream of such clarity and precise definition. Danny laughed, lifted his hand to wave to her. Molly called out to him and stretched out her arms as Danny rushed forward to embrace her. She felt him warm in her arms. She started to cry and he touched her cheek. He smiled at her and, suddenly, a covey of white doves swooped in to enclose them and she could feel the soft beating of wings around her body as she was swept dizzyingly upwards, lifted higher and higher until...

Then Molly awoke. She lay motionless, breathless, eyes wide, her skin still tingling where Danny had touched her. She sat up and looked over at the small bed tucked tight against the adjacent wall. Though its quilt of Disney characters remained as ever untouched, the bed no longer felt empty. Warmed by a glow that radiated from within, she knew for certain that Danny was still here on this earth. And that somehow, miraculously, he had been here. With her. In this trailer, this room.

She got up and showered, dressed, went through the rituals of morning as the early light of day filtered into her home and the neighborhood began to stir. This had been more than just a dream, she thought staring into the mirror and seeing the lines of worry that had etched themselves into her face.

The vision refused to leave her, lingering with Molly all through the day. She was smiling now, she realized, as she set about cleaning up her home. Confident. Optimistic. Buoyed with a hope that refused to desert her, she vacuumed and polished and tidied up her neglected home. For the first time since Danny had disappeared, she dared to open the photo album. There was Danny holding his first fish. It was a puny little thing dangling from his line, but he looked so proud that it could have been a hundred-pound tuna.

"Danny's okay," she said when Tripoli came by with sandwiches for the two of them.

"Huh?" he said with a full mouth of pastrami.

"He's okay. I'm sure of it now. He's alive."

"What makes you say that?"

"I had this dream."

Tripoli looked at her skeptically. "*Dream?*"

"No, really. Listen to me, Trip. Just hear me out."

He listened as her words excitedly cascaded into each other, but nothing she said made much sense to him.

"You think I'm looney, don't you?"

He reasoned that she was getting desperate. He knew that he certainly was.

"I can't expect you to understand. But it was like no other dream I've ever had. Everything was so sharp and clear I could make out every single little pixel. People don't dream like that. Not with that kind of resolution. Now I know, know now in my heart of hearts, that Danny's safe." She could feel her face flushing at the mere memory, feel her skin prickling again where Danny had touched her. "It's like I'm in the zone."

"Zone? What's this got to do with Danny?"

"I know my baby's okay."

"Well…all right…" He said, but it wasn't all right. He didn't have much hope left; by now he was only interested in getting Molly through this in one piece.

"I'm going to keep the checks," she said resolutely. "For Danny. When he comes home. I'll be able to buy him all those things he wanted. Or put it toward the farm. Hey, that's why I saw those animals!" she exclaimed, suddenly making the connection.

Tripoli took a sip of his Dr. Pepper and stared blankly at the wall behind Molly, chilled at what he thought might be happening to her.

"I had this dream," Molly explained when Rosie came by to visit on the weekend. "It was the most real thing in the world."

"Yeah?"

"I was immersed in these wonderful, fluffy clouds. And they kept changing shape…"

Rosie listened, transfixed. "Go on," she urged.

"…And I heard this voice singing. A high, little voice. And when I looked I—"

"Saw it was Danny," said Rosie, finishing her thought.

"Yes! But it was not like any ordinary dream. You know how when you dream you see things kind of vaguely. It's like when you close your eyes and try to imagine someone's face but you can't really see them. Well, this was different. It was like—"

"Like you were looking at a living photograph."

"Exactly! And every little detail was perfectly clear."

Rosie nodded. Her eyes were moist. "About a year ago I had this sharp dream—I guess I never told you about it—about my cousin Carlos. You remember him? He moved to Chicago. I hadn't talked to him in ages. Anyway, in the dream he wanted to talk to me. I tried to get ahold of him, but he wasn't there any more. So I went to this woman—"

Molly jerked her head. "You mean a *psychic?*"

"Wait," Rosie held up a hand. "Just let me finish. Turns out no one in my family had the faintest idea where he was. So I went to this woman and she told me exactly where I could find him. He was in Houston."

"Great. She figured it out. You know anybody can go on the Internet and do a search."

"Okay. Maybe, but it turns out that when I finally got ahold of him, he had actually been trying to get in touch with me. His wife was sick."

"I don't get it?"

"When I told that woman my dream, she told me that Carlos's wife was sick. Don't tell me she got that from the Internet."

"Look, I appreciate it." She touched Rosie's shoulder. "But this isn't for me.

"Okay, but Danny talking to you in your dreams—well, that

makes perfect sense, right?"

"Yes, it does, because we have a connection. I've always known what Danny was thinking before he even said it. And he could read my thoughts, too. And in that dream he was talking to me. Reassuring me. Directly."

"Of course he was! That's the way things work."

"I told it to Tripoli, and he just avoided my eyes. But I *really* know Danny's safe. And well. And happy." Molly's face was radiant. "Tripoli thinks I'm just deluding myself—"

"Hey, there are a lot of things people in this world just don't understand. Especially cops. They only believe in things they can touch and feel and see for themselves."

"But Tripoli's a good guy. And sensitive," Molly objected.

"Really?" asked Rosie, no slouch herself at picking up on things. "So, how long you been seeing him?"

chapter six

A little more than two and a half weeks after Danny's disappearance, Molly surprised everyone by appearing at the office. She just marched in, sat down at her desk, and flipped on her computer. Everybody came over to give her a hug and a smiling welcome back.

After a couple of weeks of seclusion, thrusting herself back into the bustle of work at the *Upstater* was jarring. She had forgotten how hectic the office could get. How the stagnant air, laced with the odor of ozone and fresh ink, vibrated from the copiers and printers running full throttle. File cabinets slammed and phones bleeped as a steady stream of messengers from UPS and FedEx swept in and out. Trays of donuts and fresh coffee kept coming through. The noise and activity, once so stimulating, now seemed disconcerting. Well, she thought, at least I'm doing something. Killing time.

Shortly after Larry Pierce had settled into work that day, he stepped out of his office to go to the kitchen and discovered Molly at her desk.

"Look, I can't sit around staring at the walls. I've got to keep busy," she explained. "Till Danny comes back." Larry winced and Molly, ignoring the look, went on. "Just tell me where we are and what I need to take care of first."

In the period of her absence, things had fallen seriously behind. The others in the office had been trying to cover for her, but they had missed a series of vital deadlines, which meant the magazine was off schedule. The data bank of subscribers hadn't been updated, the billing records for advertisers had become jumbled, and no one was attending to the Christmas ads, which had begun coming in.

"Listen, it's not the end of the world," Larry said, doing his best to put a good face on things. "So people will get their *Upstater* a little late. So what?" But this was not the Larry Pierce who sweated deadlines and bills, the Larry who had posted a sign in the office saying, "Blink and this magazine is extinct."

In trying to cover Molly's work, what's more, Doreen had stolen precious time from her editing, and she, too, had fallen behind. "Let me help you," suggested Molly in the afternoon.

"You ever do any editing?" Doreen asked, staring skeptically over the tops of her spectacles that hung low on her nose.

"No, but I think I recognize a whole sentence when I see one."

"Okay," said Doreen after a thoughtful pause. "When you have a moment, give this a try." She handed Molly an article that had just come in. It was a story about the Cayuga Drums, mysterious rumblings that periodically emerged from the bowels of the lake. "But take care of your own tasks first. I know Larry can use all the help you can give him."

Molly took the story and turned to leave.

"Hey," said Doreen, looking concerned, "are you really up to all this?"

Molly simply smiled.

She threw herself into her work. She took care of all of Larry's correspondence, negotiated permissions for photos they wanted to use in the next issue, worked with the layout people and printers, and finally, late at night, tried her hand at editing. She worked on tightening up the story about the Cayuga Drums, trimming its excesses and patching up the grammar and awkward sentences.

"Not bad. Not bad at all," said Doreen scanning the pages she had done. "But a story's always got to open with a hook. This piece is lame. It takes five paragraphs before you even know what it's about." Doreen took a red pen and started eliminating whole paragraphs with large, brutal crosses. She used arrows to move sentences from one page to the next, kept on ruthlessly cutting and chopping.

"Brevity is the name of the game. This ain't supposed to be poetry," said Doreen, who was known around the office as a bit hard-boiled. She handed the marked copy back to Molly.

"Yes!" said Molly, studying it. Suddenly it was obvious how much more there had been to it. "I think I'm beginning to get it."

In the days that followed, Molly came in early every morning, long before anyone arrived, and stayed late, often being the last to lock up and leave. Larry upgraded her computer, gave her an electronic organizer and automatic dialer—like those he had. He got her a beeper so he could reach her whenever needed. She carried it in her purse, and somehow its proximity gave her comfort. When Doreen handed her another story, Molly turned it around in a day, and it came back with noticeably fewer corrections.

"Not quite there," said Doreen, "but you're getting it. That saved me a lot of time. Now try to be just a little more merciless. Look at everything with a jaundiced eye. I do," she smiled kindly for the first time. Coming from Doreen, the encouragement was no small thing.

As long as she was working, Molly was able to fill the emptiness created by Danny's absence and drive away the demons of doubt. Her baby was alive. Safe. Happy. She kept silently repeating this mantra, reminding herself of the dream. It was only a matter of time until he was back, she told herself, and her only task was to fill that lonely vacuum. Try to sleep through the nights. Slog through the days.

During one lunch break, Tripoli came by the magazine with a bag of Chinese takeout. They drove over to Stewart Park and, after dusting off the thin layer of snow, sat on the tables and stared out at the deserted lake as they ate the still steaming lo mein.

A couple of ducks waddled by to beg for food and Molly fed them bits of her almond cookie.

"Danny always made me save old bread for these guys. He loved the way they would eat from his hand, ticking his palm."

Tripoli put his arm around her and she started to shiver. Until that moment, she didn't realize how cold it was. She nestled in close to him, his body shielding her from the cold wind that blew in from the lake.

"Thanks for lunch."

"My pleasure," he smiled, stroking her hair. There were things he wanted to say, but didn't say them. He wondered what it would have been like had he met her under normal circumstances, Molly a mother with her boy. Would she have gone for him as she had done?

"I've gotta get back to work," she said, getting up from the table.

"No problem," he said, and wished she didn't have to, that they could just spend the day together.

They pulled the newest issue together. It ended up being a last-minute affair and Molly, like the others, worked late that night, getting the final bits and pieces ready for the printer. Finally the proofs were handed to the waiting courier, people congratulated each other, and everybody took off for home. Thinking she was alone, Molly began to open the week's haul of thick manila envelopes.

"Hey, enough," said Larry, emerging from his office. "Enough is enough. It's finished. We take a breather now."

"But I've got to start the new manuscripts moving. We can make up all that lost time—"

"Not tonight you don't. Come on, let me get you some dinner."

"But—"

"But nothing. I know I'm a slave driver, but I can't allow myself to be accused of starving the slaves."

He took her out to the Glenwood Pines on Route 89, a restaurant with a smoky bar and loud country music, because he thought she'd feel comfortable there. He confessed as much after they had sat down to drinks and she had wondered about his choice.

"So, you think I'm a redneck, huh?" she asked with a knowing smile.

"No, this is a nice place. Very interesting. Excellent drinks," he said, taking a sip and smacking his lips.

"Well, I *am* a redneck, I guess. Anyway, if it's a choice between town and gown, I'm a townie. That's for sure."

"Okay, but nevertheless, I like you," he grinned. "You can be my token townie. Every office needs one."

"And you're our token city slicker."

He laughed.

"It must have been some experience, running a big magazine in the city."

"Maybe it was. But this is more exciting. There I waltzed into an established operation. It was just a matter of keeping things rolling and not making any major mistakes. But here we're creating everything from whole cloth. The upside of doing this is phenomenal— and not just for me. For all of us. The whole team." He looked her straight in the eye. "For you."

"Geez," said Molly, who didn't know how to respond.

"We're going to repeat this formula in state after state. The same mix. Same upscale audience. Keep the core human interest stories, the gourmet food and recipes, just insert local pieces. It'll look regional, but it's essentially national. Really big. And I'm counting on you to go with me. All the way. Maybe we'll move the entire operation to New York."

She tried to imagine living in New York City. Danny going to some kind of private school where they wore uniforms.

"And I thought you should be the first to know about some

good news," Larry said, lowering his voice and turning serious. The cell phone in his pocket went off and he just ignored it.

Molly waited.

"We're moving into new offices. I just signed the lease. It'll be downtown. Right on West State Street. It's a modern place. We'll finally have enough room for everything. Expansion included."

Molly was excited that Larry was sharing this with her. "When's all this going to happen?"

"Right before Thanksgiving."

The next morning, Tripoli appeared at her door. He looked unusually subdued. "I tried to reach you last night."

"I was out having dinner. With Larry Pierce. Hey, Trip, why are you looking at me like that? Don't tell me—"

"No, I'm not jealous…It's not that."

"What's up?"

"Can I come in?"

Suddenly Molly was alarmed. "You found something."

"Not necessarily."

"Out with it!"

"I was wondering. Did Danny ever see a dentist?"

Her heart was pounding and she felt weak in the knees. Before she knew it, the room was spinning and her legs had caved in under her.

Tripoli reached out to catch her, but she collapsed so fast she slipped through his arms. He stretched her out on the trailer floor and elevated her feet.

She revived quickly, her eyes opening in a flutter to stare up at him. "Let me get you some water," he said, rushing to the sink. When he was sure she was fully conscious, he propped her head up with his arm and gave her a few sips. "Take it slow," he gently urged.

Molly grunted and then pulled herself up. "Come on. Come

on!" she said irritably. "What did you find? Give it to me straight. You want dental records, right? I'm not a total idiot. Talk!"

As he groped for the right words, something that might be appropriately neutral, she grew more frantic. He didn't want to talk about bone fragments and decomposed tissue. Finally, he said, "Parts of a child's body have been found."

"Where?"

"Near Buffalo. In Batavia."

"Buffalo? That's not even near!" Molly was shaking.

"Of course, this doesn't necessarily mean it's Danny," he added, a little too hastily.

"But it's not Danny. It's not." Now she was crying. "I just know it."

"I didn't want to do this. Ask you, that is." Tripoli was fighting his own tears. "I just thought it was better me than one of the others." He didn't want to tell her about the small bones or that the state of decomposition seemed to coincide with the date of Danny's disappearance. They had a couple of fingers, some long bones. Little ones. The forensic pathologist was estimating that it came from a male child between four and five years old. They had already run a blood type on the tissue. It was the same as Danny's.

The next morning at work, Larry noticed the state Molly was in. She couldn't concentrate. Her desk was awash with photos and papers and files, so jumbled she couldn't seem to assemble them into any coherent order. Finally, he called her into his office and closed the door.

"Is it something I did yesterday—or maybe said? I have a habit of being insensitive, and the last thing in the world I'd want to do is hurt you."

"Oh, no," she said, shaking her head. "Not you, Larry," She started crying.

He got up from his desk and went to her, put his arms around her and held her. Molly simply hung on. It took her a good minute to regain control. She wiped her nose, dried her eyes, and told Larry about the body.

"Oh, God!"

"And I was so sure Danny was okay. So very sure. Now I don't know. I'm not sure of anything. I don't know if I can take it anymore."

Tripoli spent the morning rounding up Danny's medical records. When he was just a little over three, the boy had slipped from the monkey bars in Stewart Park. In the fall he had chipped a front tooth and suffered a green fracture of his left leg. The X rays of the leg were at the hospital, and Danny's dentist, who had examined the boy, was at the opposite end of the city.

Finally armed with Danny's records, Tripoli took it upon himself to deliver them to the forensic pathologist. The snow was blowing and drifting, and it took him over three hours to drive to Buffalo.

When he got there, the doctor held the X rays to the overhead lights. "Damn! Wrong bones," he said, immediately. "I've got a right fibula, not a left. And these teeth. We don't have front incisors. Looks like we're going to have to go the DNA route."

"I don't see what you've got to lose," said Rosie at about the same time Tripoli was leaving Buffalo. She had brought over a casserole and put it into Molly's oven.

"So, who is this woman, anyhow?" Molly asked.

"Her name is Evelyn Kovacs."

"Evelyn? I'd at least expect her to have a name like Madame Zhivago, or something like that."

"She looks just like you and me, kind of everyday normal, but she's got these powers. *Real* powers." Rosie was very solemn.

"Does she live in a cave surrounded by candles?"

"No, she lives in Lansing up by the mall. Look, I'm not trying to convince you. All I can say is when Ed was working a job and things were sailing along smoothly, she told me that he was going to lose his job. And then, bang the next day, Ed was out on his ass. Laid off."

"Maybe she arranged it?"

"I couldn't find my purse with my license and cards and important stuff in it. I swear I looked everywhere. Evelyn asked me, 'Did you try the garage?' Just like that."

"And where was the purse?"

Rosie grabbed a pot holder and opened the stove, squinting to see how her dish was doing. "Sitting smack on the shelf in the garage, just like she said. I couldn't remember for the life of me putting it there, but there it was. And don't tell me that Evelyn put it there, or I'll bean you with this casserole."

"Careful, it's hot," said Molly with a full mouth as they later ate. "But good! Hmmm," she smacked her lips. "One amazing cook. You ought to open a restaurant."

"So, are we going?" Rosie persisted.

"Madame Evelyn"—as Molly kept referring to her on the drive up to Lansing—lived in a split-level ranch on Burleigh Place, just behind the Triphammer Mall. She was a dowdy, middle-aged woman with frizzy black hair and thick glasses. She had three kids, a dog, and drove a rusty Subaru wagon which rested in the driveway up on blocks, waiting for new brakes. Her husband was a lecturer in Math at the University, and she did this as a sideline. "Not for the money, mind you," she offered, as she led the women towards her tiny office in her finished basement. Molly had to step over toys scattered in the playroom.

"You'll see," whispered Rosie, giving Molly a nudge. "I'll wait outside, Evelyn," she said to the psychic.

Evelyn closed the door, sat Molly in a chair, placing herself directly opposite. Then she reached behind and lowered the lights with a dimmer.

"Give me your hands," she said.

Molly obeyed, though she felt a little foolish.

Evelyn took them in hers and gripped them tightly. Evelyn's hands were reddened and rough.

"You have to close your eyes," Evelyn said. "Try to concentrate."

Molly closed her eyes. The basement smelled faintly of cat pee, and she could hear the phone ringing somewhere in the house. The family dog scampered overhead, nails scratching the floor. A door slammed.

"Block everything out. Concentrate. Think about Danny."

Molly tried. Into her mind came images of a child's decomposed body lying in the woods. She kept pushing it out of her thoughts until, finally, she could actually see Danny. He looked as he did that last day, that last moment when she had hurriedly left him at Kute Kids. She could see that eager look in his eyes as he contemplated the visit to the farm owned by Billy's Uncle.

"You had a dream…" said Evelyn with her eyes still closed. "A very clear and vivid dream."

Molly eyes popped open. She stared at the woman who sat with her head bowed, rocking in her chair.

"Danny was trying to talk to you."

Molly forced her eyes closed.

"Your boy is safe. He is warm. Cared for. Content. Peaceful. He is being prepared for something very important."

"You can see him?" Despite herself, Molly was swept up.

"Yes. Yes!" exclaimed Evelyn, gripping Molly's hands tighter. "I see him now."

"Where is he?"

"That I can't see yet. But it feels like he is in a very tranquil place. In the country somewhere. In nature."

"What's he doing?"

"Yes. Now I see him. He's in the woods. He's picking up sticks."

"Why's he doing that?" Molly asked excitedly.

"Gathering wood," said Evelyn. "You are not to worry. Wait! I hear—"

"What?"

"He is talking to me."

"What's he saying? *What?*"

"Quiet! Wait! He's saying, 'Don't worry...Mother...Don't worry."

"Mother?" Molly opened her eyes. "Danny calls me Mommy. Not *Mother!*"

"He has changed," intoned Evelyn, her eyes still sealed. "He has matured. When he returns to you he will be different. Changed." She opened her eyes and looked straight at Molly who had been watching her.

"Well...uh..." Molly stammered.

Evelyn just waited.

"This is all very...interesting," said Molly finally. For a moment there, she realized, the woman had her almost believing. "But that dream," she said. "You heard it from Rosie, didn't you?"

Evelyn shook her head and tried to speak, but Molly pushed on. "And the business about the woods..."

"Whatever you want to believe," Evelyn said calmly.

"Look, I really appreciate your effort. And I don't want to seem rude. But...I've got to run," Molly said, rising and pushing back her chair. "Thanks a lot. Maybe you've helped. I don't know." She sounded confused.

"So?" whispered Rosie eagerly as they walked arm in arm in the to the car. "What did she say? What did she tell

'k to Ithaca that evening, Tripoli picked up Molly
...о. nome and drove her to the hospital.

"We just need a sample of your blood."

"But when will I know?" she asked, turning her face up to him as the nurse slid the needle into her vein.

He didn't immediately answer and she looked down to see her blood, red and dark, spurting into the vacuum tube.

"It'll take a little time," he said finally. "I'll rush it. But in the meantime you've got to go on with your life."

"Fat chance."

He took her home and helped her into bed.

"Can you stay?" she asked.

"Sure."

"I need you to sleep here. I don't want to be alone. Not tonight."

"No problem."

He got into her bed and held her. He could feel her shivering.

"Do you love me, Trip?" she asked.

"Naw," he tried to joke. "You're just another case. I do this with all my suspects." He kissed her on the nose.

She didn't say anything.

"Of course I love you. I love you like crazy. I only wish there were something that I could do to take away the pain."

"Hold me tight," she said, and he held her tightly and stayed awake long after she had finally gone to sleep.

They moved into the new offices on State Street. The premises were clean and new, but the walls were paper thin. Everything seemed chintzy, made out of plastic rather than real wood. The move itself took a lot more effort than anybody had anticipated; and when all the excitement was over there was Thanksgiving staring Molly in the face. It was a painful time for many reasons. Rosie always made a large turkey, and Molly and Danny went over to the Greens' for the feast. Everybody in the Green and Lopez families were invited— cousins and uncles and aunts and grandparents. Although Molly had few living relatives, Danny had inherited a sprawling family through Rosie, one representing every shade in the human spectrum. Without Danny, Molly couldn't imagine taking part in the festivities.

The passing of Thanksgiving also heralded the Christmas season. All over town the stores were filling with decorations and gifts. The city itself had strung lights in the trees on the Commons, and families were starting to trim their homes. Danny had been gone now for over a month and the pain was acute as ever. There was no way to ignore the approach of the holidays, though Molly did her best to avoid the toy sections in the stores.

Danny's birthday fell on the fourteenth of December, so close to Christmas that Molly always went to great efforts to make sure that that day was not slighted because of the big holiday. For his fourth birthday she had thrown a large party for him, inviting as many little kids as could fit into the trailer. The place had been a mess, but Danny, swamped with attention and gifts, had been euphoric. After all the children had left, it had taken hours for him to settle down.

"What kind of party am I going to have this year?" he kept asking right up until the day he had disappeared from Kute Kids.

"Well, we've got to plan something, don't we," Molly had said.

But they had never had the chance.

Molly kept wondering about that little body, chopped up into pieces and abandoned to rot in the woods somewhere off the highway near Batavia. Despite herself, she couldn't resist following the story in the newspapers. The body remained unidentified and Tripoli tried to avoid talking about it. When pressed, all he would say was that the DNA results hadn't come back yet. It took time. He tried to be supportive. What else, he wondered, could he do?

Life seemed suspended as she waited for the inevitable call. It came a week later, Tripoli reaching Molly at work to inform her that the DNA didn't match.

"Aha!" she said, exhaling a loud sigh of relief. "I knew it. I was sure, Trip, just sure. Now didn't I tell you?"

"Yeah. I suppose so." There was a flatness to his tone of voice, but Molly refused to be infected by his lack of optimism.

The body was not Danny's, and that meant hope. Hope for her. She tried not to think about the other mother…Hope…Even if it was just a shred she clung to that fragment for all she was worth, and two days before Danny's birthday Molly took off during her lunch break and drove straight to the mall. She hadn't been there since the day Danny vanished and the shopping center seemed bigger, busier, more crowded than she remembered it. Danny's biggest dream was to own a remote-controlled car like the ones he had seen the older boys playing with in the park. She found them in the toy store next to J.C. Penney's and picked out the biggest, most expensive one she could find: a pickup truck souped up with flames and decals. It weighed nearly ten pounds and cost more than a week's worth of groceries.

When Molly arrived at work the next morning, Larry called her into his office to tell her that Doreen was leaving and that she was being promoted to editor. The job had a lot more responsibilities but he was sure she could handle them.

Two days later, Molly moved into Doreen's office. It was small, but had a door she could close and a window. Though it was sealed, it looked out on the garden courtyard and on days when the sun was out, it flooded the room and lifted her spirits. Part of Molly's responsibility was to train the new secretary Larry had just hired. Tasha was fresh out of school with no real experience and needed to be coached. Suddenly, here she was in a position of authority, student transformed into teacher.

Life went on. Not only at the magazine, but in the rest of the world. That was the odd thing about tragedy, thought Molly. It was like a rock dropped in the ocean—the ripples were evident only close to where it disappeared.

Tripoli was working long, irregular hours. A lot was happening in town. There were a flurry of break-ins, an attempted rape up near the campus.

"Your people are not working on Danny's case like they used to," said Molly one night, sitting at the kitchen table as Tripoli washed up the dinner plates.

"Well, I'd be lying to you if I said we were going full-steam. It's not that I've given up looking. It's just that we've got an overload of cases right now. You've gotta understand, Molly, the department works by a system of priorities."

"And Danny is now low, is that it?"

"A day doesn't go by—no, not an hour—that I don't think about Danny. Nothing in the world would make me happier than to get him back to you."

That same week, Rosie lost her job at the P&C. They fired her because she had come up short on two occasions. It was just before Christmas, a particularly bad time. Ed was still laid off, she had lost her health insurance with her job, and…

"And on top of everything," said Rosie, biting her lip, "I think I'm pregnant."

"Think?" asked Molly, putting down her pastrami sandwich. In an attempt to cheer Rosie up, she had taken her out for lunch at Hal's Deli on Aurora Street.

"Know!" she said heaving a sigh.

"But that's wonderful. Aren't you and Ed…?"

"I'd say right now we're more scared than happy. I know why I lost my baby last time. You can't imagine what that body shop was like."

Molly could. She remembered how the building was sealed in winter and the exhaust fans were ineffective. Every time she stepped in she got nauseated from the fumes.

"There were days I had these throbbing headaches. Sometimes I couldn't even breathe. I knew I should have quit right away, but…"

"But now you're out," said Molly, trying to sound upbeat.

"Two years there. All I can do is think about what they did to my body. Did permanently. And now there's some other poor sucker trapped in my place."

Molly opened her pocketbook and took out her checkbook.

"What's this?" asked Rosie, her face flushing as Molly slid a check for five hundred dollars across the Formica.

"This is for medical expenses. I want you to see a doctor."

"I can't take this."

"Oh yes you can!" said Molly fiercely. "And you will."

With the command post closed, Lou Tripoli was back in his old office on the second floor of the city police building on Clinton Street. He spent hours reviewing the videotapes they had taken from the AM/PM Minimart on Green Street, the Short Stop Deli on Seneca, even the cameras outside the bank and merchants at the Mall.

The surveillance cameras had been running continuously on the afternoon that Danny disappeared, and Tripoli began again the laborious task of watching the tapes. He was still hoping that they had overlooked something, some fleeting detail that might generate a fruitful lead.

Tripoli actually found Edna Poyer on the Minimart tape. She had cut across a corner of the station lot, and was indeed heading towards Woolworth's around three o'clock—just as she had claimed.

Tripoli pushed a button on the machine and printed out a couple of the frames.

The more Tripoli searched, the more determined he became. He was sure that if he kept at it, sooner or later he'd turn up something substantive.

It was late December. The January issue of the magazine had been put to bed, and the office was closed for an extended Christmas break. Two solid weeks. Losing Danny had been bad enough. But now, missing him at the time of year they both loved so much—that was almost too much to bear. Molly was afraid she might go to pieces. Tripoli made it his business to check up on Molly at odd hours. Once in a while they made love. At other times Molly wasn't quite up to it and he didn't push. They just slept, content to lie in each other's arms.

Molly made it through the Christmas holidays by simply staying outside and walking. It snowed incessantly that winter, the low gray clouds dumping inch upon inch onto the frigid landscape. But the snow didn't stop Molly. She kept pushing on through drifts of thigh-deep snow, across the campus, up and down the hills. Each time she spotted a small figure her heart would start racing.

"I tried to reach you yesterday," said Tripoli when he finally reached her on the phone one morning.

"I must have been out," said Molly, her voice dull and flat.

"Everything okay?"

"I'm making it."

Tripoli was going to fly down to North Carolina to bring back a guy on a warrant. "You going to be all right while I'm gone?"

"Sure. Don't worry about me."

"But I do."

That winter, Ithaca barely saw the blue of sky. At first people were merely inconvenienced, but soon farm animals had to be locked inside their barns, and the deer began dying by the hundreds. Day and night the plows kept noisily scouring the roads, and soon the trailers in Molly's park lost their form and came to resemble huge white burial mounds. The snowfall, which in one twenty-four-hour period exceeded thirty inches, had already broken all accumulation records for an entire winter. Temperatures, too, continued to plummet to all-time lows. On a Wednesday, while Molly was at work, the propane heater in her old trailer gave out, and she returned to find the pipes frozen. Although she was able to get heat again, she was without water for nearly a week. Yet Molly refused to move. How else could Danny find her?

As the days wore on, Molly continued putting in long hours at the magazine. No matter how hard she worked, however, there was still time left over, time to fill, time to think, and time to miss her boy.

Despite her growing doubts about ever seeing Danny again, her nights of despair and moments of panic, her career was taking off, reaching a level she could only have dreamed of a year earlier. She was earning a good salary, meeting critical deadlines, and having other people seeking out her counsel. She realized she was perfectly capable of holding a good job, here or maybe anywhere. By any of the external measures she had made it; she had strengths and resources greater than she ever realized. Yet without Danny, this victory felt hollow.

Frigid February yielded to a wind-whipped March. In the middle of the month it rained, then abruptly turned colder, the snow freezing into a hard and treacherous icy mass. To Molly, however, the weather became a matter of indifference. When she wasn't working, she continued her endless hunt, a bundled-up figure lumbering through the glazed and gusty streets, peering into every alley, searching every face, stopping total strangers to show them a picture, ask them questions. Somewhere, someone had to know something about Danny. It was only a matter of connecting. Always her search took her back to Green Street, to the boarded-up remains of Kute Kids, to the place she had left her little boy that morning in the late fall, entrusting him to strangers.

"What are you raising in there?" asked Molly when Rosie stopped by the trailer on a night late in March. "Elephants?"

Though Rosie was only into her sixth month of pregnancy, she was now so big that when she walked she wobbled and had trouble keeping her balance.

"It's twins," said Rosie. "We just saw them on the sonogram up at the hospital. I got the picture at home. Ed says he's framing it."

Molly kissed her. "Why that's wonderful!" she exclaimed. "I just hope you're taking care of yourself." Rosie didn't look good to her. Her skin seemed sallow. Though her stomach was distended with the pregnancy, her cheeks were a little hollow and she wasn't as lively as usual.

"I'm just very tired these days."

"It'll be fine, you'll see."

After Rosie drove off, Molly remained in the driveway. For the first time in months, the air had a distinct touch of warmth and she could hear the dripping of melting snow from the trailer roofs, the distant sound of the creek gurgling under the ice. The wind, she noticed, was coming out of the south and, when she closed her eyes, she could detect the rich smell of fecund earth. If you used your imagination, she thought, you could catch the scent of blossoms drifting up from the south. Spring was finally returning to Ithaca.

"Danny," Molly whispered into the night, caressing his name. "Danny, my dearest baby boy. Wherever you are, please come home to me."

"I think you have to let go," said Tripoli late at night as they lay in bed, sleep elusive. Molly had been talking about Danny, making plans for when he got back. May was now splendidly warm, winter but a memory. The windows in the trailer were open and the air was alive with the sound of nighttime crickets. A mosquito buzzed around Molly's room and it got her thinking of summer. When Danny got back she would take him to the Adirondacks, they would go canoeing, fishing, just like she had done with her father when she was little and he was still living at home. It was a memory that Tripoli suspected had been burnished with time. "Letting go doesn't mean giving up."

"Never," she said. "Never." She got up on an elbow to look at him in the darkness. She studied his face, tracing with a finger the line on his brow. "I'm cruel to you. It's not fair. You should find someone else, a woman who could love you full time. If you left me—"

"Never," he said with a laugh and silenced her with a quick kiss on her lips. "Never."

BOOK TWO

chapter seven

For the month of May, Tripoli was stuck working weekends. He hated leaving Molly, knowing she would be alone all day in the trailer. As usual, he left her at dawn that Sunday morning, slipping out of bed and dressing as quietly as he could, then bending over her and giving her a kiss. In her half sleep Molly reached out to caress him, then sank back into sleep.

Tripoli was long gone when she finally arose. He had made himself a hasty breakfast, and when Molly got up all that remained of their night together were a plate with crumbs and his coffee cup piled on top of last night's dishes.

Molly helped herself to the coffee he had made for her, then set to work cleaning up the kitchen. As she waited for the sudsy water to fill the sink, she thought about Tripoli, his loyalty and tenderness, and wondered why she couldn't have met him before—before Danny had disappeared. How vastly different life might have been. Danny would have had a father and…

She was facing the kitchen window when a small, distant figure near the highway caught her eye. It was a child, walking along the road near the trailer park. The water kept rising in the sink as she leaned closer to the window to see the child more clearly. It was a boy, she saw as he came around the curve of the road, a boy just about Danny's age with a sprightly gait just like Danny's. As he got closer, she thought she recognized Danny. But no, her eyes were playing tricks on her again and she squinted in the morning brilliance to see better.

The boy came closer. Then, as the water started running over the rim of the sink, running onto the floor, Molly let out a scream.

She rushed out of the trailer and down the road, barefoot, oblivious to the stones cutting into her feet. "Danny!" she was screaming. "Danny!" And the closer she came the more she was now certain that it was her child, her lost boy. His hair was long, much longer than it had been, but he was wearing the same red flannel shirt and bib jeans, and he had hung a rough woolen sweater over one shoulder. Then she could see his face more clearly, set in a broad, happy smile. He began to run toward her.

"Mother!" he laughed as Molly swooped in and scooped him up into the air. In her arms he felt feather light.

"Oh, my God, oh my God!" she said crying and laughing. "My baby! My baby!" she kept repeating as she raced with him back to the trailer, nuzzling his neck and ears and drinking in his scent. She wept so hard, held him so tight, that she could hardly breathe.

Tripoli was getting ready to head out of the office when his phone rang. Molly was sobbing and her speech so garbled he couldn't make sense of it.

"Hey. Slow down," he said, at first alarmed. "What's going on?" He had never heard her like this.

"He's back!" she gasped.

"What are you talking about?"

"Back! Back!" She kept repeating.

But all he could make out was her sobbing. She's hysterical, he thought. "Don't do anything, *please,*" he pleaded. "I'll be right over."

He burst through the door and dashed down the hall, knocking officer Lynn Spino off her feet and shouting an apology over his shoulder as he moved off. When he reached his car, he flipped on the siren and lights and took off.

"Let me just look at you!" said Molly, the phone slipping out of her hand as she fell to her knees, coming eye to eye with Danny, his face smudged with dirt. "Oh my God. You're so skinny. Are you okay? Is everything…" She took up his hands and counted every finger, lifted his shirt to examine his bony chest and belly, kissed his silky skin and again smelled his special fragrance. His ribs were showing and his arms felt like sticks and he was not particularly clean, but she could find nothing really wrong with him. "And it's you! My darling! My baby! I still can't believe you're *real*."

Danny threw back his head and laughed. "Oh, I am!"

Then she was crying again.

"Please don't cry," he said, and looked like he was about to cry himself. "I didn't mean to scare you."

"Scare me? Scare me?" she laughed hysterically. "You didn't scare me. You've made me so happy. That's why Mommy's crying. So happy!"

She kept touching him, trying to reassure herself that he was actually alive and healthy and there. "But where have you been?"

"I've been…I've been…" he gazed around the interior of the trailer.

"Yes? Yes?" she prompted, trying to catch his eyes to retain his attention. She kept combing her fingers through his hair pulling out burrs and little sticks of wood caught in it, running her fingertips over the contours of his skull as if the explanation lay in it.

"…been away."

"Yes. But how could you…? Who…? Where?"

"But I was okay," he insisted, still averting his eyes. "I didn't want you to worry."

"*Worry?* Where in the world have you been? What have you

been eating? Who's been keeping you? Don't you know that the whole world has been looking for you?"

"I'm sorry," he apologized.

"But where?" she insisted.

Every time she asked he turned away, seemed to find some new fascination in the details of the trailer.

Then they heard the wail of an approaching siren, the sound of tires squealing on the paving of the roadway, an engine racing. Danny stiffened nervously at the sound.

"It's okay, Honey," she said lifting him into her arms. "It's just a good friend coming. He's been helping me look for you all this time." She thought of Tripoli, rushing again to her rescue, of his concern for her all these months. She buried her face into the curve of Danny's neck, now wet with her tears.

When Tripoli burst into the trailer, the floor was deep in water and Molly was standing in the living room with a little blond boy clutched tightly in her arms. Her eyes were wide, pupils dilated, and she was trembling and weeping and smiling. When the boy turned and Tripoli saw his face, he froze. "Oh God, oh God," he kept murmuring. It really was the boy in the picture. The face was leaner, lacking the baby fat, yet it was clearly the image of the missing child, the boy he had given up hope of ever finding alive. Seven long months. Danny!

It took Tripoli a moment to realize that he, too, was weeping. Triumph and relief, bewilderment and awe. It was too good to be true, and all he could do was weep—weep for this sudden miracle of goodness and justice, all this for the woman he loved and whose faith had finally been rewarded. Engulfing Molly and her boy in his arms, he held them tightly, his shoulders shaking as hot tears streamed down his face.

Tripoli's car stood outside, bubble top flashing and siren shrieking. From all over the park, people started emerging from their trailers, converging on the scene. Heads peeked in the open door, bodies jostled for position, old faces and young vied to catch a glimpse of Molly's little boy—now actually back, alive and well! And of this cop, this detective, this hard-bitten sonofabitch, crying his eyes out.

People kept pressing in; the air in the trailer became hot and stuffy.

"Out," Tripoli ordered. "Come on, please. Everybody out!"

He managed to move the neighbors out and press them back to the driveway just as a familiar stringer from the *Ithaca Journal* came running up. He had a photographer in tow and Tripoli had to bark the pair back from the door of the trailer. When he returned, Molly was still clutching Danny. Though dressed in an old T-shirt and frayed shorts, Molly looked to Tripoli at that moment more beautiful than he could ever remember her, more joyous than he had ever seen her or imagined her to be. Her hair, tied up with a scarf, exposed the full arc of her radiant face and, though he knew every inch of it, it seemed suddenly radically different.

"I'm standing here doing dishes, just looking out the window. And then…" Molly gushed, "Then I see this little boy *all* the way down, near the highway."

"That's me," piped the boy and then giggled.

Tripoli glanced at the sink filled with sudsy water and dishes. The counter was soaked. The vacuum was out and stood leaning against the sofa.

She tried to explain how she had first seen the figure of a boy near the turning in to the road of the trailer park. It looked like Danny, but she couldn't believe it was really him. How she felt a burst of hope and joy and almost in the same time suspicion and disbelief.

"Then I run down the road. And it's really him, Trip. My Danny!" she uttered, and broke down again.

Tripoli looked at Danny. The kid looked scruffy. Grungy hair. His fingers were stained, dirt under his nails: he was badly in need of a good scrubbing. He was still wearing that plaid flannel shirt, the bib jeans and the sneakers with colored trim, but his shirt had tears in it at the elbows, his sneakers holes where his big toes were pushing out, his jeans worn through in the seat and knees. The boy looked, however, physically sound, basically healthy.

"Danny's grown," said Molly, patting his bottom. "He's a big boy now—aren't you!" She started to cry again and then laugh. "Just look at him!" She stretched out a leg for Tripoli's inspection. The bottom of Danny's pants hardly reached his ankle. "Must be a good two inches!"

"And I'm stronger, too. Just feel my muscles." He flexed his skinny arm, and Molly pinched the little bulge at his biceps.

"Why it's true. Just look at this, Trip."

Tripoli hung back. He felt off kilter, not knowing quite what to make of it all.

"Please, Mother," said Danny finally, "could you let me down?" His voice was sweet, high and reedy, and virtually bubbled with laughter. It suddenly reminded Molly of her dream, of Madam Evelyn, the psychic.

"*Mother?* Did you hear that?" Molly sniffled and wiped her eyes. "Hey, I'm your Mommy!" She squeezed him tight, then reluctantly let him down. "Boy you've gotten big," she marveled again, straightening her back.

Tripoli watched as Danny stood there snug to Molly, his eyes surveying the room, fastening on items of furniture, appliances in the kitchen, as if trying to recall the place. He really was a beautiful child. Finely sculpted features and big, brown eyes, a sweet bow-shaped mouth with full lips and a wonderful smile. The contrast in coloring between Danny and Molly, however, was striking; he was as blond as she was dark.

"You must be starved, Honey!" Molly exclaimed and then rushed to the fridge. "We're gonna put some meat on you."

"Where's he been?" Tripoli asked finally.

She shrugged, fumbled with a glass in the cabinet, tried to pour some milk, her hands still trembling. She kept spilling over the edges of the glass. "I don't know. Every time I ask, he just…" She came in with the milk and a bag of cookies. Tripoli continued to observe him. And Danny, he saw, was watching him. For a long moment their eyes met. The kid's look was so unwavering that Tripoli felt his spine go cold.

"Go on, drink it," Molly urged, pushing the glass into the boy's hand.

"What kind of milk is it?" he asked.

Molly did a double take and then burst out in laughter. "Did you hear that?" she said to Tripoli, then turned to Danny. "Cow's milk, silly!" she exclaimed. "What else?"

"Oh, yeah," he smiled and thirstily gulped down half the glass. "Mmmmm," he said, smacking his lips. "Cow's milk. It's cold and good. Not very creamy, though."

Molly rolled her eyes heavenward for Tripoli's benefit and handed Danny a cookie. He took it, turned it over in his hand examining it with interest. It was as if he had never seen one before.

"Go on," urged Molly.

The boy took a small, tentative bite, chewed. "Mmmmm," he marveled, "Yes, it's very sweet."

"It's Chips Ahoy," she said, showing him the package. "Your absolute favorite. Don't you remember, Honey? "

Danny wrinkled his brow in thought. "Yes…I sort of remember." Tripoli could see he didn't really, that he was trying to please her. Danny popped the rest in his mouth, and then giggled, crumbs spilling out. Molly laughed and ruffled his hair. Then she kissed him again.

"Come on, drink up," she said. "You must be starving. And take another cookie."

He hungrily dug into the bag and then polished off three in a row.

Though Tripoli had never seen the boy before, there was something remarkable about him, something he couldn't quite put his finger on. Perhaps it was the boy's poise, his air of calm self-assurance. Then he noticed the small gray sweater lying crumpled in a corner, and went over and picked it up. It was made of coarse fibers and obviously hand knitted, like one of those sweaters you could find in the Peruvian store on the Commons, but even more primitive.

"What's this?" he asked quietly, dangling it aloft by two fingers.

"Danny was carrying it when he came back." Molly's voice was still heightened with tension, high and loud. The boy seemed to wince slightly when she spoke. "Weren't you, Honey?"

Danny nodded. His eyes darted for a moment toward the windows. They were open, Tripoli noticed, and the sound of many voices drifted in on the wind that was fragrant with lilacs and spring greenery.

Tripoli brought the sweater to his nose. The wool was scratchy and smelled of livestock. It had fine seeds and tiny pieces of burdock caught in the fibers. It looked like something straight off the back of a sheep. "Okay," he said finally to Molly, "So where was he? And how did he get back?"

"Like I told you, Trip, he just walked right up the road, didn't you, Angel?" she hugged and kissed him again. The boy laughed, a happy, carefree laugh that sounded like stones tumbling in a stream. "Hey, Trip, didn't I tell you he was okay?"

"Well, you were right," Tripoli nodded. His eyes, however, were still on the boy, "How'd you find your way back here, son?" he asked.

Danny looked at him. His smile seemed to fade.

"Well?" Tripoli persisted.

Danny shrugged and turned to look up at his mother. "This is where I live," said Danny.

"Of course!" exclaimed Molly.

"Did someone bring you back here?"

"I walked."

Tripoli slowly advanced towards the boy. "Okay," he said calmly, "but from where?"

The boy's face clouded and he shifted back toward Molly, looking up at her beseechingly. Tripoli edged delicately closer. Danny searched his mother's eyes, but when he saw how she stood there waiting for his response, he turned finally back to Tripoli, his gaze meeting Tripoli's again without wavering. It was, he realized, not the look of a child.

"This is Trip, Danny," said Molly, interceding to break the silence. "He's a good friend of mine. He's also a policeman."

"I can tell that," said the boy, his smile suddenly returning. Danny extended his hand. "Hello, Mr. Trip."

The gesture caught Tripoli off guard. Taking Danny's hand, he suddenly found himself smiling, too—thinking to himself that you couldn't help liking the kid straight away. For a little guy he certainly had a way of disarming people.

"This sweater?" he asked, holding it out to the boy.

"Nice isn't it. And it's very warm in the winter," said Danny with a sincere nod.

"I'll bet it is." Tripoli squatted down in front of Danny, bringing himself eye to eye with the boy. He was still grasping the sweater. "It's a very interesting sweater," he said softly, going through the motions of examining it for the boy's benefit. "Unusual. Not the kind of thing you could buy in any store, is it?"

"Yeah," agreed the boy.

"Where did it come from?"

"From sheep, of course!" said Danny, and giggled loudly as if it were a foolish question.

Tripoli smiled. "Well, I suppose that's obvious, too. But from which sheep?"

"Oh, just regular sheep."

Molly, who was quietly listening, suppressed a laugh.

"Who made it?"

"Someone."

"Who?"

Danny looked away. First up at Molly who was staring down at him questioningly, then quickly his eyes roved around the room.

Still crouched, Tripoli could feel the strain building in his haunches as he waited. Faces were peeking in at the kitchen window, and he tried to ignore them. "Look, Danny," he said gripping the boy's hand to capture his attention, "everybody would really like to know where you've been."

Danny looked at him. "But it's just like I said," explained the boy, with a toss of his head.

"No, you haven't really said anything."

"Can we *please* already talk about something else now?" His eyes turned to Molly. "And could I maybe have another of those sweet cookies?"

Molly started to move off, and Tripoli signaled her with a raised finger to stop. "You can have a cookie, but first we want to know where you've been all these months? You know your Mommy and I were terribly worried about you."

"You didn't need to worry," Danny shook his head. "Because I was perfectly okay." He looked up at Molly and smiled. Tripoli saw that she seemed to melt under his gaze. Her short memory irritated him.

Two patrol cars had pulled up outside the trailer. Tripoli heard their sirens dying down, the crunch of tires on the driveway, then the familiar voices of officers ordering the people to stand back. "We can see that you're okay," he persevered as gently as he could. "But, son, you were gone for months. Six *whole* months. So you had to be somewhere. With someone."

"Oh, I was around," said Danny. He moved away from Tripoli and walked over to the bookshelf. He stood there with his back turned to them, running his fingers over the spines of the books.

"Around where, Honey?" asked Molly, going over and resting her hands on his shoulders. She bent over and kissed his head.

"Just around," he said, shuffling his feet and squirming impatiently under her touch.

"Here in town?" Tripoli asked, moving over to where Danny stood. He crouched down again and, positioning himself face to face with the boy, held both of the child's hands in his so he couldn't turn away. Danny squirmed, tried to turn, then finally looked at him wide-eyed. There was something so innocent and pure about the boy's look that it was difficult to be severe with him. "Maybe a far away place?" Tripoli suggested.

"No," said Danny.

"Close by?"

"Depends," Danny responded.

"Depends on what?"

"What you think is close."

Tripoli had to finally laugh and shake his head in resignation. "This kid sounds like he's going to be a criminal lawyer," he said turning to look up at Molly. "Maybe he was in law school for the last six months?"

Molly laughed. "My little lawyer," she said coming over and giving Danny a wet kiss on his cheek. When Danny glanced away, she slipped Tripoli a grazing kiss. "I'm the happiest human being on earth," she whispered in his ear.

There was a knock on the door and, when Tripoli opened it,

framed in the doorway stood two uniforms, Richie Pellegrino and Jerry Sisler. When they spotted the boy, their jaws went slack and their mouths flopped open.

"Jesus H. Christ," muttered Sisler.

"You'd better close your mouths before some flies swoop in," said Tripoli.

"Flies in your mouth!" Danny thought it funny and doubled over in laughter. Then he watched as Tripoli quietly huddled with the two cops, then handed them the sweater, and mumbled something as he escorted them outside.

When he returned, Tripoli tried to pull Molly aside, but the boy clung to her.

"We're taking him up to the hospital," he whispered.

"Hospital?" she said loudly, turning to her boy. "He's the picture of health. Just look at him. Aren't you fine, Danny?"

The boy nodded emphatically. "Better than fine."

"I don't know that," explained Tripoli, trying to exclude the boy. "I want him checked over. And then questioned."

Suddenly Molly looked frightened. "I mean, come on Trip, what difference does it make now? He's back and that's all that really matters."

Tripoli managed to break Molly free. "You wait here," he pulled Danny away from his mother, then took Molly back to the bedroom. "Maybe to you right this minute that's all that matters," he said in a low, stern voice. Danny's toys sat on his shelf as they had since the fall, the boy's bed still undisturbed. "But he's been somewhere with somebody—and been there without legal sanction— and I want to know where and who and how he got there. And what, if anything, they did to him. I want a doctor to go over him with a fine-tooth comb."

"But…"

"If he hadn't come back, would you have been quite so forgiving?"

"I'm not forgiving. Trip, I just can't take all this in so fast. I—"

"If we found his body instead—"

"Please! Don't—"

"Look," he shifted tack, "there's been at least one crime committed, and it's my job to uphold the law, to follow it to its prosecution. We're not going to casually walk away from this. What do you think the D.A.'s going to say? Forget it?"

"No. No. I understand. I just need some time to—"

"Don't you want a doctor to check him out. Make sure he's healthy?"

"Of course. I just thought we could tomorrow, or—"

"No way," he said firmly.

"Now you're just being a cop."

"You got it," he said. "Imagine this happening again. To somebody else's kid."

She raised her hands in surrender. "Okay. Okay." she said.

When Tripoli peered around the door he noticed that Danny had crept close to the bedroom and was trying to eavesdrop. The corners of his mouth were turned down. "Hey, come here," he said and, reaching out, gently lifted him up. The boy was light and rested easily on his hip. He held him for a moment and could feel the child's body melding into his. "You've got nothing to worry about, son," he said soothingly as the boy fixed him with his big doe eyes. "Your mother and I are the best of friends, and we wouldn't do anything in the world to hurt you. In fact, we'd do anything we could to help you. To make you happy. I want you to know that. Okay?"

The boy's eyes twinkled and he smiled. "Sure," he chirped, putting his arm around Tripoli's neck. "I know that!"

The boy snuggled yet closer. When Tripoli nuzzled him, he smelled of milk and leaves and wood smoke, and there was something in his touch that all but made Tripoli dissolve. Maybe that was what it was like, he thought, having a little kid of your own. "Come on, Molly," he said. "Let's get going."

"Okay," she agreed reluctantly. "He goes for the checkup. But I'm coming along. I'm not letting Danny out of my sight for a second!"

chapter eight

Tripoli phoned ahead to the hospital to alert the physician on call. Then he had Molly carefully undress Danny. She took off his shirt and dropped into a plastic evidence bag that Tripoli held open for her. Then he sealed and tagged it.

"We're going to need everything," he explained as he continued the bagging and tagging. "Socks. Shoes. Even underwear." Especially the underwear, he thought. He took each piece, put it into a evidence bag, marked the bag, and then carefully sealed its contents. When he had it all, he handed the bundle out the door to a waiting patrolman who drove it directly to the station.

When he turned, Molly was headed to the bathroom to give Danny a quick bath.

"No, no," he said, cutting her off.

"Huh? I just wanted to—"

"Just take him as he is. You can wash him up later. After."

So she dressed Danny in a pair of shorts and a polo shirt and let him wear flip-flops. None of his old shoes seemed to fit him.

"Oh, these feel really good," said Danny, wiggling his bare toes. "And they're light, too." He jumped around in them, shaking the trailer. Tripoli noticed there was mud between his toes. "Hey, how did you make them?"

"Make them?" repeated Molly. "We bought them when we went up to Syracuse. Carousel Mall. Don't you remember, Honey?"

Danny scrunched up his face in thought. "Yeah, I sort of do."

Molly changed out of her shorts, slipping on a light cotton shift. She strapped on a pair of sandals while Tripoli stood waiting at the door. He couldn't help but watch and admire.

Outside, there was now a crowd of people, maybe a hundred or more herded behind the police lines. Some were folks Molly recognized from the trailer park, others she was sure she had never seen before. There were two crews from the local TV stations and several photographers positioned on both sides of her door. Molly now realized that the story of Danny's return had to be big news: there was no way that any journalist was going to let a story like this get away.

When the people saw Danny emerge from the trailer, they started loudly clapping and whistling, and a volley of flashes went off on all sides.

"Hey, Danny!" folks shouted all at once. "Welcome home! Where've you been?"

"He's back," Molly shouted to the crowd straining at the cordon of police who had locked arms. "My little boy is back!" Taking Danny's hand, she lifted it triumphantly. Danny laughed, all the people cheered, and at that instant she felt like jumping up on the roof of her trailer and crowing out her joy, or throwing herself into the crowd and kissing every man, woman, and child who was there.

Danny seemed amused by all the attention, and Tripoli hustled him and Molly into the back seat of his car. As he drove off, he noticed a television van was right on their tail, following them. They kept up for almost a mile, then Tripoli ran a series of red lights and lost them. As they curved down the highway descending into the valley, Tripoli stole glances at Danny, whose head kept pivoting from side to side as if the boy were trying to remember where he was, where he had lived. They sped through the city where spring flowers adorning the houses gushed in colorful profusion. The magnolias in front of the court house were out in full, dazzling bloom, and Danny, who had managed to slip from his seat belt and open the window, was already leaning halfway out when Molly caught hold of him. "Be careful!" she said, pulling him back. She tried to close the window, but he took her hand away.

"No! I want the wind," he insisted. "I need the air."

"Well, okay, but stay put. And you need this seat belt."

At the west end of town the traffic was heavy as usual. "Hey, get a load of this," said Tripoli turning to Danny in the rear. He flipped on his lights and cranked the siren full volume. Magically, the tangle of cars parted and they sped through, flying over the inlet bridge, then climbing West Hill "Neat, huh?"

Danny was not impressed. His gaze, Tripoli saw, was fixed in the distance, catching through the passing trees and houses glimpses of the lake below. There were whitecaps on the surface and the water was dotted with sailboats heeling in the stiff breeze. "You like boats?" asked Tripoli.

Silence.

"I've got a friend with a big motor boat. We could all go out. Do some serious fishing, maybe, huh?"

"That sounds like fun," agreed Molly above the roar of wind in the rear seat. "Danny loves to fish," she said, recalling that picture of him with his very first fish. "Don't you, Sweetie?"

"No," he mumbled. "Not really."

"Huh?" said Molly.

"Not anymore."

"Oh…" was all she could say. "Oh…hmmm…"

Tripoli tried to turn the subject to advantage. "Is that because you did some fishing while—"

"Stop asking me!" said Danny with his childish lisp. The reflection of his resolute eyes met Tripoli's straight on in the mirror.

They rode up West Hill, and when they reached the entrance to the hospital Tripoli pulled directly into the emergency bay next to a parked ambulance.

"Emergency room," said Danny.

"What?" said Tripoli. Somehow the kid had made out the sign. Had he been here before?

"Why are you taking me to the emergency room?"

Molly and Tripoli exchanged glances.

"We're just going for a checkup. That's all. You've had them before." Molly smoothed his cowlick and fastened the top button of his shirt. "They're going to look you all over. Take your clothes off, maybe."

"What for?"

"Make sure you're healthy."

"But I am!"

"Sometimes," said Tripoli, "grownups do things to children—"

"You mean like sex?"

Tripoli tried to hide his surprise.

"Yes, Honey," said Molly, keeping her voice level.

"Well that's just silly," said Danny emphatically. "Nothing like *that* happened!"

There wasn't just one doctor waiting to examine Danny. There were three of them, one of them an obstetrician. They were as curious as everyone else in town.

"Ooooh, that's cold," he said when old Doc Wozniak put his stethoscope on his chest.

"Just want to listen to the old ticker."

"Is it really ticking?" asked Danny.

"Like a clock. You wanna hear?"

Danny wanted to hear and Doc Wozniak stuck the ends into his ear.

"More like drums," said Danny.

"Depends on the ticker." The doctor wiggled his furry white eyebrows. "Some are like clocks. Some are like drums. Some are like broken machines. So, young fella, tell us, where have you been?" asked old Dr. Wozniak, who was not one to mince words.

"Away," said Danny seriously, and then burst out laughing.

The team of doctors carefully checked Danny for any signs of injury or abuse. When little boys are raped, there are always some indications, even months later, some trauma, at the very least minute tears of tender tissues. They found nothing. They took a sample of blood and, while they waited for a quick answer from the lab, weighed and measure Danny.

"He's tall enough for his age," said Emily Glover, the pediatrician, "But he's definitely underweight," she explained to Molly. "Any idea what his diet's been?"

All eyes, including Tripoli's, went to Danny.

"Just good stuff," Danny said.

When the lab results came back, it was clear his blood values were fine. His red count high, white low, electrolytes all in balance. There were no indications of infections nor any obvious problems. In fact, despite his lean weight, the kid was in pretty good shape. About as healthy as anyone could possibly ask for, thought Molly.

As Tripoli escorted them from the hospital to his car, they were suddenly engulfed by a mob of reporters waiting at the emergency room entrance. Blinding lights flashed on and everyone began shouting questions all at once.

Amidst the pandemonium, Danny seemed overwhelmed and moved to safety in the shadows behind Molly.

Tripoli took Danny's hand and made a dash with him to the car, Molly hurrying after them. He got Danny into the back seat, but when he turned he saw that the cameras were upon them and Molly was talking to the reporters on the other side of the car.

"I was surprised, sure," Molly was explaining. "But I *always* knew he'd come back. You see, I had this dream." And she started to tell about her vivid dream. About the clouds and colors. The sheep and goats. Tripoli gunned the engine in mid-sentence. "Whoops, excuse me," said Molly and hopped into the car.

"Now we go home," explained Molly in the back seat as they drove away from the hospital.

"Not quite," said Tripoli. "We gotta make another stop. Child Protective Services is waiting for him downtown. They want him to see the juvenile psychiatrist."

"Oh, Trip," she pleaded and started to haggle with him.

He tried to explain that it was standard procedure in kidnapping cases. The boy, Tripoli noticed, was carefully watching, listening.

The evening was unusually clear and calm. In the valley below, the lights were coming on and the small city clustered below them sparkled in the valley. To Molly, the scene was picture perfect.

"Look," said Molly, leaning forward from the back seat to come close to Tripoli, "You can ask Danny all the questions you want tomorrow. He's not going anywhere." She turned to Danny, "Right, Honey?"

Oddly, the boy didn't respond. He turned to gape out the open window, his hair streaming in the wind.

"Honey?" she repeated

He turned, looked at her, and then smiled, though he still said nothing.

"Back for keeps!" She kissed him wetly on the nape of the neck. She gripped his hand tightly. Bringing it close, she examined his little fingers, kissing them one after the other. Though there was dirt embedded under his nails, they were relatively short and trim.

"Someone cut your nails," she said.

"Yup."

"Who?"

Again he turned away.

"We've got to get your hair cut."

"Do I have to?"

"But darling," She ran fingers through his tresses, "it's ridiculously long. You want people thinking you're a girl?"

"But I like it just like this."

Tripoli remained silent, listening to their conversation as they cut across town, passing Dewitt Park where a group of youngsters were sitting at the foot of the war memorial strumming guitars, lovers strolling arm in arm. Danny was back, he thought, and Molly's entire focus was on the boy. It was to be expected, of course, and he was happy for her, but he couldn't help but wonder if there would still be room for him.

Molly glanced out the window. A young mother in the park was watching her toddler running in the grass. People were standing on the street, laughing, chatting, smiling. The town suddenly seemed different to her, friendly and inviting. She thought about her neighbors who had crowded around her trailer to welcome Danny back and regretted all the miserable thoughts she had harbored. She recalled the way Larry and the folks in the office had rallied around her, supporting her all these long months, about the great friends she had in people like Rosie and Ed. And Trip. Of course Trip. Ithaca wasn't such a bad place to live after all, she suddenly realized. Not a bad place to raise a little boy.

"Come on Trip," she wheedled sweetly as they reached the center of town. "Just take us home. What difference are a few hours going to make now after all these months?"

"It just makes the trail that much colder," he said, barely audible.

"And Danny's tired. I want to clean him up. Give him some food, tuck him into bed."

"Yes," echoed Danny with his little lisp. "I'm tired. Very tired."

"Geez," Tripoli shook his head. "You're making me out to be the heavy."

"So lighten up a little," she said, resting her hand on his shoulder.

He drove them back to the trailer park. As they pulled through the police line, he was on the radio rescheduling the shrink for the morning and organizing a detail to cover Molly's home for the night.

The phone was ringing as they stepped in. Molly's answering machine was already filled with messages and was no longer picking up. Scrunching up his face, Danny stuffed his fingers in his ears to block out the incessant ringing.

"We'd better yank the cord if you want any peace tonight," said Tripoli, and then pulled out the plug.

"Whew!" sighed Danny in relief. He started wandering around the trailer.

"You remember everything here, right?" asked Molly.

"Sure!" said Danny, exploring. "Well sort of." He popped the switch on the toaster oven up and down, turned on all the burners on the stove and watched the flames ignite; he opened the refrigerator and peered in. "Ice," he said, licking the outside of the freezer compartment with his tongue. "Mmmmm. Cold."

Tripoli hung back, intrigued at the way the boy kept shifting from room to room. Danny was now in the bathroom flushing the toilet. He had his hand in the bowl and was trying to change the direction of the downward swirl.

"What in the world are you doing?" asked Molly who had been trailing him.

"Looking," said Danny.

She washed up his hands, tried to get rid of the brownish stains that had dyed his fingers and palms, took a washcloth and started scrubbing his face and neck as he squirmed around the bathroom. "Owww, not so hard."

"Hey," said Tripoli, sticking his head in the bathroom, "Okay if I leave you guys for the night?"

Danny was now working the faucets on the tub, cranking them on and off. "Look," he said to Trip, "it comes out hot!"

Molly walked Tripoli to the door. "I think he went native," she said with a laugh that sounded forced to her own ears.

"Or maybe the kid's planning on being a plumber," added Tripoli, trying to make light of it, too. But it was weird. Bizarre, but perhaps telling. There was no pushing the boy, not now, that much was obvious. The morning would be a different story. "Hey, look, if you need me," he touched her arm, "just tell one of the officers who'll be here tonight—or plug in the phone and give me a call—I'll keep my cell on, okay?"

"Thanks, Trip," she said, giving him a chaste kiss. "And thanks for everything. You're one terrific guy. And tonight I'm one of the happiest, most grateful human beings on this earth. Thanks for everything."

Tripoli took hold of her tightly and was about to plant his lips on hers when, out of the corner of his eye, he noticed Danny peeking out of the bathroom. "I gotcha!" Tripoli said pointing, a finger as if it were a gun.

The boy, caught, giggled. "You were going to smooch her, weren't you?" Danny said.

"Absolutely!" Tripoli said. "You've got one nice, smoochable Mommy."

"Mother," corrected Danny. *Mother.* And then he laughed again.

"I'll bet you're hungry," Molly said, going to the kitchen. "I'm going to make you a yummy dinner. This is going to be a celebration—just the two of us."

"Sounds great!" he chirped, tagging behind. "Isn't Mr. Trip going to eat with us, too?"

"I think he went out to catch some crooks. You like Trip, huh?" she spun around to catch him in her arms. Danny's eyes sparkled with intelligence. To her his face was the picture of goodness and purity. Even sweeter and purer than she had remembered him, if that were possible. He seemed different in other ways, too. Less impulsive. More observant. More grown up. But of course. He was six months older. Six months in which she hadn't been an influence. Six months with someone else. Who else? How could they!

"Yes. He's very nice," said Danny, breaking into her thoughts. "But he keeps bugging me with those questions. I don't like that."

Molly let it slide. "Hey, how's about a kiss before dinner?" she said leaning over. He puckered up and planted a big, wet one on her mouth. "Mmmmm, good," she uttered, gave him another for good measure and set to work. It was still almost impossible to comprehend that he was actually back. Everyone around her had long since given up and there were times, she remembered, when even she had almost abandoned hope.

"Hmmm. Let's see about dinner," Molly mumbled to herself as she hunted through the fridge and cabinets, seeing what she could scrounge up on short notice. With a free hand, she hit the button on the answering machine. The messages started reeling off. "Hello, this is Sally Wentworth with the *New York Times*, could you please give me a call at…" There was another from a reporter at the *Washington Post*. As well as people from *Time* and *Newsweek*. Tom Brokaw himself was trying to reach her, as were producers from CNN in Atlanta and ABC in New York City. The network morning shows were after her, too. As were all the wire services. And there were lots of calls from ordinary people, locals as well as folks from around the whole country.

"This is Cathy Peebles in Boise, Idaho. I just heard on the news about your boy coming home. I'm sure you're ecstatic and I wanted to tell you how happy me and my family are for you. Once, when my girl was little, just about Danny's age, I lost her in a crowd and I almost died till we found her an hour later. I can only imagine…"

In the freezer Molly found a small packet of ground beef, enough for the two of them. As she slid it in the microwave and hit defrost, she noticed that her hands were still trembling. She tried to control the temptation to fuss over Danny, but found that she couldn't resist constantly watching him. He had pulled a book off the shelf and was leafing through it. Molly noticed that it was a dictionary.

"I put your books on the lower shelf over there," she pointed.

"Oh, okay," he said. But, instead, he pulled out one of her old college books and sat with it cross-legged on the floor, neck bent as he slowly turned the pages. What was he looking at? she wondered. It had hardly any pictures.

"You know, you're going to have to tell me where you've been," she said, trying to make it sound as offhanded as she could.

Danny pretended to ignore her.

"Sooner or later," she added.

He turned a page.

"Oh, come on, Honey."

"Huh?" he said, looking up.

"You heard me," she said.

"I'm hungry."

"Hey, I'm working on it," she said, and then laughed, breaking the moment.

Reconnecting the phone, Molly dialed, then cradled the receiver against her shoulder as she washed the dishes that lay forgotten in the sink. The countertop was still soaked from when it had overflowed. What a day this had been.

"Honey," she glanced over at Danny as the phone rang on the other end, "Please don't make a mess of the shelf." He now had a dozen books spread out across the floor and was crawling amidst them. "Why don't you take out one at a…Hey, Rosie?"

"Molly!" came the shouted response on the other end.

She shut off the faucet. "Guess who's here? You're *never* going to believe this."

"Oh yes, I will! You kidding? Everybody in town is talking about it. You guys are on television. We've been trying to call, but…And I still can't believe it. My God. My God!"

"Well, Danny's really here. Sitting right next to me on the floor."

"What happened to him? Where was he?"

"Lord only knows."

"I don't get it?"

"Well, nobody does."

"But he's okay, right?"

"Yes. Perfectly! Incredibly! Of course!"

"You think I could talk to him?"

"Danny?" Molly said. He looked up from the floor. "Somebody wants to talk to you." She held out the phone. He got to his feet, came over. He stared at the receiver. "Go on already," she urged, "it's not going to bite."

Danny took the phone, turned it over in his hands. "Like this, silly!" she said, putting it to his ear.

"Oh, yeah." His face broke into a broad smile when he heard the voice. "Hi, Aunt Rosie."

"So you remember me, huh?"

"Sure I do! And Uncle Ed, too."

"Where in the world have you been? We were sick with worry about you."

"I'm sorry," he said, the corners of his mouth turning down.

"Oh don't be. We're just so happy you're back."

Molly pretended not to overhear. The meat was finally malleable and she started shaping it into a couple of thick patties. "Tell Rosie I'll call her back later when I have a chance."

"My mother says she'll talk to you later."

"I'm going to come and see you real soon, right?"

"Okay, Aunt Rosie." He handed the phone back to Molly who was pulling out a frying pan, and then plunked himself down at the pile of books.

"Rosie. Give me a chance to get settled down. I'm just in the middle of cooking." She plopped the burgers into the pan. They sizzled loudly, filling the trailer with the aroma of frying meat.

Danny looked up, sniffing the air. Cautiously he approached the stove. When he saw the frying hamburgers, his features suddenly crumpled.

The look frightened Molly. "What's the matter, Honey?"

"I'm sorry, Mother," he said pulling back "but I can't eat…"

"What can't you…?"

"It's *flesh*," he whispered, horrified. "Isn't it."

"Honey, it's ground beef! Look how nice and juicy these are." Tilting the pan, she poked a burger with a fork and the pink juices sceped out. "See, I made them extra—"

Danny backed away. "That's from an animal somebody killed!"

"But Honey, you *always* loved hamburgers."

He looked at her in disbelief. "Maybe. But I don't love it anymore." He stood pressed against the wall, arms pulled tight into his chest. *"Please,* get it away! I feel sick." He looked as if he was going to throw up—or cry.

Molly rushed out the door with the pan and chucked the meat out on the grass.

"And the smell. Yuuuch!" he said, clutching his throat.

She threw open the windows and aired out the trailer.

"I'm sorry, Angel," she said, confused. "I didn't—"

"We shouldn't hurt animals."

"Of course not. *We?*"

"People."

"But you've got to eat something…" Molly was perplexed. Hey, wait! I've got a great idea!" she exclaimed, mustering false optimism.

"How about some nice spaghetti?"

Danny eyed her warily.

"It's not meat. Believe me. It's made from grain. Just like bread."

She took a box of dried pasta from the shelf and held it out. Danny opened the package, peered in, and examined the hardened noodles. He took out a stiff strand and bit into it.

Molly waited. She could hear the sound as he crunched it in his teeth. "Well?" she inquired.

He ran his tongue over his lips. "I think this is nice."

"I can make it with a yummy tomato sauce."

"Ah, tomatoes!" His smile returned. "Yes, tomatoes. I like them. A lot."

"Okay, looks like we got something right this evening. Tomatoes…" She continued to set the table. "…and what else did they give you to eat?" she inquired as offhandedly as she could.

He hesitated. "Well…lots of things."

"Like?"

"Oh…" he hopped up into a chair and sat with his legs tucked under him. "…potatoes and cattail roots. We had lots of nuts. I like those, too. Things like hickory nuts. You know what black walnuts are? You gotta take a rock and smash them first. They're real hard. And you get this color all over your hands."

"Yeah, we used to do that as kids when we visited my uncle in the country," she said. Get him talking, she reasoned, and he would tell her everything—just like before. He had never been able to keep secrets from her. Always so open. She looked again at his hands. The stains that didn't wash out. Nut stains? Who? Where?

When she poured the tomato sauce over the steaming spaghetti in his bowl, he picked up a single strand with his fingers and held it up to the light.

"It's okay," she assured him. "They're definitely just good old-fashioned noodles. No dead animals in there." Before he had vanished, they used to playfully tease each other and Molly wondered if they would ever return to their former easygoing intimacy. Danny and his Mommy. "Trust me," she said and wondered who else he had come to trust.

Danny gave her a smile, waited for the dish to cool, and then plunged his fingers deep into the saucy noodles. She watched in astonishment as he ate in slurping gulps, tomato sauce and olive oil oozing down his hand.

"Hey, how about a fork?" she suggested, holding it out to him.

He took the shining instrument in his sticky fingers, turned it to get a better look, then placed it back on the table and continued greedily eating with his fingers. When he finished, he held out his plate for more. The poor boy was starving. What inhuman sonofabitch had kept her baby hungry and lean like this?

"What's the story?" asked Chief Matlin when he got Tripoli on his cell phone.

"I don't know yet," answered Tripoli.

"What do you mean don't know? Where the hell was the kid? Who had him?"

"He's not talking."

"That's ridiculous."

"I can't get him to talk."

"What does the juvic shrink say?"

"She hasn't seen him."

"Huh?"

"Yet. Look, the mother won't let me—"

"I don't give a shit about what the mother wants. That kids gotta be over at—"

"Hey, let me do this my way, okay. You don't have a good sense of all the details. This is no ordinary—"

"Okay, fill me in then. What details? Was the kid abused?"

"No, I don't think so. No, definitely not. Not physically."

"What does that mean?"

"The boy is apparently changed."

"Huh?"

"He's different."

"Brainwashed?"

"I don't know. Look, Chief, give me a day. One lousy day and I'll have a lot more answers, okay?"

"Let's go," said Danny, reaching for the door knob.

Molly sprang to her feet. "Go where?" she asked, positioning herself between Danny and the door.

"I dunno," he said, attempting to reach around her. "Just out."

"Out? But, Darling, we just came in a little while ago. And it's getting late and dark outside."

"I don't care. I just want to—"

"Hey, Sweetheart, I've got a better idea. How does a nice hot bath sound? We'll get you all cleaned up," she suggested brightly, taking him by the hand, "and then tuck you into bed."

"But I'm not tired," he objected as she took him into the bedroom and then pulled his shirt off over his head. "And I don't want to go to bed," he balked, sounding just like the little boy she knew.

Molly filled the tub with hot water, checked the temperature, and then settled Danny in the deep bath.

"How does that feel?" she asked.

"Mmmm, good," he admitted with a smile and, submerging deeper, arched his head back so that his long locks of hair splayed out into the water.

Sitting him up in the tub, Molly soaped a washcloth and began sudsing him. Not only were his hands callused, but his elbows, too. She worked up the length of his arms, then his chest, as he submitted willingly. His skin was smooth and silky under the soapy cloth.

When he stood in the tub, his body glistened in voluptuous flesh tones. His legs were not quite those of a stumpy little kid any more, but were longer, his thighs and buttocks firm and contoured. Though he was reedy, she also saw that he was strong, his arms and chest had actually gained muscle and definition. From carrying things? she wondered. Working? What was it they made him do?

She poured some baby shampoo into the palm of her hand and lathered his abundant hair. He leaned back in the tub, closed his eyes, relishing the attention. Did they touch him, too? Like this? Care for him in the way he needed. Did someone love him? The water in the tub turned dark from dirt.

"Did they have a bathtub where you were?" she ventured cautiously.

"No, of course, not!" he answered, eyes closed. "You don't need this much water to get clean. All you need is a bucket. But you gotta make the hot water first."

"How?" she asked, trying not to stare at him.

"On a fire, of course, silly!" He laughed.

She let the dirty water out of the tub, turned on the shower head and let him rinse under the stream until the water coming off him was clear and clean. Then she turned off the faucet, wrapped a towel around him, and helped him out of the tub, squeezing him tight.

"You know, I bought you a birthday present while you were gone." Taking him back into the bedroom, she showed him the truck

"Yes," he said, offhandedly, "I saw it."

She picked it up off the shelf and handed it to him. "It's huge, isn't it."

He held it in his arms. "Yes, it's very big."

"Maybe you'd like to play with it?"

"Yes, maybe later."

"Oh."

"But thank you for the present," he said with a smile, handing it back to her. "I know you were thinking of me. And that was nice. Very nice." Naked from the waist up, he wrapped his arms around her and pressed his head into her midsection, his ear against her womb as though trying to detect a familiar murmur. It was from here that he had sprung, she thought, the tiny, fragile infant-turned-boy. In his soul did he still feel the elemental connection of their tissues?

Molly caressed his back, and the warmth of his skin allayed her fears. "Of course I was thinking of you. I thought of you every minute of every day," she murmured, bending down and burying her face in his hair smelling of wood smoke and pine needles. And she kept wondering. Where had he been? Who had kept him all these months? And why wouldn't he talk, at least to her, his mother and life-long confidant?

"I was worried about you, too," he admitted, turning up his head so that his soft cheek was pressed against hers. "I felt bad. I kept thinking about you," he pulled slightly back to look up at her. "But I had to stay away. You understand."

"No I don't."

"I couldn't help it."

"Did someone hurt you?"

"Oh, no!"

Despite herself, Molly was crying. "Oh, Darling," she said, stroking his brow. "Promise me you'll never, ever leave me again. Promise me," she pleaded.

He clung to her, but remained ominously silent.

Molly gave him a kiss and turned off his light.

"'Night, Honey," she said.

"Good night," he said so sweetly that she had to go back yet again, nestle her face against his, breathe deeply, again inhale his familiar little-boy smell. Yet, buried under it was something darker, muskier, that no amount of soap seemed to dissolve. Foreign and complex, it smelled like wet earth and mushrooms, sunshine and leaves. "Sleep tight, darling," she uttered in his ear.

He brought his arms around her neck and held her, then snuggled under the freshly laundered covers. "Mmmmm," he murmured, "I forgot how nice and soft and cuddly this bed is."

"Sweet dreams," she said, closing the door. Danny didn't object—didn't even give so much as a peep about keeping the small night light on. This from a boy who had been so terrified of the dark.

She kept returning every few minutes to check on him, but he was always still there. In his bed. Sleeping peacefully. She stood over him, gazing down, listening to his rhythmic breathing, bringing her face so close to his that she could drink in his sweet breath. Her baby was back. Really back.

Later in the night she called Tripoli.

"Well, how's it going?" he inquired.

She told him about the scene with the hamburger, his needing to get out, his indifference to toys. "It's like my kid was abducted by aliens."

"Or someone."

"I didn't mean to neglect you today. And argue. I mean—"

"Hey, that's what I'm here for."

"This is just all so...so strange."

"The boy's going to need time to readjust," he tried to reassure her. "But kids are flexible."

"Hey, it's not him. He's doing great. It's me. His 'mother.' I'm the one that needs time to adjust!"

Molly woke up with a start. At first she thought it was a noise, but everything was silent and dark. She turned to look at Danny's bed and her heart leaped in panic. The covers were pulled back, but all she could see was the pillow that bore the imprint of his head. She leapt out of bed. After a dizzying, terrifying moment of indecision, she detected footsteps in the living room and she rushed out.

"My God, what's the matter?" she whispered as she saw the pale form of Danny in the darkness.

"I couldn't sleep," he answered in a whisper of his own. Outside it was now so quiet you could hear the frogs croaking in the swamp behind the park. He kept moving around in the darkened room.

"Did you have a bad dream?"

"No. I just couldn't sleep. I think I've got to get used to this place again."

Molly pulled him close. Every muscle and sinew in his body was tense. "What was the other place like?"

"Different," he said.

"How?"

"It was quieter. And it had more air. Not so stuffy."

"Would you like to go out? Is that it?"

"Yes. *Please.*" Something like desperation in his voice tugged at her guilt.

Unlocking the trailer door, she led him out onto the cold metal steps. The night was crisp and clear; the air was still and lightly perfumed with the fragrance of spring. Beyond the immediate lights of the trailer park, the sky was dark and moonless. In the distance, a big truck droned down the highway. Danny took a series of long, deep breaths, exhaling slowly, and Molly could feel the tension in his body dissipating.

She waited, keeping him warm against her side. "Better now?" she finally inquired.

"Yeah," he nodded. "Much better."

The sound of the truck had faded, and now all they could hear was the buzzing from the mercury vapor lamp that sat on the power pole overhead. One hundred feet from the house stood a patrol car. A cop sat in the front seat, staring out at them, and she pulled her nightgown tight around her.

"Could I sleep out here?" asked Danny.

She looked at him. Hesitated. "Sure, Honey," she said finally, went back into the trailer, gathered his blankets and pillow and made him a bed on the grass. Happily, he crawled under the covers.

"Think you can sleep now?"

"I'm sure."

"Good," she said, tucking him in.

Molly went back again, put on a coat, and lugged out an aluminum chaise lounge. She unfolded it, stationing herself beside his bed, wondering what the cop would say about this to the others in the morning. She closed her eyes and tried to sleep, but her mind was in turmoil; she could not drive off the indefinable sense of dread that gnawed away at the edges of her consciousness. The same questions kept circling in her mind. Who had kept him? How did they get him? How did he get away? And why? Why? *Why?* Only with the approach of daybreak did she fall asleep.

When she opened her eyes, Tripoli was standing over her, blocking the glaring sun. She squinted in the brightness, trying to orient herself.

"Where's Danny?" she asked, leaping to her feet.

"Right here, Mother," he laughed, smiling at her. He was sitting cross-legged on his mattress, naked.

It took Molly a moment to take in the scene. The neighbors gawking. The new cop on duty, leaning up against his squad car, arms folded, watching them.

"Jesus," muttered Molly, and she scooped up Danny and headed into the trailer.

Tripoli gathered up the mattress and carried it in behind her.

"I'm not going to ask," he said with a smile.

"There's nothing to ask," said Molly with a shrug. "We were camping out."

"That's what I told them when they called last night."

"Huh? Who?" Molly fumbled with the coffee maker, popping in a filter.

"My men."

"Oh, I'm sorry," she said. "I didn't get a lot of sleep last night. Hey, what time is it, anyhow?" Molly answered her own question, checking the clock. "Cripes. It already nine!" She picked up the phone while scooping coffee.

"Hey, make enough for the both of us."

"Larry," she said, "I meant to call you last night, but—"

"My God," exclaimed Larry. "I heard. The papers and news services are full of it. It's extraordinary. I mean, incredible. Wonderful! What happened to him? Where was he?"

She looked over at Danny leaning over his pile of books, his naked little butt in the air. "Hey, how about getting some clothes on."

"Huh?" said Larry.

"I meant Danny," she laughed. "Look, I really can't go into details now."

"Sure. I understand. Just curious."

"Look, I won't be in today."

"Well, of course not!"

"Let me call you when—"

"Whenever. I'm sure it's crazy on your end. Just one piece of advice. Don't sign anything. Don't agree to anything—"

"What?"

"Without having a lawyer or an agent. Danny's story might be worth big bucks." His other line was ringing. "Hey, we'll talk later. Just don't do anything without talking to me first."

"We've got an appointment, remember?" said Tripoli as soon as she hung up.

"Oh…"

He fixed her with his bright green eyes. "And there's no weaseling out of it."

"Weaseling!" said Danny and laughed. He obviously liked the word. "Weaseling," he kept saying as Molly took him back into the bedroom. "Trip said *weaseling*. Isn't that funny!"

"Hilarious. Now go brush your teeth. And use the toothpaste."

"You mean with that minty stuff?"

A few minutes later, Tripoli could hear the shower pelting the sides of the metal stall and Danny came out dressed, his hair combed, looking a lot cleaner than the day before. He plunked himself into the middle of the pile of books.

Tripoli poured himself some coffee and then ambled over to where Danny sat. "Hey, whatta you got there?"

Danny looked up. "A book," he said.

Tripoli sat down next to the boy and put his arm around him. Danny nestled in close.

"Hmmm, seems to me like kind of heavy stuff," remarked Tripoli, looking closer. It was one of Molly's old textbooks, a psych book, and it was open to a section on nonverbal communication. "Can you read some of the words for me?" he inquired curiously.

"I could try," said Danny, looking up with his big doe eyes.

"Well just try this," said Tripoli, pointing to a paragraph.

"Okay, let me see," said Danny. Pulling the heavy volume closer, Danny began haltingly to sound out the words, his fingers following the text. "All of us…communicate non-verb-ally as well as verb-ally." He turned to look back at Tripoli, a proud smile on his face.

"Wow that's terrific!" Tripoli said. "I'm impressed. Keep going."

Danny read on. Sometimes he stumbled or mispronounced a word, "If irritated, we may—may t-t-tense our bodies or…or press our lips together. With a gaze, aver- averted glance or stare we comm- communicate inti-mecy—no, missy, sub-mission, or dom- dom- dom-"

"Dominance," Tripoli prompted.

"Yeah, dominance."

"That's wonderful," Tripoli said.

Molly, her hair still wet from the shower, had quietly slipped into the room, and stood watching, her jaw slack with surprise. "Holy moly," she muttered.

Danny smiled eagerly again. "I can read more—if you want."

"I've got a better idea," Tripoli said. "Let's give you the real test."

"Okay," piped Danny, anxious to play along. "Give me the test. I like tests!"

"All right then. Just what does all that mean?" He knew that children could be taught to read at an early age, just how early he wasn't sure, nor how much, but the true question was the degree of their comprehension

"Well," Danny began, "I think it means something like…you can speak to people without using words."

Tripoli was speechless. He looked over to Molly who shook her head in amazement.

"It's just like that funny look on your face right now. And my mother's, too. You're surprised that I can read so well, aren't you." And then Danny laughed.

"Yes. Yes I am," said Tripoli clearing his throat. "How did you learn this? *Where* did you learn this?"

"Oh, I don't know," Danny casually moved his head back and forth. "Just around."

"Did he mention anything else last night?" he said in a low voice, after Danny got into the car. He closed the door and turned to Molly.

"Nothing really. Just that you don't need whole bathtubs of water. You can use a bucket. But you've got to make a fire. A *fire?*"

"We went through Danny's clothes. There some things we found in his pockets that weren't in the original report. Can you recall what he had when you dropped him off at daycare?"

"I'm not sure any more. It was so long ago." Danny was tapping at the closed window and Molly lifted a finger asking him to wait. Then she looked back at Tripoli. "Well, tell me, what'd you find?"

Tripoli positioned himself with his back to Danny. Blocking his view, he reached into his coat pocket and pulled out three plastic evidence bags, handing them to her one at a time.

"He found some pennies."

"He might have had those." She shook the bag and then stared up into the lightness of Tripoli's green eyes. "He always liked the sound of money jingling in his pockets. Given the state of his mother's finances, you can't blame him, can you?"

"We found this string, a yellow piece of Lego, and a stone."

"Yeah, sure," Molly said, "this is his lucky stone. He loved it and always carried it with him. And this is probably a piece of his Lego— looks like it came from this little tow truck he has. And the string?" she turned the bag around to examine it in the light. "I don't know. I think he had it. Looks like some kite string, maybe. I can't be sure."

"Now, was there anything you can think of, something that might be missing?"

"Hmmmm." Molly wrinkled her forehead.

"Think hard."

"He used to carry this damn whistle he found."

"What kind?"

"Like a police whistle—you know with a ball in it. It was plastic. Red and white. He was always going around blowing it, driving everybody crazy. Mrs. Oltz kept warning him that if he took it out once more at Kute Kids she was going to confiscate it."

"Did she?"

"Not that I know of. But..." Molly cut herself off in mid-sentence.

Tripoli saw that Danny was leaning over the front seat to see what they were doing. Quickly, he took back the bags and stuffed them into his pocket.

Tripoli drove Molly and Danny into Ithaca. The sun-drenched streets of downtown were filled with people in shorts and tank tops and summer dresses relishing the mild spring day. Parking in front of the old County Jail on Court Street, he led them upstairs to what the Child Protective Services referred to simply as "The Room." It was an oblong space filled with toys and colorful cushions, and it was equipped with a one-way mirror. The juvenile psychiatrist, a matronly woman of indeterminate age with short-cropped hair and big-hooped earrings, was waiting when they arrived.

"This is Mrs. Barrie," said Tripoli.

"And you must be Danny?" she said brightly, stretching out her hand. The woman had a soft smile, and Tripoli hoped she wouldn't be condescending.

"No. Daniel."

"Yes, Daniel."

Danny shook her hand. Tripoli could tell that he didn't quite trust her; he wondered if she would have better luck than he or Molly had.

"Why don't you just call me Joan?" she suggested cozily, putting an arm around him and leading him deeper into the room.

"Okay," he said, *"Joan."*

"Would you like to play with some of the nice toys we have here?" she asked.

Danny looked them over, then shrugged. "Not particularly, *Joan,* he said. Tripoli had to suppress a smile.

"I've got some really neat trucks and…" She didn't go much further. It was apparent that Danny was not going to tolerate being indulged with childish distractions.

"Can I please go now?" asked Danny, looking beseechingly toward Molly. Then Tripoli.

"I was thinking that perhaps we could have a little chat," said the woman.

"I don't really like it in here," said Danny.

"Maybe your mother and Mr. Tripoli could…" the psychiatrist lifted an eyebrow in Tripoli's direction.

"Yes, of course," said Tripoli, taking Molly by the arm.

Molly started to stiffen, but Tripoli held on tight and escorted her toward the door. "Don't worry, Honey," Molly called over her shoulder. "I'll be right outside waiting for you."

Danny looked apprehensive. He kept staring at the door after it was closed.

"Now," Mrs. Barrie said when they were alone and she had Danny settled on the floor beside her on puffy cushions. "I understand that you were away from your Mommy for quite a while."

Danny turned from the closed door and stared at her. Then, slowly, he gazed around the room. At the doll house. The puzzles. The low table with a big box of crayons on it.

"Did you do some traveling? Did you go far away?"

He didn't answer. His eyes were still scanning the brightly lit space. There were two dolls sitting on a shelf, a boy doll and a girl doll, each with prominent sexual organs. He stared at them. Then at the woman.

Mrs. Barrie waited.

Danny began to hum to himself. It was a strange-sounding melody, the woman noted. In fact, to her ear it seemed hardly melodic. Just a series of atonal, disconnected notes. His voice was high, reedy, almost flute-like.

"When a young man disappears, grownups can't help but wonder where he went," she continued, still trying to engage him.

Danny stopped humming and sighed impatiently, still avoiding her gaze.

Tripoli and Molly sat behind the one-way mirror, leaning forward and watching. Beside them stood a young man dressed in black jeans and a sweater, panning with a video camera and taping Danny's every move. As the psychiatrist spoke, her voice issued through the overhead speaker thin and distant.

Danny got up and moved around the room. The woman continued to let time pass. He walked a full circle and then came back to where she sat on the cushion and looked down at her.

"Are we finished?" he asked quietly.

"Not quite," she smiled.

"I don't like the questions you want to ask me," he said pointedly, hands perched on his hips.

"Well, maybe I could ask some questions that you'd like?"

"I don't think so," he said in his high little voice. "How long do I have to be here, anyway?"

"Just a little while."

"What does 'a little while' mean?"

"Let's say an hour."

"That's too long," said Danny. There was now not a hint of humor in his voice.

Mrs. Barrie laughed good-naturedly.

"A half hour," he said. He kept staring at the mirror.

"Okay. A half hour," she agreed. "That sounds fair."

Danny wanted to know exactly what time it was and precisely what time this meeting would over.

"Do you know what a half hour is?"

"Yes. Thirty minutes."

"Good!" said Mrs. Barrie. "Come, sit down," she urged, patting a neighboring cushion. "Please."

Danny finally slumped down next to her.

"Well, now that we're alone like this, just the two of us, I thought it would be nice if we could talk. Talk honestly. Openly."

"But we're not alone," said Danny, looking her hard in the eye.

"Why do you say that?" inquired the woman.

"Because my mother and her policeman friend, Mr. Trip, are behind that mirror," he said, pointing directly at them. "And so's that man with the machine."

The woman spun around to face the mirror. All she could make out were the reflections of herself and the boy.

Molly could see that she was flabbergasted. She kept staring at them through the mirror, her face flushed. Molly wasn't sure if it was embarrassment at being caught or just plain shock.

Tripoli said not a word, just sat nodding to himself, his hands folded in his lap.

"Why do you think that?" asked Mrs. Barrie, finally regaining her composure.

"I can see them," Danny said with a shrug. "Please, can I go out? I don't like it in here. There're no windows and…and it's smelly!"

"Like what?"

"I don't know. Like chemicals."

"Chemicals?" she echoed.

"Yes!"

"So you would rather be outdoors?"

"Yes," he said, furrowing his eyebrows.

"Like where?"

"Like in the air," said Danny.

"Do you mean just out in the street or in the country?"

"Yes," he answered smiling with his faint lisp. "The country. I like that."

"You were living on a farm, then?"

"In the forest," he corrected.

"Where in the forest?"

He shrugged.

"With a man?"

Danny nodded. He stared at the mirror and seemed to be looking right through it.

"What did the man look like? Was he old? Young?"

Danny didn't respond.

"Did he maybe have a mustache?"

"He had a beard. A big one. It was all white." He answered, still staring at the mirror.

"Oh, that's very interesting. And what did you do with him—the man?"

"Nothing special. Just talked a lot. And things."

"And did he touch you?"

Danny looked annoyed. He glanced at the naked dolls, then looked straight back at her. "Not the way you think." His unwavering stare unnerved the woman.

"And did you live in a house?"

"Sort of," he said, getting more and more restless.

"Come over here, Danny," She led him to the small table, opened a box of crayons and spread them out. Then she gave Danny a big sheet of paper.

"Can you draw for me a picture of the man and his house?" she asked.

"I suppose."

"I think that would be very, very interesting," she said, and held out a bunch of crayons. "Now what color should we start with?"

Danny looked at her somewhat incredulously. "I can do this," he said, then went to work. He drew intently, picking crayons of different colors.

Molly and Tripoli stood up to get a better look.

Danny was drawing what appeared to be some kind of hut. It was made with sticks and branches, its roof thatched. Not a bad job for a five-year-old, thought Tripoli. There were animals around it, what looked like goats and sheep, and there were trees and steep hills in the background. The scene was flooded with long, golden rays from a somewhat out-sized sun. A man stood near the hut, holding hands with what was clearly a little boy. He held a walking staff in his free hand, and his hair and beard and mustache were silver. The boy's hair was the same yellow as the sun.

"Okay," said Danny, handing Joan Barrie the picture and getting to his feet. "Can I please get out of this place now?"

"I just wanted to ask you a few more—"

"The time is up. You promised. And I don't want to talk anymore," said Danny. "I need to get out. *Please!*"

The psychiatrist slowly got up, turned to the mirror with a shrug, and led Danny back to his mother.

"How about a few straight answers, huh?" said Tripoli when they got back to his car. He had placed Danny in the front seat next to him with Molly in the back. The radio was turned down, crackling in the background.

"Sweetie," Molly implored, leaning forward, "Couldn't you just tell Trip and me where you've been?"

"I did. I made the picture for you." Danny turned to Tripoli.

"I know you didn't like that lady."

"No, she was okay. Just a little silly is all." He grinned.

"Listen, Smiley," Tripoli warned, "I like you a lot. You're a swell kid. The picture was beautiful. But you're not going to squirm out of this. Not that easily."

"We don't want to nag you," said Molly. Tripoli and his dogged insistence was making her edgy. "But—"

"I want to get out of this car! I hate these smelly machines!" Without warning, Danny suddenly lunged for the door handle.

Moving fast, Tripoli caught his hand before he could pop open the door.

"Owww!"

"Trip!" shouted Molly.

"Hey, you want him to run out into traffic?" he turned and looked harshly at her, then back at Danny. "Okay, what do you say we cut the baloney, and you start telling me and your mother the truth?" Tripoli hung onto the boy's thin wrist. "I think your mother especially deserves some honest answers. For six months she hasn't slept for worry about you."

"Come on, take it easy, Trip," warned Molly, nervously.

Tripoli silenced her with a raised eyebrow. "We're doing this my way now," he said. "No more pampering. Now we get some straight answers." The people from the State Police lab had taken fibers from the carpet in Kute Kids and would be over at Molly's in the afternoon pulling samples from the trailer. Forensics in Albany would subtract them out from what they found on Danny's clothes, and then they'd have something substantive. Old man. A hut. The boy was opening up. But he seemed to do it only when pushed.

"You promised me, Mother," said Danny, struggling to turn around and catch sight of her above the high back. "that we'd go for a hike, and—"

"You can go for the biggest hike in the world," said Tripoli. "You can go all the way to Katmandu. But first you're going to help me a little, okay?"

"No!" Danny banged his fist against the door.

"The sooner you help me, the sooner we can all be outside having fun."

"I don't want *fun*," Danny spat back. "I just want to be out of this *thing*."

"Same difference," said Tripoli.

Molly moved again to intervene. "Trip, you—"

"Please," said Tripoli with an abrupt insistence that left no room. "My department has spent six whole months on this—a lot of manpower and a lot of dough. We've had every agency in the state look-

ing for Danny. We've turned this county upside down." Tripoli could feel his face burning and knew he was losing it, but couldn't help himself. "I think we all deserve an explanation." He turned to look straight at Danny, then released the boy's arm. "You understand what I'm talking about, don't you?" he said harshly.

Danny looked cowed.

"I don't like you when you're like this!" His lower lip was jutting out and he looked like he was going to cry.

"Well, that's the breaks," Tripoli said, curtly.

Danny started to cry quietly.

Tripoli started the engine and began to roll. He kept glancing at the boy as they moved down Court Street. They took a left on Cayuga and got caught at the light. A line of children from the elementary school crossed the street in front of them holding hands in pairs. The kids were not much older than Danny, but he didn't seem to take notice of them. He was staring at the dashboard, his eyes wet.

Tripoli took a series of long breaths and slow exhalations. "Look," he said finally. "I'm sorry. I didn't mean to jump on you like that, son."

"I know," said Danny in a tight voice. With the back of his hand he wiped the tears from his eyes.

"I'm only a stupid grownup," he said deliberately, though still a little gruffly. "We lose our patience sometimes." He caught the reflection of Molly in the back seat. Her eyes were wet and she was biting her lip. "You understand that, right?"

Danny didn't answer.

"Come on, let's try to work together on this. Okay?"

Danny bit his lip, just like Molly. Two peas in a pod. Same body language. Same way of tilting their heads when they were curious, fluttering their eyelids when they were tense.

It was a risk. A gamble. Taking the kid back to Kute Kids. Who knew what he had really been through?

The building stood vacant, its windows boarded up with sheets of delaminating plywood, closed down by the state after finding it rife with violations. Tripoli dug through the keys he had gotten from the landlord. Across the street, Sonny Makarainen was supervising a delivery man rolling silver kegs into his bar.

Tripoli turned the key and the door swung open, creaking on hinges that hadn't been used since Mrs. Oltz had been ordered to shut the daycare center down. Inside it was dark and dank. Cold. Tripoli switched on the lights. The florescents came on with a loud sparking snap then settled into a hum. A couple of weak bulbs continued blinking.

The place was the same as it had been the day state officials had forced Mrs. Oltz to shut down her facility. A little pair of rubber boots lay abandoned in the hall closet that stood ajar; a single mitten lay forgotten on the floor. A half-dozen plastic cups caked with the dried residue of what looked to be cocoa sat on a tray near the entryway.

"Come on," said Tripoli gently, shepherding Danny into the room. Molly closed the door behind them, muting the street sounds. Inside, except for the buzz of the lights, it was deathly quiet. A shiver passed through her as she took in the once familiar surroundings. The open basement door.

Tripoli got down on a knee, bringing himself to eye level with Danny. "You remember this place?"

Danny shrugged.

"Of course you remember," Molly said plaintively, and softly squeezed his shoulder. "You used to go here every day. With Stevie Lifsey and the twins and…You remember? It's Kute Kids."

"Yeah, maybe," Danny said, unconvincingly.

Crayons and paper cluttered the little tables. The matching chairs stood askew as if they had been hurriedly deserted. Blocks and toys littered the floor. How could I ever have put him in this dump? thought Molly.

Danny's eyes slowly swept the room, fastening for a moment on a model hanging down from a string. The plane rotated slowly, stirred into life by their presence. Danny kept looking around the playroom.

Outside, a heavy truck rolled by, then stopped at the corner. When it started again, the whole building shook. Then, again, the place was relatively quiet, just the swish of traffic.

"Maybe you want to sit down?" Molly suggested, hoping to jog Danny's memory. If only he would talk, they could end all this. Why all the secrecy?

"Yeah," Tripoli agreed. "Where did you usually sit?"

Danny shrugged. Molly pointed, and they took him over to one of the tables and got him to sit down.

He sat there looking up at Tripoli questioningly.

"Hey, look, here's a crayon. A nice big red one. Maybe you'd like to draw something," urged Tripoli. "You know, like you used to?

Danny took the crayon.

They waited.

"Hey, look at all these," Danny said, suddenly fascinated by the spider webs strung between the neighboring chairs.

"Come on, Danny," she said. "Tell us. How did you get out? Did someone take you out?"

He just looked up at her.

"Maybe you snuck out? I know about Cheryl locking you in the basement. I'm so sorry about that." Molly waited. "Honey, tell us," she said, *"Please."*

Danny reached up, put his fingers on her lips to quiet her.

"Come on, let's get out of here already," Molly said. "This place gives me the creeps."

Turning away from her, Tripoli tried to hide his frustration.

"Come on, we're not getting anywhere like this."

Wordlessly, he picked up the keys and headed for the door.

Once they were back out on the street, Danny refused to get back into Tripoli's car.

Tripoli coaxed and Molly pleaded.

"We can walk," Danny suggested. "I don't mind walking."

"You, maybe," Tripoli said trying to make light of it, "but I'm getting old."

Danny didn't smile.

Finally, they got him into the car. Tripoli put him in the seat belt, locked the doors, and started the engine.

"You used to go here. To daycare. You know that, Danny, as well as I do."

"Well…maybe," he conceded.

"Not maybe. You *did!*" Tripoli was nearing the end of his patience, and knew it.

"Trip, please," Molly said. "Go easy."

He ignored her and went on. "And you somehow snuck out of here, right?"

"Apparently."

"Apparently, nothing!"

"If you're not nice to me, I won't even talk to you," Danny warned.

"Geez," Tripoli said scratching his head in irritation. "Come on, Danny, cut me some slack, huh? I'm your friend, not your enemy."

"Then why do you keep bothering me?"

"Well, then I'm acting like a policeman now. Okay, you said you went to the woods, right? And you were in this little house-like thing—a hut? And there was this hermit."

"*Hermit?*" repeated Danny, wrinkling his brow. For the first time, he was showing interest.

"Honey, a hermit," explained Molly, "is a guy who lives all by himself in the woods."

"Hermit," repeated Danny thoughtfully. "Yes."

"And this hermit had a name, right?" asked Tripoli.

Danny turned to look at him. Paused. "He had many names."

"Oh?"

"He just never told me what they were."

Tripoli traded looks with Molly. Was this kid playing games? If nothing else, the boy was systematically driving a wedge between him and Molly—and she was letting him get away with it.

"But what did you call him?" Molly prompted.

"Father," he said finally.

"Father?" she repeated.

"And sometimes John."

Silence.

Tripoli waited. John. John? He looked at Molly and she shook her head.

The engine kept idling. When you came down to it, the boy was right, thought Tripoli. It did stink in the car. Probably needed a new exhaust. Tripoli rolled down his window and waited.

"You want to know where I went, right?" Danny said, finally breaking the silence.

"Well, of course!" Tripoli gestured.

"I went out."

"Okay. Out where?"

"Up there." Danny motioned vaguely up Green Street.

"Ah, now we're getting somewhere." Tripoli put the car into gear and started rolling.

Molly remained silent in the back seat. My God, he was finally talking. In a way, she was afraid of what Danny might reveal.

They crept slowly up Green Street, traffic eddying around them.

"Okay?" Tripoli asked as they passed the Minimart.

Danny nodded. He seemed again self-possessed.

"Did you cross Cayuga Street?"

"Yes," he answered. "This street."

They drove through the intersection. Coasted right past the front of Woolworth's.

"Here, too?"

"Uh-huh."

"And you saw this old lady," Tripoli said more than asked.

Danny looked startled, and Tripoli knew he had him slightly off balance. So, the old woman really had seen him in front of Woolworth's.

"And she talked to you, didn't you? Asked you what you were doing out alone on the street?"

The question caught Molly by surprise, too. So Tripoli had really questioned Edna Poyer after all.

"Okay, then what?" persisted Tripoli.

"Then up there." Danny motioned to the overpass that was Aurora Street.

Tripoli had to drive under the bridge and make a complete circle through the "tuning fork" until he came up on Aurora Street. He took a left and started up the steep incline. A tanker truck loaded with milk was in front, partially blocking the view. Tripoli let it creep ahead, black diesel smoke puffing out of it's exhaust pipe as traffic began jamming up behind him.

"And then where'd you go?"

"Hmmm," Danny wagged his head. "I went somewhere through," he said motioning to a yard.

So, he did it on his own, thought Molly. Snuck out somehow. Cheryl was so spacey and Danny was such a quick little guy that he could easily have slipped past her while a parent was entering or leaving Kute Kids.

But where was he headed? Did he know? Had he been lured out or did the man just stumble upon him and take him? Keep him. Six whole months?

"You cut through this side or that?"

"I'm not sure. I don't remember."

"Where'd you come out?" They were still moving up the hill, passing where the old Southside Coal Company used to sit. Then the Italian restaurant with its umbrella-topped tables on the deck overlooking the highway and the gas station.

Silence.

"Do you remember anything. A building? A house? Something."

"The school." Danny smiled at the reminiscence. "Yes. I passed the school with lots of children outside. They had this real big ball. I watched them."

"South Hill School!" exclaimed Molly from the back seat, and Tripoli quickly turned around, went down a few blocks and cut a right onto Hudson Street.

"This look familiar?" he kept asking. "Or this?"

They started again up South Hill, now parallel to the main route.

When they came abreast of a big white house, Danny pointed, "Yes. I remember this one with the funny tower." Then he recognized the school yard. Oak Hill Manor, where old Edna resided, was just above it.

"And then which way?"

Danny motioned vaguely further up South Hill. "I kept going up," he said.

They continued climbing until they came to the edge of the Ithaca College campus. "And then what?"

"I just kept going," said Danny. "Up and up and up..."

"Where? Which way?"

"I don't know."

"You must remember more. Come on. Think."

Molly could see Danny was becoming progressively more agitated. Tripoli was again losing his patience, trying to back Danny into a corner. "Please, Trip, he's just a little boy," she implored.

"Please nothing," said Tripoli. "I've got to get to the bottom of this. Don't you see? We're close. So close."

The boy had tears again in his eyes. "I can't breathe. Can you open the windows? All of them. There's not enough air in here."

"Where, Danny? *Where* did you go?"

"I need more fresh air."

"Where? *Where?*"

"To the woods," he said.

"Which woods?"

"The forest."

"Which forest?"

"I don't know! I don't know and I can't tell you. Now take me home! Or else."

"Or else what?"

Molly became frightened. She began to speak, but Tripoli cut her short with a withering stare. She could see the lines on his jaw turning sharply defined as he clenched his teeth. He was like a man possessed.

Danny turned stone silent. An ominous silence filled the car, and when Tripoli turned to look, he saw that the boy's skin had suddenly blanched a deathly white. His breathing had turned rapid but shallow, fluttering, like a wounded deer going into shock.

"I'm going to die if you don't get me some air," the boy gasped.

"This has got to stop!" shouted Molly in alarm. Reaching over the seat, she unsnapped the belt and lifted Danny over the seat. "My poor baby," she said cradling him in her arms and stroking his pale face. His eyes were blank and unblinking. "Just hang on. We're going home. Right this instant!"

"Okay, okay," Tripoli relented, frightened by the boy's appearance. He flipped on his red lights, swerved the car around, and hurried back down the hill, windows opened wide. Aside from the wind rushing through the car all he could hear was the boy gulping for air like a fish out of water.

chapter nine

The investigation was now picking up steam. So, too, was the media hype. It was being treated as a kidnapping, and the Feds, their interest rekindled, were suddenly back on the case. Tripoli spent over an hour with two FBI agents, briefing them. They wanted to question the boy. So did investigators from the sheriff's department, and, of course, the State Police BCI. It was big news, and everybody felt they had to be in on it.

"I've been running this investigation for six fucking months when nobody else gave a shit!" Tripoli said, standing in front of the chief's desk with his hands on his hips. "And now—"

"You've got more than enough on your plate, Trip. Why not step aside and let the State Police or Feds take over? They've got the resources. The manpower. You could continue to work with them. Just let them manage the case, take the heat off the department."

"Fuck the heat. Either I'm the lead on this or I'm not. And if I'm not, I'm not walking into that press conference." He pointed a thumb upstairs. "You can answer all the questions. Bullshit them like you're bullshitting me."

"Now just calm down. Don't get your balls in such an uproar." Chief Harry Matlin got up. A regal-looking man with wavy white hair and year-round tan, he always struck Tripoli as more the politician than a cop. He rested his hand on Tripoli's shoulder, but Tripoli shrugged it off.

"This is our jurisdiction and you're rolling over for—"

"Nobody's rolling over for anybody."

"So I'm in charge then, right?"

"If you feel that passionate about it…Okay. It's yours."

"In that case, I want hands off the kid, too. Nobody grills the boy without my say-so."

The Chief thought about it. "Alright. As long as you make progress."

"I'm close. I'm sure of it. Don't worry about my end."

"Right now I'm worried about this press conference. I don't want us coming off as a bunch of small-town hicks," he said, checking his watch. "Damn it! We're late. Come on. Let's get a move on it." He strode out of the office, Tripoli on his heels. "You know they're all waiting to eat us alive." The Chief repeatedly punched the elevator button, waited an impatient second, then took to the stairs. "The kid's home now, and if we don't crack this nut we're going to look pretty stupid. You'd better bring me up to speed."

"The kid walked," said Tripoli, as they hurried up the two flights, their footsteps echoing on the steel stairs. "I'm pretty sure. Though how he got out is a mystery." Tripoli was talking fast now. "I've got a gut feeling that he ended up somewhere south of town. He keeps talking about the woods. The forest. My best guess is the Danby State Forest. I'm ordering the State Police to do a flyover. Also, I've got the kid's clothes up in Albany. Something's gotta give. Somewhere. Somehow."

"No abuse, no kiddy diddling."

"Nothing far as they could see. He was in good shape. A little dirty around the edges, a little skinny, but no."

"The father?" asked the chief as he moved down the corridor, Tripoli at his side.

"Nah. I doubt it. But we're still following that, too."

The chief stopped at the double doors leading to the conference

room, his hand resting on the handle. "Are you sure you can sepa-
rate your job and your personal feelings?"

"Huh?" Tripoli avoided his eyes. Through the wooden doors, he
could hear the din of competing voices, the shuffling of dozens of
feet.

Tilting his head, the chief stared at him knowingly.

"Christ," muttered Tripoli.

"Well, it's a small town. You know that. Just be—"

"What?"

"Careful. Discreet. You know the drill. I just don't want any gossip circulating. Come on," he said, yanking open the door and
motioning for Tripoli to move ahead, "let's get this show over with."

All eyes in the crowded room snapped to attention as Tripoli and
the chief entered, and the room lit up in a blazing array of lights as
cameras started rolling and reporters and cameramen jockeyed for
position. Tripoli followed Matlin as he mounted the elevated plat-
form and approached the jumbled bank of microphones that had
been hastily mounted on the lectern. The air in the room was thick
with noise and sweat. Gazing out over the sea of people, Tripoli did
a quick head count. There were twenty-five people, maybe thirty. In
addition to the usual locals from Syracuse and Elmira, lots of out-of-
towners. The big name networks, too; even a camera crew from
Japanese television. Nothing like this since that family out in Ellis
Hollow got butchered and burned ten years ago.

The chief moved close to the microphone and cleared his throat.
The room quickly quieted.

"First of all, I want to thank you for the stories you carried in
the past…"

Tripoli watched Matlin as he spoke. Though he was masterful at
stroking the press, Tripoli could see that the muscles in his face were
taut. It didn't take much imagination to comprehend what he was
going through. What he said earlier was true. They had plenty of

cases to handle. Besides the usual run of robberies and drug busts and assaults, they had those leaky barrels of low-level radioactive waste just discovered in a lot off Cherry Street. A witness claimed to have seen a truck from a Buffalo company unloading something just the night before. Up on Gun Hill Road, the residents had been complaining about a strange smell coming from storm drains. It turned out to be pure TCE, trichloroethylene, a potent carcinogen. It was not clear if it was leaking from the old Ithaca Gun Plant or if someone was actually dumping the stuff. Of course, none of the reporters really gave a crap about that. The kid was what they were after. Danny. Human interest.

"…And over six long months this department has dedicated exhaustive resources…"

Before coming to Ithaca, Matlin had been a lieutenant on the force in Hoboken. He moved the family here after his daughter fell chronically ill with lung and blood problems, here to what he had thought was pristine Ithaca, hoping to escape the poisons of New Jersey. This was getting to look more and more like Hoboken, thought Tripoli as he watched the Chief serenading the press.

"So let me introduce you to Louis Tripoli, our senior investigator, who's been heading up this case since its inception. I'll turn this over to him. Lou?"

Tripoli stepped up to the bank of mikes. Swallowed. "Because of the nature of this ongoing investigation, I'm not at liberty to answer all of your questions," he said, sensing the weight of cameras and stares. "But I can tell you that the boy is in good health. He doesn't appear to have been physically harmed in any way."

"Physically?" A woman reporter in the rear picked up immediately on it.

"I'm not a psychiatrist. And we really haven't had a comprehensive evaluation yet. Though we will. We wanted to give the boy and his—"

"So where was he all these months?" was the next question shot out from the crowd.

"Well, that's the sixty-four-thousand-dollar question," admitted Tripoli. "We suspect that he was living somewhere in the countryside. We think it might have been in a forested region, in all likelihood somewhere south of Ithaca, possibly in the Danby area. Indications are that the boy may have been living in a rather primitive type of housing. Perhaps a hut or a shack. We think the boy may have been kept by an older or elderly man who had a full beard and mustache."

"What does the boy say?"

"Errr…" Tripoli turned to Matlin, who looked back at him deadpan. "He's reluctant to talk."

"Why?"

"You're asking questions I can't answer right now. But we're going to need the public's help to resolve some of the issues. We're asking anybody who has any information regarding the whereabouts of this site or such a person to contact us immediately. We still have the same hotline number here at headquarters. Or people can contact their local State Police barracks. Or the FBI—who are also investigating."

The questions followed in rapid fire. What has the boy said? Has he said anything? Is he happy to be back? Unhappy? Traumatized? Any truth to the story that a cult had held him captive? That he was brainwashed? Tripoli had to keep deferring answers, continually repeating, "We don't know. We *just* don't know yet. You're going to have to be a little patient."

"We're hoping to have a quick resolution to this case," said Chief Matlin, moving in to take over. "At which time we'll provide you with all the pertinent details. Once again, I'd like to thank you all for coming." And with that he quickly exited the room with Tripoli close behind.

Late that same afternoon, Tripoli climbed into the rear seat of a State

Police chopper. It lifted off from its helipad at the new barracks in Dryden, tilted forward, and skimmed over Turkey Hill. The vibrations from the engine pulsed through his whole body. Scant minutes later they reached the edge of the Danby State Forest. Below Tripoli spread the tops of the newly leafed trees. Following the contours of the hill, they formed undulating waves of soft, light green. In the lowlands, the skeletons of drowned trees angled out of the shimmering water.

The pilot let the machine hover while he checked his map, then consulted over the intercom with the spotter sitting beside him. Then, following a carefully mapped grid, he started the search, skimming mere yards above the trees. The spotter kept alternating between his binoculars and checking the screen of their infrared detector penetrating the foliage. When Tripoli leaned over the front seat to peer at the eerily glowing screen, he realized the device was so sensitive that he could see a squirrel hidden by the dense canopy as it darted across the ground.

On their first pass, the spotter signaled the pilot and he made a tight circle and maneuvered the craft over a small opening. Tripoli strained to see what they were looking at.

"What's up?" he shouted above the roar.

The pilot angled the chopper so he could see. It was a patch of marijuana, a good three dozen plants. The troopers marked it on his map, swung around in a tight arc, and swept the next strip. Tripoli kept trying to look through the breaks in the canopy of trees, sure that they would find some signs of life. Hot spots of deer and coyote, a whole line of wild turkey kept popping up on their screen, but no old man.

Halfway through the search, they spotted a poacher dragging a deer carcass out of a ravine deep in the forest. When the guy heard the helicopter and saw the machine above his head, he made a desperate run for it, tripping over logs and plummeting through the underbrush. No matter where he ducked, the chopper was right on top of him. By the time he finally stumbled back to his pickup, two armed rangers were already waiting for him and Tripoli and the troopers watched as they slammed the man up against the hood of their vehicle and handcuffed him. If it was this easy to nail a poacher, why couldn't they find the hermit? Maybe he wasn't in the Danby woods after all? Was Danny misleading him? No. He *had* gone up South Hill. Tripoli was sure of it. The boy had cited too many landmarks.

Later, they spotted a group of men who were illegally cutting valuable nut trees, then stumbled upon an embarrassed couple making love near the edge of the woods. There was, however, no sign of a hut, much less an old man with a white beard. But the state lands were dense and vast, low swamps thick with reeds and cattails alternating with steep, densely wooded hills. He could have been in a cave or underground, in which case they might have flown right over him. Technology was not always perfect, Tripoli realized. And they certainly didn't have ground-penetrating radar.

When they had finished, the pilot turned around in his seat. "There's nothing down there," he called back to Tripoli.

"Do it again!" Tripoli ordered.

The men looked at each other. The light was already waning and there was a menacing front of dark clouds moving rapidly in from the west.

"Go on!" shouted Tripoli above the deafening noise. "He's got to be here!"

The pilot shrugged, mumbled something into his microphone and started all over again, moving in lines perpendicular to their previous path.

Twenty minutes later the pilot was again shaking his head. But this time he didn't bother to inform Tripoli that he was abandoning the search. He simply pulled up the bird to a higher altitude and then skimmed back toward Dryden. As they came settling down on the pad near Route 366, Tripoli understood that nothing short of a foot-by-foot search of the scattered forested lands could rule out all possibilities. Maybe the old man just happened to be out of the woods for the moment? And who was to say, he thought ducking down as he exited the chopper, that the boy had been in the woods at all? Maybe he had just been somewhere in the country? Danny was smart, very smart. He had a lively imagination. Perhaps he really thought he had been living in a forest? The dust, whipped up by the spinning blades, flew into his eyes as he headed for his car.

Clearly, Danny was protecting whoever it was, Tripoli concluded as he drove back into the city. But why? The sky now had turned prematurely dark. The air was getting cold and it looked like rain.

By the time he reached the city line, the first drops were already pelting his windshield. Rolling up the windows, he mulled over the same questions. What was the grip that his captor still had on Danny? Over the years, Tripoli had been involved in dozens of juvenile investigations. Usually the kids who had things done to them seemed spooked. Terrified. Or they were in complete denial, without affect, near zombies. Some never really recovered. But this was different. If Danny hadn't been harmed or coerced, why the secrecy? And what was this business about getting enough air? If he hadn't been physically abused, then what had been done to him?

Back in his office, Tripoli called forensics again.

"Come on, what are you people doing over there?" he fumed. "The press is all over us, the chief's tearing a new asshole and you're sitting on evidence."

"We're not magicians" said the woman who ran the lab in Albany. "You want careful lab work? Then you've gotta wait. We'll call you when we're ready. So just cool it, huh?"

Chief Matlin summoned him again. He wanted to know about the results of the flyover. What did forensics have to say? And the kid, had his mother gotten him talking yet?

"Why don't we get one of our female officers to question the boy? Liz Spino is really great with kids."

Tripoli shook his head.

"Or Loretta Drake? She's got a little boy of her own just about his age."

"They're going to spook the boy," he said, adamantly. "Danny'll talk. He wants to talk, but he's conflicted. The kid needs time. A little space. Look, you're just going to have to trust my instincts on this."

"So now you're a big child psychologist?"

When Tripoli got back to his office, there was a message from the mayor's office demanding an update. Slips from news agencies kept piling up in his message box. No matter how many he tossed away, every time he turned around the box was full again.

That night he called Molly. There had been a severe downpour, over four inches in a matter of an hour. Some of the roadways were underwater. There had been a bunch of accidents out on Routes 34 and 89. Yet as fast as the rain had come, it had cleared, and a cold front had moved in. Now the sky was clear

Tripoli could hear Danny babbling in the background. "So, how're things going?"

"Who is that?" asked Danny.

"It's Trip."

"Oh, it's him. Your boyfriend. The policeman," he said and laughed.

"Apparently he's not angry at me for today."

"I don't think so. Just let's not have a repeat performance. Okay?"

"Anything new?"

"Status quo."

"What does that mean?" asked Danny, coming close to the phone.

"It's Latin," said Molly. "It means M.Y.O.B."

"M.Y.O....? I got it! Mind your own business!" exclaimed Danny and burst into gales of laughter.

"I was thinking of maybe coming over," he ventured. He looked out his office window at the darkness, the wet pavement glistening in the street lamps, the stream of cars hissing past on Clinton street.

"Not such a good idea."

"Oh..."

"Let's just..."

"Yes?" he asked, trying not to sound too anxious.

"Just cool it a little bit."

"You sleeping out again tonight?"

"Not if I can help it."

"It's gotten really chilly," said Molly as she went out to join Danny on the trailer steps. The weather seemed so unstable lately, she thought. One minute it was broiling hot, the next it was freezing. And this was supposed to be the end of May. She took a blanket and wrapped it around his shoulders. "I don't want you getting sick, Honey."

"I'm fine, Mother," he said. "I just like it out here."

Molly sat down beside him. She had been reading under the glare of the kitchen lamp and it took a long moment for her eyes to adjust to the darkness. The air was damp and a slight wind was blowing, making it feel even colder.

Danny sat quietly with his head arched back, staring up at the black sky.

The night was dark, moonless, the air so clear you could make out the multitude of stars glistening against the backdrop of the heavens. The band forming the galaxy of the Milky Way stretched above them.

"Come on, Sweetie, let's go back in," she said finally, her teeth beginning to chatter.

"No, wait," he took hold of her arm. "Please." He offered her a part of his blanket, and she snuggled under it close to him.

"Wait for what?" she asked.

Danny just kept gazing up into the velvety blackness as the sound of croaking frogs traveled in from the swamp. She wondered what it was that he saw, that could hold his attention like this. Watching him in profile, Molly felt overcome by waves of love. She was about to kiss him when he jerked upright.

"Okay...Now!" he exclaimed, pointing up over the roof of the Dolph's trailer. "Look!"

Molly stared up. "Huh? I don't..." An instant later a meteor suddenly appeared in the western sky. Moving with surprising slowness, it swept across the dome above them, growing ever brighter in intensity and illuminating a brilliant swath in its long wake. It was white and yellow and blue all at the same time, and the colors reminded Molly of her dream about Danny.

"Holy Christmas!" she gasped as it traveled across the heavens

Finally, the meteor plunged into the line of the horizon, disappearing as if it were a nugget of white hot metal doused in an ocean at the distant edge of the continent. An instant later, the sky was pitch dark as before.

Stunned, she turned to Danny, his features visible in the light from the kitchen. On his face was a proud grin.

"Hey," she whispered, "Now how in the world did you know—"

"I just did." He laughed at her look of astonishment.

"But you had to know somehow. Did you read about it?"

"No."

"Or did someone tell you? Maybe it was in the newspapers, huh?"

"Nope, I just listened."

"Listened to what?"

"The firmament," he replied, then turned to his mother and smiled.

It rained buckets again that night. It was still drizzling in the morning, but before noon the clouds dispersed, the sky turned a crisp blue, and the air felt as though it had been scrubbed clean. Molly followed the path that skirted the swamp behind the trailer park, Danny dashing ahead.

"Wait for me, Honey," she called, as she hurried to keep up with him. The trail curved and he disappeared behind a wall of cattails. "Please," she said, taking his hand as she caught her breath, "don't go so far ahead."

"I'm okay," he said and smiled up at her reassuringly. "I won't get lost."

Earlier that morning, they had dropped by Rosie's place to say hello. Dr. Wozniak had ordered Rosie to bed. She was anemic, exceptionally tired, and, given her history, he wanted to insure that the babies would be carried to term.

Nonetheless, Rosie had stumbled out of bed in her nightgown to greet them.

"Sweetheart!" she cried as Danny let out a whoop and rushed to her. He flung wide his arms and tried to clasp Rosie around her enormous waist. "My darling baby! Angel, let me take a good look at you." She held him at arm's length. "Why you've grown two feet taller!"

Danny laughed.

"What have they been feeding you?"

"Food!" Danny giggled, and refused to let her go. "The same thing they've been giving you," he said, patting the contours of her distended stomach.

"Still the comedian, huh? So, are you going to tell your old Aunt Rosie where you've been?"

"Nope," Danny had said with a smile.

Now, Danny was again dashing far ahead and Molly charged after him as they left the lowlands surrounding the trailer park and started up the long, steady incline. When she caught up with him, he finally slowed, staying by her side as they cut through a dense grove of trees and then burst out into open, sloping meadows. Reaching a high, wooded ridge, they stopped and turned around to take in the view.

"Wow, what a view," she remarked.

Sprawled below them lay the whole of the University, the tall towers of the biotech complex, the old Armory that looked like a medieval fort, austere glass and steel modern structures squeezed up against the old ivy covered buildings of stone. From the distance it all looked so small, like a play village constructed for a child.

They climbed yet higher and, finding an open patch of dry grass at the top, Molly lay down. Danny plopped down beside her and then lay back, resting his head on her stomach.

"Mother..." he began.

"Hmm?"

"Is Rosie sick?"

"No, no," she said quickly. "Why do you say that?"

"I dunno."

"She's just very tired. I suppose she's using all her strength to make the babies... Two of them!"

"Deer have twins all the time. Sometimes triplets! I saw it myself. Three babies. The mother was licking them clean. And then they just jumped up and ran."

Molly smiled at him. The moment felt so peaceful that she was afraid to say anything that might spoil it. Danny looked up as the wind soughed through the branches above his head. She stroked his face and could feel him purring under her caress. High on the hill, they seemed suspended timelessly above all the anxieties of everyday life.

"It's going to take us a little time to get to know each other again," said Molly finally. A fly buzzed by and settled on her leg. She shooed it away.

Danny, chewing on a long stem of grass, was watching the white clouds scudding past. They reminded Molly of her dream. She thought about Evelyn and her insight. Somehow the woman had actually been right. Could she really have *seen* Danny gathering wood—or had it been just a lucky guess? She had predicted that Danny would return and, when he did, he would call her "Mother." And Molly could still hear the woman intoning: "When he returns to you he will be different. Changed."

Molly looked down at her boy. With a fingertip she traced the lines of his profile, so noble, so pure, so possessed of angelic comeliness. She ran her fingers through his hair, and saw him close his eyes in pleasure.

"Maybe things feel a little strange now," she said. His eyes remained shut. "But I want you to know that I love you. And I always, always will love you. You're my boy forever and ever."

He reached up and innocently rested his hand on her breast. "And I love you, too."

"But you're not exactly the same little boy that I once knew."

"I've grown up," he said, quietly.

She kept combing his locks with her fingers. "Well, yes. But you've changed. A lot, it seems."

"Yes, I have. But you've changed, too."

She looked at him askance. "You think so?"

"Yes." He opened his eyes and peered up at her seriously.

"How?"

"I don't exactly know how. You're just different, too—I think."

"For better or worse?" asked Molly getting up on an elbow.

"Just different."

"Because of Trip?"

He shrugged. "I dunno."

Molly let time pass. "You know," she said finally, "I want us to be together just like it was before. Close. The two of us. You remember?"

He looked at her with an expression she couldn't quite read. He seemed to be observing, studying the nuances in her expression in a way that felt cognizant beyond his years.

"Unless we talk about what happened," Molly went on. "I'm worried that there'll be something between us, always separating us. You know what I mean?"

He didn't answer—which was uncharacteristic of the impulsive Danny she knew, the boy who could never keep quiet, much less hold a secret.

"Is it that you're afraid of talking about it?"

"No," he resolutely. "I'm not really afraid of anything."

"No one hurt you, or scared you, or—"

"Of course not!" he said, jumping to his feet. "Come on, let's keep going. I want to see more things."

Later, they wandered down the back side of the hill, curving around the base as they headed home. This time Danny remained close to her side. For the first time since coming home he seemed truly content and, despite his reticence, Molly could sense a touch of their old intimacy returning.

"What made you come back?" she ventured as they hit the low ground and neared the swamp.

"Oh, I wanted to…I missed you." He looked up at her, smiling with his eyes, his whole face.

"And you'll never know how much I missed you, Darling." She tugged him close, squeezed him tight.

"I knew. That's why I didn't just want to stay…"

She tried not to react.

"At first he didn't want me to leave. He said I wasn't ready. But…"

Molly forced herself to keep walking. "Oh?" She could feel her heart fluttering, and strained to keep her tone calm. "Ready for what?"

"Just not ready yet." Danny tossed his head. "I needed to learn lots and lots of new things. He said that I had this job to do. And that he was now too old to do it."

Molly's chest was so tight, she found it hard to breathe, much less force a smile. She had come to a halt, but had not realized it until now. "What kind of job?"

"That I needed to learn enough so I could go around and teach other people. And that's why I should stay with him—come on, let's keep going," he tugged at her hand. "I want to see if there are any ducks or birds in the water."

Molly stood rooted to the ground. "But you didn't stay?"

"No. I could feel you were worried."

"Oh, I was. I was." Finally, she continued to walk. "Terribly worried."

"But you didn't have to be. I was fine. Really I was."

The thudding in her chest slowed, though her fear seemed only intensified. "Did you like the old man?"

"Sure. Of course!" Danny's eyes twinkled. "And he told me that you had someone—someone you liked, too." He stopped and looked up at her.

What he said caught her completely off guard, and it took her a moment to gather her wits. "Yes. I like Trip a lot, yeah. But he could never, ever take the place of my little boy." She took his face between her hands and kissed his lips. She could feel that she was in danger of crying and bit the side of her tongue.

They continued on. The wind had suddenly picked up, and now it was whistling through the cattails. It blew Molly's hair into her face, and she pulled it back so she could see Danny clearly. "But he let you go?" she asked finally, almost afraid of his answer.

"Huh?" he asked distractedly.

"The old man. The Hermit. John. He let you go."

"Oh, yes! In the end he even wanted me to go home for a visit."

"Visit," she echoed with a choked voice. *"Visit?"*

When he saw the mask of terror etched on her face, Danny became alarmed. Molly understood. He had said more than he was allowed to. She tried to stem her swelling panic. "What does a visit mean?"

"I dunno," he said and turned and ran ahead to the edge of the swamp. Kicking off his flip-flops, he waded into the mud. "There's a big mother frog in here!" he called out.

Shoes and all, she stepped right in after him. "You mean you're supposed to go back?" she persisted, grabbing him roughly by the shoulder and turning him to face her.

He struggled to turn away. "But the frog—" he said.

"Talk to me!" she begged.

"Huh?"

"A visit," she persisted. "What does that mean?"

"Look," he squirmed out of her grasp, "they're tadpoles here, too. And they've got little legs."

"Talk to me!" she demanded, catching his hand and jerking him tight.

"Owww!" he looked up at her. "You're hurting me."

"A visit!" she whispered, her voice tremulous. Danny was back in the bathroom washing his hands for lunch.

Tripoli listened intently,

"I don't know what the hell he's talking about. It's insane. He said that he had all these things he had to learn, then something about the job he had to do because the man was too old to do it. Job?"

When she finished there was a long silence.

"You still there?" she asked.

"Yes. Of course. I'm just trying to take it in."

"It sounds like some cult got their hands on him. Trip, they've got him programmed."

"They? Or is it him, the old man…Look, I want you to do two things. First, you've got to stop worrying."

"That's easy for you to say."

"As long as I'm on this Earth, Danny's not going anywhere you don't want him to go."

"How can you promise that?"

"We're going to nail this fucker and that'll be the end of it."

"Oh, Trip, I wish I could believe that."

"Second, keep Danny talking. Just listen. Whatever you do, don't let him see you're scared or he'll clam up on you. Just get as much info as you can. The more you can glean, the more we've got to go on, the sooner we'll have this guy locked up where he belongs. He's not going to be grabbing any more kids. You can count on that."

"I'll bet you're hungry," she said as he came out of the bathroom.

"Oh, I'm starved!" He hung out his tongue. "That melted cheese stuff we had for breakfast this morning I really liked."

"Okay, but dry your hands."

"I like them wet. They're nice and cool then." He waved them in the air.

"And you didn't even wash your face," she said inspecting him. "Come here," she took him back to the mirror. "See this," she pointed to the smudges on his cheeks. "And here. Now, go back and try again and I'll make lunch."

He came back a minute later, clean but dripping.

"You know we're going to have to get you some new clothes," she said slicing two bagels.

"But I *have* clothes." He jumped up on a chair at the kitchen table and sat swinging his legs.

"I know, but they're too small. And the only shoes you've got are flip-flops. We *need* to go shopping."

"More cheese," he said, watching as she laid on slices of Mozzarella.

"I'd like to take you up to the mall."

"The mall?" Danny hopped off the chair and came over to the counter where he snatched a piece of cheese and popped it into his mouth.

"You know on Triphammer Road. Where all the stores are."

"The stores," he chewed thoughtfully. He didn't seem to remember the mall.

"We'll get you some nice new sneakers—the kind that are really bouncy. Maybe a new pair of *Nikes*. The ones with the wings."

"The kind you can run fast in?"

"Very fast. Or even fly!"

"There's too much stuff in here," said Danny as they wended their way through harshly lit aisles of the Ames Store stacked with discount clothes and boots and auto parts. "And it smells horrible!" His nose was twitching like a rabbit's. "And my head hurts. Bad."

It was true. It did smell of plastics and synthetics, insecticides and bags of fertilizer with weed killer—though she had never really noticed it before. "Okay, Honey," she said, taking his hand and hurrying him out of Ames. "We'll go over to Sears. It's nicer there."

Cutting through the throngs of people in Cafe Square, the smells of Chinese fast food and pizza and baking cookies mixing with the odor of newly manufactured goods, Danny's features were hanging and his shoulders were hunched forward as if he were being whipped. "Oh, the noise," he said covering his ears as we was overwhelmed by the swirl of sound, the cacophony of echoing voices and footsteps, cash registers ringing, toys beeping, music spilling out from a dozen different sources. Molly realized that after his months in the woods, bringing him here was a big mistake. But, having come this far, she was loathe to give up. "Can you hang on just a few more minutes?"

His eyes seemed to be swimming in his head, and he didn't seem to hear her.

When she bent down and took him in her arms, Danny burrowed himself into her breasts, blocking out all the light and sound.

"Just tough it out a little longer Sweetie, okay?

He nodded, his face pressed into her. "Yes," he said, his voice muffled.

Molly looked up to discover that she was kneeling amidst a circle of people crowding in close; men, women, children smiling and pointing and craning their necks in curiosity.

"Mommy is that the boy who…?" asked a little girl.

"Danny! Hey, Danny!" called out an old man waving to get his attention.

"Excuse me. Please," she said, plucked Danny up, and lugged him over to Sears, a few people still trailing behind, curious.

"Ugh," she said, putting him down in the section with children's clothes. "You've got to walk now. You're just getting too big for me."

"I feel dizzy," he murmured. He staggered and she wondered if he was maybe laying it on a little for her benefit.

"Look, how's this? And this one?" she asked, pulling short sleeve knits off the counters and holding them in front of him. "This'll fit, I think. And this green is a nice color for you."

Danny was swaying from side to side as if trying to keep his balance.

"What's the matter?"

"I dunno know. Just dizzy. From the smells."

"But it's better in here, isn't it?" Molly hurried on, grabbing two pairs of jeans off the rack with hardly a second look. "We're almost done. Please try to hang in there," she said, rushing him over to the shoe department.

A salesman wandered by. "Excuse me," she caught his attention. "could you help me. I need some sneakers for him. Do you have a pair of these in size?…"

Danny slumped down in one of the chairs, closing his eyes. His face was chalk white. He was salivating profusely, a thin line of drool creeping out of the corner of his mouth.

When the man finally came out with a box of sneakers, they looked to be a size too large but Molly took them anyhow. "Can I just pay for everything here. I'm in a hurry and—"

"Hey, isn't he the boy who…? Danny right?" The man's face lit up. "And, wait! You must be Molly—"

"Please, my boy's not feeling well. Can you just ring up everything here and…"

He looked at Danny and saw that he really did look sick. "Yes. Of course!" he said.

Molly got a handful of bills out of her purse, paid, took the packages in one hand and Danny in the other. "Come on, this way," she said, pulling him along. "This is the fast way out." But, turning a corner, she found herself dead-ended in a maze of mowers and air conditioners, freezers and water softeners. Danny's knees began to cave in, and she scooped him up and rushed down the aisle, past the electronics section where a half-dozen stereos were going full blast, racks of TVs running on different channels, people playing with the computers.

Danny lay limp in her arms, his head lolling to one side. Her shoulders ached and her muscles cramped. "Come on, Angel, hold on a little, please," she begged as she came full circle right back to the clothing department.

Molly finally found an exterior door. "Whew!" she said, bursting out into the brightness of daylight. Propping Danny up on top of a concrete abutment she bent close to examine at him. "You all right?"

Danny opened his eyes and smiled weakly. "I'm fine now," he said softly, then turned his head and threw up, vomit gushing out explosively. It kept coming. And coming. Until all that remained was a slimy green bile.

"Oh, darling, oh darling," she repeated, holding his head as he continued to retch. "I'm so sorry."

When his spasms finally ceased, she found a tissue and wiped his mouth. His breathing was shallow and rapid and Molly suddenly hated herself for dragging him through the mall. His breathing began to slow and he took a series of deep breaths. "Better?" she asked nervously. Maybe he needed to see a doctor. She wondered if they had found anything in all those tests at the hospital that they hadn't told her about? Blood diseases, parasites, her imagination began to run away. What the hell did he pick up in those goddamn woods? What did that old creep do to him?

"Yes," he murmured with his faint hint of a lisp. "Much better. I'm sorry," he uttered and looked like he was going to cry.

"Sorry for what? Don't be silly. It's my fault."

Slowly the color began returning to his face, but Molly now felt herself sickened. "It was those smells," he tried to explain. "And all that noise. They gave me a bad headache. And then. Then…"

"Yes. Yes. I understand," she said. "Your mother just wasn't thinking…I'm so terribly sorry, Honey. I just didn't realize…" The sun was broiling and her clothes were damp with sweat. "You think you can make it to the car on your own?"

"Maybe things aren't quite the way we think they are," whispered Tripoli into the darkness after Molly told him about Danny anticipating that shooting star.

It was close to midnight and the trailer was quiet, as quiet as it ever got. They lay on the living room floor, clothes twisted about them, their half-naked bodies still entwined. Their heat had dissipated and the perspiration from their passion now lay chilling on Molly's body.

"Whatta you mean?"

"I don't know. Maybe I've been looking at this thing the wrong way."

"I really don't know what you're talking about."

"I don't think I do either." He laughed at himself, shook his head.

"What happened today at the mall was frightening," she said, beginning to shiver. "You should have seen him." Molly reached out and pulled the blanket over them. She glanced over at the bedroom door and listened for an instant. When they were still she could make out Danny's breathing. Exhausted, he'd gone to sleep directly after dinner. Hadn't even insisted on sleeping outside again—thank God. "He used to love it there at the mall," she said turning back to Tripoli. "He'd be bugging me every day that he wanted to go to the game room. And he was really excited whenever I bought him new clothes."

"Something extraordinary happened," he said, thinking aloud and Molly regretted now having told him about the meteor.

Tripoli sat up and Molly draped part of the blanket over him, her hands lingering on his shoulders.

"It's like he's been totally programmed. My baby!" she uttered angrily. "I want Danny back. Like he was. I just want a normal little kid. I don't want to have to keep worrying that someone is going to come and snatch him again. A *visit?* Oh, God, Trip!"

He took her in his arms and held her quietly.

"I keep going over the same things. " he said later after she had calmed. "Old Edna spotted Danny. Alone. I'm sure of it now. Which means he must have somehow gotten out of Kute Kids—on his own. He was headed up towards South Hill. I'm somehow sure of that, too. You know," he turned to look at her in the streaks of faint light filtering in through the blinds, "I think Danny knew where he was going right from the start."

"What do you mean?" Her hand slipped away from him, then the blanket fell loose and he was sitting up alone. "How could he?"

"I don't know. I'm just speculating," he said into the darkness. "Supposing he was somehow drawn to the kidnapper, the old man, the Hermit, whatever he is."

"That's ridiculous," she said and thought about the meteor.

"Hey, did Danny spend any time around South Hill? Or Danby?"

"No. Never. We never had any occasion to go out there. Whenever we went out for trips and stuff it was usually towards Lansing or Freeville. Sometimes the lake."

"Maybe you knew somebody who…?"

"No. I'm telling you. *Never*," she said peevishly.

"Okay. Okay." Tripoli fell silent, lost in thought. "He had many names," he murmured.

"Huh?"

He turned to her. "That's what Danny said. Do you remember?"

"Aliases?" She pulled him back down, snuggled closer to gain warmth from his body.

"He called him father…"

"A priest?"

"Or God."

"Trip, get real!"

"John," he uttered thoughtfully. "John…How many Johns do you know?"

"Hundreds," she said. "Zillions!"

"The old man kept him," he went on, still caught up in his conjecture. "Educated him. You've got to grant him that."

"Infected him," she injected. "Poisoned him so he couldn't even go into a lousy department store!"

"But what were his intentions?"

"To steal my child!"

"Right. But at the same time the old man tried to give him something—"

"Hey!" She pulled abruptly away. "Who the hell's side are you on, any way?"

"Yours. Danny's and yours, of course. I'm just trying to put myself in the old guy's head."

"You'd better not, because I'd like to smash his fucking skull," she said vehemently.

"I understand."

"No you don't understand. Can't. Not quite. No one can."

After Tripoli left, Molly headed directly for her bed. Restless in his sleep, Danny had kicked off his the blanket and one of his legs hung half out of the bed. Molly gently slid him back into place, straightened the covers, and tucked him in tight. Immediately she fell into a deep slumber. Her dreams were jumbled. She was in the office and Larry was saying something. The next instant she was with Danny in the woods. There was snow on the ground, and he was standing in front of an outdoor fire warming his hands. A tall figure was lurking in the distance behind them, watching him, watching her. He began to move forward, his feet dragging through the snow with a shuffling, dragging, hissing sound. No it was a scrambling sound. A rubbing. A… No, wait, it was real, not a dream.

Molly awoke with a start. It took her a moment to focus. Something was moving outside the trailer. Cocking an ear, she could make out a slight rustling, a faint scratching noise below the window by Danny's bed. The old man, was her immediate thought. He's come to take Danny back.

Crouching down on the floor where she couldn't be seen, she quickly crept over to Danny's bed. He was tossing in his sleep, muttering and, when she locked her arms around him, she could feel his pulse racing. Her own heart was pounding, too. She hung by the bed, paralyzed in the darkness, straining to listen, afraid to move.

Then the noise was gone and all she could hear were the normal nighttime sounds of the trailer park, a door slamming somewhere in the distance, a baby whimpering. Maybe it was just a cat digging under the trailer? she told herself. Or one of those raccoons that were always raiding the dumpsters. Yet as she tried to calm herself, she could have sworn she still felt a presence hovering just outside the thin walls of her home, watching them.

Finally, she got up from her crouch, lifted Danny, and carried him back to her own bed.

"Huh? What?" he asked as she settled him under the covers close to her.

"Shhh," she whispered under her breath, clutching him close. "It's okay. Just go back to sleep." She stroked his cheek and in an instant he was back asleep, his body tucked warm against hers. His pulse was even now, and she could feel his little heart beating next to hers.

chapter ten

"He was here," said Molly first thing in the morning when she got Tripoli on his cell phone. He was just driving into the office. The day was dark and drizzling and she was standing in front of the trailer in her bathrobe getting soaked. It always seemed to be raining, more than ever, more than she could remember.

"Who?" he asked.

"The old man."

"You *saw* him?"

"No. No." She told him about the sounds.

"Okay. Fine. But how do you know it was the old guy?"

"I could feel it."

"Molly—"

"And Danny felt it, too. His heart was racing away and—"

"I had a guy posted right in front of your place. He didn't see anything. And if you heard something, why didn't you call him? He'd have been on your doorstep in a second. Or call me."

"I was so scared," she said, "I wasn't thinking."

"Next time you call me."

"There better not be a next time. Anyway, I'm getting a gun," she said.

"You know how to use one?"

"No."

"Well, forget it. It's a lousy idea. You're going to end up shooting someone. Could even be one of my guys. A gun? No way! You don't want one. Not with a little kid in your trailer."

Shortly after ten, Molly had an unexpected visit from Larry Pierce.

"Just thought I'd drop off a little welcome home present for our young friend." He went back to his car and returned with a big, gift-wrapped box. Molly noticed that he had brought along his briefcase, too.

Danny came wandering curiously out of the bedroom.

"Oh, hello there young man!" exclaimed Larry. He turned to Molly, "Boy, he looks really wonderful!"

"Do you remember Mr. Pierce, Honey?" She rested both hands on his shoulders. "Larry's my boss at the magazine you were looking at yesterday."

"Oh, yeah," Danny nodded. "The one I read with that story about grapes."

"Read?" Larry laughed.

"Larry's been a big help to me while you've been gone." She moved Danny closer to him. "He's a good friend, too," she smiled up at Larry, resting a hand on his arm. Danny's eye was on her hand.

"I brought a little something for you." Larry plunked the package down on the floor.

"Maybe you want to open it, Honey?" suggested Molly.

"Come on, let's take a look." Larry knelt down and unwrapped the carton. Inside was a metal box. He swung open its doors to display the contents.

Danny's face lit up.

"You know what this is?"

"Sure I do!" said Danny. "It's a thing to magnify very tiny objects."

"Exactly! A microscope. And this is the deluxe model. I didn't know if you were too young—"

"Oh no, I'm not." Danny already had the microscope positioned on the floor, and he was angling the mirror, trying to catch the light.

"I heard you were really grown up now and—"

"Look, it's got just everything." Danny opened the small drawers, examining the contents.

"Right. Slides. Stains here. Forceps and scalpels—you have to be very careful with this, though, it's sharp. And it's got some ready-made slides, like these? I think…" Larry held one up to the light, "…this is a sliver of a bird's feather, right?"

"Oooh," cried Danny, squinting into the eyepiece. "You can see everything. All the little lines and…Hey take a look!" Molly hadn't seen him this excited since he had come back.

"Well, I've got to run off." Larry reached for his briefcase and headed for the door, then hesitated. "Look," he turned to face her. The gesture seemed a little too rehearsed. "I know things must be topsy-turvy for you right now…So I *really* hate to ask anything…" he sounded terribly reluctant.

"Well, go on," Molly urged, "at least ask."

"If you could just take a quick look at some things—maybe when you have a few spare minutes." He reached into his briefcase and pulled out a thick manila envelope, then a bunch of files and laid them on the table. "We're stymied. None of us can make heads or tails of these."

Molly opened the envelope. Inside were stacks of bills, accounts payable, contracts, and requests for reprint rights. "Don't worry, I'll take care of it," she said, and couldn't help but note his smile of relief.

"And these files," he pulled out some more from his briefcase. "They're the writers' fees for—"

"Yes, yes, I know," she said. "Don't worry. I'll be back soon."

Danny looked abruptly up from the floor, kept watching, his eyes still on the door as Larry gave his mother a peck and finally left.

"He's a nice man, isn't he," said Molly.

Danny chewed on his lip, then turned back to his new microscope, peering into the eyepiece. "I don't really like him so much," he said without looking up.

"What? Why do you say that. He certainly was thinking of you when he brought this nice present, right?"

"Yes."

"So?"

Danny carefully adjusted the knurled focus knob back and forth. "I don't think he tells the truth."

"About what?"

Danny looked up at her and shrugged.

"And he's done so much for me. For us. Why, without the magazine job, I don't know what we'd do. And your Mommy — Mother—needs to do things she likes, too. You want that, don't you?"

"Sure." He looked up and smiled at her. "Sure."

Late that morning, the lab report came back from Albany. Tripoli was on the phone in his office when Sisler dropped it on his desk.

"Hey, what's this?" he asked, covering the mouthpiece as he leaned far back in his chair and continued to listen.

"Forensics," said Sisler.

Tripoli popped upright. "Hey, Pete, let me call you back," he said, snapping the receiver into its cradle.

He ripped open the envelope and quickly scanned it with Sisler hanging over his shoulder. Forensics had done a thorough job, examined everything. The boy's underwear. No pubic hairs. No signs of ongoing sexual abuse. The soil caught in the treads of Danny's sneakers. The lint in his pockets, the fibers and stains on his clothes. When they had eliminated all the knowns, they discovered lots of fibers from domestic animals—fleece from sheep, hair from goats. But they also detected filaments from the wilds—the unmistakable fur of rabbits and deer and squirrel. All his clothes contained significant amounts of charcoal and wood ash. The stains on his pants were vegetable in origin, the residue of native wild grapes, raspberries, blueberries; his shirt sleeves had spots of tannin found in the bark of trees. It might have come from a solution used to tan skins or simply from the outer coating of hickory and black walnuts. The sweater assay was just as Tripoli expected, made from hand-carded wool.

"Well?" asked Tripoli, turning to Sisler. "What does it tell you?"

"I don't know. I suppose that the kid hasn't been shitting us. He didn't spend six months hanging out in a ranchburger in suburbia—at least not one that had carpets and drapes."

"And?"

"There really is a hermit out there somewhere?"

"Exactly!"

"Okay," said Sisler. "Now how do we find him? Where do we start? Even if we're sure it's south of here, there's one hell of a lot of land out there between Ithaca and Key West."

Tripoli's officers did a good job of keeping unwanted visitors away from Molly's trailer, but almost every time she left home there was at least one reporter dogging her heels.

A camera crew ambushed them while shopping at Tops Friendly Market.

"We just want to talk to Danny for a minute," said the TV reporter with her moussed hair and perfect makeup as she stood in the middle of the cereal aisles, blocking Molly's cart.

"Well, Danny doesn't want to," Molly tried to shield Danny from the cameraman.

"Where were you all this time?" the reporter persisted.

Danny peeked out from behind his mother, smiled, then scooted back out of sight.

"What did the old Hermit—"

"Please!" said Molly, taking Danny by the hand and abandoning her groceries. She crossed the parking lot and started shopping all over again at Wegman's.

Given the amount of media focus, the whole town was abuzz with talk of Danny's return. There was hardly a living soul who didn't have a theory about his disappearance.

Siddhartha, the Norwegian hippie cook in the kitchen of the Moosewood Restaurant, suggested to Dansingtree, the waitress, that Danny had gone off to be raised by wild animals. "You know, just like in the story of Romulus and Remus.

"Yeah. That makes sense," Dansingtree agreed. Especially since Romulus, New York, was just a quick thirty miles up the road.

"One of those cursed fanatical religious sects kidnapped him!" exclaimed the Reverend Glen Thorne, shooting an index finger heavenward as he stood at the pulpit, exhorting his followers to be wary of the danger of worshipping false prophets. As pastor of the United Society of Christ, an evangelical splinter sect that held services in an old garage at the edge of town, he felt it his duty to warn his parishioners of the evil lurking in their very midst. "They programmed that boy and then turned him loose to snare new converts for their satanic beliefs."

Others were convinced that a large ransom had been paid to a gang of professional kidnappers, while still others who worked in construction and were less prone to wild speculation surmised that the father had swiped the kid. Those who had been screwed by Chuck in some business deal figured nothing was beneath him, even hurting an innocent woman like Molly.

When one of the weekly supermarket tabloids hit the stands, it confirmed what a small but vocal segment of the population had suspected all along:

"Danny was kidnapped by aliens!" said Mrs. Song Hong, reading aloud as the cashier at the P&C beeped her groceries through the scanner.

"Aliens?" repeated Annie Hubbel, swiping a carton of eggs past the intersecting red beams of light. "Does it say what kind of aliens?"

One late afternoon Wally Schuman from the *Journal* managed to talk his way through the police protection and stood in Molly's kitchen. After all the help he had given her, it was hard for Molly to turn him away.

"I don't want him to be pressured," she said.

"Of course not," he responded emphatically.

"You start asking questions about where the Hermit is and he gets very—"

"I understand. Frankly, I'm really much more interested in Danny than the old man. Everybody is. I heard such wonderful things."

"If you write a story, then there'll be just more folks hanging around."

Schuman took a long thoughtful pause. "You're worried about the Hermit coming and somehow taking the boy back, right?"

Molly guessed the tack he was taking. "So your story is going to help flush the guy out, is that it?"

"Well, yes, that's a distinct possibility."

Molly looked at him. He had crow's-feet at his eyes and lines in his face that gave him a perpetual smile, a kindly face. "You know you're pressuring me."

"I'm aware of that. Unfortunately, it goes with the job."

"If I don't let you—" she started to say.

"Then the story becomes a lot of speculation, secondhand information."

"Okay," she said finally. "Just remember the ground rules."

And she let him sit with Danny out on the stoop and talk without interference. Maybe, she told herself, maybe he can elicit something that Danny hasn't told me. She stood at the kitchen window watching Schuman, saw how he put his arm around her boy, the way Danny smiled and looked comfortable with him, and she finally relaxed.

"I heard," said Schuman softly, "about that shooting star."

Danny turned to him and smiled with a touch of pride.

"Your neighbor, Mrs. Dolph, saw you with your mother sitting out there that night."

The boy didn't in the least seem surprised. "Yes. I know. I saw her."

"You see a lot don't you?"

"Not really," he said. "It's all there."

"Let me tell you, what you did was pretty impressive. How did you do that?"

"Oh, just listened." He got up, and starting poking his toe into the ground. "I'm going to make a garden right here." he said. "I need to dig all this stuff up. Wanna help?"

"Well, maybe yes. But not right now…That man. The Hermit. He taught you that trick."

"But it's not a trick. You could do it, too."

Wally Schuman looked very surprised. "I could?"

"You just need to open your mind's eye."

The newspaper man did a double take. "Is that what he taught you?"

"Everything is there. To see. To hear. You have a lot of powers in you." He touched his own chest. "You just have to use them, that's all."

"But how?"

"Just do like me!" said Danny and laughed. "You gonna help me dig?"

A half-hour later, Wally came back in. He stood in front of Molly, absorbed in thought.

"How strange," he said finally, shaking his head. "Talking to him…Well…I found myself at times completely forgetting that he's just a little boy. He sometimes seems so…" he struggled for the right words, "so wise beyond his years. He seems to see so much."

"See what?"

"Just the world around us." Wally looked entranced.

Rosie, still confined to bed, had theories of her own, and she called Molly about them during the course of the day.

"As I see it," Rosie explained. "Danny wasn't kidnapped at all. And he didn't just haphazardly wander off into the woods. If you examine all the evidence—"

"You know you're beginning to sound more and more like Tripoli."

"A cop?" she laughed. "That's an insult! Hey, maybe he's sounding more and more like me." Molly could hear a toilet flush. Rosie was on her wireless phone, her voice fading in and out as she moved around. "Anyway," she went on, breathing heavily, "I'm just basing my theory on facts."

"Like what?"

"Just think about all the things you've been telling me, the incredible things Danny learned. Maybe…" she went on, getting carried away in her conjecture, "maybe Danny was chosen."

"Chosen for *what?*"

"Something special. Like the Dalai Lama. To be like a leader. Or maybe to be like a some kind of wizard who can—"

"Rosie, that kind of speculation just makes me nervous."

"I don't see why."

"I'll tell you why." And finally, she told Rosie about Danny talking about being home only for a visit, about the sounds outside her trailer that night.

"Oh… That would make me jumpy, too. I'm sorry. I didn't mean to worry you. I was just thinking about the positive side of things."

"And its like everybody wants a piece of Danny."

"Whatta you mean?"

"I don't know. They just want to be around him. Talk to him. Wally Schuman was just here. I let him spend some time with Danny and the guy came away mesmerized. Everybody's so—"

"Well, Danny is unusual. And what's happened to him, well you've got to admit—"

"There's nothing to admit! I just want people to leave us alone."

"I didn't mean to call so much. I'm—"

"No. No! Not you, Rosie. Never you. I mean *other* people."

Tripoli stopped at the trailer while Molly was getting Danny ready for bed. He had been in the neighborhood following up a report on a burglary and thought he'd just say hello. Or that's the explanation that he had prepared if Molly was going to put him on the spot. He tried not to think of himself as being marginalized since Danny's return, but what could you expect, he told himself. She and her boy need time to get to know each other again. And though their relationship might never be quite the same, he hoped she would begin to miss him the way he ached for her.

"Come on in. It's open," she called through the bathroom window. He could hear water running in the tub. "I'm just fixing Danny's bath. I'll be right out."

Tripoli patiently waited in the living room as the windows in the trailer began to steam up; finally he opened a couple. He paced up and down the single aisle. He took a glass of water and drank it slowly.

Five minutes later Molly emerged, the fine hairs at the nape of her neck and temples damp and sticking to her skin. She was carrying a handful of bath toys. "Got any use for these?" she asked, holding them out. She was wearing a tank top and frayed shorts, which he found appealing.

"I've got plenty of boats," he said with a laugh, "But I could probably use this duck," he picked it up and played with it. "Yeah, this is perfect." He gave Molly a kiss on the cheek. He was moving in for a longer, more serious kiss and could feel her pull back slightly.

"What's the matter?" he asked, looking offended.

"Nothing," she said. "Give me a second, and let me dump these." She tossed the wet toys into the kitchen sink. "Danny tells me he's too grown up for nonsense like this. If he's going to have ducks, they've got to be real ones. And his latest pronouncement? He doesn't want me calling him Danny anymore. Now he's *Daniel.*" She rolled her eyes heavenward.

The door to the bathroom was open and Tripoli could hear the boy splashing and churning around in the tub.

"Swimming lessons," she said with a toss of her head.

"Come here," he said and stood his ground, waiting.

"What is this?" she asked. "A test?"

"Of course it is. I want to know if you still remember me."

"Oh, poor Trip. Have I been neglecting you?" She came over, wrapped her arms around his neck and planted her mouth on his. "Well, better?" she asked.

He licked his lips and smiled. "A little better."

"Want a glass of wine?" She was already moving towards the fridge. "I've got an open bottle of white."

"Theoretically I'm still on duty," he said, "but…what the hell!"

"We were given a case of Swedish Hill at the magazine." Molly hunted through the fridge. "We carried this story on local wines, and they…Oh, here it is."

She poured him a glass. He took a sip and let it roll around his palate. "Hmmm," he said, thoughtfully smacking his lips. "Not bad. Not too dry. Not too fruity. A little outspoken, but—"

Molly poked playfully at his ribs. "Larry tells us we've got our principles. We can't be bought. At least not with money. Wine apparently is a different story…" She filled her own glass and took a sip. "So, Mr. Policeman, howya doing?" She glanced in the direction of the bathroom, then came again close to Tripoli, pressed her hips tight against him and kissed him long and hard. "Mmmm," she hummed appreciatively, her mouth moving on his.

He couldn't help himself and quickly had his hands all over her. "Ooooh…Nice…Has anybody ever told you what a gorgeous ass you've got?" he whispered conspiratorially, tracing its curve from the small of her back to her thighs.

"It's been mentioned, I think," she said, sliding in yet tighter to him. She ran her hands over his chest. Through his clothes she could feel his muscles ripple.

Tripoli took a long drink. He could feel it warming his insides as he moved back and forth against her. His heart was thumping and his mind was racing. Where? How? "What time does Danny go sleep?" he asked hoarsely.

Suddenly she stiffened. Then went pale.

"Wait!" she said, pushing him back.

"Huh? What's the matter?"

"It's too quiet!" She cocked an ear.

Immediately, he realized it, too. There hadn't been a solitary sound from the bathroom in minutes.

Molly scrambled toward the bathroom and Tripoli was right behind her. When she reached the door, she let out an agonized scream. "Oh God!" she cried.

Danny was lying submerged on the bottom of the tub, motionless. Through the soapy water, Tripoli could make out the boy's features. They were totally slack and he looked unconscious. Pushing past Molly, Tripoli plunged his arms into the water and took hold of Danny. His body was completely limp, and in a flash Tripoli had him sprawled out on the floor and was prying open his jaw when Danny eyes fluttered open and he looked up.

"What's the matter?" he asked as he sat up, water dripping off him.

"Jesus, Danny!" gasped Molly standing in the puddle, both relieved and furious. "You scared the living daylights out of us!"

"I'm sorry," chirped Danny.

"Sorry?"

"I was just practicing."

"Practicing?" echoed Tripoli. He was still breathing hard, and his shirt and shoes were soaked.

"To hold my breath," Danny explained as he climbed back into the tub. "I'm okay. I can do it. Watch!"

The two watched as Danny, crossing his arms, slid again under the sudsy surface.

They gaped into the tub as he lay there on the bottom. He remained there motionless and continued to stay there. At first just a minute. Then what seemed another full minute. Little bubbles formed at his nostrils.

"Holy shit!" uttered Tripoli under his breath.

"That's enough!" cried Molly finally, plunging her hands into the water and pulling him up. "Okay, enough, *Daniel,* Honey," she called out loudly. "You don't want to give Mommy—I mean your *Mother*—a heart attack, now do you?"

chapter eleven

"You'll like it at our new office," said Molly as she helped Danny fill his backpack with crayons and paper and packages of clay.

A full week had passed since Danny's return and Molly felt there was no way she could postpone going back to work. But there was also no way in the world that she was going to leave Danny out of her sight—not with that crazy man on the loose.

"Can I take these books, too?" he asked.

"Sure. Let's see if we can fit them in."

He seemed curious and eager to accompany her to work.

"And Ben and Sandy—you remember them?—they're all excited about seeing you again." She kept up a constant babble as they drove down Route 13, and for once he didn't complain about getting into a car.

Giving Tasha at the front desk a wave, she took Danny by the hand and led him directly into her office. "Big, huh?" she asked.

"Yup," he said, looking around. He eyes went right for the window.

"And it's all ours." She bent over and nuzzled his neck. Straightening up, Molly flipped on the overhead florescents and went to her desk. Awaiting her was an intimidating heap of mail and papers nearly a foot high. Her heart began to sink. It would take her days merely to organize and look through this morass.

She hurriedly fingered through the pile. "I leave and everything grinds to a major halt," she muttered in frustration. "Just look at this mess!" In the neighboring copy room, the Xerox came on with a high-pitched whine. Then it started clanking through copies, shaking the floor.

Danny, who was standing with his backpack still strapped to his shoulders, watched as his mother marched into the outer office.

"Tasha," she called out, waving a bunch of envelopes. "Doesn't anybody believe in opening the mail? Look at this. These are checks. Money. From advertisers. New subscriptions. And here's a second notice from the electric company. You want them to cut the power?"

"But nobody told me to open the mail."

Molly resisted the urge to say something, just shook her head and strode back into her office.

"Oh, there you are," she said with a laugh, seeing Danny still waiting. "You think your mother forgot you, right?"

"I don't know," he said, quietly.

"Of course not! Come on, let's take care of first things first. And that means you. Let's get you set up." She cleared off a small table, fetched a chair from the waiting room, and started helping Danny unpack. The phone rang. It was the outfit that did the color separations. Someone had sent them the wrong cover photo. As she helped Danny unpack, Molly kept talking, using a shoulder to pin the phone against her ear. "Look what nice crayons Rosie got you," she whispered to him. "You've got every color under the sun. And take a look at these books!"

After she hung up, she scribbled a reminder on a Post-it and stuck it to her computer screen. Then another.

Danny hung back.

"Come on, Sweetie, let's take off this jacket. It's hot in here." He obeyed and shed his jacket. "Now, why don't you sit over here." She patted the chair.

Danny came over and sat down.

The office seemed to Molly more tumultuous than ever: the copier spitting out pages, Larry's TV blasting away, the phones and faxes hissing and beeping. And the place smelled, too, of carpets and cleaners and electronic machines—her senses heightened by apprehensiveness.

"I know it's noisy out there," she said, "but in here it's kind of cozy, isn't it?" she asked, worriedly.

"I suppose so." Though he managed a sweet smile, his voice was flat. She feared a repeat of the scene at the mall. But Danny seemed as if he could handle it, and Molly decided it was best not to fuss over him.

"Would you like to read or make some pictures first?"

"What would you like me to do?" he asked.

Finally, she got him drawing. He worked on a picture, but kept stopping, his gaze drifting toward the window.

Turning on her computer, Molly held her breath as the whining hard disk gathered speed. Danny looked over in her direction. Their eyes met briefly; then he turned and went back to his picture. She silently exhaled.

But she had hardly started work when Sandy dropped in. "I've been dying to say hello to Danny!"

Then there was Ben.

"Hey watcha drawing? Well, look at this!" Danny had drawn a small person encased in a tight, vice-like box, arms pressing against the confining walls. "Whew, looks like we've got another Edvard Munch in the making," he said, trying to laugh it off.

"Would you like a lollipop?" asked Sandy ten minutes later, waving a big, red, cherry-flavored pop. Danny accepted it with a smile, took a lick, and then, when Sandy was gone, laid the sticky candy on his desk.

Maybe, if everybody just left him alone, thought Molly. The staff, however, kept finding excuses to drop in.

"This is getting to be like Grand Central Station," she said when Tasha found an excuse to stop in for the third time. "Come on, you've got work to do and so do I."

"Sorry," said Tasha. "I just can't help myself. He's so sweet that you just want to be around him, and—"

"Well, let me help you," said Molly, leading the girl out and finally closing the door.

"Back to work," she said, pointing at Danny who was watching her. "You do yours. I do mine."

Dutifully, Danny picked up a book. He started to read, but a minute later it lay forgotten in his lap as he stared blankly out into space. The color had drained from his face, and he was beginning to look ill.

"You okay, Honey?" She stooped behind him and draped her arm around his shoulder.

"What?" he said without even turning. He seemed almost in a daze.

Molly tried to focus on her work, but Danny's silent pressure was unnerving.

Later in the morning, Larry dropped by. He was surprised to see Danny in the office.

"Hi Danny," he said, but his eyes were on Molly, and she could read the look on his face: was this just a visit or was she thinking of keeping Danny here as a regular fixture?

"Where are we on those proofs?" he asked, swinging by once more shortly before lunch. Again she sensed that he was checking up on her.

"You must be joking, Larry. I'm still missing some of the stories."

"Well, we've got to get cracking." Leaning against the wall, he drummed his fingers on the door. "Yeah, yeah. I know," he smiled, catching himself. "It's only the first day back. Well," he said throwing up his hands, "goes to show. Without you, things just don't function." He turned to Danny. "Hey kiddo, no more disappearing acts, please. You'll destroy my magazine." Then he laughed—a little too loudly, Molly thought.

"Huh?" said Danny, shaken from his reverie.

Molly laughed. "Larry's just making a joke," she explained.

"Oh…" said Danny and gave a small, polite chuckle.

Tripoli decided to divide up the county between Sisler and himself. He would scour the outlying areas of the southern and eastern townships, and Sisler would cover the rest. It would take them at least a few days to do a cursory search, but it seemed time well invested. The chief, together with the mayor and the press, were still yapping at his heels. And Molly would never have any peace until the old Hermit was under lock and key. Then, too, there was his own intense curiosity.

"I don't get it," said Sisler, leaning over Tripoli's desk to get a closer look at the contoured map. Shaded in red were all the areas that were uninhabited or heavily wooded. It included the state forests in Caroline, Danby, Dryden, Newfield, the vast Hector Land Use area, the Connecticut Hill Wildlife Management Area, as well as a number of abandoned farms. There was more land out there than a person could walk around in a year. And steep hills. Tons of them. "What are we supposed to do? Climb mountains and become marathon walkers?"

"Talk to people—the folks who live on the edge of these areas," Tripoli encircled the marked dwellings with his finger. "Maybe they've seen the old guy. Or noticed something unusual in the woods. This isn't Christ walking on water. He eats and shits like everybody else, and he can't exist without leaving a trace. Wherever he is, he's near livestock. Sheep for sure. Goats. They make noise. Goats eat every fucking thing in sight. Leave droppings. And we know he's got a fire."

Sisler looked a little overwhelmed. "Why don't we just at least stick to the south? That's where the kid says he went."

"He could be trying to throw us off."

"That little boy?"

"He may be little, but he's not stupid."

"But look at all this area!" complained Sisler with a plaintive whine.

"All right, all right, I'm taking the lion's share. I'll even cover Connecticut Hill since I live out there. All you've got to do is…"

Molly took Danny outside for lunch.

As soon as they were out on the street, Danny sprang back to life. He had a hop in his gait and his cheeks were pink. Molly picked up a couple of vegetarian pitas on the Commons, and they went over to the green that was Dewitt Park and sat in the cool shade under a broad oak and ate.

"It's much better here," said Danny chewing eagerly. "And this is yummy, too."

"I'm glad you like it."

A puppy came by and jumped right into Danny's lap. He wrapped his arms around the squirming puppy's neck and giggled as it swept his face with its long, wet tongue.

"Maybe…" he ventured later as they relaxed on the lawn, a beseeching look in his eyes, "…maybe we can just stay out here instead of going back?"

"In this world you don't make money sitting under a tree and munching sandwiches."

"It was just an idea," he said backing off.

"Oh, Sweetie," she uttered, and kissed him on lips that tasted of balsamic vinegar.

Danny seemed to be trying—trying his darndest that afternoon not to make any demands on Molly, attempting to melt into the routine of her office. He was quiet and didn't complain; mostly just stood by her window staring down at the flowers in the courtyard below.

Larry, too, was obviously doing his best to be accommodating. He could see that having Danny around was making Molly tense. In the late afternoon, he took Danny by the hand and showed him the big-screened computer in his private office.

"I've got a high-speed link to the Internet," he explained eagerly. "Much faster than your Mommy's. Just take a look at this."

Danny hung back, reluctant.

"You see, you type in a word here. Anything in the world that interests you, and up comes—wait, name something for me. Anything."

"I don't know," Danny murmured.

"Just the first thing that pops into your head."

Danny wrinkled his brow as Larry waited. "Earth," he said, finally.

"Perfect!" Larry typed in the word, went through a couple of links and… "Voila!" A film clip of the earth taken from space filled the screen.

Intrigued, Danny took a step forward.

"You can find almost anything you want," he explained as Danny edged yet closer. He lifted the boy to his lap.

"And look at this! Here's Saturn with its rings. And now…" He showed Danny the pocked terrain that was the moon. "With a click of a mouse you can put yourself into the Amazon rain forest or even out in the Gobi desert!"

"I'd rather be there," admitted Danny a little sadly, "than just look at a picture."

"Maybe one day you will. Or maybe you'll be an astronaut in space."

Danny laughed at the notion.

"Well, you just never know."

"But I know," answered Danny with conviction.

Tripoli checked with Herb Jensen, the local forester. He found him marking cull trees on the side of the hill close to Shindagin Hollow in the Danby State Forest. The black flies were incredible, circling Herb's head in an angry cloud. He had a paint canister in one hand and with his free hand he kept snatching flies out of the air and squishing them.

"Well," said Herb, putting down his sprayer and wiping his palms on his green fatigues. "We had a hermit like that. Living over in the state lands in Dryden."

"When was this?"

"A couple of months ago. Turns out he was an ex-con who decided not to report to his probation officer. He had built himself a little hideout made from scraps of lumber and shit."

"How old?"

"Oh, 'bout forty, maybe. He was having quite a time of it. His girlfriend used to come out and visit, bring him food and stuff. He was poaching, too, naturally."

It didn't sound anything like Danny's hermit.

"Damn these flies!" cursed the forester, digging a pair of them out of his ear. "Never seen a year like it. Usually they don't bother me like this…It's this weird weather. I don't know what's going on, but these buggers are having a ball. Oh yeah, your Hermit," he said turning back to Tripoli.

"Well, I'm looking for a guy who's probably older. Gray hair. Full beard."

"The kidnapper. Right. I heard about the flyover by the troopers. Glad you nailed those dirtballs cutting our trees. Appreciate it."

"My guy has got to be living out somewhere here in the woods," Tripoli pushed on. "He made it through the winter so he's got to have some kind of shelter, got to be leaving some trails. Something."

"I'll grant you that." Herb took off his hat and wiped the sweat from his forehead. Though his face was tanned, there was a line of white that began just above his eyebrows. "But if you want to get lost there's one hell of a lot of territory out here."

Tripoli kept swatting around his head. His exposed arms and neck were already covered with red welts and the flies were trying to crawl into his ears and nose. He wondered how the Hermit was faring with these clouds of bugs.

"We could really use a hand," Tripoli ventured. "Maybe if your people could take a good look around."

"You must be joking! Before the state cutbacks we were short-handed as it was. Now all we've got are two people to cover all of this," he swept his arms in a circle. "Two lousy guys! Can you believe it?"

chapter twelve

The next day was a total waste. Tripoli was tied up in court. He was supposed to testify in a rape case, but the lawyers and prosecutors kept him waiting outside on a courtroom bench. Then when he tried to pass the time reading a book he had brought along, he couldn't concentrate. He kept thinking about the Hermit. Where the hell was the old guy? How could this keep going on? Why hadn't Sisler at least picked up a lead? Somebody. Something.

Across the hall from him an *Ithaca Journal* was half sticking out of a trash can, and he pulled it out to look at the baseball scores. The front page had a color picture of Danny, apparently shot somewhere in the city without Molly's knowledge. Top left was the story by Wally Schuman. It told about Danny's mysterious life in the woods, his return to town, dramatically transformed, and the reporter's observation that there was something remarkable about him, not just his capacity to read, but his uncanny ability to tune into his surroundings. The article kept referring to "the opening of the mind's eye," whatever the hell that was. For a level-headed and normally serious newspaperman, thought Tripoli, Schuman seemed to have gotten a bit carried away.

Tripoli paced the corridors of the courthouse, then returned to his bench, picked up the paper, and thumbed desultorily through it. There was a picture of a farmer in northern China shoveling blowing sand away from his house. A broad band of new desert was sweeping across a wide swath of once fertile land. The farmer, Tse Rangji, was quoted as saying, "The pastures here used to be green and rich." Millions of herders and farmers who had no other place to go were now stranded. He turned the page and found an article about dry lightning sparking hundreds of wildfires across the drought-stricken southern and western states of the U.S. On another page there was an account of a new malarial type of disease discovered last summer in North Carolina. New cases were now springing up as far north as Pennsylvania. He thought about standing in the woods with Herb Jensen the forester and being bitten by those black flies.

It seemed that everywhere he turned there was a story about the world going to pieces. You had to be leery about the air you breathed and the water you drank; there were alarms about the need to wear bug repellent and sunscreen, and to minimize the use of your car to save gasoline almost to the point of giving it up and walking. Christ, thought Tripoli, if you did all that how could you find time just to live?

Finally, close to the end of the day, a clerk emerged from the courtroom to inform him that there wouldn't be time for Tripoli's testimony. They'd call him back tomorrow or the next day. He should please make himself available.

Tripoli trudged back to his office, worked on a couple of reports, and then headed over to Molly's. Cutting his way across the intersecting roads of the trailer park, Tripoli's eyes swept over the familiar homes of sheet metal now looking softer in the evening light. Given the warm weather, the place was abuzz with people: little children with dirty faces, a trio of stoned-looking teens, young mothers, gaunt or obese but most looking old before their time.

He caught a glimpse of Chris Moody getting out of his truck and heading into a new double-wide. Moody, his powerful arms solid blue and red with tattoos, had just been released from Auburn and was out on probation after breaking into ATM machines. He was driving a brand new Chevy pickup. King cab. Four wheel drive. Not bad for an ex-con. I've got to get Molly out of here, he thought, as he reached the rear of the park and her old trailer came into view. Danny was out in front wrestling with a big spade. As soon as he spotted Tripoli's car, he dropped the shovel and ran up to the open window.

"Hi, Trip!" he shouted. Tripoli could feel his dour mood dissolving.

"What are you up to?" he asked, getting out and stretching his legs.

"Oh, I'm just trying to get the earth ready for my garden." Danny led him to the trailer and a patch of ground that looked more like a broken-up macadam road than soil. Danny picked up his shovel and went back to digging. But the earth was impenetrable to his efforts and when he managed to turn over a small scoop, it was nothing but subsoil and rubbery clay. Tripoli could hardly bear to watch him struggle with the hardpan.

"This is not exactly the ideal spot to plant stuff," said Tripoli.

"I know, but my mother says I can't do it any farther away than this." He jerked a thumb in the direction of Molly.

"Hi, Trip," she called through the open window. "Are you going to stick around for a few minutes?"

"Sure."

"I just wanted to go...well, I'll be right with you."

"Yeah. Don't worry. I'm here. Take your time."

"See what I mean," said Danny, leaning on the spade.

"Well, Daniel, you've got to understand..." Tripoli's use of the name caused the boy to brighten perceptibly. "Your mother's worried. You can't blame her, now can you?"

"No. I suppose not," he allowed, jutting out his lip and returning to his digging.

Tripoli leaned against the side of the trailer and continued watching. With every grunt, Danny was penetrating at most an inch or two into the unyielding earth. Then the boy got down on his knees and started breaking up the lumps with his hands. When he bent over, Tripoli noticed the small birthmark on the back of his neck that had been hidden by his hair. It was just as Molly had described it, like a star with six points.

"Here," Tripoli said finally, reaching for the shovel. "Let me give you a hand. You've got to go deep so the roots will have moisture."

Tripoli used his full weight, jumping on the edge of the spade. It was ridiculous: the stuff was like concrete, but he kept at it while Danny watched. "My Dad used to have a big garden. You know, what you really need in here is some organic matter," he explained, stopping to rest. Perspiration was running down his face and he was already winded. Boy was he out of shape! "You ought to mix in some leaves. Or I'll get you some peat moss."

"That would be great!" Danny jumped on the offer. "You mean it? You promise?" he asked.

"Hey, it's a promise."

"Then I could *really* grow stuff."

"And I'll get you some seeds, too."

"Good! But lots of them."

The kid was so elated that Tripoli kept working, though it seemed hopeless. He finished opening up a big section that curved around the trailer, then handed the shovel back to Danny. "Now all you need to do is break up these lumps. Try to get the earth fine and smooth."

Danny went right to work, his small hands gripping the long shaft of the shovel.

"By the way, I want to apologize," said Tripoli as Danny whacked away at the lumps. "I didn't mean to push you like that— you know, that morning when we were driving up South Hill and I was forcing you—"

"I'm not mad at you, if that's what you think."

"Well, I just wanted to be sure."

"My mother says that you were just doing your job."

"And what do you think?"

"I don't think. I know."

"Know what?"

Danny stopped, leaned on the shovel and stared at him. "You want to catch my friend," he said, his eyes narrowing.

"Well, the old man's done something very wrong. You're not allowed to keep children—"

"You'll hurt him."

"No, we won't hurt him. I can promise you that."

"You want to put him in jail."

"That's not my decision. That would have to be decided in court. We have laws for that."

"Those are just the laws of people."

"Well. Yes. Sure," answered Tripoli, caught off guard. "People make up the laws. They do it so that they can live together in society. Not hurt each other."

"But there are other laws. More important ones."

"Like?"

"Just others," answered Danny evasively, leaning over to study the point of the shovel as he ground it into the earth. "And I'm not going to tell you about him anyway. So you shouldn't ask anymore. And you should leave him alone!" He whacked the earth with the back of his shovel. "He's a nice man." He turned to look back up at Tripoli, "And he was always, always, *always* nice to me."

"Okay. I gotcha. I'm not going to push. But maybe, if one day you feel like—"

"Well, maybe," answered Danny vaguely. He cleaved his spade into the earth, and then jumped on it's edge.

"Fine." Tripoli raised his hands in surrender. "Case closed. Lips sealed." He pinched his lips and Danny, watching him through the corner of his eyes, softened and then laughed. "You know, if you really want to grow things, I've got a place in the country with good soil. It's deep and rich."

Danny's eyes lit up. *"Really?"*

"Hey, Trip," called Molly, leaning out the window, "you want to come in and talk to me for a change?"

"Not really," he gave Danny a wink. "But, okay, I'll come in for a minute."

He went in and gave Molly a kiss.

"Ugh," she said. "You're all wet."

"I was just going to help him for a minute, but he's a little slave driver."

"You look tired. Rough day?"

"Ah, just tied up all day in bureaucratic bullshit," he said. He kissed her long and hard, noticing as he did the way her eyes kept darting to the window. "Let me borrow your sink," he said.

"Just as long as you return it," she quipped.

He washed up in the bathroom and came back, his face bright, hair combed. "I've been thinking," he said, broaching the subject slowly. "About Danny. And you. And living here."

"What are you trying to say."

"Look, I want you guys to move out to my place."

"That's nice of you," said, "But…"

"But what."

"There are a lot of buts."

"Well, go on."

"For one, do you think I want to sit out alone in the sticks isolated with this crazy guy out there in the woods somewhere."

"You wouldn't be alone."

"Yeah? What happens when you're working nights? And don't tell me that you—"

"Well, some nights. But I'd try and work it out so—"

"Trip…" she said, taking his hands in hers. "You're so sweet."

"And we're going to find this guy. It's just a matter of time."

She didn't respond.

"Obviously there's more," he said, looking hurt.

"Okay. It's like getting married," she said bluntly.

"And what's wrong with that?"

"I'm not ready to do that. Give up my life. My career."

"Hey, no one is asking you to give up anything."

"Oh yes you are. My independence."

"I don't get it."

"I did that once."

"Okay. And you got screwed. But I'm not Chuck."

"No one said you are."

Outside, Danny's shovel kept going. Chop-chop-chop.

This time there was no mistaking the sound. Danny was sitting bolt upright in bed, listening in the darkness, too. Someone was creeping around the back of the trailer.

The adrenaline was rushing into her system so fast that Molly could hardly breathe. "You stay put!" she ordered in a whisper.

She grabbed a mop handle and in a flash was out the door, weapon in hand. She shouted for the cop on duty in his car. All around the park, dogs started barking. She moved in a tight circle around her home. In the rear of her trailer, away from the overhead lights, it was nearly pitch black. Silently she waded through the deep grass, moving back and forth, poised to strike. At first she saw nothing and heard nothing except the yelping of the dogs. Then she heard a rustling and thought she saw something, a dark figure hunched over and scuffling through the bushes a few yards from the trailer.

Rushing towards the crouched figure she lifted the stick high over her head. "You bastard!" she cried, bringing the mop handle down with all her might.

"Ugh!" cried the figure as it broke in two over his back.

Then she was on top of the man, blindly pummeling him with her fists in the dark, scratching and biting. Lights went on in the neighboring trailers, and the dogs were now frantic. A baby started crying, and a woman shouted out her window, "Shut up! I'm trying to sleep!"

"Stop! Stop!" the man was crying, struggling to his feet as she desperately clung to him. hearing his clothes rip as he broke free. "I'm a police officer!" he said, spinning around and taking tight hold of her wrists.

Then she looked straight into the face of Billy Van Ostrand.

"Oh, shit," she muttered as he relaxed his grip. "I heard something and I thought you were—"

"I saw something, too," he said rubbing the sore spot on his back. "I was trying to sneak up on it and then you…" He flipped on his flashlight and shone it around.

"I'm sorry. I didn't know." Molly was still shaking. "I didn't mean to hurt you."

"It's okay," he said, circling the trailer as she followed him. But clearly it wasn't. In the light Molly could see that he had a pair of bloody scratches running down his cheek. His shirt, hanging loose out of his belt, had three long rents right down the front. "You're just lucky I didn't pop you one," he said, waving his light. "Stay put," he ordered when they got back to the front and Molly, spent, sunk down on the front stoop.

She remained huddled in her nightgown at the front door as the young cop made another quick circle around her place, then sprinted around the other trailers, a hand poised on his gun. He even checked the roofs. Then the surroundings, in an ever-widening loop.

Danny tried to come out.

"No way!" said Molly, holding the door fast.

"I just wanted to—" He called from the other side.

"You stay inside. And I mean it!" Her entire body was still shaking.

Then the cop was back, now down on his knees, poking his light through the chinks in the lattice skirting the foundation to her trailer.

"I don't see anything," he called out from his prone position.

She came closer and stood over him. "He was here. The old man."

"Well," Van Ostrand admitted. "I thought I saw something, too. That's why I came over."

The cop went back to the rear of the trailer and Molly trailed behind him as he stooped down to examine the ground. By the bedroom window he noticed that the deep grass and weeds were trampled.

"Did you come through this way?" he asked, his light going to her.

She realized that, in her night gown, she was essentially naked, but she was still too upset to care. She tried to remember. "I don't know. I was moving fast. I came close to here, but…"

Later, when she got back into the trailer, Danny was sitting in the darkened living room waiting for her.

"It was him, wasn't it?" she asked accusingly. "The old man. The Hermit."

"I don't know," he said earnestly. Then, as she continued to stare at him, he added, "Really."

"But you heard something, didn't you?"

"Yes," he said with his faint lisp. "Something."

"Hey, what's all this?" asked Molly as they stepped out the door the following morning, nearly tripping over two big bales of peat moss.

Sitting on top were packets of bean, pea, and squash seeds, herbs, and flowers. There were trays filled with seedlings of tomatoes and broccoli and eggplant. Then she smiled. "Tripoli's work, huh?"

"Yup, he promised," explained Danny as he lugged one of the bales towards his garden. "Oh, do we *really* have to go right to that office?" asked Danny, canting his head pleadingly. "I mean, couldn't we just go a little teensy-wheensy bit later?"

"I've really got to—" said Molly.

"Please," wheedled Danny, wrapping his arms around her legs and looking up at her with his dream eyes.

"Oh... well...what the heck!" she said, finally. "Go ahead. Plant the stuff."

Danny ran to get the shovel hidden under the trailer.

"Listen, I don't want you to be disappointed," said Molly as she helped, fluffing up the peat and spreading it as Danny worked it between the lumps of clay. If he were planning on leaving, she wondered, would he be planting seeds? "I just want to prepare you. This is not exactly going to be the Garden of Eden."

"Oh, you just wait and see," said Danny. "It'll be just perfect! I know it."

"It's going to take a long time to grow," she said and watched for his reaction.

"Oh, no," he said sweetly. "It'll grow fast. You'll see."

A few weeks later, Tripoli invited himself over for dinner and made it clear that he wasn't taking no for an answer. "I hardly see you any more," he said as he washed the spinach that had come from Danny's garden. "I'm afraid we're drifting apart."

"I know. I'm sorry, but I have my hands full."

He glanced out the window. Danny was in his garden, tying up squash vines and tomatoes. Vines? he thought. It seemed awfully quick. He had been so frustrated, so focused on confronting Molly that he had walked right past the garden without paying attention. He tried to count the days since he'd given Danny the seeds and plants. It seemed like yesterday. Yet everything was already so big and lush.

Molly came and put her arm around his waist. "I've been neglecting you, I know."

"I just wish we could get closer. I care for Danny, too, you know."

"I know that. And we will get closer. It's just that I'm so exhausted. Give me some time. Some space."

"And look, dragging Danny to the office is not helping things. It's not fair to him. And it's not fair to you."

"Until you find the old man, I can't let him out of my sight. Anyway, he's not always disruptive. Sometimes he's actually very quiet."

Quiet, she thought to herself. Unnervingly quiet. Was he longing to go back to the old man?

chapter thirteen

"Look, we've got to talk," said Larry as he stepped into her office. His lips were drawn tight and his eyes narrowed. It was the beginning of the third week of having Danny hanging around, and Molly feared that Larry was about to object. "Can you come into my office?"

"Of course. Danny, come on," she signaled the boy as he stood leaning against the window, his chin cradled in his hand.

He didn't react.

"Danny," she repeated.

"No, no," said Larry firmly, "I meant...*alone*. He can stay by himself for three minutes. Right, Danny?"

Once inside, Larry closed the door and offered her a seat, but she preferred to stand.

Larry sat down, but then stood up, came around and leaned up against the desk, putting himself at eye level to her.

"Hey, I know what you're thinking," she said, preempting him.

"Good, then you know what I'm feeling, too."

"Larry, this is not just another mother trying to balance home and—"

"Maybe not, but—"

"I can't leave him alone. You know that."

"I don't know anything. For christsake, get some decent daycare. There are these wonderful places."

"No way," she said, holding her ground.

"Having him here is making you crazy. How can you work this way?"

"I'm working. I'm working!" she could feel herself beginning to lose control. "I'm doing as much as I can! There's not a night I haven't taken tons of stuff home."

Larry could see her mood shifting from defensive to combative, and he tried to soften his stance. "I know you're trying hard. But I'm worried—and not just for the magazine's sake."

"Well, I can handle it!" she snapped.

"Molly, Molly," he said with a conciliatory note in his voice. "Please, understand. We're trying to run a business here."

"I understand that better than anyone else. Look, if you want, I'll resign," she said and felt viscerally sick at the prospect. Molly could hardly imagine looking for a job again, finding a position that paid a livable wage, gave her flex time, a boss halfway as decent as Larry. Jobless again? Well, if that's what needed to happen, so be it. She had faced worse before. And Danny came first.

"Resignation's never been the issue."

"Then what is?" she asked.

"Don't you see? You've grown to a point where you're key to this operation. We *need* you. I need you. Need you desperately."

Despite herself, Molly was flattered and knew she was probably blushing. "Look, right now I don't dare take my eyes off Danny. Once they catch this hermit, I'll be able to relax. And then at the end of the summer, Danny starts school and everything will be—"

"The *end* of the summer?" he exclaimed. "That's two more months!"

"What caught her eye," said Sisler on the other end of the phone, "was that it looked like a human hand sticking out of the ground."

"Where'd she find it?" Tripoli, in his kitchen making dinner, was already on his feet. He knew a break in the case would emerge sooner or later, and here it was, finally.

"Right there in the woods. Like in a stream bed. Must have been washed down in the rains. It's hard for her to say how long it was sitting there, but—"

"So who's got it?" The ancient refrigerator in his kitchen came on with a clank, and started vibrating noisily. He gave it a kick and it settled down.

"It's over at the Hinkley Museum. But they've got to be closed at this hour."

"Well, tell the curator—or whoever is running the show—that I'm on my way and I want to see them there in twenty minutes."

"No problem."

And I need to talk to the woman who found it. What's her name?"

"Tillson. Marge Tillson. The realtor. You know, the one who's always running those big ads in the paper."

"Well, see if you can set up a meeting for me. It's too late now, it's going to be dark soon, but…Well, just tell her it's important and we need to go back tomorrow to the place where she found it. God, I hope she can find it."

"You want me to come back in?"

Tripoli checked his watch. "Nah. I can handle things from here. Go enjoy your dinner. Hey, you've certainly earned your day's keep."

Sisler laughed. "I wouldn't get too excited yet. I mean it's just a long shot."

"No, no. This sounds perfect, right on target to me. It's the old guy for sure."

Molly took her eyes off the road and glanced up at the soupy sky. "Maybe we should turn around. We're going to get caught in a downpour," she said as they drove up the west shore of the lake.

"No," said Danny. "It's not going to rain."

"No?"

"Not till later. When it's really dark," he said with assurance.

"You sure?"

"Positive."

Amazingly, Danny was always on target. He'd predict a cold front or rain shower and, sure enough, there it was, right on schedule. You could pack an umbrella according to his forecasts.

"But how do you always know?" She pulled in at the parking area at Taughannock Park.

"Oh, just by listening."

"Listening? But to what?"

"Just the clouds. And the wind...and stuff."

"Could I do it?"

"Sure!"

"Then I could quit my job and work for the weather channel."

"Really?" he asked sincerely. And she just laughed and kissed his cheek.

She had hardly cut off the engine before Danny had slipped free from his seatbelt and was out the door. A minute later he was running up along the stream. Molly hurried after him as he pranced over the flat-rocked bottom of the gorge.

Though the evening was unbearably hot in town, as they moved ever deeper into the chasm, the damp walls of the narrowing canyon towering high above their heads, it turned cool and moist, the earth was covered with ferns and moss and the air smelled of primordial mold and vegetation.

"Be careful!" she called ahead. "It's slippery. And boulders sometimes fall from the cliffs. So stay away from the sides!"

"Don't worry, I'm watching!" he shouted back, his high voice echoing up and down the canyon.

The stone floor, shaped by eons of rushing spring floods, was wavy and slippery and Molly had to tread carefully in her slick shoes and office clothes.

"Mother, look here!" Danny exclaimed when she caught up with him. He was pointing up into a tall tree.

Molly stared upward into the dimming light, but couldn't see anything.

"No, there. There. Higher. Higher." When she crouched down next to him, trying to catch the same angle, he took her head and positioned it. Finally she saw what he was looking at: a mother raccoon half hidden in the trunk of the tree with four tiny babies huddled close.

"Boy, you've got good eyes!" she said. And it was true. On their hikes he could find the concealed nest of a grouse or a spotted fawn lying camouflaged in deep grass.

"Look at this," he said a little later, showing her a perfectly formed trilobite fossil he found on the floor of the gorge. "Once these animals lived everywhere. Then they died. Like dinosaurs. Lots of things died. And never came back. Because the earth changed," he said, placing the fossil in the palm of Molly's hand.

"You know," he said as they walked now hand in hand, "this gorge and all the other ones were scooped out by ice. Just like the lake." Molly listened in awe as he explained how the small, circuitous creeks and tributaries merged in their flow to the big lake; how in prehistoric times huge glaciers had traveled across the land, gouging out deep rocky gorges and depositing rock and soil that would become the hills encircling the town. Danny even knew about the Indians, how they had lived in the area for centuries, roaming the hills and valleys and tending their orchards—which was news to Molly. She had never realized that the Iroquois had actually grown fruit. Obviously, the old man had taught him a lot. And Danny had retained it.

"Oh, yes," said Danny, "Apples. All along the lake."

As they crossed the bridge of the rushing stream, Danny told her about the infamous General Sullivan and his soldiers. How the peaceful Indians were driven from this land, their crops and long houses burned, how they were ultimately starved and slaughtered.

This was terribly heavy stuff coming from a little boy. "But, Honey, people do good things, too."

"Of course. But now they're destroying our Earth."

These were not the words of a child. "Who's *they?*"

"We."

"You mean everybody? Do you mean me and you?"

Danny shrugged. "I don't know…I didn't find out. But unless we do something, something terrible is going to happen to us."

The way Danny said it, the way he looked at her wide-eyed and worried, frightened her.

"Little boys are supposed to be happy. Carefree. Just have a good time. Play. Have fun."

"Uh-uh." He shook his head. "Not me."

Sisler really was a piece of work, thought Tripoli, navigating his car down the winding country road leading from his house. There were times he moved so slowly you just wanted to take hold of the guy and shake him. Then, unexpectedly, he'd make the most improbable of connections—something like this that verged on brilliance. One day he'd make a first-rate detective.

As Tripoli descended into the valley, the evening air became thick and he was glad he lived in the hills outside of town. He squeaked through two lights on State Street, then took a quick turn onto Seneca where the Hinkley Museum was housed in a spiffied up old Greek Revival. The curator, a wiry guy with gray goatee and spectacles, sat on the front steps waiting for Tripoli.

"Marge Tillson—you know, the realtor over at Remax Associates—brought it in," he said unlocking the door. "It's a pretty amazing piece of work. She thought she had found this real old relic, but…this way," he said, snapping on lights as they went. They passed through the main display room housing a collection of farm and household implements that looked to be from the eighteenth and nineteenth centuries. Tripoli followed his guide into a large work-room at the rear. As soon as the lights came on, he saw what he was looking for.

"Oh my God," uttered Tripoli, approaching the bench where it lay.

"Yes. Beautiful, isn't it. We've kept it even though it doesn't belong in our collection."

It was a wooden pitchfork, but unlike any Tripoli had ever seen. Carved from a single piece of ash, the shaft was as big around as a child's wrist. The tines had been created by making four splits which separated the shaft into five distinct pieces. Each tine had been individually steamed and bent, forming a graceful curve.

"Anthropomorphic, isn't it?" added the curator.

Yes, thought Tripoli, it did look just like a human hand. Four slender fingers and a thumb. There were even knuckle joints as well as nails carved into the back of the tines. "Extraordinary," he whispered in awe.

"And just look at this handle," said the curator. He shifted a lamp closer, his glasses glinting in the light. "Whoever made this had remarkable skill—not the kind of thing you see these days."

The handle had been created by splitting the wood down the middle and bending the two pieces into a U. Holes had been drilled and a dowel inserted. "The dowel was made of cured wood, but the body was still green when it was made so that, when it dried, it shrunk and fit tightly. Look, there's no sign of any glue."

Tripoli could hardly take his eyes off the graceful tool. He picked it up. It was light and perfectly balanced, ideal for forking hay or leaves, or any dry material. "So how did she find this?" he asked finally.

"You know Marge. She's a fanatical birder."

Tripoli nodded. He had seen her weekly column in the paper.

"Well, she was out in the woods, crossing a stream bed. It lay completely buried except for this end. It was really dirty and soaked when she brought it in—which is why she thought it was very old."

Tripoli's eyes went to the window. Outside it was slowly starting to get dark. "Which stream are we talking about?"

"I don't really know. Somewhere in the Danby State Forest. I think off the Comfort Road Extension. You'd really have to talk to Marge. Say, what's this all about, anyhow? I mean the police and—"

"Mind if I hang on to this for a while?" asked Tripoli, moving toward the door. Behind him the man was turning off lights and locking up. He followed Tripoli out.

"By any chance has it got anything to do with that Driscoll boy disappearing?"

Tripoli shrugged, avoiding the question.

"I hear the kid's pretty amazing."

"I guess so," said Tripoli finally. "So they say."

Late that night, as Molly sat alone in the kitchen, the table lit by a narrow cone of light, there was a sudden downpour just as Danny promised. As the rain beat down on the roof, she struggled to focus on the work spread before her, but her mind kept drifting off; nagging thoughts about Danny kept stealing into her consciousness. She recalled the old days, the days before Danny had disappeared, before he had lost his childish innocence.

She went to the shelf, took down the photo album, and began leafing through the forgotten pages. There was Danny a week old, his face still scrunched up. She turned a page and now he was as a toddler in diapers standing with his little, chubby legs stuck into her tall boots, laughing at the silliness of it. Then, Danny at his birthday party, standing on a chair so he could blow out the three candles. His cheeks were puffed up with air, and there were little faces gathered around him, watching. What happened to the little boy she had known? She continued leafing through the album, the pictures of his early life cascading before her. She lovingly touched the photo of beaming Danny with his first fish, caressed another of him dog-paddling in the shallows of the lake, splashing to stay afloat. Always that guileless, carefree little boy with no secrets. Danny at the Apple Festival. Danny at…

Molly didn't realize she was crying until she saw the wet splotches on the snapshots. She dabbed at the spots, trying to blot up her tears and ended up marring the photos, leaving indelible blotches on the shiny surfaces.

Marge Tillson was a busy woman. She had two showings of a new listing, an open house in the afternoon and a late-day closing.

"Like I told your detective," said Marge when Tripoli called her at home in the morning, "I'd love to help you, but there's no way I can reschedule. Is it life threatening or could we just do this around dinnertime?"

Tripoli relented and agreed to meet her at dinnertime on the Comfort Road Extension where the dirt road hit the Danby Forest. At the appointed time, he was sitting on the hood of his car sipping from a can of Sprite when Marge pulled up.

She was a big-breasted woman in her late forties, bristling with energy. "I've got to warn you that I don't know how much help I can be." She sat with the door open, changing out of her heels into a pair of hiking boots. She took off her realtor's jacket and tossed it onto the passenger seat. "In fact, I'm not sure I can even quite remember where…"

They climbed a series of ridges. The horseflies were unbearable, and Tripoli kept crushing them on his neck. They didn't seem half as interested in Marge.

"I was following a pair of pilleated woodpeckers. They had a nest right down there and…let me see…I was walking."

"You're now sure it was this creek?"

"Well, pretty sure…Wait! There. I found it right over there."

Tripoli went over. The stream was now but a trickle. He could see that someone had moved rocks: there was still a deep hole in the dried silt.

"When I dug it out, I thought it was really old and valuable. That's why I took it over to the Hinkley," she explained as Tripoli's eyes scanned up the sloping waterway. From the looks of things, it seemed to Tripoli that the pitchfork had washed down while the water was high. Maybe in the late fall or early spring.

"I'm going to follow this stream," he said turning back to her. "Think you can make it back out on your own?"

"No problem. I'm used to hiking. Hey, do you think this is connected with that missing boy and the old hermit?"

"Who said that?"

"You kidding?" Marge let out a loud guffaw that echoed through the woods. "Everybody is talking about it. It's the biggest thing to happen since that Cessna crashed into that house in Lansing. And that was one of my listings!"

Molly finished work late that day. There wasn't much time for the usual hike, so she took Danny out to the ornithology lab at nearby Sapsucker Woods. They parked at the entrance near the pond and walked in along the looping trails. Dusk was approaching, and the air was filled with a cacophony of sounds as the waterfowl on the pond chased each other, flapping wings and screeching. Overhead, the tree dwellers busily chirped and fluttered back and forth in the woodland canopy, utilizing the last remnants of daylight for feeding and breeding and nest building.

Molly clutched Danny's hand as they walked along the path. His head was tilted back, his eyes searching the high branches. He made an odd noise, "Eeeerk-Eeeerk-Eeeerk," and the birds actually seemed to be answering him.

By the time they neared the pavilion, the sun was resting just on the lip of the horizon, flooding the landscape in a shower of yellowish-red. Everything glowed with warmth. They stood together on the deck overlooking the water. The evening was soft, and a faint wind was soughing out of the west, singing through the pines and deciduous trees.

"Funny," said Molly, "I've always been so busy doing the laundry and trying to make a living that I never really stopped to see how beautiful all this is." She felt a chill run up her spine and couldn't resist kissing Danny. He looked up at her with love brimming in his eyes and squeezed her hand.

They shared a long moment of silence. Molly observed him as he peacefully gazed down into the water, intently watching a dense school of baby fish moving like a cloud below them. Finally Molly broke the silence. "What else did the old man tell you, besides about listening?"

"Oh, I don't know." He shook his head and then looked up at her. "Stuff like you shouldn't hurt people or other living things."

"That sounds nice."

"He talked about footsteps on the forest floor."

"Footsteps," she echoed.

"Yes. How you shouldn't use things up. Or wear things out. Like the bunny rabbit that leaves footprints in the snow. And then, when the snow melts, it's just like the rabbit wasn't ever there."

"That's a beautiful thought," she said, genuinely touched.

She began to walk on, but Danny remained behind, standing where they had stopped.

"Come on," she gently urged and noticed how Danny seemed to be staring off into the distance. He seemed fixed on some memory of pleasure, something that moved him to longing, she thought, with regret.

Upstream, the creek seemed to go on forever. Tripoli struggled to trace its path as it meandered through tangled brush and undergrowth. With the light in the dense forest quickly failing, he decided finally to give up. Breaking off branches to mark the trail as he left, he made his way back to his car. Immersed in thought, he slowly drove back down into the valley and then, for no apparent reason, took a detour to Sapsucker Woods.

Molly's old car stood alone in the parking lot and Tripoli pulled up beside it. He got out and waited. A bank of clouds had moved in and a few light drops started to fall. Tripoli felt grungy and tired, and the cool rain felt soothing on his hot, bug-bitten skin.

A few minutes later Molly and Danny came wandering back toward the car.

"Hi, Trip!" exclaimed Danny. He ran up to greet him, wrapping his arms around Tripoli's waist. "Did you see my garden?"

"Yeah, the last time I was there I was really impressed."

"No, I meant *now*. All the plants. Everything's much bigger!"

"Well, I'm coming over," He ruffled the boy's hair and glanced over at Molly, who looked surprised to see him.

"How'd you know we were here?"

"Intuition," he said, though the truth was that he didn't know, couldn't have known. It must have been sheer coincidence.

"Boy, you look a mess." She began pulling burrs and nettles from his sleeve; ran her fingers through his hair, combing out fragments of leaves. "Where on God's earth have you been?"

"Oh, playing in the woods," said Tripoli. Danny laughed. "And I found something really neat. Take a look." He popped the trunk of his car.

Danny came around the back of the car, but when he saw the

pitchfork his head jerked sharply, and almost immediately he looked away. His face flushed and he started licking his lips nervously. Tripoli watched him through the corner of his eye. One look and Molly knew where it had come from.

"Pretty nice, isn't it, Daniel?" Tripoli persisted, hefting it in his hand.

"I suppose so," Danny said, drifting steadily away from the car.

Molly waited, still staring at the tool.

"So," she whispered sharply when Danny was finally out of earshot, "you know where he is?"

"Not quite." He hedged and could see from her expression that she was let down. "But this takes us right to his doorstep."

He explained how Sisler turned up this lead at the Hinkley Museum, about Marge Tillson finding it, and his own search up the stream in the Danby Forest.

"Don't you see," he put his arm around her. "I'm so close I can almost feel the guy's breath. Please," he said. "Try to trust me. Danny's safe. We've still got a guy posted at your place."

She pulled away. "You going to post someone at work, too? And someone trailing us in the supermarket when I go shopping?"

"If need be."

"Oh, yeah. Sure. And how much longer before they pull your guys off that detail?"

"Then I'll sleep over."

"Thanks but no thanks."

"I don't get it," he said looking hurt. "What's come between us?"

"Nothing. Nothing but this guy who sunk his claws in my kid. He may have done Danny some good. I'd have to be completely blind not to see that. But that old bastard stole his innocence. Put all this end-of-the-world crap into his head." She balled her right hand into a fist. "And for that I really resent him. For what he put me through. And keeps putting me through."

Tripoli put the pitchfork back into his car as Danny wandered to the other car.

"I just want you to get him," she said under her breath. "Just get him before he gets Danny."

chapter fourteen

On the morning that Mildred Oltz and her husband were killed in a head-on crash, Wally Schuman called Tripoli at his office.

"I heard about the pitchfork," Wally said.

"You and half the county." It was a lousy, hot day, and Tripoli was in a foul mood.

"You know it's been almost two months now."

"So, you're keeping score, too? We'll get the old man, don't worry. It's just a matter of—"

"That's not the only thing that interests us."

"Us?"

"The paper. We're thinking of another piece. A feature, really. It's a pretty incredible story."

Tripoli didn't like the direction the conversation was going. He was thinking of Danny and Molly. Schuman's article had been full of conjecture and wild speculation. Molly didn't need more people bugging her about Danny. The last thing she needed was more public attention. "Whatta you say we just leave it alone for a while? Cut the mother and kid some slack."

"Come on, Lou, we can't just sit on a story like this. The whole town's buzzing about it. You can't even go in and get a burger without hearing about it."

"About *what?*"

"The boy, of course. Danny. The kid can do all kinds of amazing things.

"Hey, just hold on!"

"And the old man—"

Tripoli cut him short. "You mean the kidnapper."

"I talked to Danny myself," Schuman pushed on. "He's extraordinary. That little boy can read like an adult. And when you speak to him…well, you have the strange sense that he's in touch with life in a way that we never are."

"I think you're getting a little carried away." Absently, Tripoli picked up a cold cup of coffee sitting on his desk; the cream had already gone sour. Not knowing what to do with the mouthful, he ended up swallowing it.

"I heard about that meteor."

For an instant, Tripoli was stunned into silence. Was Molly foolishly talking about it at work? Or was it Rosie? Yeah, had to be Rosie, who was something of a motor mouth. Damn!

"How'd you know about that?" Tripoli blurted out the question before he realized he was simply confirming the story.

"Oh, we have our sources," Wally chuckled. "Listen, the main reason I called is…you know that picture Danny drew for the juvie shrink? We heard you're still holding it in evidence."

Tripoli thought about the Troopers and Matlin and the slugs working in the Sheriff's office. None of them were any help. "And you want to run it, is that it?"

"Well…yes."

Tripoli weighed the matter. It was obvious the *Journal* was going to publish their story regardless of what he did or said.

"Okay. Sure." Well, he thought, if it helps catch the Hermit. "Yeah, why not? The deal is, however, that you stop playing up the business about Danny's gifts—or whatever you want to call them."

"We'll just stick to the facts," said Schuman.

Tripoli wasn't sure of what that really meant.

"By the way," asked the journalist, "what's the story on the Oltz woman?"

The story was the Oltzes' car had gone out of its lane and slammed head-on into a pickup. Pellegrino was still out there picking up the pieces. Orson Oltz, the driver, had been drunk, way above the limit, as was the driver of the other vehicle. Mrs. Oltz, who wasn't wearing a seat belt, had been catapulted through the windshield and landed on the crumpled hood of the truck, killed upon impact.

"As far as I'm concerned, it's all pretty straightforward." Tripoli tossed the remains of his coffee at the garbage can and missed. "Two drunks hit each other. Bad luck. Or good luck, depending on how you figure it. And *please* don't quote me on that!"

More than a few people in town, however, felt that there was more to the story, much more.

"If you ask me," said Nadine Warren, who worked in the law office next to the courthouse; she had bumped into Tripoli as he was going up the front steps to make an appearance, "this was punishment, pure and simple. Retribution. God doesn't fuck around."

"That Driscoll boy," said Barry Hollenbeck, the paunched old guard recognizing Tripoli and waving him around the metal detector in the courthouse lobby. "I hear he can hold his breath under water for an hour. And talks to the animals. And they talk to—"

"Give me a break, Barry, willya."

"No. No. This is serious shit," he said, pulling his bulldog face so close that Tripoli could smell the garlic on his breath. "And that crash with the Oltzes." He dropped his voice. "That didn't just happen by chance."

"No, it didn't," answered Tripoli, raising his voice so loud in the marbled halls it caused heads to turn. "Both idiot drivers went out and first got falling down, stinking drunk. Then they arranged to meet on Route 13. In a head-on. Just as Venus and Mars were aligning. Come on, Barry, get real," he shouted, storming off down the corridor, "I wish everybody in town would stop gossiping and get a life!"

As coincidence would have it, though, the crash did occur at precisely the same moment that Rosie Lopez Green was giving birth to the first of her twin sons. By the time Mrs. Oltz's mangled body was slid into a morgue locker in the hospital basement, Rosie was already settled into the maternity ward, a squawking boy tucked under each arm. According to old Dr. Wozniak, the infants were healthy and well.

"Are you sure?" pleaded Rosie, shedding tears of relief and exhaustion. Ed kept stroking her arm, blinking his own misty eyes.

"I've been doing this for years," said Dr. Wozniak, "And they're perfectly healthy. Believe me. What do you want, that I should guarantee they're going to win a Nobel Prize?"

chapter fifteen

"Will you look at who's here!" exclaimed Ed, opening the door to his house on Spencer Street to discover Molly and Danny. "Our local TV star!" Danny flew into Ed's arms, and Ed swung him up into the air.

"Uncle Ed!" cried Danny, gripping him with both arms and legs.

"So, you missed old Uncle Eddie, huh?"

"Of course!" Danny giggled and waggled his head.

Ed leaned to one side to give Molly a kiss. "We were wondering when you guys were gonna come by."

"I'm just on a lunch break and we thought we'd say a quick hello. Maybe take a peek at the twins?"

He showed them in and Molly could hear the babies wailing above the rattle of Rosie's old washer dancing on the kitchen floor.

The Greens' house on the south side of town was a clapboard affair that sat squeezed against the road. The foundation was sagging, causing the floors to slant in all directions, and there was still plastic on the windows left over from the winter. An old refrigerator and a broken sofa stood on the front porch as they had for as long as Molly could remember.

"Rosie!" called Ed, as he moved down the hallway, Danny still in his arms. "We've got company!"

Rosie came out of the bedroom, dark circles under her eyes, the top of her dress soaked with milk. "Danny, sweetheart!" she exclaimed with a big smile.

Danny reached out from his perch on Ed and grabbed Rosie around the neck, pulling her close. She smothered him with wet kisses.

"Yuck!" he laughed, wiping his face.

Molly gave her a hug. "Hey, how are things?" The babies were still crying.

"They're a couple of handfuls," she heaved a long sigh, "but we're happy."

"How about something to eat?" asked Ed. "I just made this great, big, scrumptious chocolate cake."

Molly shook her head. "We really can't stay that long—just wanted to take a look at the little guys. Sounds to me like they're awake."

"They're always awake!" Rosie laughed. "I think they're on speed. Come on," she led the way, shuffling slowly in her bedroom slippers. "Follow me to the menagerie."

The twins were lying in the same crib, loudly protesting, their faces scrunched up and red with fury.

Danny went to the crib and bent over to take a closer look. "Ooooh, they're so tiny."

"They're only two weeks old. You were little like that once, too," said Rosie, resting her hand on his shoulder.

"Before you became an adult," added Molly with a laugh. The babies kept going full blast, and Molly noticed that Danny didn't seem in the least bothered by it. "Oh, they're lovely. Perfect," she said cooing over them. Their skin was a smooth, dark olive, and Molly could see in them Rosie's even features and Ed's long lashes.

"Yeah, but I just don't know what it is with them. Since I got back from the hospital it's been solid crying." Rosie checked their diapers. "They're both perfectly dry, see? And I just fed them. I just don't know what gives." She picked one up in each arm and rocked them, but the twins kept crying. Danny watched, intrigued, as Rosie placed them back down on their stomachs and patted their backs. Finally, she turned them over. "This is Fernando," said Rosie above the racket, "and this other troublemaker here, this is Alonso."

"But you can call them Freddy and Al," added Ed, his big head leaning in over the crib.

"Can I touch them?" inquired Danny.

"Well of course!" exclaimed Rosie. "They're your new cousins, aren't they?"

Danny rested his hand on Freddy's midsection and began moving it in small circles. Almost immediately the infant fell quiet.

Rosie looked awestruck. "I don't believe this."

"Holy Christmas," echoed Ed.

"Can you do the same thing with Fernando?" she asked.

Danny placed his other hand on the second twin. The baby kept crying for a moment, but then he opened his eyes, stared curiously up at Danny and fell equally silent. The washer came to an abrupt stop, and the only sound in the room was a talk show filtering in from the TV.

"Can I hold them, maybe?" ventured Danny.

"You kidding?" laughed Rosie. "We're keeping you here. At least till they're in college."

They seated Danny in the big armchair and brought him the infants. He held them gently, cradling one in each arm and gazing down at them with a blissful smile on his face.

Rosie and Molly wandered out to the kitchen.

"How are you feeling?" asked Molly.

"So, so," said Rosie. "Seems like I'm just dragging all the time."

"Twins will do it," said Molly, commiserating. Rosie really didn't look too hot. Since the beginning of the pregnancy, she seemed to be deteriorating.

"But I hear you got bigger problems," she said.

Molly tried to brush it off.

"He's miserable in the office, huh?"

Molly looked surprised.

"Small town. No secrets here. You keep bumping into the same people." Rosie smiled. "A guy loses his brakes coming down State Street and ends up hitting his ex-wife's new boyfriend."

Molly laughed. "Okay, I'm getting desperate," she admitted, her eyes going to the bedroom. She told her about Larry's complaints and all the extra work at the office.

"What an insensitive sonofabitch!"

"Well, it's not that he's so bad," said Molly, springing to his defense. "He was good to me when I needed help most."

"Or good to himself."

"And I suppose you've got to see it from his point of view."

"You need a break," said Rosie. "Or you're going to break. Why don't I—"

"No way!" said Molly. "You're the one who needs the break."

"It's purely selfish. It's like hiring the perfect babysitter." She tossed her head in the direction of the bedroom and laughed.

"I found the hut!" exclaimed the man, breathlessly. "The Hermit's hideout!"

The call had come in to the State Police barracks in Varna in the first hours after dawn on Wednesday. Sgt. Vernon Peters, who was covering the switchboard, took the call.

"It was just like that kid's drawing. You know. In the paper. Made out of branches and—I was out hunting and—I just couldn't believe it!" the man sounded as though he had hit the jackpot on the state lottery. "Like in the middle of the woods, in this clearing. It's hidden all the way in the brush. A clearing. It's got sheep. Animals. And he's there. The guy with the white beard. I saw him myself!"

To Peters, this had the ring of authenticity. "Where?"

"The State Forest. Danby."

"Okay. Right, but where?"

"You go beyond Comfort Road. Maybe a mile or so, and then head in. Almost directly east. On the left."

Sgt. Peters took down the man's number, put him on hold, and immediately put a call through to the Ithaca City Police.

"Is Lou Tripoli there?" he asked Carol Halperin, the civilian dispatcher, who had picked up on the switchboard.

"He's out, but I can try to get him."

"Yeah. Please."

Peters hung on as she tried to raise Tripoli on the radio. She made three attempts, but had no luck.

"He must have his radio off," she said.

"Okay, give him a message."

She took down the message, then pigeonholed the note in Lou Tripoli's box.

Peters informed his lieutenant, who waited thirty minutes, then tried the City Police's lead investigator.

"He's still not responding," explained the same dispatcher. "I think he's out on a drug bust."

When the lieutenant explained about the hut, the dispatcher put Dave Meese on the line. He was one of the batch of new officers who had just joined the city force.

"I'll leave him a note," said Meese.

The lieutenant put down the phone and shook his head. "I don't get it."

"Yeah," echoed Peters. "No one over there seems to give a shit."

And with that, the lieutenant took it upon himself to mobilize his resources.

"Get me a chopper. I want a SWAT team out there. Also get on the horn and notify the Tompkins County Sheriff and State DEC Rangers."

In a matter of minutes the word was out, crackling over the air-waves and land lines: someone had spotted the Hermit, the man who had imprisoned the Driscoll boy. They had him zeroed in.

Tripoli was so mad he could hardly speak. Mad at himself for forgetting to turn on his mobile radio when he stepped out of the car, pissed at the people on dispatch for failing to make every effort to get him. What the hell were they thinking? Or not thinking!

With the message still crumpled in his fist, he grabbed Jerry Sisler and they ran out to the car. Sirens going and lights flashing, they tore up South Hill. Five minutes later they were at Benjamin's general store in Danby, taking a sharp right onto Bald Hill Road.

"Where the hell are they?" growled Tripoli as they bounced over the hilly roadway that cut through the public forest. They were well beyond the Comfort Road area where the pitchfork had been found.

"They've got to be somewhere here," Sisler said, unnerved by his boss's burgeoning anger.

Tripoli kept his foot heavy on the gas. The paved road ended and turned to gravel. A hail of stones kicked up, pelting the undercarriage of the car as a plume of dust trailed in their wake. He was beginning to suspect that they had somehow overshot the location when he spotted ahead a bevy of official cars lining both sides of the road.

"Holy shit!" muttered Sisler, "Looks like they've got a fucking army here." It seemed like every agency in the tri-county area was on the scene.

Tripoli pulled up and, grabbing his radio, ran across the roadway with Sisler on his heels. It was easy to follow the route that the party had taken. There were fresh tracks on a logging road heading off into the woods on the left, and Tripoli could see where the four-wheel-drives and ATVs had entered.

The two took off at a sprint, following the path that had been churned to mud by tires and feet, speeding up as the road dropped into a deep gully, then forging ahead where the road ascended steeply. Deep into the woods, they finally stopped for a breather. Tripoli arched his head back and looked up into the high canopy. The maples and beeches had long since blossomed out, but he could see hints of sky and sun filtering through.

"Come on, let's go," he urged Sisler, and they pushed on. Tripoli's radio, tuned to the assault team's frequency, was now barking furiously.

"What the hell's going on?" asked Sisler breathlessly.

The road split, then the branch they took narrowed as the woods became more dense. Sisler started to fall behind, but Tripoli kept moving. Reaching the place where the group had abandoned their jeeps, he could hear the whop-whop-whop of an approaching helicopter. A bullhorn echoed and dogs barked. In front of him, the brush and low-lying vegetation was nearly impenetrable, and it took him a moment to find the spot where the men had hacked their way through.

Scampering up the last rise, Tripoli suddenly caught the reflections of chrome and steel, guns and equipment. There must have been at least two dozen highly armed men forming a perimeter, their weapons trained on a small dwelling that stood in the grassy clearing ahead. Behind the hut, a flock of sheep and goats huddled tightly against a rear line of thicket that was as dense as a wall.

"Goddamn," muttered Tripoli, "You'd think they were fighting the Red fucking Army!"

They were all focused on the hut. Meticulously constructed of small logs and saplings, with small handmade shutters and a roof of woven, dried vegetation, the hut blended right into the landscape. Despite the troopers' advanced gear—the infrared scopes, the sensing devices, the parabolic mikes—they could easily have walked past the hut without noticing it. The hut, Tripoli realized, was almost precisely as Danny had drawn it.

Tripoli's attention shifted to the police. The troopers' Dynamic Entry Team, off to his right, was huddled tight, whispering tensely. Three ranking officials stood behind a big tree arguing—a State Police lieutenant, the sheriff, and a Fed out of Elmira.

"Rush him!" voted the trooper.

"I say hit him with gas!" said the sheriff.

"Can you get those guys with the bullhorn to shut up?" the red-faced Fed yelled at the trooper. "And pull that fucking bird back!"

The helicopter was moving in and the roar was deafening.

"My men are ready to go," announced the SWAT team's leader, trotting up to join the trio.

"Hey! Wait!" cried Tripoli, wading in.

"Who the hell are you?" demanded the Fed, staring hard at Tripoli.

"Tripoli's IPD," interjected the sheriff. "He's lead investigator."

"Well, that doesn't count for shit now," sneered the trooper as he turned to face Tripoli. "We're calling the shots here."

"Like hell," shouted the Fed. "This is a kidnapping, and—"

"Who have you got in there?" said Tripoli to the sheriff, ignoring the trooper. He was vaguely aware that Sisler had finally caught up and was slumped down on a log, panting.

"It's the kidnapper," explained the Sheriff. "He's barricaded himself in there."

"And the perp's armed," added the SWAT man.

"We've already had one man killed this year screwing around—negotiating—with a holed-up psycho," said the trooper. "No way am I going to risk any of my men—"

"How do you know he's armed?" asked Tripoli.

"Because he's holding a fucking rifle!" snapped the trooper.

Tripoli grabbed the binoculars out of the man's hand. It was dark in the interior of the hut, but Tripoli could make out a shadowy figure moving around. He was holding something long in his hand. "How do you know it's a weapon?" he asked, turning back to the men.

"When we first got here," explained the sheriff, "he poked it out the window. One of my guys spotted it. Looked like an old 303. He keeps sneaking around in there. And he won't talk."

"That phone's not working," argued the Fed. "That's why we gotta toss him another."

"Yeah?" said the trooper. "You go toss it."

"Well, pull your guys back then! This is totally nuts," he turned to Tripoli, appealing to him with hands outstretched. "We don't have a serial killer in there. Just an old geezer. I saw him. He looks harmless."

"Yeah, harmless with a high-powered rifle," injected the trooper.

"Look," said Tripoli steadily, trying to wrest control. "Why don't we just slow things down a notch."

"Christ, that's what I've been trying to say," said the Fed. The sheriff looked as if he could be persuaded and Tripoli could feel a more sane coalition beginning to form.

"And just look at this place," implored the Fed, "Do you think a maniac would build something like this?"

But then, suddenly, it was too late for talk. One of the sheriff's men on the perimeter had taken it upon himself to blast a tear gas shell through the open window. It went off with a dull whomp and the tiny hut immediately started filling with gas. Tripoli already could see it beginning to ooze out of the lower edges of the window frames.

Every set of eyes turned to look.

The bullhorn fell silent.

Even the dogs stopped their howling.

Tripoli left the group and moved right up to the front line close

to the hut. He squatted down and watched, thinking about his decision to give Wally Schuman that drawing.

Everybody waited.

"Shit," said a deputy hidden behind the tree. "He's not even
coughing."

Suddenly, from where he crouched, Tripoli caught a glimpse of
the old man. His hair and beard were as white as snow, though his
face was surprisingly unlined, his skin as smooth and unfurrowed as
a child's. His eyes were discs of light gray, tender and wise and
remarkably untroubled. For an instant, their eyes met and Tripoli
could have sworn that there was a look on the old man's face as if
he had recognized him, knew him. Shivers went down Tripoli's
spine.

"Hold it!" pleaded Tripoli, rising to his feet.

"Fire another," urged a trooper.

"No, don't!" shouted Tripoli, "It's enough already. You've got an
old man in there. You'll kill him."

The mortar, however, was already launched. It catapulted through
the other window, exploding an instant later with a hiss of gas.

Again there was silence.

Tripoli waited. And waited.

"Damn you all!" he finally cried and, tearing through the line of
flak-jacketed people, raced toward the hut.

"Hey, come back!" someone shouted from behind.

"You idiot, watch out! He's armed!"

But Tripoli, like a man possessed, kicked in the door. It collapsed
with his first blow and the tear gas came billowing out. Holding his
breath and closing his eyes, Tripoli bolted in.

Someone was lying on the floor and Tripoli stumbled over him.
Groping blindly, he took hold of the still body and started to drag.
The man was surprisingly light and Tripoli managed to pull him
quickly through the doorway out into the fresh air.

Tripoli's eyes and nose were running copiously as he knelt above the old man who lay inert on the earth. There were shouts all around him, and he could feel the pounding of feet as the cops rushed in from the woods. He kept blinking and wiping his eyes, and when his vision had finally cleared he saw a thin old man lying before him on the ground. His skin was as pale as his beard. Barefoot, he was dressed in loose fitting, homespun garments. His eyes were closed and his arms were folded in a rigid position, clasped protectively across his chest.

The snipers and deputies and troopers moved out from their hiding places in the woods, converging in a tight circle around Tripoli as he knelt over the old man.

"Jesus," uttered someone, "the old guy's dead."

"And he didn't even cough!" exclaimed another voice. "Hey, did you hear him cough?"

"Oh my God," whispered Tripoli, "Oh my God. What have we done?"

Molly and Danny had hardly gotten back and settled into the office, when Tasha came bursting in on them.

"Did you hear?" she cried.

"Hear what?" asked Molly.

"The Hermit."

Danny's head snapped around. "Huh?"

"They got him! He's dead. I just heard on the radio. They've even got a special report on TV. Larry's got it on his set."

Sisler and Tripoli took control of the scene as the rest of the men started to disperse, slinking off into the woods. The helicopter carrying the state coroner came in close and settled down into the opening, blades still beating the air, the animals scurrying away to the far side of the hut. People with television cameras kept emerging from the woods, and the remaining troopers and deputies kept them confined to the far end of the clearing, away from the old man's body just outside the hut.

When the coroner was finished, Tripoli assisted him in slipping the hermit's corpse into a body bag. They zipped it closed, and then the two of them, with Sisler's help, lugged the plastic pouch toward the helicopter. Jimmy Teeter from IPD helped them hoist it into the craft, then climbed in to accompany it back to the morgue. The old man was now merely evidence and the law required that it be continuously guarded right up through the required autopsy.

"I want you to get his prints as soon as you can!" Tripoli shouted to Teeter above the roar of engines as they revved up, beating the grass flat.

"His what?" called Teeter.

"Prints! Prints!" Tripoli wiggled his fingers.

Teeter nodded, giving a thumbs-up as the machine lifted and then whirled above the trees.

Tripoli wandered around the site. The goats and sheep nervously shuffled back and forth against the wall of overgrowth, bleating and baahing, keeping their distance. Within the clearing he found a small fence of interwoven saplings, and within its protective confines a garden. There were neat lines of beans and peas, some nice-sized heads of cabbage. At the north side of the hut, Tripoli found a mounded section of earth with a trap door. Opening it, he discovered a small, rock-lined cellar containing old potatoes and newly picked mushrooms, all neatly arranged. There were other things in there that appeared to be root crops Tripoli couldn't identify.

When the last remnants of acrid gas had finally dissipated, Tripoli went inside the hut and looked around. It was finely crafted. Every piece of the structure had been painstakingly fitted, giving it a marvelous solidity. The walls, Tripoli noted, had been furred out and loosely packed with grass to form an insulating barrier. In the center of the hut, there was a fireplace made of fieldstone, hand fitted without a hint of mortar. A chimney of similar stone ascended through the roof. It, too, was a work of art. The dwelling reminded Tripoli of pictures he had seen of native huts in Africa, the thatch tight and perfectly aligned.

On the floor, where the old hermit had let it drop, lay his weapon—nothing more than a gnarled walking stick carved to fit his hand. Lining a side wall were cups and bowls made of fired clay, larger containers holding hickory nuts and shell beans and what appeared to be wheat berries. He found balls of white stuff that had a rubbery consistency and smelt like some kind of cheese.

On a corner shelf that had been made of parallel sticks bound with vines, Tripoli discovered a line of old bound volumes. He picked up the closest and carefully opened it. The paper, which felt like parchment, was like nothing he had ever seen before. The pages were all handwritten, printed in an elaborate and laborious style. Some of it was in English that seemed stilted and old. Much of it was in foreign languages. Among the volumes there were books on plants illustrated with sketches, illuminated drawings of the Earth and solar system, directions for the making of tools and the construction of root cellars, diagrams of dams, methods of food preparation and storage. One book contained intricate drawings of insects and flowers and animals, hand-colored and virtual works of art. Awed, Tripoli could not help but feel as though he and his fellow police officers had clumsily stumbled into a hallowed place, a church in which the high priest had just been senselessly murdered.

"What did you find?" asked Sisler bending down to enter the hut.

"Oh?" said Tripoli, startled out of his reverie.

"Get a load of these, will you," said Sisler, grabbing up one of the volumes and thumbing roughly through it. "Looks like it was written by some monks or something."

"Hey, take it easy!" Tripoli pulled the book away from Sisler and cradled it tenderly in his large hands. "It's evidence."

Tripoli kept moving around the hut.

"What are you looking for?"

"I don't know. I just got this vague feeling that I'm missing something—hey, get me a light," he said. When Sisler came back with a flashlight, Tripoli found it. Hanging from a wooden peg on the wall was a whistle. It was red and white and made of plastic.

"The sheep," said Tripoli as they were packing up and getting ready for the trek out of the woods. "And these goats." Tripoli counted them. There were two ewes and three lambs, a ram circling around them; a mother goat with a pair of twins, the trio pressed tight against an old billy with a beard.

"Yeah, what about them?" asked Sisler.

A man from State Police forensics had arrived and was shooting pictures of the interior of the Hermit's hut. A couple of the guys from IPD were carrying the old man's possessions out to the road. There certainly would be a grand jury investigation, and Tripoli knew the troopers and sheriff were already figuring out ways to cover their respective and collective asses.

"We can't just leave these poor animals here," said Tripoli.

The creatures still seemed terrified from all the commotion. They made him think of Danny. Leaving them would be like abandoning the boy here in the forest. How was he ever going to explain to Danny what they had done to the old man?

"Why not?" said Sisler. "Let them just eat the fucking grass—or whatever they do."

"Chrissake Jerry, they're domestic animals!"

"So?"

"I'll keep them out at my place."

"Yeah? Okay. How we gonna get 'em there?"

"I don't know," muttered Tripoli, preoccupied. "Get one of the rookies. Billy Van Ostrand's got a big four-wheeler, doesn't he? "

"Oh, the poor old man," said Sandy.

"He had it coming to him," said Larry as the office crew hunched in front of his TV.

Molly chewed on the nail of her thumb as she watched CNN's footage of troopers and the SWAT team and the sheriff's people emerging from the woods with their equipment and dogs.

"You'd think with that army of people," said Ben, "they'd be able to capture a harmless old man without killing him."

Then there was a long shot of the old man's hut and a sheet-covered lump close to the door that she guessed was his body. A close-up of the hut, a flimsy thing made of out of nothing more than branches and a roof of what looked to be thatch. My God, she thought, this was where he held Danny through a whole miserable winter!

Tasha stuck her head in the office. "There's a bunch of reporters here to see Molly and Danny."

"We're not here," said Molly and hurried back to her office. Danny stood at the window, pressing his cheek against the glass. Gently closing the door, she came up behind him and put her face near to his.

He turned to her and his mouth came close to her ear. "But why?" he whispered, his lips quivering, "Why did they have to bother him? He never hurt anyone. I liked him. I liked being with him. And he taught me *everything.*"

As he started to cry, her own eyes welled with tears. "Darling, darling," she murmured. "My poor baby."

Danny turned and, burying his face in her breast, wept bitterly. Molly clung to him tightly, bringing her face close to his. Though she felt pity for Danny, hers were the tears of relief. It was over. The nightmare had come to an end.

"He promised me," said Danny between the sobs wracking his small frame. "He promised me that he wouldn't hurt the man. Trip promised me."

"Oh, Sweetie, I know he didn't mean to hurt him. He's a—"

"He's a liar!" said Danny now pulling away angrily. "He's a dirty liar!"

"No, Honey. You're so wrong. Trip's a good man. I don't know if you can understand right now. I know you're upset, but I think you'll come to understand things better. I've been so worried, so terribly worried. That I'd lose you again. And now there's no one who can take you away from me."

He stood staring at her.

"Why are you looking at me like that?"

He continued to stare at her unblinkingly.

"Oh, no!" she cried. She stopped breathing and her mind raced. "There are others. Is that it?"

He didn't answer. Just looked at her wide-eyed.

"Tell me! Are there?" She grabbed him by the shoulders and shook him. "Well, are there? Answer me for God sakes!"

With the back of his hand, he wiped his eyes and, looking down at his feet, murmured in the tiniest voice, "I think so."

Tripoli kept trying to reach Molly at the office, but the lines were tied up. He drove over, but the girl at the front desk said Molly had already left. Finally, he found she wasn't at the trailer either, though there a contingent of reporters had camped out waiting for her and Danny.

"I want everybody out of here!" he said, but the reporters just stared back at him. They knew their rights—or thought they did. "I'm not getting into a pissing contest with you guys. You're on private property. Get off the fucking lawn or I'm going to have you all arrested. And I mean now!"

Tripoli called for backups and three minutes later two patrol cars pulled up. Pellegrino was in one of them. Then Sisler arrived in his car.

"I want them all back. Back a hundred yards."

The reporters bitched and moaned as the officers cleared them away from Molly's trailer.

"Quite a garden she's got here," said Sisler, admiring the lush vines of squash and bushy tomato plants.

"It's the boy's," Tripoli said absently.

"No kidding. He must have planted stuff real early. His beans are way ahead of ours."

Tripoli kept pacing aimlessly in front of the trailer. Where was Molly? He needed to talk to her. And Danny. He wanted to explain what had happened. He glanced over at Danny's garden. Sisler was right. It was amazingly advanced. The first thing that struck him was the color and sheer size of the leaves. They were a startling bright green and enormous. When he gingerly stepped into the patch, he realized that the trellised vines supported by old branches created a space shielded from the rest of the trailers, a kind of mystical, fragrant space that seemed a world away from the squalor of the park. This from a little boy, he marveled.

Then he noticed the arrangement. Danny had planted his vegetables in groups, his eggplants sat clustered with potatoes. Shallow rooting onions sat side by side with peppers. Tripoli's father had been an avid gardener, and this was precisely what he had sworn by: companion planting. Danny had even known what to do with the marigold seeds Tripoli had left. The bright yellow blossoms formed a protective ring around the garden, warding off bean beetles and nematodes and cabbage worm.

Hastily scribbling a note, Tripoli called out to Pellegrino.

"Do me a favor and stay put, okay?" He tore the paper from his pad. "And give this to her if she comes back," he said.

A few minutes after Tripoli left, Molly drove into the park and was beset upon by the crowd of cameramen clogging the road. Two officers cleared a way for her car and, when she reached her trailer, Pellegrino handed her Tripoli's note.

She lead Danny into the trailer and a minute later she was back out in front with her phone, anxiously pacing back and forth.

"I never forget to turn on my radio," Tripoli said. He was just driving out of town and heading to his farm in Newfield. "When I'm in the car, I can't have both radios on—they interfere with each other. You get feedback when you transmit. But as soon as I step out, I always, *always* turn on my mobile." His sounded frazzled, unhinged, as if he were ready to cry. This wasn't the Tripoli she knew. "If I had just had the brains to turn the goddamn thing on, this would never have happened. Never!"

"Listen," she said in a clipped voice. "I don't feel guilty. And I don't see why you should, either. I don't give a shit if they're all dead."

What she said stopped him short. "All?"

"There are others!"

"Others?"

"I thought it was just the old man. Get rid of him and—"

"What are you talking about?"

She told him what had happened.

"Did Danny actually see other people out there?"

"Yes. No. I don't know. He won't talk. Just that there were others."

"I'm coming over."

"No way!" she said. "You're the last person in the world he wants to talk to."

"Oh damn, I really fucked up, didn't I?"

"No you didn't," she kept insisting. "What happened is right. He deserved it."

"No one deserves that.'"

"The others," she said, coming full circle. "They could be any-body. Anywhere."

"Let me at least—"

"No!" she all but shouted. "Stay where you are. Everybody should just leave Danny alone."

The sun, a blazing globe, seemed enormous, dramatic, brighter and bigger than he could ever recall. Winding up the drive leading to his hilltop house, it flooded his house and barn with a brilliant hue of reddish yellow, inflaming the colors and making the place look as though it were stage-lit.

Set against a backdrop of dense, dark woods, the old Greek Revival looked better than he knew it was with its rundown barn and neglected five acres. It had lots of "possibilities," as Kim used to say. But the paint was peeling and part of the roof was missing, a tarp held down with boards the only protection from storms. It needed just about everything: new siding, gutters, interior walls. Yeah, it had possibilities, endless possibilities for work. A place like this craved a family, not a single, divorced cop who was hardly ever around to take care of it or enjoy it, he thought bitterly.

Yet, against his better judgment, he had hung on to the property. Abutting the Connecticut Hill wilderness area, it possessed a sense of space and tranquility. Returning here at the end of the day, Tripoli ruminated as he bounced up his potholed drive, he could leave behind the city and all its problems. He had always hoped that Molly would one day come out here with the boy, live with him, marry him. Hoped.

Things now, however, just seemed to be going from bad to worse. Since the day that Danny had returned, he could feel Molly slipping away. And now, now he had let Danny down. Tripoli wondered if he could ever repair the damage he had done to the boy's trust. He thought about Danny's need to be outdoors and now he understood it perfectly. The way he felt, Tripoli didn't care if he ever set foot again in that station house. What had transpired today sickened him, made him ashamed of being a cop. A peaceful old man had been killed. And in his doggedness he had been the catalyst, the one who kept instigating the other agencies to take action; he had led that trigger-happy pack right to the old guy's doorstep. And then—at the most critical moment—carelessly let his attention lapse.

When he got out of the car, Tripoli heard the shouts of men in the field mingling with the forlorn cries of the sheep and goats locked in his old barn. Billy Van Ostrand's truck stood near the kitchen door caked with mud. Sisler and Van Ostrand were out in the meadow trying to tackle a billy goat that kept making end-runs around them.

"Christ, you'll never get him like that!" snapped Tripoli coming up behind them, "You've got to use your brains—not brute force."

"Well," said Sisler brushing off his clothes. "What do you say we let you use your brains?"

"Fine," said Tripoli. "I'll take care of this."

A moment later he regretted his brusqueness. "I didn't mean to jump down your throat like that. I really appreciate the help."

"Yeah, any time," said Sisler, hardly hiding his sarcasm, "Just say the word."

Young Van Ostrand, the knees of his uniform soaked with ooze, looked a little disgusted himself. "Got a hose so I can wash out the truck?" he asked tersely as Tripoli walked them back down the hill. "It's new. Used to be, at least."

It took nothing more than a bucket of grain and a measure of patience to entice the goat back to his friends. After he was sequestered in the barn, Tripoli went down to the local Agway. Talking his way into the just-closed store, he went right to the steel posts.

"I'll need a few dozen of these. And what have you got in the way of fencing?" he said moving quickly. "Got anything with woven wire?"

He next found a big trough. "I'll take this, too."

With the clerk's reluctant help, he managed to tie a couple of big rolls of the fencing to the roof of his car. And even as the two jockeyed the trough into the trunk, Tripoli kept thinking about the "others." A cult, he wondered? Or had Danny just been imagining others? Finally, he tossed two sacks of cracked corn into the rear seat, then, tying down the lid of the trunk with a bungie cord, took off.

With his car nearly scraping bottom, he headed out the Trumansburg Road toward the hospital, recalling images of the old Hermit lying in front of his hut. He remembered what Danny had said, about laws, human laws. Justice? The whole thing was sickening.

As he drove onto the hospital grounds overlooking the lake, his mind went back to the hut. So perfectly constructed, it had been more like a nest than a house. He thought about how much the old man had taught Danny, thought about those old hand-lettered books, those beautifully illustrated texts, and felt like a grave robber who had stumbled upon an ancient find.

The medical examiner's office sat secluded in the basement of the main building, in the rear behind the labs. Phil Yerka, the M.E., was in his office with Jimmy Teeter, who had flown in with the old Hermit's body. Teeter, settled in for the long haul, was sitting off to one side, his feet propped up on a desk. He was reading one of Yerka's hunting magazines, a cup of coffee perched in his lap. Yerka was at his desk, filling out papers. He glanced up at Tripoli, lifting his bushy, gray eyebrows in acknowledgment. The place smelled of formalin and antiseptic. Usually it didn't bother Tripoli, but today it made him queasy.

"Hey, Jimmy," he asked, "You got someone lined up to cover for you on the next shift?" Tying up precious manpower around the clock for a dead body seemed like an awful waste, but he didn't make the rules.

"They'll be sending up Paolangeli tonight," said Teeter, looking up.

"And the prints?"

"We took 'em already. I was thinking that I'd bring them down when Paolangeli relieves me. That fast enough?"

"Yeah, sure. No big rush at this point, is there?" he said, a note of sadness creeping into his voice.

"Hey, how's the farming going?" asked Teeter with a knowing grin. One thing about the department: gossip spread fast. But Tripoli wasn't in the mood for jokes and he turned to Yerka. "What's with the autopsy?" he asked.

Yerka got up and stretched. Standing, he was more than a good head taller than Tripoli. When he took off his glasses, his eyes looked sunken and owl-like. "Day after tomorrow," said the pathologist. "Might be late in the morning. Around eleven, say? I've got a slew of other bodies lined up. You want to be present, Trip? Of course, we'll videotape it for posterity."

"Nah, I think I prefer to catch the movie," said Tripoli in a wan attempt at humor. He couldn't bear the thought of seeing the old man split up the middle and disemboweled, his brain and liver lying in a pan.

"You want some coffee?"

Tripoli thought about it.

"You look like you need it," Yerka added kindly. "Come on, my treat."

They walked to the hospital cafeteria and each got a coffee and a cheese Danish. It was only when he took a bite that Tripoli realized he hadn't eaten a thing since early morning. It had been a hell of a long day. He glanced around. A group of nurses who were on break sat at a nearby table gossiping and laughing. A young guy with a stethoscope slung around his neck sat down and joined them, and they all laughed at something he said. Tripoli was in a foul mood. Even here, he noticed, the place smelled of hospital. He tried eating without breathing through his nose.

"So what the hell happened out there?" inquired Yerka, finally.

"Don't ask," Tripoli played with the empty Styrofoam cup, breaking it up into little pieces. "They were out of fucking control. All these chiefs and no Indians. Every asshole with his finger on a trigger. I think they were dying for an adrenal rush, maybe some target practice, too."

Tripoli told Yerka how someone had lobbed in gas, twice. How the old man had never even coughed.

"Yeah, that's what Tecter was telling me," said the doctor.

"And?"

"Well," said Yerka with a lift of his heavy eyebrows, "I took a quick look when the body came in. There was no mucus at all. Nothing in the nose or throat. Clean. And he looks like he was a healthy guy—for his age."

"Do you think he had a heart attack maybe?" he asked.

"It's always a possibility. But I'm not God. I've got to do the autopsy first."

"I'm just speculating, that's all."

"A little prematurely, I'd say. Give me a day."

"Sure. Sure." Tripoli scooped up the pieces of the broken cup. "But…well…I just keep thinking about this. It's got me stymied. Everything about it. Everything!" He was thinking, too, about Danny. The boy popping up after six months in the woods with the old man.

"Obviously you're taking this hard."

"*Obviously?* What are you talking about?" he sat up straight.

"Hard? I'm fine!"

"Trip, how many years have we known each other?"

Tripoli couldn't even begin counting. Yerka had been the M.E. since he had started with IPD, and that was almost twenty years ago.

A couple of young doctors still in scrubs came in and got in line for some food. Tripoli caught the nurses stealing glances in their direction. It was always interesting the way women sized men up. He thought of Molly as he watched the men get their meal, then shifted his eyes back to Yerka. "Do you think," he began, "think that the old man could have died just by holding his breath?"

"Yeah, sure," said the pathologist with an indulgent laugh. "Have you ever tried it? Go on, let me see you hold your breath. I'll be back and check on you in a half hour." He got to his feet. "I don't know about you, but I've still got some real work to get done today."

Tripoli followed Yerka out of the cafeteria and down the corridor toward the labs and his office.

"What about someone willing himself dead?"

"Trip, you're moving way out of my realm. Listen, when I'm ready to retire, I'll put that on a death certificate: 'Resolved themselves dead.' Then they'll cart me off to Willard Psychiatric Center and I'll have a nice vacation." He laughed boisterously, then caught himself when he saw how serious Tripoli remained. "Come on, man," he said taking hold of Tripoli's shoulder. "Pull yourself together. This is not exactly the first corpse you've brought me."

Danny was so miserable he refused dinner.

"I'm not sitting down!" he said standing by the table with folded arms. "And I'm not eating. I don't like this kind of store food. And I don't have to eat it and nobody can make me!"

"But, Honey, you have to eat. You haven't had anything since—"

"I'm not eating until they bring him back! I want to talk to my friend. I want to see him." He shoved his lower lip out and then started to cry again.

"But, Darling," Molly moved to comfort him, but he pulled abruptly away. "I know it must be horrible for you, but there's no way—"

"I want to see him," he said, staring at the floor and continuing to weep.

"Probably right at this moment he's in heaven, happy and—"

Danny stamped his foot on the floor. "No he's not! I want to talk to him!"

Finally, she got him to sit at the table. She held a glass of juice to his lips and reluctantly he started to drink. First a few sips. Then he took hold of the glass and emptied it in a series of quick gulps. Molly pretended not to notice. She made a melted cheese sandwich and fed Danny morsel by morsel, all the while keeping up a distracting chatter.

After he had eaten, his mood seemed a bit more elevated.

She turned on the tub faucets, put in some bubble bath, and filled the tub with hot water.

"What's this?" he asked, his eyes lighting up when he discovered the billowing mounds of suds.

She let him play in the tub, made a white beard and mustache for herself that got him laughing. "Make one for me, too!" he exclaimed and then giggled when he stood and saw himself in the mirror.

Molly sat on the seat of the commode watching him play.

"The others," she ventured cautiously.

"Huh?" he looked up at her.

"The others. With the old man. Did you see them?"

"No," he said, and scooping up a huge handful of suds and piling them on his head. "Hey, do I look silly like this?"

"So," Molly persisted, "how do you know that there are any?"

"I dunno," gathering up more suds and heaping them too on his head. "He just talked about them."

chapter sixteen

"There's plenty of blame to go around," wrote Wally Schuman in an *Ithaca Journal* editorial that appeared in the early morning edition. "Had there been a little less haste and a bit more coordination by police agencies, one poor soul who lived in the woods would still be alive today."

"It's simply horrible," said Kelly Scutt, leaning across the aisle of pumps at Chuck's Mobil as she filled up the tank of her SUV.

"Imagine being gassed to death in your own home," said Carla Shaeffer, cleaning her windshield.

"Like a bunch of Nazi storm troopers," said old Marv Firestein, who had just pulled up in his Jetta and caught the tail end of their conversation. Born in a concentration camp in Poland, he knew what he was talking about.

"The old man was extraordinary," Kelly raised her face skyward. "He gave the boy all kinds of magical gifts. To see things that no one else can see."

"I heard he can predict the future."

"And heal sick people just with his touch," added Chuck, wiping his greasy hands on a rag as he stepped away from the repair bay to join the conversation.

"The world's going to hell in a handbasket," said Jeff Potter climbing out of his Mustang convertible. "And the old man knew how to save it. And us."

"And for that he deserved to die?" asked Carla.

"Everybody who hears about this is simply appalled!" added Kelly.

Carla dipped her squeegee back into the soapy water. "But I don't know what we can do."

"We have to let the authorities know." Marv dug through his worn wallet hunting for his credit card, then ran it through the pump. "Protest so this never happens again!" he said, getting authorization and lifting the nozzle.

The reaction among the cops in town was ostensibly different.

"Maybe the Hermit should have opened a daycare center," said Ron Weaver, leader of the SWAT team. He was sitting with another off-duty trooper in the dimly lit The Wooden Nickel Bar off Meadow Street working on his fourth beer. "You know, you drop your kid off for six months!"

"How many Hermits does it take to screw in a light bulb?" asked Sheriff's Deputy Wayne Pruitt, who had been part of the assault force. "None. There's no electricity in the woods!"

Tripoli spent the day on his farm. He laid out a section around the barn and then, picking up a heavy sledge, pounded in one post after another, the sharp ring of steel on steel punctuating the silence. The roll of woven wire was heavy, and he became bathed in sweat when he unrolled it, wrestling it down the line of vertical supports. He hadn't labored on the land in years, and he had forgotten how satisfying the simple act of building a fence could be. He thought of the days off he had spent in a stupor on the couch, watching grown men beating their heads against each other on TV.

Lured by the perspiration that dripped from his face, flies buzzed around him, but he remained unfazed. From inside the barn came the bleating and restless hooves of the flock; and when he stopped to wipe the sweat from his brow, he could see little furry snouts poking through the slats, pairs of curious eyes watching him. As he labored on, unsettling thoughts of the old man returned. There was far more to all this than he could fathom. Who was this peculiar old man? Why had he kept Danny? Where in the world did he come from? The prints, of course, might be the key.

Finally, in the late afternoon, he took a break. He ate a bologna sandwich and had a cool beer, lay down on the couch for a few minutes of rest and fell deeply asleep. By the time he awoke it was evening. He reached for the phone near the couch and called Molly. She was already home from work.

"How's Danny taking it?"

"He seems a lot better. I got him eating. We ate some of the peas and spinach from his garden and that made him very proud and happy," she said. "He's working in his garden again—and that's always a good sign." She glanced out the window to check on him. Danny had gathered more sticks from the woods in the back and was building small teepee-like structures to support his tomatoes.

"And he's still angry at me?" he asked, stretching and stifling a yawn.

"He doesn't talk about you. Doesn't want to. Or about the Hermit. What's odd is that he refuses to believe that the old man is dead."

"Maybe it's just as well," said Tripoli.

There was a long silence on the phone.

"And you?" he asked, finally.

"Hanging in there. Trying to." Molly exhaled a long breath. "What I said about being glad he was dead. I didn't really mean that."

"I know you didn't."

"I don't want to wish anybody dead. And I just don't want to keep worrying. But if there are others," she said finally, "then I'm back to square one. I can't turn my back. They could be anywhere.

Anybody. Not just living somewhere in the woods, but people right here in town. My neighbors. My—"

"Hey, slow down," he said. "Did Danny see other people when he was out there?"

"He says no."

"So how do you know—"

"The Hermit talked to him about others."

"Okay. Supposing there are others. Or were others."

"Huh?"

"Maybe there were others—before him. Who says they're now living?"

"Then why would he talk about them? I don't get it, Trip. What are you thinking?"

"Frankly," he paused, "I don't know. I just don't think you have any basis for panic. You're starting to worry about things that may be pure conjecture."

"You think so?" She wanted some fragment of hope.

"Sure!" he said, trying to reassure her.

A few minutes later he roused himself and went back out to the barn. He stretched a section of fencing, yanking on it with all his weight until the buckles and bows were gone, then wired it tight. He moved on from section to section, but always there was that lingering sense of loss and grief and guilt hanging over him, muting the pleasure he took in his labor. There was no way to deny it; he had broken his solemn promise to the boy. They had hurt and killed the old Hermit.

The lingering light of the summer evening was golden and seemed to last forever. By the time he finally had a section of deep grass enclosed at the mouth of the barn, the sun was below the horizon. He slid open the barn door, moved away, and sat down to watch. "Come on, boys and girls," he coaxed. "Nothing to worry about. You're home."

Cautiously, in the soft blue light of the evening, they began to emerge—the bold billy goat leading the way, then a ewe with her lambs. They looked around, sniffed the air. He counted. There were nearly a dozen of them all told. Eleven to be exact.

Tripoli filled the trough with water and gave them a generous helping of corn. He took a quick shower and shave and then headed for town. Whether they wanted it or not, Tripoli felt he needed to be near Molly and Danny.

Tripoli was coming in from Newfield, cutting through the downtown, when he spotted the large crowd moving slowly up the road that overlooked the eastern shore of the lake. He couldn't believe his eyes. There must have been more than three hundred people assembled, carrying little candles, their hands sheltering the fragile flames.

He circled them, drove ahead, then pulled off far to one side where he could observe without being noticed. He got out of his car, leaning against the open door, and watched as the procession snaked its way towards him. There were men and women, even children in the crowd, and no one uttered a word. Though it was night, the city streets were still broiling hot; waves of heat rose up from the pavement. Without the faintest hint of a breeze, the air was so still he could make out the shuffling of hundreds of pairs of approaching feet. He scanned the nearing cortege. In its ranks were matrons from up on the Hill, laborers in coveralls, punks with spiked hair and pierced bodies, a smattering of students and professionals.

As the procession got closer, Tripoli also saw familiar faces. There was a teacher he knew from Boynton Middle School and a vice president from the Trust Company. Wally Schuman from the *Journal* was there, too, as were some of the people who worked in the Moosewood Restaurant. And there were lots of people that Tripoli didn't recognize, dressed a little too formally for locals. The women were in heels, the men is sport jackets and suits. Definitely out-of-towners, plenty of them. Downstate city types.

Tripoli kept to the shadows, watching. There was something about the procession that unnerved him. It felt as if the people in their silence were accusing him of killing the Hermit. Having locked his car, he followed at a distance, slipping from one dark area of the streets to another.

In the end, as he suspected, the long line of people snaked their way into Molly's trailer park, where the crowd coalesced into a tight but silent throng near Molly's trailer.

Someone started singing "Amazing Grace," and soon everyone joined in. Those who didn't know the words just hummed along.

"What's that?" asked Danny, looking up when he heard the singing voices.

"Sounds like some kind of religious service," said Molly. When she peered out the window, she couldn't believe the number of people squeezed in the small grassy space. The neighbors from the other mobile homes, she saw, were leaning out their windows as well, staring curiously.

Then there was a knock. Molly opened the door to find Wally Schuman on the front steps.

"We're all very upset," he said with lowered eyes, his hands clasped together. "About what happened to the old man."

"Yes, I understand," said Molly. Some of the voices were now singing in harmony, high and low merging into a consonance that was quite beautiful. "I…We…Danny and I…" Danny was at her side, his head cocked listening to the voices.

"Maybe Danny could join our memorial for a moment? It would be nice if…" Schuman trailed off.

Uncertain, Molly turned to Danny.

"People want to express their concern about what happened to your friend," said Schuman, kneeling down in front of Danny.

"Okay," Danny nodded. He stepped forward and Molly

followed, grasping his hand tightly in hers. Danny followed Schuman as the crowd parted to let the trio into their midst, then closed in on them until they were surrounded in the darkness by a sea of flickering candles.

When the song ended, there was a long moment of silence, and in the air hung a palpable, rising sense of anticipation.

Molly gripped Danny's hand yet tighter. Her palm, she realized, was wet.

"Say something," called a voice from the crowd.

"Tell us…tell us about him," murmured a young girl, stooping down so close to Danny that Molly instinctively pulled him back.

The crowd tightened, all eyes on Danny. Molly clung to him.

"Look, it's getting late and I think I'd better…" said Molly, trying to edge her way out. She pushed against two of the young people directly in front of her, and though they tried to move out of the way, the throng behind refused to budge. All she could see was a wall of faces illuminated fitfully by the lights. "Please, do you think you could…?"

Molly began to panic. But when she looked down at Danny, she saw there was not the slightest hint of fear on his face.

By now Tripoli had started moving in. But it was hard for him to penetrate without creating a fuss. He stopped deep in the knot of people, watching, uncertain how to proceed, how to oppose the will that held the crowd.

"Let the boy speak!" cried out an elderly man leaning on a cane.

"The boy!" called another, craning for a view above the forest of heads.

"Danny!"

There was a hungry, needy look in the people's faces that frightened Molly. Thoughts of the "others" flashed through her mind and she drew Danny tight to her side.

Wally Schuman held up his hands and gradually the people fell silent. Bending down, he whispered something into the boy's ear. Danny nodded and then he lifted Danny up, Molly still holding on to his hand as Schuman hoisted him high on his tall shoulders so all could view him.

From his vantage, Tripoli could see how the mere appearance of the boy stirred the crowd, as if the people had taken a collective deep breath. Tripoli tried to imagine what might have developed if Danny had remained with the Hermit, stayed until he was "ready."

"What do they want?" whispered Danny, holding on to Schuman's head for support.

"Just say something," he urged.

Everybody waited.

"Go on," Schuman appealed.

Finally, his eyes sweeping the crowd, Danny spoke. "They should have left my friend alone!"

Heads nodded up and down the lines. "Yes, yes," the people agreed.

"He was nice to me, and he knows many things. Important things."

"What did the old man tell you?" asked a nearby woman with long braids.

"What did he teach you?" asked a teenage girl with braces.

"What are we supposed to do?" asked the woman with braids.

Danny looked at her. Looked at the others. The people around him seemed genuinely worried, a bit frightened. Danny tilted his head. "He said that the whole world's in trouble."

"Yes."

"Yes."

"Yes!"

Tripoli suddenly thought back on all the calamities he had been reading about in the papers, the floods and droughts, crop failures and fires; he recalled the extreme cold of the previous winter, the

unprecedented snow that had buried the town, then the constant
rains and heat of this summer, the strange weather patterns he had
himself been witness to without making the connections. What if,
he thought, as the people around him started shushing, what if the
doom and gloom were not the figments of alarmists' imagination?
What if the old man had been right? And these signs had been fore-
warnings of impending calamity?

The crowd settled down, became so expectantly still that Molly
could hear the distant rumble of the coal train leaving the power
plant halfway up the lake. This was no good, she thought. Why can't
they just leave us alone? "Danny," she said, trying to get his attention, but he didn't seem to hear her. She squeezed his hand, so hard
she must have been hurting him, but he continued to stare out at the
crowd.

"And we're supposed to?" prompted Schuman.

"Listen," uttered Danny. "Just listen."

"Listen…Listen…" His word spread, sweeping back and forth.

"But you have to *hear*, not just listen. That's what my friend
taught me."

"Listen to *what?*" asked a serious young man with glasses.

Danny looked surprised, as if mystified by the power of his own
words. "We have to listen to the earth." A faint smile crossed his face
as if he were remembering something.

"And what do you hear when you listen?" called out an old,
creaky voice.

"I hear…" replied Danny, cocking an ear, "I hear the earth crying." He squinted in concentration. "And…and I hear a storm." His
eyes went wide. "A big, bad storm."

"Where?"

"Here!" he cried and the crowd pushed in so tight that Molly
had trouble breathing. She could smell and taste the mingled breath
of the people, and it felt as though they wanted to consume Danny.

Enough, thought Tripoli. Enough!

Elbowing his way through the knot of people, he called for reinforcements.

"Come on, let me through. Excuse me. Excuse me." To Tripoli it was all beginning to pull together: the hut and its contents, the boy's uncanny gifts, his ability to see what others were blind to, hear what other mortals could not detect, his potential to affect people and the world. Someone had to realize it, understand its far-reaching implications; someone had to protect the boy, help him attain his potential—if it was not already too late. When he reached the nucleus of the crowd, he pulled Danny from Schuman's shoulders, grabbed Molly by her arm, and propelled them briskly through the crowd, the wail of sirens now filling the air.

"It's that cop," said someone, leveling a finger at Tripoli and nearly poking him in the eye.

"They murdered the old man!"

"Killer!" cried an anonymous voice. Someone grabbed the back of his shirt and he could hear it tear as he jerked loose.

"Murderers!"

There was hissing and booing, some in the crowd turning mean. As the first squad car was pulling into the park, Tripoli guided Molly and Danny through the last of the angry throng, rushing them back toward the trailer.

"Thank God you're here," said Molly, as the heckling trailed off in the distance.

"Hurry. Go inside," he said, holding the door for them.

Danny ignored him.

"Go already!" he ordered.

Tripoli pushed in behind them, then closed the door and locked it. A moment later they could hear the shouts of the cops dispersing the crowd.

"Ooohhh," sighed Molly. She pulled a series of long deep

breaths, then her shoulders slumped forward.

Danny stood with his arms folded, his back turned to Tripoli.

"Geez," said Tripoli, "what the hell were you doing going out into a mob?"

"I wasn't really thinking. Their singing sounded so…And Danny…You okay, Honey?" She bent down, stroked his head.

Danny nodded, but refused to turn around to face Tripoli.

"So, Daniel," he said, trying to catch the boy's attention as another squad car screeched up in front of the trailer, its turret flashing red in the windows. "You're mad at me, right?"

Slowly, Danny turned his head, looked up at him, his eyes narrowed to wrathful slits. "You're a liar," he grumbled low, his voice laced with indignation, "and I'm *never* going to move to your horrible place!" Then he jerked his head away and marched back into the bedroom, slamming the door behind him.

Tripoli could be moody at times—colleagues often reminded him—but depression was uncharacteristic of him. What he needed, he told himself, was some space, some unstructured time to sort things out. He had not had any significant leave in years, not since Kim had left him.

Later that night, while the city was deep in sleep, he drove to the station and went through the procedures of taking an extended leave, cashing in all the accumulated sick days and vacation. Then he turned in his service revolver, shut off his radio, and went back home to Newfield.

That night he slept erratically, repeatedly waking up and then lapsing back into a sleep punctuated by bursts of intense dreams. Once he found himself locked in a dark cabinet and couldn't get out. Another time the billy goat was caught with its horns wedged in the mesh of the new fence. None of it made much sense.

He was sitting at his kitchen table the next morning, watching the animals grazing, when the phone rang.

"I tried calling you at the station, but they told me that you're going to be out on leave."

"Yeah. I felt I needed a break. Needed some time to do some stuff."

"Like?"

"Like thinking," he said. His voice sounded odd to Molly, flat and lacking its usual edge.

"Okay," she said. "Thinking about what?"

"I'm thinking about life and death."

This was not the Lou Tripoli she knew. "Danny'll get over it. He didn't really mean to sound that nasty. I told him afterward that you don't call people liars."

"It's not just that."

"The old man, huh?"

"Yeah, that, but a lot of other things, too," he admitted.

"Tell me," she said.

"What can I tell you?"

Molly tried to imagine him at the other end of the line, but couldn't, not in his present state. It worried her hearing him like this. "It's us, right? I know our relationship hasn't been exactly stellar. Not a lot of fireworks. But I'm just so exhausted these days. Try to—"

"It's not just that, either."

"Okay, then what is it?" she urged.

"I suppose I'm just thinking and evaluating everything."

"Like?"

"Like my life," he said with a grim laugh. "You know, I spend all my time chasing down people. Bad guys. Two days ago I was up in Collegetown busting some poor suckers who had some weed and mushrooms instead of being out at that hut. I was so focused on bullshit that I couldn't even remember to…The old man would still be alive today if…"

"You're being hard on yourself."

"No, I think I'm beginning, for the first time in my fucked-up life, to do what Daniel said last night. To listen."

"Oh…" said Molly. Oh, God, she thought, Not him, too. Was everyone in town losing it?

"And I'm wondering. I'm hassling the bad guys, but how bad are the bad guys? They're using drugs. But what are a lot of these drugs? They're Prozac for the poor. Most of the people I hassle are impoverished and depressed. They're self-medicating is what I think. And what am I doing in all this, dragging in potheads? I'm not doing anybody a favor. I'm not making the world a better place. I've got the feeling I've wasted precious time. You know, Molly…"

"Yes?"

"I became a cop because I really wanted to help people. Can you believe that?"

"Of course," she said softly.

"Who am I helping, huh?"

"Me," she said. "Me and my boy."

chapter seventeen

It was the sharp crack of thunder slicing through the early hours of morning that startled Molly out of her sleep. The wind-driven rain was flooding the windows and the trailer was rocking on its foundation like a ship pitching on a stormy sea. The howling wind kept gathering in intensity. By the time she was on her feet looking for Danny, the roar of wind had built to a deafening pitch. It sounded as if a huge freight train was running right through the middle of her home.

She found Danny at the kitchen window and dragged him under the table as the sound of metal crashing against metal and wood snapping filled the air. She could make out people screaming as the sky flashed with a blinding brightness and a bolt of thunder exploded with an impact that hit her in the chest.

"It's okay," she said, clutching Danny.

He seemed more curious than frightened. "I want to see," he kept saying, trying to squirm loose.

Then, but a minute later, the rain trailed off into a drizzle, the sky began to lighten, and the dawn was now filled with an eerie silence.

Molly relaxed her grip. Danny slipped through her hands, opened the door, and stepped outside, the damp trailing wind blowing back his hair. "It's okay now," he said, his eyes on the sky. "It's gone." He stepped barefoot out into the squishy yard.

Molly was right behind him.

The trailer park was littered with debris; tree limbs and toys and garbage strewn all over the place. The other residents of the park, looking stunned, were staggering out of their homes. The shed behind the Dolphs' trailer was nothing but a heap of rubble, two trailers lay on their side, and people were helping the families out of the windows. There was blood streaming down Charlotte Moody's forehead. Her daughter was cradling an arm and crying. A limb had been spiked right through the windshield of the Pakkala's new truck. A tree had toppled and crushed a new Grand Am. A dead dog lay in the road and the other animals in the park were still cowering in the corners.

"It was a tornado!" exclaimed the man who lived in the big double wide near the entrance.

"Tornado?" said Mrs. Dolph. Her hair was wet and plastered to her head as if it were a skullcap.

Tornado? thought Molly. They had them in the Midwest. The South. But never, ever, in Ithaca.

"I was going to work and I saw it," continued the man. He looked almost as if he were going to cry. "A funnel. I couldn't believe it!"

"I think it touched down north of us," cried a woman. "Did you hear it? It sounded like cars crashing."

Molly could make out the sound of fire and rescue trucks moving in all directions.

"The boy," said someone pointing at Molly's child.

All eyes went immediately to Danny.

"He knew there was a storm coming!"

"He made it come!" cried Mrs. Dolph, leveling a finger at Danny.

"Don't be ridiculous," said Molly and hustled Danny back into the trailer.

"You're going to Rosie's today," Molly announced as she put down the phone. "How does that sound?"

"Much better than your office." Danny had his hand deep in a box of Raisin Bran and was digging out single raisins. Other than that, he refused breakfast.

"And nobody will know you're there. We don't have to worry about people bothering you."

"They're not bothering me."

He still seemed subdued, a bit morose, and she wondered how long it would take before he forgot the old man.

Molly called the office and got Ben on the line. Somebody had left a window ajar and there was a flood in the copy room, a section of roof shingles had been peeled off. Otherwise, things were operational.

"You should see what happened in Lansing and up by the mall," said Ben. "I've never seen the likes of it—and I've lived here almost forty years. A *tornado?*"

Molly gathered up her briefcase and waited while Danny packed some of his books into his knapsack. Locking the trailer, she had just turned to go to her car when she bumped into an older couple with a young boy nestled between them. The boy was about Danny's age. He was wearing a wool hat and though it covered his head it was evident that he was hairless. His skin was deathly white except for splotchy blue bruises on his arms and legs, and his eyes had such a feverish look that Molly had to restrain herself from overtly pulling Danny away from the boy.

"Excuse me," said the man, politely. Though it was hot and sticky outside he was wearing a jacket and tie. "If I could ask a favor…"

The woman, dressed in a flowery tent of a dress that could hardly hide her obesity, had her tiny eyes riveted on Danny.

"This is my wife Adelaide. And our boy, Tim."

"Hello," said Adelaide. She had an arm around the boy and it looked as if she was supporting the child to keep him from toppling over.

"Hi," said Tim It hurt Molly just to see them.

"Tim's got leukemia," the man blurted out.

The trio stood blocking her path. "He's gone through chemo twice," began the woman and then suddenly her tiny eyes welled with tears. The man, though struggling to hide his emotions, was now dabbing at his eyes as well. "And it didn't work. He still has got these fevers and his white count…"

Danny silently watched the exchange, intrigued, his eyes shifting from the family to Molly and back again. Molly looked for a way around them to her car.

"Look, I'm terribly sorry, really. But I don't see what I can…" she tried to go on but couldn't. She suspected what was coming.

"If Danny could just…" said the mother, outstretched hands imploring Danny.

"Just touch Tim," added the father.

"It's not going to do anything," said Molly. "Believe me."

"What can it hurt?" asked the man. "He's not contagious."

"No. No. It's not that," objected Molly.

"Please," said the woman, "I'm begging you as one mother to another. I'll get down on my knees, if that will—" and she struggled to lower herself to the ground.

"No! Don't!" cried Molly mortified as she caught the woman by her elbows and held her up.

"I can touch him," said Danny, and before Molly could respond, Danny had already wrapped his arms around the frail frame of the other little boy. He stood there holding him as Molly looked on awkwardly, watching the two little boys locked in an embrace.

Both parents stared down at Tim, anxiously waiting.

The boy, looking Danny in the eye, began to slowly grin.

"How do you feel?" inquired the mother.

"Tim?" asked the father bending down to get a closer look.

Then, suddenly, turning his face up to his parents, Tim broke into a big, beaming smile. "Better," said the boy, shaking his head earnestly. "I feel much better. Really!"

He did look better, thought Molly. At least happier. What the hell, she thought. "Look, I gotta run. I'm late for work."

"Oh, thank you!" cried the mother as Molly took Danny and hurried to her car.

"How can we ever repay you?" she heard the father calling after her. Molly could have sworn he was reaching for his wallet as she pushed Danny into the car and snapped on his seat belt. When the engine sprang to life on the first try, she was more than a little relieved.

As they drove to Rosie's downtown house, Molly saw a clear swath of destruction. The tornado had touched down on the Eastern Heights near Molly's trailer park. Approaching the mall, she could see how it had sliced across the western edge of the shopping center, through Sears and Hoyt's Cinema, pulverizing the buildings and scattering their contents. Everywhere, the ground was littered with heavy timbers and big sheets of corrugated steel. Clothes and toys, linens and tires and tools, whole store counters were dispersed over the near backyards, parking lots, and fields. Bras and nightgowns hung from the trees like Christmas ornaments. The power of the storm must have been beyond anything that she had ever witnessed, she thought.

Danny was fascinated by the intensity of the storm. "Look!" he said, pointing to a pair of seats from the movie theater which sat perched high in a tree as if waiting for occupants.

Molly turned on the local news as they headed down into the valley paralleling the storm's path. There was talk of numerous injuries. A still uncounted number of deaths.

"Oh, poor trees," sighed Danny, sighting the twisted remains of the old, majestic willow trees that had once lined the shore. They had been torn up by their roots and scattered as though they were flowers plucked by a cruel hand. In the marina, pleasure craft lay in sloppy heaps amidst chunks of concrete and pieces of wooden dock.

Shifting in her seat, Molly turned to Danny. "You didn't *really* know this storm was going to happen, did you?"

"Yes," he said with his childish lisp. "But not this big. Just look at that!" he motioned towards the top of West Hill; and when Molly took her eyes from the road, she saw a huge yacht perched upright on top of the hill.

"But *how* did you know?"

"I could feel it. The warming," he said, still staring in wonderment up at the big boat.

"You mean the summer?"

"No. No," he shook his head. "The earth." It was almost as if he were blaming himself.

"Okay," she said. "What are we supposed to do about it?"

He turned to her, shook his head worriedly. "I don't know," he said. "I just don't know. He never told me."

"Did you see what the storm did?" asked Rosie when they got to her place. "There's this big ship sitting on top of West Hill!"

"I saw it, too, Aunt Rosie!"

"It's just like in the Bible, Honey. Noah's ark."

"Before or after the flood?" asked Molly with a touch of sarcasm. She hoped Rosie would not be filling his head with a lot of nonsense.

Rosie laughed good-naturedly. "Well, looking on the bright side, there'll be plenty of work for masons. Ed just got called out on a big repair job." She turned to Danny, stroking his neck. "So it's just going to be you and me and the twins, Pudding."

"Okay," said Danny.

Molly stood there watching, reluctant to leave.

"So go to work already," said Rosie, finally.

"You'll be all right, Honey?" she asked Danny.

"Of course we will!" Rosie rested her hand on Danny's shoulder. "Have you had breakfast yet?"

"Yes," Danny nodded. "I had some raisins."

Molly shook her head.

"Oh, so you wouldn't want some nice hot pancakes with maple syrup and melted butter, would you?"

"I'm not that hungry, really."

After Molly left, Rosie fixed him some pancakes. "They call these silver dollars, because—"

"I know," he said, watching the butter melt in puddles that dripped down the edges of the stack.

"Go on," she coaxed.

"I'm not really hungry."

"Just give it a taste, okay? Aunt Rosie went to all this trouble and…" She poured syrup on top. "This is *real* stuff, right from the maple trees. None of this supermarket junk. Uncle Ed has this friend in Candor who's got this big farm with sugar maples." Rosie kept up a steady patter all the while shoveling food into his mouth. "It's good, isn't it?"

"Yes, Aunt Rosie," he said sweetly.

"Oh, Pumpkin," she cooed and kissed the back of his head, "I don't want you being sad like this."

"I'm okay."

"I know you liked the old man. It's terrible what happened. But, well, people don't live forever anyhow. We're here on earth for, well, like a visit, wearing our body suits. And then we just take them off and go somewhere else that's nice, too. Maybe nicer."

He gazed up and looked at her intently.

"You want to play with the babies?" she suggested when he got up from the table and went to the window to look out. A pair of deer were standing in the backyard staring at him. "Will you look at that!" said Rosie. "Deer in the middle of the city. Boy those guys aren't afraid of anything these days." A buck with a full rack leaped into the yard. "Look at him!" she exclaimed. "Isn't he beautiful?"

Danny pressed his face against the glass, and Rosie noted how the buck stepped boldly closer.

Later, he went into the nursery and held the babies while Rosie did the laundry and tried to straighten up the house. When Rosie went to check on him, Danny was talking to the babies.

"…and why couldn't people just leave him alone?" she overheard him say. "But I don't care what they say. I know he's not dead. He couldn't be dead. He promised me he wouldn't die until I was ready."

"I don't want you to panic," said Rosie when she got Molly at the office just before lunch, "but—"

"But what?" Molly held her breath.

"But I can't find Danny."

"Oh, God!" she gasped. "No!"

"I've looked everywhere around the block, but I can't go very far with the twins. And Ed's working somewhere up on—"

"I'll be right over," said Molly, grabbing her keys. She brushed right past Larry who was headed her way.

"Hey, what's up?" he called after her, but she was already out the door.

She found Rosie standing on her porch, crying and tearing at her clothes.

"I don't know how he got out," Rosie kept wailing. "First day he's here and then he disappears into thin air. And I was watching him like a hawk—you've gotta believe me! He had just helped me put the twins to sleep. I was making lunch and I looked around…and…and he was just gone!" She broke into sobs again.

Molly tried calling Tripoli at his home, but he didn't pick up. His cell phone was off, too. She tried the station, but in her panic forgot he was on leave. She called his house again. She let it keep ringing as Rosie stood behind her rattling on and on.

Finally, after a dozen or more rings, he picked up.

"Trip. You've got to help me."

The day in town was torrid again. As Tripoli pulled up on Rosie's block, Molly ran to his car, her face flushed and streaked with sweat.

"Oh, Trip!" she sighed, leaning in the window.

The air rushing in from the streets was so oppressive he felt like he was in the tropics. "Let's try not to panic on this one," he said.

Molly noticed that he had a growth of stubble on his face—which was unusual for a fastidious guy like Tripoli. He was wearing jeans and a T-shirt, and his forehead glistened with perspiration. "Look, I'm going to cruise around. You work the neighborhood. Whoever finds Danny first, calls the other. All right?" Through the open window, he handed Molly his cell phone.

"I'm sorry to have to drag you in again like this…"

"No problem," he said, "Better than sitting home and brooding. You can leave a message for me with IPD. They'll call me. I'll keep my radio on. I just don't want to call out all the troops yet, okay?"

It wasn't quite okay, but Molly had no choice.

"Stay calm. I got a hunch where to look." As she turned to hurry off, he peeled away from the sidewalk, took a right, and went east on Green Street. Running a series of red lights, he took a sharp left on Aurora and headed up the incline.

Tripoli spent a good ten minutes snaking around lower South Hill, checking backyards and alleys. Then, finally, he spotted Danny cutting up Hudson Street. Except for his sneakers, the boy didn't have a stitch of clothes on. And, sure enough, he was headed south.

Tripoli pulled up alongside the naked boy and threw the door open. "Come, hop in," he said.

Danny, ignoring him, continued moving. Tripoli switched on his lights and kept pace with him, letting the car slowly creep ahead, signaling a van behind him to pass.

"Well, where do you think you're going?" he called out the window.

"I'm not talking to you," Danny said, pouting.

"Okay, don't talk to me. Your mother just called me. She was worried. Wanted me to find you. *She* wanted to know where you're going?"

"I'm going to see the hut." The breeze was carrying the car's exhaust in his direction and Danny reacted with a grimace of pain.

"Yeah, I figured so. Come on, give me a break and get in. You're making your mother sick with worry. Is that what you want?"

Danny stopped.

"Come on, *please,* we all feel bad enough as it is." Tripoli opened the door again and finally Danny climbed in. He sat on the front seat beside Tripoli, staring straight ahead.

"So, where are your clothes?"

"I don't know." Frowning, he turned to the side window. "I forget. It was hot so I took them off."

"Well, you can't go around like that."

"Why not?"

Tripoli chuckled. He didn't have a good answer. It was so hot and sticky he wished he were naked himself. He drove down the hill and stopped at the first phone booth.

"Hey, you can relax," he said to Molly when she answered his cell phone. She was all the way up North Cayuga Street near Fall Creek. "I've got your little escapee." He looked over at Danny and smiled. Danny glared at him.

Tripoli cut across town and toward the high school. Molly had gone there, figuring that maybe the heat had gotten to Danny and he had headed for the cool waters of Fall Creek. Except for a pair of teenagers wading in the stream, the place was deserted.

As they pulled up, Molly stood waiting in the shade of a tree, her hands on her hips. Scattered at her feet lay branches broken by the storm. She was livid as she slid into the front seat, shoving Danny closer to Tripoli.

Danny peered at her sheepishly. This time it was clear she was in no mood for forgiveness. "You can't keep doing this to me!" she exploded, grabbing Danny by the arm and shaking him. "You'll get me fired. Don't you understand? And then what will we do?"

"Go easy," said Tripoli.

"Easy nothing!" she snapped.

Molly's teeth were clenched, her features hard, and Danny looked at her, puzzled, frightened, as if she were a stranger. Tripoli had never seen her angry like this, certainly not at her boy.

"Why don't you let me take him for the rest of the day," he suggested.

Molly looked at him, then turned back to Danny. "Be my guest. He's all yours. I'm getting so tired of all this."

As Tripoli drove down Cayuga Street toward her office, she stared mutely out the windshield. He could feel her wrath slowly beginning to subside.

"I'm sorry I got upset like that," she muttered later without looking at either of them.

"We understand, don't we?" Tripoli glanced over at Danny who looked small and still cowed by her fury.

"I wouldn't be so sure," she said and turned to Danny. He looked up at her, his eyes welling with innocence. "Oh God," she uttered with a sigh, and finally embraced him. "What am I going to do with you?"

Tripoli found Danny's clothes on a bench on the east side of the

Commons. He tossed the clothes to Danny in the front seat, then headed out of town, crossing the bridge spanning the inlet.

"There's a little something I want to show you," he said as the boy dressed.

"Is it a long drive in this machine?" He turned his underpants inside out and put them on, one leg at a time. "I don't like being in cars, you know."

"Not very long. Just chill out and enjoy the view." The radio in his car was clamoring about the pursuit of a suspect on foot, three cops boxing in a man who had just swiped some steaks from the supermarket. He turned it off, and the space in the car suddenly became more habitable. Daniel was certainly right about one thing, he thought, and that was silence.

"How much longer?" Danny kept asking as they cut onto Route 327. There were cows grazing out in fields, and when Danny saw them, he became less fidgety.

As they started to climb Tripoli's rock-strewn driveway, Danny suddenly spotted the animals and his face broke into a big smile.

"You got them!" Danny shouted and clapped his hands. He had the door open before Tripoli had come to a complete stop.

"Rescued them," Tripoli chuckled.

"I was scared that those policemen had..."

The animals all eagerly turned their heads to watch as Danny raced toward the barn. He squirmed through a tiny gap in the enclosure, ran straight up to the old billy who stood as if waiting for him. Wrapping his arms around the goat's neck, Danny kissed him right on the nose. Then he ran around and greeted every one of the sheep and goats, calling them by strange names. They seemed to recognize him as well. His sudden happiness was such a relief, so infectious, that Tripoli had to laugh.

Next Tripoli gave Danny a quick tour of the grounds, then took him inside to make him a sandwich. All he had on hand was a package of bologna, peanut butter, and a little moldy jelly left at the bottom of a jar. The choice was obvious. He made the boy a peanut butter sandwich and took the balogna for himself after slathering it with mayonnaise. Then he popped open a beer. When he couldn't find any milk for the boy, he made up some juice from a can of concentrate.

Danny took his sandwich and explored the house, checking out all the rooms, upstairs and down.

"This is better here," he said, coming back into the kitchen.

Tripoli took a swig of his beer. "Better than what?"

"My mother never lets me eat and walk around. I have to always sit at the table. She says I make crumbs."

"Well," said Tripoli surveying the balls of dust that had accumulated in the corners, "in this house we firmly believe in feeding the mice."

Danny looked at him. He wasn't sure if Tripoli was kidding or not. When Tripoli finally winked, he smiled. "I like mice, too."

"Well, of course. We're all God's creatures," said Tripoli. At first he said it as a joke, but when he thought about it, it rang true. Why not let the mice partake? "And they want to live like everybody else."

Danny looked at him askance.

There was a long moment of silence.

"Yeah, I know," Tripoli said finally, "a promise is supposed to be a promise."

Danny just continued to stare at him.

"Nobody meant to hurt him. Really. Least of all me."

Danny stood there with the last bite of his sandwich in his hand.

"Go on, finish up your food and we'll go out."

In town, the heat was searing, the air was perfectly still, and the fumes from the cars and factories hung in a thick haze in the valley.

In the magazine offices, the air conditioners in the windows were laboring full blast.

"What was that all about?" asked Larry as Molly sat under the vent of her air conditioner trying to dry out.

"Nothing. Just an old friend who had a problem."

"Oh," said Larry, who hardly look convinced. "You mean a *Danny* problem."

"Larry, you've got to understand."

"What I understand is that half the people in this town have lost their ever-loving minds. This mumbo jumbo with the Hermit and the boy creating storms, healing people and the —"

"I never said anything like that."

"But everybody else is saying it. And you need to put a stop to it before it gets out of control. No, it's already out of control and it's fucking up our office."

And with that he turned on his heels and left before she could try to explain.

"It's the heat," said Ben, after Larry stormed off. "It's making everybody a little crazy. Larry'll get over it. He'll be back in five minutes saying he's sorry. You'll see."

He wasn't back in five minutes, or even ten, but there was a pale man in a blue suit who was sitting in the reception area waiting to see her. He would not tell Tasha who he was, only that he was from a government agency in Washington.

"Sorry to take up your time," he said, opening a briefcase and taking out a notebook. He wore a pencil-thin mustache, and his dark hair was buzzed in a military brush cut.

"What government agency?" she asked.

"Well, I work for a number of agencies. I'm on loan you might say," he answered vaguely. "I just need to ask you a couple of questions."

"Is this about my taxes?" she asked, and he laughed, not sure if

Molly was joking.

"I've been asked to follow up on some reports we've been getting about your boy."

Molly felt her stomach slide. "Reports?"

"Nothing to worry about. The newspapers have been filled with all this stuff about your boy being able to sense the weather, predict—"

"Listen," said Molly, cutting him short. "There's been a lot of nonsense floating around."

"Well, we assumed that. But, you know, we have to follow this thing up. There are stranger things in life. We've got porpoises that can defuse mines and bees that carry messages. So you just never really know."

Molly had no idea what he was talking about, and didn't care. All she knew was that this man and whoever he represented was a threat to Danny. "Danny's just a regular, happy little boy. No extrasensory perception. He doesn't heal by laying on of hands. He can't read minds. He doesn't—"

"Well, that's what we figured," he said amiably, closing his pad. "Just had to follow it up. Anyway, it was a good excuse to fly out of Washington. The heat there's been a real killer. Between the pollution and the temperatures, people have been dropping in the streets like flies. During the day the streets are like a ghost town. You should be glad you're living up in a nice, cool place like this."

Out in Newfield it was frying, too, but there was a breeze wafting across the tops of the high hills creating a sun-drenched afternoon that was still tolerable. Danny helped Tripoli carry buckets of fresh water to the animals and watched as they greedily drank. Kept busy around the animals, Danny appeared to be distracted from his grief—and his anger at Tripoli.

Tripoli found an old wooden-handled scythe in the barn, honed the blade to a razor finish, and then, with Danny trailing behind, waded out into the high meadow to a point where the grass was still dense and lush.

As they left the animals, Tripoli could feel the boy's mood steadily sinking again. Silently, he watched as Danny sauntered off, finding a cool spot under a nearby tree and plopping down in the shade. Sitting with his back propped up against the trunk, he stared glumly out at the rolling hills.

Ignoring him, Tripoli set to work and, grasping the wooden handle of the scythe, he drew the blade in a long arc, slicing neatly through the succulent growth. It fell in a neat fan-like line. Then he took another pass. And yet another. As he worked, each stroke became more fluid and Tripoli quickly developed an easy, elegant rhythm. Soon the air was filled with the smell of freshly cut pasturage. This was the quiet way that people used to work, he thought as he left in his wake a long path of flattened stalks. This was how it was done before the advent of riding mowers and weed whackers. How quiet it must have been before we had cars and planes. He glanced over at Danny who was lying under the tree, his chin cradled morosely in his hands. What could he do to get him to forgive him?

Peeling off his shirt, Tripoli set back to work. The heat of the sun soaking into his pale skin seemed to infuse him with energy and warm his soul. He had actually forgotten how good it could feel to do simple but honest labor, to be outdoors instead of cruising in mindless circles through city streets. He had almost forgotten Danny, when he heard a shout from the boy. Tripoli turned to see him leaping to his feet and making a strange, chirping noise. Danny was staring into the line of woods and then flapping his arms as though he were a bird. Tripoli watched, startled, as Danny threw himself against the tree and hugged it.

He hurried over to where the boy stood. "What's up?" he asked.

Danny's face was glowing. Tripoli scanned the field, then the edge of the neighboring woods, but could see nothing unusual.

"What happened?"

"Oh, nothing special." His eyes were now suddenly bright and untroubled, and there was a broad grin on his face.

"In that case, how's about your giving this old man a hand?"

"Sure," said Danny, and happily bounced along at Tripoli's side back to the work site.

They spent the next hour gathering grass and carrying it back to the barn. Danny, his arms laden, didn't walk, but seemed to prance, bounding across the meadow with the gait of an animal.

"Hey, Pal!" Tripoli called after him, "you're not supposed to lose half of it on the way."

The boy just laughed and kept dancing along. Tripoli had never seen him quite so happy and was at a loss to explain how his grief could have dissolved so abruptly.

The man stood in the doorway of Molly's office holding a straw hat in his hand. Tasha must have been in the ladies room. "I just gotta talk to the boy," he said. He was dressed in a heavy flannel shirt and overalls. "I just need to know when I should make my next cutting of hay. And I gotta know soon if I should plant winter wheat or—"

"Danny's not here," she said, ushering him towards the door, "and he doesn't know about farming."

"But I heard—"

"Well, you heard wrong." said Molly, hoping to shuffle him out the door before Larry saw him. The farmer stood with his feet rooted wide on the ground as if he wasn't going to budge. "Look, if you don't leave now I'm going to call the police."

All afternoon people tried to get ahold of Molly—or actually Danny. They tied up the phones or just planted themselves in the outside office. They urgently needed to see the boy, to ask him questions about their future. The paralyzed wanted to walk, and the blind wanted to see. Stock and commodity traders wanted tips for the futures markets. A poultry farmer offered to hire Danny because his hens had all but stopped laying eggs. Maybe if Danny talked to them real nice, they could increase production.

"I'd certainly be willing to share profits with you and the boy," he offered, caught up in his excitement.

Molly was beside herself with distraction. Trying to control her fear, she summoned Tasha to her desk. "I want you to field every call. If it's not about magazine business, then get rid of them. And no unwanted visitors, please Tasha, please. And whatever you do, don't give out my private number."

"You can count on me," said Tasha.

Nevertheless, somehow Wally Schuman got through on her direct line.

"I'd like to come over and see Danny."

"Well, he's not here," she answered

"Maybe later then. I could drop by your place."

"Please don't," she said, tersely.

"The boy. He knew about the storm."

"All he said was that he heard a storm. I hear storms all the time. Does that make me—"

"Look, Mrs. Driscoll. Molly. I'm not a religious nut or anything. Given what I've seen in life, I'm not sure I even believe in God. I'm strictly a newsman. I only trust what I can hear and see for myself. If you read the news or even watch the—"

"I don't have time to follow the news. I'm just trying to keep my job and—"

"...see what's going on around the world," he kept on, "Look carefully and you begin to realize that something terrible is happening."

Molly didn't know what he was talking about.

"With the weather," he added, "the climate."

"What's Danny got to do with that?" she asked. Again she could feel that queasy feeling unfolding in her stomach.

"More than just predicting that tornado, I think he—"

"Look, please…" Molly fidgeted with the cord on her phone, snarling it around her fingers.

"I think that Danny may have something important to tell people. Not just here in Ithaca. But the country. The world."

"Please," she said. "I've got to get back to work." And she hung up.

Later, when the pasturage was all in and the animals were contentedly munching away, they rested in the shade of the porch. Tripoli lay in a hammock nursing an icy beer while Danny gulped down a big glass of orange soda.

"I like the bubbles," he said. "They tickle my nose. How do they get them into the water?"

"I think they put the carbon dioxide in under pressure."

"Oh, I see," said Danny.

"You know what carbon dioxide is?"

"I think it's the stuff that plants breathe in."

Tripoli was mildly surprised. "The Old Man. He taught you that, too, huh?"

"I'm not sure," said Danny. A neighbor's cat came by and jumped up on the deck. It was a big calico and Danny crept over to it and petted it. "Maybe he did."

"You know, Daniel, I keep wondering."

"Hmmm?" The cat was now in his lap, licking Danny's fingers. Danny giggled.

"How did you get to him?"

"I walked," he said, matter-of-factly. "Oooh, feel her tongue. It's so rough."

"Was he waiting for you?"

"Huh?" He turned the cat over on its back and stroked its belly. "The Old Man?"

"Oh, not really." The cat was purring like an engine. "But he did say I was waiting to find him."

"How did you know where to go?"

He stroked the cat under its chin. "I dunno. I just did."

"He taught you a lot, didn't he?"

"Yup!"

"I mean besides reading."

"Yup!" Danny was now on all fours, pretending to be an animal. The cat, tail high, was snaking in and out between his limbs, rubbing itself against the boy. "He told me a lot of stories. And had me tell him stories, too."

"What kind of stories did you tell him?"

"About things."

"Like?"

"Oh," Danny lowered his head to rub his nose against the cat's, "he wanted to know what life was like. Things we did. You know, here. In town."

"So what did you tell him about?"

"Oh, television. He wanted to know about the things I could see on it. And video games. What my mother had learned in her school and about her computer and stuff."

The boy was suddenly opening up in a way he never had before, and Tripoli decided it was safe to gently prod him. "And what else?"

"He wanted to know about phones that didn't use wires. He had seen someone using one, but I didn't know anything about them—not then. You know, like that little black phone you always have in your pocket."

"He didn't like those things—computers and television and such—did he?"

"Oh, no, he did!" said Danny looking up. "He was very interested in them. He wanted to know *all* about them. How they worked. But I didn't know. Not yet."

"So why didn't he just come and look for himself?"

"He just didn't like being in the city with the noise and machines and stuff."

"Like you?"

"It doesn't bother me as much."

"And the stories he told you? What were they about?"

"Oh, just everything." The cat leaped off the porch and crawled underneath it. Danny jumped down and crept along the ground, peering into the darkness under the porch.

He was now out of Tripoli's vision. "Like for instance?"

"He would make up these stories. Like once he told me about a lady who lost her way. She was nice and everything, but she was at this place where there were all these roads and she was all mixed up and…and…and didn't know which one to take. She couldn't read the signs."

"You mean they were not in English?"

"No! Not like that!" his head popped into view above the edge of the porch. "The signs. The signs!"

"Oh?"

"The kind you have to look for carefully. Or listen for. They're always there. It's just that the lady didn't see them. Now where's that crazy kitty?"

When Tripoli went in to get another beer from the fridge, the phone was ringing. He hesitated, debated, then, figuring it might be Molly, picked it up.

"I've been trying to get ahold of you all day," said Sisler. Your answering machine isn't picking up. Your cell's off…Where the hell have you been?"

"Out."

"Out where?"

He sat down, leaned back in his chair far enough to reach the fridge door. The beer was sitting on the top shelf. He popped the top and took a long, thirsty drink. "Oh, just out wandering...walking and ruminating," he said with a laugh.

"Hey, are you okay?" asked Sisler.

"Sure. I'm fine. What's up?" He lifted a hand to wipe his face and noticed that it smelled pleasantly of fresh grass.

"*What's up?* Haven't you heard?"

"Heard what?"

"The body's missing."

"What body?" It took him a moment. "You mean the *Hermit?*"

"Yeah!"

"What the hell do you mean *missing?*"

"Just that. The old guy's body is gone. Disappeared."

It took all of Tripoli's effort to pull his mind out of the barnyard and back into focus. He sat up on the edge of his chair and leaned into the phone as if to cover it. Danny was on the other side of the screen door, lying on the porch, his head over the edge. He was dangling a piece of string, laughing excitedly every time the cat lunged for it.

"So when did all this happen?"

"No one knows. Yerka went to begin the autopsy and the locker was empty."

"You're kidding!" said Tripoli.

"Hey, I don't make jokes like that. And the chief is going ballistic."

"Jesus H. Christ!" uttered Tripoli.

"Yeah, exactly," said Sisler with a snort.

Tripoli was perplexed. "I don't get it. I mean, Jimmy Teeter was there from the beginning. And Paolangeli was supposed to—"

"Yup, he took over. And then Pellegrino. There was a man there right up until Yerka opened the locker."

"So somebody swiped the body?"

"You tell me how."

Tripoli didn't know what to tell him.

"Oh, and the prints!" He could almost hear Sisler slapping his forehead.

"They came back?" Tripoli was now on his feet.

"Yeah. That's another reason I called."

"Go on, go on," Tripoli urged impatiently.

"They came up as a missing person."

"And?" Tripoli knew there was more.

"They came up in the FBI registry. They're the prints of a *kid*. Missing from Watertown."

Tripoli listened expectantly. He knew there was still more. A great deal more.

"Now this is the weird part. The kid disappeared in *1939.*"

"How old?"

"Six. I think a little over six."

"Yes!" trumpeted Tripoli, snapping his fingers triumphantly. "That's what I thought!"

Danny glanced up from where he lay on the porch.

"What are you talking about?" asked Sisler.

"I don't really know—but I think I'm starting to get it. Does this guy have a name?"

"Of course. Matthew Roland."

"Matthew? Huh? *Matthew?*"

"Yeah. Yeah. Matthew."

"Did he have a middle name?"

"Like what?"

"You know, a middle name." Like John, he thought.

Tripoli could hear papers rattling on the other end. "Errr…Wait. Here. I got it. Matthew Peter Roland."

"What else have you got?" Tripoli noticed that Danny had stopped playing with the cat and was looking his way. Although the boy couldn't hear Sisler's end of the conversation, Tripoli had the uncanny sensation that he somehow knew what they were talking about.

"Nothing else. That's it. Period. I mean you're talking here ancient history. More than sixty years ago. That's before the invention of the typewriter, isn't it?"

"Some swell babysitter you are," muttered Molly when Tripoli appeared at her office. Danny was with Ben in the kitchen getting an ice cream. It was 4:30, her desk was awash in paper: she still had hours of work left. "I thought you were keeping him until dinner so I could get stuff done," she shuffled through a lower drawer looking for a file. "I was hoping..." She glanced up from her desk as Danny stepped into the office, a chocolate-covered popsicle in his hand and a big smile encircled by chocolate. He looked happier than she had seen him in days.

"I wanted to stay, too," piped Danny. "Trip's got all our animals!"

"I really *was* planning on keeping him. But—look, something urgent just came up." Tripoli was clean-shaven and dressed in a freshly pressed shirt and slacks.

"Great, between two great au pairs, you and Rosie..." She said in mock complaint, realizing that whatever it was that Tripoli had done it had broken the spell that had plagued Danny since the old man's death.

"Look, I gotta run." He reached for the door, then turned. "Daniel and I had a swell time, didn't we?"

Danny nodded. "Can't I come with you? *Please?*" He wrapped his arms around Tripoli's waist.

It was hard to pull away from the boy. "Not now. But I'll make it up to you. You'll come out again. And real soon. We'll do more stuff together. You'll see." Tripoli ruffled his hair, gave Molly a quick kiss, and then was back on the street.

Tripoli drove across the inlet bridge and went straight up to the hospital, cutting across the line where the tornado had ripped through a section of dense woods. Stately oaks and towering maples lay deposited in heaps as if they were matchsticks.

"Not you, too," said a disheveled Yerka when he stepped into the M.E.'s office. "I've already had visits from the D.A., your beloved chief, the State BCI people, and the governor's office is even sending in an emissary. And now you!"

"Well, it's not every day you lose a body," said Tripoli.

"Please," Yerka held up his hands in surrender, "do me a favor. No jokes this afternoon. It's brutally hot. I'm bone tired. My sailboat was wrecked in that storm. I've had just about—"

"Look, Phil, the body had to get out of here some way, right?"

"Okay. But why is everybody talking to *me?*" Yerka poked himself in the chest. "It was *your* fucking guys who were here continuously—or were supposed to be. It's not my job to guard a corpse. I'm a physician, not a cop. And the door to the morgue was locked. With God as my witness, I locked it when I left last night." As he described the scene, Yerka's long arms were waving comically in all directions. "The body was there. I know that for a fact. And Paolangeli was sitting right here in the front office playing solitaire when I took off at seven. No one could go into the morgue without running into him—or whoever the hell was on duty."

"Hmmm, I suppose not," muttered Tripoli.

"Come on, I'll show you," said Yerka grabbing his arm and starting to lead him into the morgue.

"Okay, but just hold your horses."

Tripoli kneeled to examine the entry lock to the morgue door. It didn't appear to have been tampered with, but then the place wasn't exactly Fort Knox. It could easily have been picked by somebody with a modicum of skill.

He joined Yerka who stood waiting in the morgue room.

"See?" said the pathologist, pulling the lever and opening the refrigerated locker. He slid out the tray. The sheet that had been covering the old Hermit's corpse lay crumpled to one side of the stainless steel drawer, just as Yerka had found it.

Tripoli examined the door to the locker. The latching mechanism was controlled from the outside. Then, to Yerka's surprise, he stooped down and carefully examined the inside of the door.

"What are you thinking? Listen, Trip, they don't put handles on the inside of these things."

"Okay, okay. I'm just looking at everything."

"Let me slide you in and see if *you* can get out," said Yerka angrily.

Tripoli actually contemplated it for a moment, then smiled. "No thanks, Phil. I don't want to catch cold. Besides, I can see enough like this."

"Trip, the guy was dead as a doorknob. Believe me. They don't come any deader. And unless you're Houdini, there's only one way to open this locker—and that's from the outside. It's very simple. Some idiot came in here and helped himself to a dead body. The old guy didn't rise from the dead. He didn't pass through walls. Somebody picked him up and schlepped him out of here. Period."

"Yeah, okay. I'll buy that. But then the question is who? And *why?*"

"What are you doing, asking *me?*" Yerka raised his voice and was almost shouting. "I'm a doctor, not a fucking detective! You want to know who? I'll tell you who. It was probably one of those religious nuts. This town is crawling with borderline crazies. And with this spiritual hermit nonsense, the whole fucking city is rapidly going off the deep end."

"We'll get this thing figured out," said Tripoli calmly.

"I don't even care if you figure it out. Far as I'm concerned, just get me my corpse back and I'll be happy."

"We can't have this," said Ozmun, the landlord of the trailer park. She had just returned home and was getting ready to prepare a stir fry for dinner when Ozmun opened the door to her trailer without so much as a knock. Nobody ever saw him unless there was trouble.

A former bouncer at the Wooden Nickel, Ozmun was huge, hairy, and not particularly bright.

Danny was out in the garden tying up the vines that had been torn away by the storm, and when the door handle turned, she was sure it was him. The man's menacing presence frightened her.

"Hey, don't you believe in knocking?" she said, trying not to appear cowed.

He simply glared at her.

"Okay, what do you want?"

"This has gotta stop. I'm getting all kinds of complaints. People comin' and goin' at all hours. You've got the cops here all the time."

"They're here protecting my boy. And I certainly didn't invite these other people. They—"

"I don't want to hear no more bullshit about the boy." He swiveled in the doorway so he could face Danny. "And he's dug up the lawn. You don't have permission!" He leveled an accusing finger at Danny, who slid down amidst his tomatoes. "I want all this crap ripped out and reseeded."

"It's my garden," the boy said quietly, standing up. Molly felt a brief flash of pride at his fearlessness. She pushed right past Ozmun and stood defiantly beside Danny.

"You call this pile of rock a lawn?" She spat back.

"This keeps up, I'm gonna have you evicted."

"Hey, don't worry. I'm going to move out of this overpriced rathole, all right. But I'm going to do it when *I'm* good and ready."

"I'm going to talk to my lawyer."

"Go ahead. Be my guest. But right now this is *my place. I* pay the rent. So get the hell off my 'lawn' before I have you arrested for trespassing. "

Her hands on Danny's shoulders kept shaking long after Ozmun had left.

"Is he going to rip out my garden?" asked Danny, looking up at her.

"Don't be silly, Honey. He's just a stupid man who makes a lot of noise and doesn't scare anybody."

But Molly knew she was worried.

"Well, what have we got?" he asked Sisler when Tripoli found him downstairs in the supply room. They were just issuing new pistols and Sisler was signing out a shiny Glock with two clips and a couple of boxes of 40mm ammo.

"Hey, I thought you were taking a vacation?"

"I am and I'm not."

They walked up from the basement level.

"We're not supposed to touch this case any more, you know," said Sisler, hefting the new weapon admiringly in his hand. "The Attorney General's office has got an independent counsel coming in to investigate…"

"So, who's touching it?" Taking the stairs again instead of waiting for an elevator, he held the steel door for Sisler. "I'm just asking a few questions."

"There's all kinds of shit already hitting the fan, and if we're not careful, we're going to get splattered. That dumb-assed raid. The old man dropping dead. Now this body crap. This is all going to a grand jury. You can count on that. And Matlin's already shitting a brick."

"And you're not in the least curious, huh?" he said, giving a sideways glance at Sisler as they entered Tripoli's upstairs office.

"Well…" Sisler finally smiled slowly. "Yeah…of course. Sure." He grinned.

"Good!" Tripoli closed the door.

Sisler pointed the empty Glock out the window, closed one eye, and tried sighting it on a distant tree. "I heard you went to see Yerka."

Tripoli told him about the vault, how it was constructed.

"So somebody swiped the body." Sisler loaded the Glock's clip, feeding in one shiny cartridge after the next until he had inserted all seventeen rounds, then slammed the clip into the butt. A southpaw, he holstered the gun under his right arm. "We ought to get a list. Access."

"Now you're talking."

"The chief already questioned Teeter and Paolangeli and Pellegrino. It was the three of them that were on rotation and they're all insisting they never budged for a second."

"Why don't you talk to them yourself," suggested Tripoli. "But informally. You know, pull them aside. Or take them out for a beer or something."

Sisler started to load the second clip for his belt, then stopped and looked up. "Are you going back to the hospital?"

"You're becoming a regular mind reader, Sisler, you know that?"

"Please Rosie, forget it already," Molly juggled the phone as she sliced onions, her eyes watering.

"Are you crying?" she asked.

"No. It's onions. Look, it's not your fault. It's nobody's fault. This has just been the day from hell."

"If I hadn't gone into the kitchen and left him alone," said Rosie, "Danny would never have slipped away."

"Don't count on it." Turning the fire up under her wok, she shot a glance out the window to check on Danny. Through her watery vision she could see him barefoot in his little garden hoeing weeds. Remarkably, the garden, sheltered by the trailer, had hardly been touched by the storm. She poured oil into the hot wok, letting it sizzle, all the while her ears keyed in the sound of Danny's repetitive strokes.

"From now on, I swear," said Rosie emphatically, "I'm not taking my eyes off him."

"Rosie. I can't do this to you. You've got enough to worry about."

Rosie started to object.

"Or to me," Molly added.

"But then what are you going to do?"

The question hung for a moment in the air. "Danny stays with me," she said resolutely. "There's just too much craziness going on. Another month, things'll be settling down, and then he'll be starting school."

"School?" echoed Rosie.

The sound of hoeing had stopped, and Molly turned to see Danny standing close to the open window. How much had he heard?

"You can't do that to a boy like Danny," Rosie was saying. "And the people at school wouldn't understand him. He couldn't take it. Can't you see that—"

"Rosie, I can't talk now," she said. "Let me call you back later, okay?"

The evening was still steamy, a palpable soup of humidity and grit hung suspended in the air.

"This summer's getting to be a real killer," mumbled Sisler as they left the station and marched to the parking lot. "I heard it broke a hundred again today. All afternoon the ambulances have been running people with heat stroke up to the hospital. Paolangeli told me that two old people and a baby died. They're packing people in ice in the hospital like they were corpses. Can't even get enough ice."

In the short hike to the parking lot, Tripoli's shirt was completely drenched, and Sisler, walking a yard away from him, reeked from sweat.

"Let's take yours," said Tripoli motioning towards Sisler newer Caprice. The cooling system in Tripoli's car was worthless in this heat, and Sisler's had a powerful air conditioner.

They drove out through the West End. Although the sun had set, the concrete was still baking and the whole neighborhood was out on their stoops drinking beer and soda. Everyone looked drained. The kids who would usually be playing in the street were hunched listlessly on the curbs. On State and Plain, where a lot of the drug deals took place, a bunch of tough-looking adolescents were clustered in front of the pizza parlor. Ordinarily when one of the unmarked cars approached, someone would always yell "Five-O," and the young men in baggy gangsta attire would quickly be sauntering off in all directions. Tonight they didn't have the energy to turn their heads.

Tripoli and Sisler caught Valerie Hagen, the chief hospital administrator, just as she was getting ready to leave. She had her key in the door and looked annoyed.

"But the D.A.'s people were just here," she objected. "I've spent two hours with them!"

"Well, we're investigating this, too."

"I've got to pick up my daughter. I was supposed to be out of here ages ago!"

"We'll try to make it fast," said Tripoli.

"Just a couple of questions," chimed in Sisler.

She shook her dark, tight curls, reopened the office, and turned on the lights.

"If you could," said Sisler, "we'd like a list of everyone who had a key giving them access to the morgue room."

"Okay," she said, opening her drawer and handing them the list. "Here. This is what I gave to the D.A.'s people."

With Tripoli leaning over his shoulder, Sisler studied the sheet. It included supervisory personnel, nursing, and janitorial staff.

"Anybody else that ought to be on here?" asked Sisler as Tripoli hung back and let him handle it.

"That's it."

"What about you?"

The woman's face flushed. *"Me?"*

"Yes," said Sisler. Now it was his turn to sound annoyed. "Do you have access?"

"Well…yes…but I never go down there."

"We need everybody."

"And anybody," Tripoli chimed in.

"You don't think that *I* would steal a body, do you?"

"I would hope not," said Tripoli affably. "But maybe you want to go back to the beginning and make this list all inclusive."

Flustered, Hagen sat down at her computer and went to work. Fifteen minutes later she had come up with a comprehensive list which included a number of resident physicians, orderlies, and cleaning staff who had escaped her first pass. All told, there were an extra dozen.

"You don't ask, you don't get," said Tripoli, studying the two page list as they cruised back down West Hill to the station.

"Hey, I thought you were so depressed," said Sisler, slowing for a red light.

"Who said I was depressed?"

Sisler crept forward and managed to reach the light just as it changed to green. "Well, you were down." He kept his eyes on the road.

"So now I'm up, okay."

"Fine. No complaint from me. Just wondering is all."

"I'm stimulated," said Tripoli with a faint smile.

"Huh?"

"You know the cloud lifts, things start to make a little bit of sense, the chase quickens the heart."

Sisler finally turned to face him. "What are you talking about?"

"Supposing the old man didn't kidnap the kid."

"What? You mean the kid just stumbled onto him?"

"Something like that…"

"All these months, in all that space—we've got helicopters with electronic surveillance gear, rangers, and search parties tramping through the woods—we couldn't find the Old Man, much less a goat. So how does the kid find him?"

"Maybe he knows right from the beginning where to go?"

Sisler looked obliquely at him.

"Please don't stare at me like that. I'm not crazy. All I'm asking you to do is to employ a little imagination, be inventive. We keep driving in the same ruts, seeing the same things, and in the process fail to spot the obvious that's just a little off the road."

From the look on Sisler's face, it was clear he just didn't get it. For the moment it was better to leave it be. When they reached the parking lot, Tripoli handed Sisler the list the hospital administrator had compiled. "Okay. This is your department."

"Huh?" Sisler looked dumbfounded.

"Check them out."

"You mean I've got to do all this? Alone? Come on, man, I thought we're working on this together?"

"We are. We are. It's just that you're just going to have to handle this end of it, that's all. Meantime, I've got a few other fish to fry."

"Try to be quiet," said Molly when Tripoli came by that night. "I finally got Danny asleep. He was all worked up about being with you today. He kept going on about his old friends the animals."

Tripoli eased the front door closed, then tiptoed in.

"No I'm not asleep!" piped Danny, bounding out of his room. "Hi, Trip!" He sprang into Tripoli's arms as if launched from springs.

Tripoli laughed. "Howya doing, big fella? Have a good time today?"

"It was great! The best day in the whole world!"

"I thought you were sleeping," said Molly, less than enthused to see him up.

"I was," said Danny. "But then I remembered something important. I forgot to tell you, Trip," he snuggled close, "you can milk the mother goat and the sheep, you know. The milk is very good to drink."

"Well," said Tripoli, weighing the matter. "I'll think about that."

"And you can make yummy cheese, too."

There was such an endearing innocence to the boy that Tripoli couldn't resist giving him a kiss. Danny locked arms and legs tightly around Tripoli's torso and clung tightly.

"Come on, go back to bed. *Please*, Honey," said Molly wearily. "It's been a long day for all of us."

"And I want Trip to have some of my vegetables, too."

Heaped on the counter were a cornucopia of cherry tomatoes and green onions, fresh young potatoes and eggplants.

"Boy, these look beautiful," said Tripoli, leaning over to get a better look. "Wow, they're humungous!"

"And we've got lots of beans in the fridge," Danny added.

"Yes, they're beautiful," said Molly, "but could you go to sleep already?"

Tripoli carried Danny to the bedroom and, when he lowered him to his bed, the boy clung to his neck, pulling him close. Tripoli buried his face in the curve of his throat and inhaled. His skin had a wonderful fragrance to it, the essence of milk and greenery, of clothes dried in the sun, of flowers and fresh-turned earth.

"Please," Danny whispered in his ear. "Don't let them put me there."

"Where?"

"School. They want to put me in school."

"Huh? Who?"

"My mother. Larry. *Everybody!*"

"Oh…" uttered Tripoli, ambushed.

"But you won't let them, will you."

"Well…But…" he stammered, "It's not really for me to…I mean, that's the way it is. All children have to go to school."

"But Trip, I won't like it there," said Danny under his breath. "Please. You gotta help me," he begged.

"No way!" Pellegrino exploded, flinging his fork into his beef stew and sending a splash of gravy out in all directions. Kesh, the owner of the State Diner, came over from the grill and wiped the counter. He offered Sisler a wet cloth for his shirt. Pellegrino was still in uniform and the dark blue had a way of hiding stains. His face, however, was beet red. "I never so much as budged a fucking inch."

"What time did you get on?"

"I got there at eight in the morning. Took over from Paolangeli. I did a crossword I found in Yerka's *Times*. It was a real bitch. I couldn't get half of it."

Kesh continued to linger, cleaning the counter, an ear cocked.

"I don't get this. Why the fuck are you grilling *me?*" Pellegrino spat at Sisler.

"Ssshhh, come on. Lower your voice," he said, which just irritated Pellegrino more. "Hey, you're not being singled out. I'm talking to everyone."

"And it's not even your goddamn case! I heard the state's sending in a special investigator."

Everybody in the diner was looking their way. "Easy. Easy," muttered Sisler under his breath.

"The body," said Kesh, nodding his head.

Pellegrino turned on him. "What the hell do you know about it?"

"Know? Ha!" Kesh tossed a shoulder. "Everybody knows."

"Yeah?" said Sisler.

Kesh drew close to the cops, looked around. "About the boy. How he can make storms. About the Old Man. How he can pass through the walls," he whispered, "like a ghost."

"Are you *nuts?*" exclaimed Sisler.

"No. No. I'm serious," said Kesh, earnestly. "Things like that happen all the time."

"Maybe," said Pellegrino. "but not in Ithaca."

"I never even thanked you for today," said Molly.

They were sitting on the couch with their feet up on the low coffee table. Molly had reheated the noodles and veggies from dinner. Tripoli had taken a few bites before settling back with a cold beer. It was almost beginning to feel like old times, he thought to himself, when they were close and always had their hands on each other. Yet it had been so long since he touched her, really touched her, that this intimacy now felt slightly awkward, almost new. They would have to go back, he feared, start again from the beginning,

"Nothing to it. It was my pleasure. Daniel's great to have around. I even got him working," he chuckled, playing with a silky lock of her hair. She had turned the TV down so Danny could sleep. Running faintly in the background was a news program about crop failures in the Midwest, but Tripoli was too intent on Molly to give it much attention.

"I didn't mean to snap at you about bringing Danny back early. And I still feel terrible for jumping on Danny back in the car. I was so frustrated. I don't want to lose my job, and I'm already in hot water as it is."

"Daniel understands."

"I was grateful that you took him today. Really. Hey," she interrupted herself, "I don't know what kind of miracle you performed, but I haven't seem him this happy in days."

"It took me by surprise, too." He told her about Danny sulking under the tree and then breaking into gales of laughter.

She looked at him. "So what happened?"

"Nothing that I could see. That's the amazing thing."

"After you left, he kept going on the whole evening. The sheep this, and the goats that. How you guys cut lots of grass for them. Then fixed the fence, and met the cat that lives under the porch."

Tripoli risked letting his hand trace the curve of her buttocks, followed the soft voluptuousness of her thigh.

"That feels nice," she said.

His hands slid down the length of her long legs.

"Hey, you're diverting my thoughts."

Tripoli smiled. *"Me?"* he said, feigning innocence, "Now why would I…" and kissed her deeply.

Molly turned to check the bedroom door, then took the remote and flipped off the TV. "At least turn down the lights," she murmured.

Tripoli got up and switched off the kitchen light.

"That one, too." She pointed to the lamp near the book shelf.

It was almost pitch black in the trailer. Tripoli's eyes hadn't adjusted to the darkness, and he kept bumping into things as he groped his way back to the sofa.

"Oh, there you are," he laughed, making contact with her. He kissed her. She kissed him back, pressing tightly against him. He helped her undress, and when she was naked he eagerly slipped out of his clothes. Turning her on her stomach, he spent a long time caressing the length of her back. The more he massaged her, the more excited he became.

"I love having you close like this," she murmured, turning back around, his tumescence obvious. "It feels good just having you hold me," she said, but she was clearly positioning herself away from it. "Let's be like this for a while, okay?"

His hand came to a reluctant halt on her hip. "Sure," he muttered, surrendering with a disappointed groan. "You've got lots of things on your mind. I understand."

They lay in silence, their bodies interwoven.

"I thought that once Danny was back everything would be just perfect. But it wasn't and it isn't," she said bitterly. "I was deluding myself, thinking that we could just pick up where we had left off. I kept thinking, too, that well, if the Hermit was locked up and out of the way, I'd finally have Danny to myself." She was working herself up; she knew it but couldn't stop. "Even dead, he still has his claws in my boy. It's always the old man this. The old man that. Everything Danny does and says always refers back to him. When Danny's happy, why is he happy? It's *not* because he's with me. Or even with you. It's because he's with the old man's sheep and goats. Or he's back out in the woods—where the old man kept him."

"Six months is a long time in a kid's life."

"You know, I'll turn to Danny and sometimes he's got this faraway look in his eyes. Or he's pulled into himself as if he were unconscious, or dead. And it's scary. Creepy. All this time now, and I still can't *really* break through. Oh, Trip," she said, plaintively, "I can't turn my back for an instant. I'm always afraid somebody is going to grab him again. Everybody wants something from him. Oh, I want people to just leave us already alone. I just want Danny to have a normal life. Play Little League or just hang out with friends his own age. Is that so unreasonable?"

Tripoli swallowed, cleared his throat. "This thing with Daniel is really wearing you out," he said, the implication clear.

"Nah. It's not just Danny. It's the job, too. And Larry. And the people who keep…"

"But no one is forcing you to stay there."

"You mean quit and move out with you, is that it?"

"Well, that's a reasonable option," he said and could feel her stiffen.

"I'm paying my own way in life, thank you."

Though Tripoli had her in his arms, he could feel her slipping away. He took a long breath and slowly exhaled. "You know, I don't quite understand how things between us have gotten so…"

"Sour?"

"I just can't get it straight in my head. We were so close, so intimate. Then, bang, it's like we're almost strangers."

She pulled away. "Ever think that maybe you're putting pressure on me?"

"I am? I thought I'm trying to help."

"You are helping, but you don't quite understand where I'm coming from."

Tripoli hesitated, thought about it. "Maybe," he ventured, "maybe the problem is that you're trying to force him into a mold he can't fit."

"Force him?" She jerked upright and immediately he knew he had misspoken. "Everybody has got plans for him. But remember, I'm his mother."

"Of course you are."

"And I just want what's best for him."

"Well, then you've got to take into account who he is."

"Oh, no," she groaned, turning away from him. "You're not going to start that crap with me. I've been beating away people all day who—"

"People aren't blind. They can see that Daniel's very special."

"Oh, Trip! Please, not you, *too.*" She thought back on the night of the vigil. The way that crowd had craved Danny. That morning of the storm. Those angry faces directed at him. It still gave her goose bumps. In her mind's eye, she saw Danny pointing towards the sky, illuminated by a blazing meteor.

"Okay," she said into the dark. "I see. He's different. But that's not necessarily going to make him a happier person. Which is *all* that I ever wanted him to be. Or us. The two of us. Don't you see?"

"I see what you want. Yes."

"For his own selfish purposes, that old Hermit stole Danny's childhood. I'm telling you right now, I can't and *won't* allow it. I'm not going to permit every fool in this town to get their grubby hands on him! Poor Danny's been through enough already."

He waited for her rage to subside. "Molly…The Hermit…I don't think he just some crazy old geezer who kept him captive. I believe Daniel was being prepared for something incredibly important."

"*Prepared?* All he did was fill poor Danny's head with this doomsday shit."

Tripoli stared out into the darkness. He was thinking about the books, those elaborate volumes he had found in the hut. Those sheaves of parchment touched by the hands of unknown scribes.

"I don't want my boy being taken for a messiah and nailed up on any cross!" Molly all but spat out. "Prophets get killed. Even false ones. And I don't want Danny dying for someone else's sins." She kept seeing those hungry faces of the vigil, hearing their beseeching voices. "The world's going to pot. Okay. But is my little boy supposed to be the answer to everybody's problems? For God's sake," she cried out, "he's not even six years old yet! Can't the people just leave us alone!"

Disentangling herself from Tripoli, she got up, went to the bedroom, and got her robe. Slipping it on, she tied it tightly at the waist and stood glaring down at him as he lay there exposed in his nakedness.

"I really wish that you—you of all people—would stop. You're feeding this thing like all the rest. And Danny'll never have a chance for a normal life unless this ceases. He's just a regular…Little! Boy!" she said, her hand slicing the air with each word. "Yes, he can read. And he's smart—damn smart! And he knows big words. And he can talk bird talk. Or squirrel talk—or whatever. But he's going to have to live like the rest of us cruddy human beings in this shitty world. And his name is Danny, do you hear me, DANNY! NOT Daniel! Not yet at least. He's still just a little boy."

"I didn't mean to upset you," he mumbled as he hunted for his clothes. She snapped on the lamp, and Tripoli winced in the brightness. "Where are my shorts?" he asked, still searching for them.

They were behind the sofa, and Molly tossed them at him.

"This is all crazy. Everyone is going totally nuts—including me," she said, holding out his trousers in her clenched fist. "You're guilt-stricken and depressed about the old man dying. Half the town thinks he's risen from the grave and that my little Danny is the next Mohammed or Francis of Assisi or God knows what. I'm tiptoeing around, trying to hold a job with Larry breathing down my neck and Danny whining about the noise of the florescent lights. I can't even step into McDonald's anymore and have a lousy hamburger without being condemned as a flesh-eating murderer by my own son!" Molly was on the verge of hysterics. She knew she was being unreasonable, but she could no longer hold herself back.

"I think I'd better go," said Tripoli, buttoning up his shirt.

"Look, I'm sorry," she murmured as he reached for the front door of the trailer.

He pulled the door shut behind him and a moment later could hear Molly turning the lock.

The night was sultry, still beastly hot. The crickets and peepers and toads in the nearby swamp were going full blast. A half moon had risen over the Dolph's trailer, and the park was quiet. The only sounds were the buzz of overhead lamps, vast clouds of moths flocking in their white aura.

In the light he could make out Danny's garden. Despite the drought, the tomatoes were swollen and red and looked luscious. Gingerly, he twisted one until it came free of the vine. It was the smallest of the lot, yet it was so large that he could barely contain it in his hand. When he bit into it's supple flesh, the juices running down his hand and chin, he was suddenly overcome, the intensity of sweetness and tartness assaulting him.

chapter eighteen

In the early hours of daylight, Tripoli set off on the journey to Watertown. It was a straight shot directly north on Route 81, almost to the Canadian border. He hadn't been there since he was a kid, and the only thing he remembered about it was that it was one godforsaken place in winter with deep, drifting snow, blinding whiteouts, and temperatures that plunged a good twenty degrees lower than even those in Ithaca. Whenever the weather reports were citing the lows for the state, it was always Massena or Watertown that won the booby prize.

Yet now, in the middle of August, the sky was blazing blue with not a cloud in sight. The heat from outside was pouring in his window and the fields he glided past were all parched and brown. The corn was stunted, less than knee high, and it looked spindly and wilted. The trees, stressed by the heat and lack of moisture, had prematurely turned color and some were already shedding their leaves. Apparently, the drought was more severe here in the north.

With traffic zipping past, Tripoli hugged the right lane, driving slowly as he continued to observe the countryside. Twice he ended up on the gravel shoulder and once he almost went off the road.

Watertown was smaller than Ithaca, and it was easy for Tripoli to find the offices of the Jefferson County Sheriff.

"Well, well. The Ithaca Police Department?" said the sheriff, getting to his feet when Tripoli was shown in. "Not often we get to see you people up here."

The sheriff held out his hand. He was a big, beefy man with a bulbous nose and eyes so small they were little more than slits. In his polished boots and uniform, he looked more the image of a southern sheriff than an upstate cop. When they shook, his hand was twice the size of Tripoli's.

"Take a load off your feet," he said, showing Tripoli a seat. The sheriff put his feet up on his desk and leaned far back; the springs in his chair creaked.

"So, what brings you here?" he asked, knotting his huge hands behind his head and revealing stains of sweat under his arms.

"I'm looking for some information," explained Tripoli. He told the sheriff how, on a kidnapping warrant, they had raided a hut on state lands. An old man was dead, and they had taken prints.

"Yeah, I heard something about that. You had the troopers and Feds down there, right?"

Tripoli nodded.

"I don't get it. What's this got to do with Watertown?" The sheriff offered him a cigarette and, when Tripoli refused, lit one up himself.

"The old man's prints," said Tripoli, "they came back as a missing person from Watertown."

"Missing?" The sheriff took a long, thoughtful drag. The smoke oozed slowly out his nostrils. Tripoli could see he was searching his memory.

"It's not exactly recent." Tripoli handed across the desk the report that Sisler had obtained.

The sheriff studied it. "*1939?*" he exclaimed, sitting up and looking straight at Tripoli. "You must be joking."

"I know it was a long time ago, but I was hoping you guys might have some sort of record."

"No way," said the sheriff waving away the notion. He handed back the papers. "Nowadays all our files are computerized. We've got stuff that goes back to the seventies if you want. But this, this is way before the advent of—"

"I realize that," said Tripoli patiently.

"We could try and dig, I suppose," admitted the sheriff begrudgingly. "But those old files down there in the basement are a regular mess. Chances are you'd never find…Hey, wait," he said, interrupting himself. He rubbed his chin. "'39 it says, huh?"

"Yes."

"That was the time when…" he got up and went to the outer office.

Tripoli jumped to his feet and hurried behind.

"Hey, Emery," he called out, addressing a uniformed man old enough to be Tripoli's father. He sat at a cluttered desk in the corner, doing paper work. "1939."

"Yeah?" asked the Deputy, slowly looking up. "What about it?"

"Who was sheriff, then? Your Dad was on the force in 1939, right?"

Tripoli stood observing the exchange.

"'39?" the old Deputy scratched his head. "Must have been Denny Holbrow was sheriff. I think Dad worked for him before Frank Chapman took over. Yeah, yeah. It's gotta be Denny."

"That's what I thought," said the Sheriff, nodding to himself. "Denny Holbrow," he repeated, turning to Tripoli.

"So?" said Tripoli.

"He's still alive and kicking—well, sort of."

Molly didn't hear it from Larry. She got the news from Ben. Which is what worried her.

"We're taking on two new people," explained Ben as she rinsed some grapes for Danny in the office kitchen. "Somebody in marketing and another person in editorial."

"But we can handle the editorial." Her heart was fluttering in her chest.

"Larry says we're growing and we're going to need the extra staff." Ben shrugged, avoiding her eyes.

"Couldn't I just take the grapes down in the courtyard and eat them there?" asked Danny, watching as the forgotten faucet continued to gush.

"What?" said Molly, distracted.

"The grapes. Can I eat them outside?"

"No. No. You've got to...Ben?" she turned, but he was already gone.

Molly took Danny back into the office. "Now read one of your books. You've got plenty of new books." She slumped down into her chair, stared blankly at the pattern of multicolored helixes intertwining on her screen.

"But I'll just sit down there, and you can watch me from here. I promise I'll be good. I'll just stay really close."

"The answer is *no!*" said Molly loudly. "And I want you to stop nagging me. I've got tons of work to do and I can't keep getting disturbed." What was Larry up to? Was he positioning himself so he could get rid of her? In the pinch, when he needed her, she had always come through for him. Why was he doing this?

Hunched over his desk, Danny looked to her like a whipped dog. "Oh, Honey, I'm sorry. I didn't mean to yell at you like that. But I've got something serious on my mind and..."

He got up and edged close to her, put his arm around her neck. "Can't I help you?" he offered.

"Honey, if you could just occupy yourself for a couple of minutes so I could think, that would be the biggest help of all."

Danny slunk off.

Molly sat at her terminal, tried to concentrate on the screen, but her mind was still in turmoil. Her first impulse was to walk right into Larry's office and confront him, ask him what he *really* was up to. The business was growing, that was true, but where was the money for the new salaries? Was he contemplating growth or protecting himself for the time when he would have to let her go? Marketing and editorial. That's what *she* did.

Molly just couldn't get a decent night's sleep. She couldn't get to sleep until late, and she was up early in the morning just after dawn. While Danny slept, she waxed the floors, cleaned windows, took out the recyclables, and emptied the trash. Outside, the sun was already up and a hot, dry wind was blowing, gathering up small vortices of dust.

On her way back from the dumpster, the beefsteak tomatoes in Danny's garden caught her eye. Nearly ripe, they were enormous, not only for the time of year, but double the size of any she had ever seen. As she stepped among the plants to take a closer look, something caught her eye, something dangling from one of the trellised vines. It was a kind of earth-colored pouch, and when she opened it she discovered inside a piece of coarse paper. Unfolding it, she immediately recognized what it was: a map.

The others!

"Leave him alone!" she cried and in a frenzy she tore it all into little bits and threw them into the air. Watching as the hot wind scattered the pieces across the park, she realized her mistake and regretted it.

Tripoli found the old sheriff in the Hillview Nursing Home on the outskirts of Watertown. It was a long, low complex that looked more like a motel than an old age home.

Denny Holbrow appeared to be in his late nineties. He was a shriveled piece of humanity, little more than a shroud of leathery skin hung on a long frame of bones. Holbrow had severe emphysema and sat in a chair with an oxygen cannula hooked into his nostrils. When he spoke, he did so in short bursts, needing to pause repeatedly to catch his breath. Tripoli pulled a chair close, facing him. He introduced himself. Asked the man how he was feeling. The old sheriff gave his bony shoulders a heave and stared back at Tripoli with rheumy eyes.

"I understand," Tripoli went on, "that you were sheriff in 1939."

The old man suddenly seemed to take interest. "Yeah. Yeah." His features became animated and his eyes turned bright. "1936 to 1952. To be exact," he said. "Right through...the war."

Tripoli could hear the oxygen hissing from the tube; when the old sheriff spoke, his voice was gravelly. Although his physical condition was poor, his mind was obviously sharp.

"There was a case in October of 1939," Tripoli prompted, becoming hopeful. "A boy was missing."

"Matthew Roland," retorted the old guy, not missing a beat.

Tripoli smiled. "So you remember."

"Hell, yes!" He sat up at attention. "Damnedest thing!"

"Tell me," said Tripoli eagerly.

"Boy just disappeared. Into thin air."

"And?"

"Wasn't the first time, though."

"Oh?" Tripoli couldn't hide his surprise.

"First time was the big news," he said, shaking his head at the recollection. "I was just a young fella then. Full of piss and vinegar." Holbrow gave a raspy laugh and, staring out the window, he seemed to drift off into a reverie.

"Go on, please. How old was he? I mean the first time he disappeared?"

The old sheriff turned back. His eyes, Tripoli noticed, were actually a light green, just like his own. "I think Matthew was five. Six? Something...like that."

"And?"

The old man took a couple of slow breaths, then continued. "Vanished. The boy lived…right in town…with the mother. Nice woman. Mary, I think it was. Yeah. Mary. Died 'bout three years after Matthew disappeared."

"And the father?"

"Died. When the boy was little. Accident with a tractor or something. I can't remember so well…anymore."

"You're doing great. Really. Please, go on."

"Well…" The old man started coughing violently. It took him a good minute to clear his chest.

"Sorry," he apologized hoarsely, when the fit had passed. "Goddamned cigarettes," he muttered. "Devil's invention." He coughed and spit a gob of thick phlegm into a handkerchief. "'Scuse me."

Tripoli nodded. "Relax. I've got plenty of time."

"Where were we?"

"The boy, Matthew, disappeared. Age five or six."

"Yeah," nodded Holbrow. "The mother, a widow…worked as a waitress…at the diner. Not exactly prosperous. She was frantic. Desperate."

"It's her only kid," said Tripoli, filling in with a guess. He already suspected what was coming next.

"That's right. She's at her…wit's end. We, our department and the troopers, we're sure…the boy's gotta be dead. It's going into deep winter, see? You know what it's like. Here?"

"Fucking cold," said Tripoli.

"Yeah! Now here's the…crazy part. We're all sure…Matthew's dead. Not a chance he's alive. But, come summer, boy waltzes right into his…his Mom's diner!"

"Where's he been?"

"No one knows. But there he is. Hell of a nice kid. Like

sunshine. Kid'd walk into a room and the place…well, it'd just light up. I didn't know him before…"

"But he's changed, right?"'

"Can say that again. His mother tells me he doesn't like noise. Doesn't want to be cooped up…inside. Regular nature boy. Talking to the chipmunks. And rabbits." The old sheriff started to laugh, but it turned to a cough.

"Mother couldn't…" he started hacking again.

"Yeah?"

"Handle him."

"Why?"

"Kept…Can you?" he motioned to a pitcher. Tripoli poured the man a glass of water and watched him as he took deliberate sips. His hands were shaking and Tripoli helped him steady the glass. The old sheriff swallowed. "Hmmm. That's better," his face creased in a smile showing teeth that were surprisingly even and bright.

"You were saying the mother couldn't handle him."

"Kept disappearing."

"Where?"

"Just going off."

"Seeing somebody?"

He shrugged. "Who knows? Then he'd come back."

"And?"

"His teacher even had trouble hanging on to him in school." The old sheriff looked like he was getting exhausted from the exertion. His features were sagging, and his skin had developed a lifeless blue tinge.

"Take your time," said Tripoli softly. "I've got all day and more if you need it."

The sheriff rested. Slowly the color returned to his face.

"School?" coaxed Tripoli.

"Yeah. That's where he disappeared from."

"And in the end?"

"Yup. Again."

"And?"

"And that's it. I suppose you can read…all about it…in the papers."

"I will," said Tripoli, getting to his feet. "By the way, did the kid have a nickname? Like, what did the mother call him?"

"Matty…I mean, Matthew. Before it was Matty. After, he kept insisting that Matthew was his name."

"No other name? Maybe the kids in school called him something else?"

"None that I know of," he said, looking up at Tripoli with his watery blue eyes.

"You've been a big help, sir. Believe me." He took the old man's bony hands in his.

"So, you finally caught up with Matthew, huh?"

"Yeah. It looks that way. The prints certainly match." Tripoli was reluctant to go on.

"So, he's dead, huh? Well, figured that's why…you're here. Real shame, huh?"

"Don't be so unhappy" said Danny, coming up to her as she sat at her desk staring out the window. He brought his head close, pressed his cheek against hers.

"It's nothing, Sweetie" she murmured. "I'm just in one of my moods."

Molly had decided that the prudent thing was not to put Larry on the spot. Let it go, she had kept telling herself, trying to focus on her work—though it all now had a bitter taste. In a matter of little more than a day, her perspective had shifted from long term to the immediate, from career advancement to basic survival. When Larry was ready, he would call her in and inform her of the changes he had made. She wondered who else in the office knew. Had everyone but her been told ? Why was he holding off?

"We could grow our own food," said Danny.

"What do you mean?" she asked, swiveling in her chair so she could see him.

"You know, if you lose your job."

"Who said anything about—"

"I heard what Ben said. About the new people. I'm sorry." There were tears in his eyes. "I didn't mean to get you in trouble."

"Oh my darling," she said with tears in her own eyes. She took him into her arms and held him against her breast. "It's not your fault, Angel. Don't even think that. It's this lousy business world. That's what it is."

Tripoli spent the remainder of the afternoon at the *Watertown Daily Times*, sifting through their archives.

The first mention of Matthew Roland was on a microfilmed edition of the *Times* dated November 3, 1938.

"Five-year-old missing"—the headlines read. There was a large picture of the boy on the front page: an attractive kid with dark hair slicked down and combed in a sharp part, a big smile on his round face. He was wearing a white shirt and an oversized bow tie. The photo looked like a Christmas picture taken the previous year when the boy would have been four. The resemblance to Daniel was striking: Matthew was Daniel cast in dark details. He had the same large almond eyes and high cheeks, so close that Tripoli couldn't help but wonder if his mind were playing tricks on him. Maybe there was a common denominator to five-year-olds.

He read on. The boy had disappeared from the downtown elementary school that cold November morning. His kindergarten teacher, Lydia Munson, was baffled. One minute he was there, she claimed, the next he was gone. She couldn't recall Matthew leaving the room at any time, nor did the children as a group leave the class-room. Matthew had simply vanished without explanation or trace.

Through successive editions, Tripoli could follow the progres-sion of the investigation. Matthew's classmates had been questioned, but to no avail. Search parties had been organized, dogs employed, rivers and lakes dragged. The FBI had been called in, and Matthew's name had been entered into their national registry of missing persons.

Much like the hunt for Danny, Tripoli could follow the same trajectory of public concern: first the intense search, then the inter-est falling off as the days progressed into weeks of fruitless efforts. As the search dwindled, the articles shifted their focus to the poor widow and the toll that her son's loss was exacting. Neighbors were quoted as saying what a nice boy Matthew had been, how friendly and smart, how promising. The quotations all had an eulogistic ring to them, as if everyone was now certain that Matthew was dead.

Tripoli traced the story, moving in chronological order through the papers. Now and then there appeared a brief mention of Matthew or his mother. Mary, Matthew's mother, was repeatedly quoted as saying she remained unwavering in her conviction that her child was still alive. In February, there was mention of a bake sale to raise funds for the mother, who had been briefly hospitalized with a "nervous condition." Then there was nothing in the papers. Not a single mention of Matthew, or his mother, or the case. Tripoli raced through the spools of microfilm.

Then, suddenly, on June 17, 1939, a huge and jubilant banner headline:

"Missing Boy Returns!"

This time the paper had a photo of a somewhat older Matthew, the beaming boy clutched in his mother's arms, the pair surrounded by a crowd of cops and city officials.

"Presumed dead by police after his disappearance seven months

earlier, Matthew Roland, aged 6, walked into his mother's diner..."
Tripoli raced through the article. The boy, still wearing the clothes
he had disappeared in, was apparently in perfect health. But there
was still no explanation of where he had been.

Tripoli jumped to the next day's edition. The police questioning
Matthew seemed to have elicited no solid information. "Matthew
provided no explanation other than to say that he had been living in
the woods."

"The Mystery Widens"—the next issue of the paper
announced. The article was full of wild speculation about where the
child had been. People were suggesting everything from his having
been abducted by Gypsies seen traveling in the Watertown area to
his being nursed through the winter by wild animals. Aside from the
slightly dated language, the article might easily have described the
events surrounding Daniel's return.

Tripoli kept winding through the film, his pulse racing as he hit
upon article after article. Interest in Matthew was obviously growing. According to his mother, Matthew had undergone a drastic
transformation. "He can read just about anything," marveled Mrs.
Mary Roland. "He can even understand books meant for
grownups." But that was only part of it. He seemed exquisitely
tuned in to his surroundings, to people, to animals. But with all that,
his mother explained, clearly troubled, he had also become intoler-
ant of any modern contrivances. He couldn't stand the glare of electric lights. He had pulled out the plug of her new refrigerator
because the sound of its motor disturbed him, causing all their food
to spoil. He refused to ride in an automobile, eat meat, or drink milk
that was in any way processed. Nor would he talk on the phone or
permit a radio to play in his presence.

Tripoli sped on through the papers, the print streaking past as he
flew forward in time—Matthew still there on the first pages. Word
of the boy was spreading. People were claiming that he had

supernatural powers. That he could read minds. Foretell the future. Predict the weather. That he could heal with the simple touch of his small hands.

In one account, Dr. Oskar Friedmann, an expert in child psychiatry who had worked with the famous Sigmund Freud in his native Vienna, traveled all the way from New York City to Watertown. Following two days of extensive examinations, Dr. Friedmann announced that the boy had undergone a severe trauma initiating a marked transformation of personality. The article was couched in a lot of psycho babble, but its net result, from what Tripoli could fathom, was that this episode had propelled Matthew into a heightened state of nervous receptivity. "It is like the volume control on your radio set," explained the psychiatrist. "Imagine turning it all the way up so you could hear absolutely everything. And I mean every little sound, every station. It would make you crazy, wouldn't it?"

Then, as quickly as the news had ballooned, it tailed off again. By the end of August, two months after Matthew miraculously walked into his mother's diner, there was nothing. Public interest had moved on to more pressing matters: the proposal for a new municipal water system, the County Board working on its new budget, the movement of German troops in Eastern Europe.

Tripoli vainly searched through the days of September. Then, October 7, 1939: "Matthew Roland Missing Again!"

"So when was all this decided?" Molly asked when she was finally alone with Larry in the early evening. Everyone but she and Danny had finally left the office, and she simply couldn't take the waiting any longer.

"I'm sorry. I've been so busy I didn't have a chance to talk to you."

"But you did have time to talk to Ben."

He got up from his chair. "Molly dear," he intoned, approaching with outstretched hands.

"Molly, nothing." She jumped back, refusing to be placated. "Just level with me. Please."

"The business is growing," he explained. "We need to expand the staff. You know that as well as anybody."

"And you've got the money?"

"Well…" he paused, "I think I'm getting additional financing. We've got some V.C.s who are interested. And revenues are moving up nicely." He was talking fast and Molly knew that usually meant a smoke screen. "And I'm going to need you to train the new people."

"Larry," she finally confronted him straight out, "are you thinking of firing me?"

He didn't answer.

"Well?" she persisted.

The question hung in the air.

He turned away from her, pretended to busy himself examining some papers, but Molly kept her eyes on him.

Finally he turned back. "Let's face it," he said. "No one is indispensable."

"Well, that's pretty clear."

He went to shut the door, then hesitated.

Molly stuck her head out in the corridor. Danny was waiting in the hallway, ready to go. "One minute, Honey, and we'll take off," she said. "Okay, Sweetie?" He nodded and she gently nudged the door closed.

"I'm willing to work with you on this," said Larry in a lowered voice. Now he was close, looking her right in the eye, and she could feel the edge to her anger blunting. She tried to calculate how long her savings might last if she was out of work. Her mind flooded with memories of being poor and needing food stamps, her furniture out on the street in the pouring rain, going to that lawyer, Mr. Greenhut, for help. Her hands were trembling, and she clasped them together.

"I'll give you another couple of weeks until Danny starts school," said Larry. "But then this nonsense has got to cease."

The word "nonsense" stung. Molly bit her lip to keep her eyes from tearing up. "I've worked my ass off for you," she said through clenched teeth.

"Maybe, but these days little is getting done. Molly," he tried to put his hand on her shoulder, but she jerked away. "You think I don't know what's up when you streak out of this office because Danny has bolted again? Or those endless lunches? Or the kid nagging at you all afternoon to take him out? People coming and going like Grand Central Station. Molly, Molly, you used to be a real power-house. You did the work of ten."

"No, two."

"Please," he pleaded, "You've got to understand. This magazine," he said and she could have sworn there were tears in his eyes, "this is my *baby*. I've got my whole life wrapped up in it. All my chips are on the table. If I lost it…well, I'd be almost as devastated as you were when Danny disappeared. Can you understand that?"

Molly tried. "Well, I suppose so," she said hoarsely and had to keep clearing her throat.

"And I want to keep you. I really and truly do."

"What about the new people?"

"I need you to train them."

Train my replacements? she thought.

"You'll have a new slot," he said, anticipating her thoughts. "You'll be in a supervisory position. Next quarter we'll do a salary review. But you've got to get your life straightened out, get Danny into school and resume a normal existence. Everyone has a breaking point. Including me."

The evening in Watertown was sticky, and Tripoli, with a bit of time

on his hands, ambled aimlessly through the quiet streets, peering in
store windows and thinking…pondering the history of Matthew
Roland…the circumstances surrounding the boy's vanishing the
second time. By the time he decided to check in with Sisler at headquarters, Sisler had already signed out. Tripoli tried him at home, and
Sisler's wife, Tracy, picked up the phone.

"Oh, hi Trip," she said, recognizing his voice.

"Is Jerry around?

"No. Did you try at the station?"

"Yeah. But he just left."

"Can I have him call you when he gets in? I know he really
wanted to talk to you."

"He might not be able to reach me. I'll have to try him later."

"Sure. By the way, have you found out anything about that old
man?

"Naw," he answered vaguely. "Nothing very much yet."

"I mean it's none of my business, but everybody in town's been
talking about Danny and that—Whoops, hang on, there's a car coming up the drive. That could be Jerry."

There was a pause and Tripoli could hear Tracy in the background, calling out to her husband. A door slamming. Footsteps.

"Hey, Trip," said Sisler, coming on an instant later and sounding
a little winded. "Glad you called."

"What's cooking?"

"There was a nurse. Wait…" Sisler took a moment to catch his
breath.

"What nurse?"

"There was a nurse who went into the morgue that morning of
the day the body disappeared. Around five. She had a key."

"And? What was she doing in there?"

"Some old lady on the medical ward croaked and they took her
down to put her in a locker."

Tripoli waited.

"Now the interesting thing is that this nurse claims there was no officer on duty. She was sure of it. And she's sure of the time, too. There's a death certificate. I took a look at her patients' charts and the entries are bracketed in time—before and after she went down to the morgue."

"Five? That was before Pellegrino took over. Paolangeli's shift, right?"

"Yeah. And I talked to him. He insists that he never left his post."

Tripoli didn't say anything. He was thinking.

"Now somebody's not telling the truth. Trip?"

"Go on, I'm listening."

"They both can't be right. I hate to say this, but I think I believe the nurse. I mean, why should she distort anything? I think he went to take a dump or smoke or whatever, and now he doesn't want to own up to it. The nurse is pretty sure she locked the door, but who knows? It starts to explain everything—well, almost everything."

There was a prolonged silence, and it was Tripoli who finally broke it.

"I'm not so sure," he said.

"*Huh?* What do you mean? It's perfectly clear. Paolangeli takes a hike. The door is open, the place unguarded. Someone slips in—or maybe they got a key, I don't know—they grab the old man's body. And bingo, that's it, he's gone. Right?"

"Well, that's certainly one explanation," said Tripoli.

"*One?* Okay, how many others do you have?"

Tripoli had checked into a motel on the outskirts of Watertown and he found a diner nearby. That its parking lot was jammed with tractor trailers Tripoli took as a propitious sign. Once seated in the corner booth, he couldn't decide between the meat loaf and the spinach lasagna; finally he went for the lasagna special. Even though it was meatless it was surprisingly tasty, and for $6.95 it came with everything from salad to dessert, coffee included. There was a bunch of truckers sitting in a nearby booth and Tripoli eavesdropped on their conversation. They were griping about their loss of haulage. Something about milk production being sharply down. New environmental regulations that were costing them a fortune. They were being so squeezed they could hardly make a living anymore. After dinner, he had a couple of beers in a dark corner of a nearby tavern. Finally, he went to the pay phone and called Molly. It was well after eleven.

"Sorry to call so late."

"No, no. No problem. I was trying to catch up on some work."

"I just wanted to hear how Daniel is."

"Fine, of course. And why shouldn't he be?" she asked and there was an edge to her voice.

"Oh…no reason at all. I was just calling to see how you guys were doing."

"Trip, this line sounds strange. Where are you?" She could hear loud music playing in the background.

"In Watertown."

"*Watertown?* What are you doing up there?"

"Following up some leads to a case."

Silence. He took a gulp of his beer and Molly could hear him swallowing.

"You still angry at me?" he inquired cautiously.

"Never was. Just annoyed. I'm under a lot of stress at the office."

"Yeah, I figured as much."

"And then you start in with this stuff about how Danny's the second coming."

"I never said quite that. I just—"

"Or whatever. You know, you and Rosie ought to get together. She keeps telling me that Danny is some kind of saint. And on top of it, all everybody and his brother has got advice for me."

Tripoli remained silent. He knew that anything he said carried the risk of inflaming her further. But how could they keep any relationship going if he had to censor his every thought?

"You still there?"

"Yeah," he said, softly, "still here."

"We shouldn't be arguing." Molly heaved a long sigh. "You're not just my lover. I think of you as my friend, Trip."

"And I am. For life. You can always count on me."

"Then take it easy on me."

"Sure."

"I'll make you a deal. You don't hammer me about Danny being in contact with the angels, and I won't get pissed. How's that for a bargain?"

"Sorry, but I'm not making any promises," he said, quietly.

"Oh, Trip," she sighed.

"Not until I know what this is all about."

"I wish you were here," she said longingly. "But then, when you're here, I get so furious. It's not like me." What she didn't dare say was that she didn't quite trust him anymore. Couldn't trust anybody. Everybody had their own agenda.

"I know," he growled comfortingly. "I know that."

"Something odd happened," she said finally.

"What happened?"

"I found something." She told him about the pouch and the map.

"I want to see it as soon as I get back."

"You can't."

"Huh?"

"I tore it up."

"Oh, Jesus!" he groaned.

"I know. I know it was stupid. But I was so enraged—and afraid.

Afterward, I kept having this creepy feeling. Like the old man has been watching us, trying to lure Danny back."

"Hey," Tripoli cut her off. "He's dead. I saw him. Touched him. Believe me. Just ask Yerka, the medical examiner. Look, Molly, I'll be back as soon as I can," he said. "Just stay calm."

After she hung up, Molly sat staring at the phone. Some fool in a souped-up Camaro was burning rubber on the road by her trailer, screeching to a halt and then accelerating with a squeal. Back and forth he went. Danny was trying to sleep, and she debated going out and yelling at the jerk.

Molly made a cup of coffee, then sat at the kitchen table listening to the sounds in the night. Thumbing through the newspaper, she came upon an article on the OpEd page by the Reverend Glen Thorne. He had written a piece on the danger of what he called "pernicious cultism." That people, he wrote, "witnessing the endemic corruption and wickedness swirling around them, seeing before their very eyes the breakdown of the earth's fragile ecology, are turning in their desperation to false prophets. The day of reckoning is upon us today. It is Sodom and Gomorrah revisited. And those who worship the Antichrist are doomed to eternal damnation." Though he didn't specifically say it, Molly knew what exactly he was writing about: he was talking about Danny.

Tripoli went back to the motel and flipped on the TV. He lay down on the lumpy mattress and, still dressed in his clothes, fell soundly asleep.

He awoke the next morning with rumpled clothes, a bad taste in his mouth, and the television running. The morning news seemed to be filled with nothing but disasters. A preseason hurricane had ripped through the Florida panhandle, destroying countless citrus orchards and dairy farms in the central region. Another early storm was brewing in the Gulf of Mexico and threatening Galveston.

He showered and put on fresh clothes, the television droning on in the background.

Catching his reflection in the speckled motel mirror, he saw how haggard he looked and blamed his restless night on the heavy dinner and late beers; the sagging mattress hadn't helped things either.

As he reached for the remote to cut off the TV, the news anchor was just starting in on a story about the wheat crop that was failing in Canada.

Tripoli grabbed a quick cup of coffee and a muffin in the lobby of the motel and drove over to the courthouse. His plan was to research the Roland family, to see what he could dig up along the lines of birth and death certificates, deeds and property transfers.

Inside the courthouse, he descended the marble steps to the basement where he found the records room. Neatly arranged on tiers of wooden shelves that ran from floor to ceiling sat the dusty and daunting ledgers that were the cumulative history of Jefferson County and its inhabitants. As he wrestled a large tome off the shelf, the county clerk appeared almost magically at his side.

"Can I help you?" asked Carol Ellis, her intelligent eyes twinkling behind a pair of thick lenses. She was extremely short, and had pudgy cheeks and an upturned nose that gave her an elf-like appearance.

Tripoli explained that he was looking for some information on a family who had lived in town around 1939.

"Well, if they were bonafide residents, we should certainly be able to uncover something. She pulled a pencil from behind her ear and got ready to write. "Now what's the name?"

"Roland," he said, and saw a flash of recognition cross the woman's face.

"Roland?" she repeated, the pencil forgotten in her hand. "You mean *Matthew* Roland?"

"Why, *yes,*" answered Tripoli, who couldn't hide his own surprise. "You know about him then?"

"To work in this job you've got to be a bit of a history buff. And Mary Roland and her son Matthew—well," she waggled her head, "they created quite a sensation in their time."

"What I was hoping to find," said Tripoli eagerly, "is someone who might actually have known the boy personally."

The woman studied Tripoli through her thick lenses. "Why are you so curious about Matthew?"

A man dressed in a pinstriped suit came down the aisle towards them carrying one of the volumes, and they stepped aside to let him pass.

"There's another boy like him," said Tripoli in a lowered voice. "A boy who vanished and then came back."

"Oh, heavens." Her smile vanished. Suddenly she made the connection. "Yes. But of course! I read about him. In Ithaca, right?"

He nodded.

"You're a policeman then?"

He nodded again. She was quick.

"Look, can you think of anyone…*anyone* who might remember Matthew? Maybe a neighbor or a friend of the family?"

"Hmmm…" She scratched her head with the point of the pencil. "Wait. Mrs. Francis!"

Tripoli tried to remember if he had read her name in the paper.

"Flossie Francis. She was Matthew's teacher. She taught in the old elementary school. She was an active member of our Historical Society. She was just starting out as a young teacher then and—"

"Is she alive?" interrupted Tripoli, who couldn't wait for the clerk to get around to it. "Where is she?"

"She moved to Sarasota, Florida about six years ago. Had enough of our winters," she joked, but Tripoli was already heading for the door.

"I heard," said Sandy, lowering her voice so it was barely audible above the clatter in the copy room. The machine was flashing and spitting out pages at a blinding rate.

"Yeah, I'm supposed to train my own assassins," said Molly.

"Oh, don't be silly!" Sandy placed her hand on Molly's arm and leaned in close. "You don't have anything to worry about. Larry needs you. We *all* do."

"No one's irreplaceable," said Molly, quoting Larry.

"Aww, that's just Larry making noises. You've got to understand. He's sitting there in that pressure cooker."

"Sure I understand."

"Good." Sandy smiled. "Without you, this place would fall apart. Believe me."

chapter nineteen

For the duration of the flight to Sarasota, Tripoli kept trying to envision his meeting with Flossie Francis. On the phone she had sounded suspicious. Who was he? Why did he want to know about Matthew Roland? Hadn't enough gone on about that poor boy to last a lifetime? She was just plain heartsick about the whole affair and preferred to leave it alone.

"Look, could I come down and see you?" Tripoli had persisted. He was obviously getting nowhere on the phone.

"I don't see how that can be worth your trouble. Or time. It's a long trip."

"*Please,* it's important," he had pleaded and she had reluctantly given in.

So here he was, flying over the heartland of Florida. As the plane continued its gradual descent, Tripoli could make out stretches of low-lying land still flooded from the hurricane, farm buildings half submerged, orchards leveled. The jet then banked, skimming a tropical landscape turned suburban—a meshwork of highways and shopping centers, little backyard pools of aquamarine embedded like fake jewels in an endless carpet of tract housing.

When Tripoli stepped out of the terminal to pick up his rental car, the afternoon hit him with a sweltering blast. Then, with his windows sealed and the air conditioning on high, he drove out along the palm-lined coast. Though the storm had skirted the city, there were toppled signs along the highway and branches and coconuts still down on the ground.

Flossie Francis lived on the fifteenth floor of a sparkling white condominium that catered to the elderly. When she opened her door, Tripoli was expecting to find a hunched-over little eighty-year-old, but the woman who greeted him was tall and stately with a regal crown of silver hair.

"Mr. Tripoli," she said with a smile that disarmed him. "Won't you come in." She was well spoken and had an air of elegance that shattered his hasty conclusion that Watertown was a hick town. Her apartment was simply but tastefully furnished in bright colors and white rugs. They went into a living room decorated with wall hangings that looked like those made by American Indians, woodcarvings from around the world, and shelves lined with books.

"I'm afraid I was being difficult with you," she apologized, seating herself opposite him. "You see, this thing is still terribly distressing for me." She gave a hurt smile. "I normally don't talk to people about it—and frankly don't care to."

Tripoli just nodded.

"And I don't really understand what your interest in Matthew could be. Now, after all these years. My goodness, it must be—what is it?—about sixty years now since Matthew came back?"

"I'm a police officer with the Ithaca Police Department."

"Yes, you told me that. But this is so long ago now."

"Well, I've been working on a recent case—"

"Oh my!" Alarm registered on her face. "You know something about Matthew, don't you?"

"Yes, I do," Tripoli admitted. She was watching him carefully, he noticed. Color had risen to her neck and face.

"You found him finally?"

He paused and said gently, "Yes."

She read the look on Tripoli's face. "Oh Lord, he's dead." It was a question that was asked and answered.

"I'm sorry."

Flossie Francis' facade crumbled before him, and she started to weep. "Forgive me," she kept apologizing, but couldn't quite stem the flow of tears. Finally, she got up and left the room. Tripoli went to the large window and stared out at the hazy horizon lingering over the sea. Then she returned with a handkerchief, dabbing her eyes, somewhat more composed.

"I'm sorry to be the one to bring you the bad news," he said, turning from the window.

"Oh, it's not your fault," she said, and saw how Tripoli winced. She blew her nose. "So, Matthew was alive *all* this time?" Her smile returned. "Now that's good news to me. I was always worried about him. He was so innocent and sweet. Do you want to tell me what happened? How you found out about him?"

"I don't quite know where to begin," admitted Tripoli.

"Well," she said, as if coaxing a child. "Why don't we start at the beginning? When you first learned about him?"

He paused, glanced again at the Gulf, then turned back to her. "I didn't at first learn about Matthew. You see, there's another little boy," he said.

She pressed a slender, vein-lined hand to her mouth, "Oh no!" she exclaimed. "Another."

Tripoli found himself opening up to the old school teacher in a way that surprised him. "You see, I blame myself for Matthew's death," he said finally.

"But why? What happened?"

He explained about the raid. "I let things get out of control. But, look," he said, "tell me about Matthew, Miss Francis." He could never imagine calling her by her first name. "That's what I need to know. If I can learn something about Matthew, maybe it'll help me understand Daniel."

"Now it's my turn to wonder about where to begin," she said.

"When did you first get to know Matthew?"

"I had heard about him, of course. But I didn't really come into contact with Matthew until September."

"This is September of '39?"

"Yes," she nodded. "September of 1939. I was teaching the first grade in the elementary school. Of course, like everyone else in Watertown, I knew about Matthew. There were all these reporters coming to town. His mother, Mary Roland, was a simple woman, a widow, a very modest person. She just wanted Matthew to be a normal boy and go to school and fit into the world. That's what she always talked about. 'Fitting in.'"

Cool air was blowing in through a vent above Tripoli's head; he could feel it on his damp skin.

"I'll always remember that first day of school, right after Labor Day, it was. Some parents sent their children off on the bus. Others walked them to the school grounds, then left. But Mrs. Roland brought Matthew directly to me in the classroom and then plunked herself down right outside the door. She took a chair and just sat there for the *whole* school day. At first I thought she was maybe a little deranged from all that had happened. But it didn't take me long to figure out why she was there."

"What was the boy like?" prompted Tripoli.

"Oh, Matthew was brilliant—exceptional in every respect. He read just about anything he could get his hands on. And he seemed possessed of an innate understanding of people and the world around him—the natural world. He spoke about things like preserving the earth, but back then no one knew what he was talking about. He was just far ahead of the times. Sometimes I catch myself thinking, what if he were around today, what with all the scary stuff that's going on with the climate changes and…maybe people would finally understand, listen."

For a moment she gazed wistfully off into the distance. Tripoli waited for her return.

"But for all of his wonderful gifts, Matthew was a handful. He was…But wait," she stopped short. "I've got some photos. Would you like to— "

"Of course!" he said eagerly.

Miss Francis went to the closet and brought down a box from the top shelf. It was brimming with old pictures.

"Here," she handed Tripoli a large print. It was a portrait with a couple of dozen young children lined up in stacked rows. Watertown Elementary School, first grade class, 1939, said the label at the bottom.

Tripoli instantly picked the boy out of the class. He was standing next to his young teacher, The old teacher handed Tripoli another picture. A snapshot. The young teacher was in a playground with a few of her students. She had both hands on Matthew's shoulder and his head was turned from the camera.

"It wasn't easy getting him to pose," she laughed.

Tripoli continued to stare at the second picture. "This spot here," he said, pointing to the boy's neck. "What is it?"

She took a second look, furrowed her brow as she searched her memory. "If I remember right…he had a small birthmark."

"What did it look like?"

She shrugged. "Sort of reddish."

"You got a magnifying glass somewhere?" he asked anxiously.

A moment later she was back with a big lens.

"Oh," said Miss Francis, leaning over Tripoli's shoulder. "Now I remember. It looked almost like a—"

"A star," Tripoli uttered, completing her sentence, things finally beginning to jell.

"Got any other pictures?"

"I don't believe so." She rummaged through the box. "No, that's all."

Tripoli went back to the second photo. "From the looks of things here it seems you're trying to keep him from taking off?"

"To say the least," agreed Miss Francis. "Every time I turned around he was gone. You couldn't keep that boy in the classroom. From that first day, Matthew was like a caged animal. You could almost see him literally panting for air. Craving to get out. That's, of course, why his mother was sitting there. I'd turn my back, he'd be out the door, and she'd catch him and drag him right back in.

"But Mrs. Roland was a working woman. She couldn't sit there forever. After a couple of weeks, she thought she would try to go back to the luncheonette. I even suggested it."

"And then?"

"And then I was alone with Matthew. Thirty-one children and Matthew. It was an almost impossible situation to handle. I had to teach a class—not neglect the other children—and also attempt to deal with him." Miss Francis bit her lip.

"Matthew tried everything. Even climbed out of windows. Going to the lunchroom, I'd have to hold his hand to make sure he didn't break away. I certainly couldn't let him go to the boys' room unac-companied. I used to have to call Mr. Carpenter, the gym teacher."

"Where was he going?"

"Into the air. Outside."

"Like Daniel," remarked Tripoli, nodding to himself.

She took a long breath. "You have to understand. I was exceed-ingly young then. Fresh out of teachers' college, where in those days they emphasized discipline in the classroom. I was beside myself. I had a conference with Matthew's mother in the principal's office. 'Please,' she begged us, 'don't give up on my Matthew. If he doesn't go to school, how's he *ever* going to make a life in this world?'"

"I kept him after school for hours—which, of course, only made matters worse." Miss Francis began to pace the white carpet as she spoke. "I made him sit still right in front of me while I graded papers and prepared lesson plans. Mrs. Roland, at her wits' end, resorted to spanking the poor child. Between us, we kept Matthew imprisoned—yes, that's what it was." Her eyes brimmed with tears. "Excuse me," she said and blew her nose.

Flossie Francis took back the photo and stared at it for the longest moment, then turned to look back at her visitor.

"I remember the day he disappeared. The hour. He had just tried to crawl out of the window again, and I had caught him by the tail of his shirt and pulled him back into the classroom. The other children were laughing and I fed their laughter, asking them what kind of animals climb out of windows and up trees. 'Monkeys!' they were all shouting. *Monkeys!*'" she raised her own voice, and Tripoli could almost hear the cries of the children.

"'And what do we do with monkeys?' I asked, hanging onto Matthew and dragging him toward my desk. I was angry. So angry that I did something unconscionable. I took some rope, tied it around his waist, and leashed him to my desk."

Her hands were trembling, and she clasped them together in an attempt to control them.

"By the time I finished with him, Matthew really did look like an animal. A beaten, hurt creature. He had the most pitiful look on his face. But at that moment I just didn't care, didn't see. Didn't hear his whimper. Didn't *listen!*

"After he was gone, a great but inexplicable sadness descended on our town. It felt as if something vital were suddenly missing—and, of course, it was. His mother died a few years later, still a young woman. I don't know if you believe in broken hearts?"

"I've seen it happen," Tripoli said with compassion.

"Matthew had a gift for us, but we just weren't ready for it. It was only much later, after he was gone, that I understood the extent of his message."

"Yes?"

"Even then, we lived in a tumultuous world. There was a world war going on. We were all too busy, life was too noisy for us to listen. To listen to each other, to the natural world around us, and—most importantly—to listen to our own hearts. Tell me, Mr. Tripoli, what could be more simple or true than that?"

Danny was way ahead of Rosie, pushing the carriage with the twins over the bed of black cinders.

"Let me at least give you a break for a couple of hours," Rosie had said when she rang up Molly at the office. Molly had hesitated, but had finally given in.

They went south from the Spencer Road and ended up on the old, abandoned railroad bed that switchbacked up the hill.

"I wish there were trains again," Danny said when Rosie caught up with him and took hold of the handlebar.

"Oh?"

"Well, there used to be trains here," said Danny. "And they were nice."

She looked at him puzzled. "Now when did you ever ride on a train?"

"I didn't!" he laughed. "But this is a good way to go. You know," he said, leaning into the carriage to check on the babies as they slept. "You can follow these and get just about anywhere. And no one can see you." He turned to gaze up at her. "It's like you're invisible."

"And you know your way around, huh?"

"Sure we do."

"We?" asked Rosie as they pushed on. "You mean the old Hermit?"

"Uh-huh. He knows everything. And the others do, too."

chapter twenty

On his return flight from Florida, Tripoli got stranded in the Newark Airport. It was hardly the first time he got stuck on the last leg home. The airline kept Tripoli and the six other Ithaca passengers waiting in a congested and sweltering lounge as planes taxied noisily past the open gates. The room was low ceilinged and smelled of kerosene, stale pizza, and sweat. He picked up a *USA Today* that someone had discarded. There was a front page story on a vast forest burning in Thailand.

Tripoli's thoughts turned to the weeks and months he had spent looking for Danny. The leads and dead ends. He remembered how he had fallen in love with Molly. That first time they made love—how sweet it had felt in those bitterest of times. He recalled the raid in the forest, that look of recognition in the old Hermit's eyes as they made fleeting contact. And he thought about the people in Watertown who had been touched by Matthew—and about Flossie Francis. *It was only when Matthew was gone, that we—no, that I—began to comprehend just what we had all lost.*

He stared out at the expanse of shimmering tarmac and the long lines of planes that stood idling in the August sun, and he wondered...wondered if the legacy had been broken, if that accumulated wisdom could still be salvaged. If Daniel could still be made ready? Was it all there in the books?

"What's up?" asked Curly Donahue as he hunted through his big ring of keys. It was still early in the morning; he had had only his first cup of coffee, and here was Tripoli, standing over him, hustling him.

The books were locked away in the Evidence Room, and Curly was the man in charge. Having joined the department as a young officer back in the early sixties, he had been the one to oversee the station's security for the last thirty-five years. Except for a couple of wisps of hair, Curly was bald. Even his eyebrows were all but absent.

As he unlocked the cage, he stopped and turned. "You'll bring them back, right?"

"No," said Tripoli, "I'm going to eat them."

"They can't leave this building. Not till the investigation is over."

"Will you give me the fucking books?"

Tripoli took them up the stairs and out the station house door.

The pages felt like parchment but were not made of animal skin; they had the texture of a wood product yet were not paper. Tripoli remembered seeing some material like it once at an exhibition at the university museum. Tapa cloth, it was called, and it was made by the Polynesians from the bark of mulberry trees. The leaves of these ancient volumes sitting on Tripoli's kitchen table had the exact same feel. Tissue thin, yet strong.

Outside, the wind suddenly picked up and began whistling around his isolated farmhouse, rocking the trees as the sky darkened and flashes of electrical discharge illuminated the distant hills. Oblivious to the weather, he hunched over the books that sat nestled in the small ring of yellow light spilling from his lamp.

The bindings on the books—and there were five of them in all—were hand-sewn. Each gathering had been stitched together, then connected to make the whole. Tripoli's father had been a collector of old books. What a pity that he was no longer alive, he would have relished seeing these.

The five books were all of different lengths. The first was the shortest, a little more than one hundred pages. The third was the longest, almost three hundred pages. Some of the entries in the books were simply a couple of paragraphs long, others went on for pages. Using the differences in penmanship and ink colors, Tripoli tried to gauge the number of different authors who had made entries into the text and complex tabulations, and lost count after three dozen. There could easily have been fifty authors. If one attributed to each scribe thirty years of entries, that made the books more than one thousand years old. Perhaps two thousand!

Tripoli began on what he guessed to be the first volume. It was not easy going. The books were in a multiple of languages, both ancient and modern. They were written in what looked to be Hebrew and Greek, English that spanned the gamut from old to medieval to modern. There were even portions written in Chinese-looking characters, and other sections in what might be Sanskrit.

He concentrated on the portions that were in English. They were handwritten in a florid style that was difficult to decipher, and the language was old-fashioned and strange.

The first book appeared to be about the world, the greater world, not just the sun and planets but other galaxies and solar systems. There were drawings of orbits, endless charts with numbered entries. Interspersed through the book were elaborate illustrations adorned with gold leaf and colored with hues of lapis lazuli and the most dazzling of red-orange pigments. There were pages covered with what could have been mathematical formulas, though the symbols were like none that he had ever seen; and diagrams, too, plans and schematics for what looked like machines and odd contraptions.

Once Tripoli started, everything around him seemed to fall away; the day vanished into night, then dawn broke through with its early, pink light.

Slowly, very slowly, he began to understand—or thought he

understood. Here, locked away in these precious books, was a virtual treasure trove of accumulated wisdom, a merging of philosophy and science, psychology and engineering. Whoever these anonymous scribes had been, they had attempted to come to grips with the mysteries that had bedeviled human beings in all times, the very meaning of life—or, at any rate, how to invest life with meaning. They had come to understand how one could live in harmony with nature, both receiving her bounty and returning it in kind; how to live a fulfilling and productive life free from stress and disease, exhaustion and despair. Somehow it all fit together, worked together, the practical and the theoretical, art and technology, music and poetry dovetailed into mathematics and physics to create a single body of knowledge that offered a unified theory of life. And here it was, sitting on his kitchen table. If only he could truly penetrate these works, do more than pick up intelligible fragments from what to him were all but hieroglyphics. If only he could plumb their depths, tap into this enlightenment.

Tripoli pushed on through the next day, breaking only to give the animals some water and fresh fodder, reading until his eyes burned and his head ached. Jumping ahead to the more recent volumes, he discovered small inserts attached in strategic places where gaps had been left in the text. When he ran his fingers over the surface of these attachments, he discovered that the paper was different from the surrounding pages, crisper, newer. The ink, too, seemed fresher. When he put his nose close to the paper, it smelled of bark and berries. The notations contained some kind of ideograms commingled with numbers. One of the images looked like that of a little boy. It was Danny, he was sure. The old man had been keeping a record of Danny's visit, a log of his progress, plotting the trajectory of their encounter.

That evening as he wandered the fields and forests surrounding his home, he thought about the ancient texts. Here, distilled for the reader, was what poets have written about, musicians composed, and artists painted. The more he thought about it, the simpler it all became. It was what Daniel was always speaking about. If you listen, you can hear. And if you can hear the natural world outside yourself, you begin to love it, to get an inkling of what love actually is, come to grips with the core of existence, come to care about the planet, other creatures, other people. For that, the books seemed to say to Tripoli, was the meaning of life, and societies that failed to heed these meanings were ultimately doomed.

As he continued to plow his way through the books, sifting back and forth between the pages of the old scribes and those of recent insertion, laying one volume aside while cross-referencing yet another, it was obvious to Tripoli that the people who had worked on these books were not superstitious, fumbling amateurs, but surprisingly advanced. They spoke of how to use the earth's renewable sources of energy; they had proposed ways of harnessing the wave action of large bodies of waters, devised means of tapping the heat reservoir that was the ocean, appeared to have built solar collectors that were connected to devices that were capable of storing electricity in very small and transportable packages. These were certainly not a people opposed to innovation. On the contrary, they were prophets and scholars who recognized the value of technology but also realized that a society that became too highly centralized, too dependent on vast quantities of energy, and too wasteful was ultimately programmed for catastrophic collapse.

Though Tripoli could but scratch the surface, he now thought he knew why Daniel had disappeared. Daniel was an integral part of this legacy of prophets, the newest disciple to be indoctrinated and trained and granted the wisdom of this succession of sages. Once mature, he too would be charged with the responsibility of carrying forth this knowledge and making salvation available to the greater world when it was ready—ready to listen.

For some still mysterious reason, Daniel had interrupted his studies to return to the modern world. Or maybe it wasn't an interruption? Perhaps, Tripoli speculated, this was an integral part of his learning: perhaps he had been sent back to the modern world to learn, gather information about the new technologies and devices so that they, too, could be integrated into the old? Whatever the purpose, killing the old Hermit had broken the chain, disrupted the continuity. Yet here were these priceless books, the awesome legacy to be passed on to the next visionary, now in Tripoli's hands.

"I've got a question for you," Tripoli said.

Outside, the air was perfectly still and the last days of August were brutally hot. The gardens around Ithaca that weren't scrupulously watered had all but dried up. In the vineyards along the shores of the lake, the grapes that would be squeezed for wine were few and far between. Only the fruit trees in the orchards scattered outside of town seemed to be faring better. With their deep roots, they were still able to tap into deep levels of ground water. Yet, though there was fruit to be had, many of the late varieties seemed stunted. The summer had turned exceptionally dry and every day it felt as though it were going to rain—yet it never did.

"I've got a question," Tripoli repeated. His face was covered with the beginnings of a beard and his eyes were bloodshot and heavy-lidded.

He had found the old priest in his sacristy, hanging up his vestments. Although he hadn't seen Tripoli in years, the priest didn't seem at all surprised by the sudden visit. In the intervening years, his thinning hair had turned snow white and his eyebrows had grown long and bushy. Sticking out of his ears were tufts of white hair that looked like puffs of cotton. Tripoli followed him as he shuffled back to his office. Tripoli hadn't stepped into this church since his wedding to Kim.

"You're a man of wisdom, a real scholar, and I figured maybe you're the right person to ask."

"I'm flattered, Lou, but I wouldn't go that far." The old man laughed. Although his face was deeply furrowed and his features sagged, his eyes were a clear, bright blue.

"Enlightenment," Tripoli said. His hands were knotted together and he shook them as he searched for the right words. "How long does it take?"

"Take?"

"Till someone is ready?"

"Ready?"

Tripoli struggled to formulate his question. "I mean if you look back in history at the prophets."

"Oh…" said the priest, sinking down into his chair. "That's quite a question."

Tripoli stood hovering over him, waiting.

The old man drew a long, deep breath. He studied his own hands and brought his furry brow together in contemplation. "Well," he said finally glancing up at Tripoli, "If you look at the prophets…if you read the Bible or the Koran or the Bahgavad Gita, it's really unclear whether they gained enlightenment in a single moment or over a period of years."

"Christ. Mohammed. Buddha sitting under his tree," persisted Tripoli. "How long did it take?"

"Forty days in the desert or a lifetime under a tree. As long as it takes," said the priest with a chuckle. Then seeing the look on Tripoli's face asked, "You're not kidding about this, are you?"

Tripoli didn't respond, but pushed on. "When I say the name John, who do you think of?"

"The Bible's full of Johns. And there are numerous Popes named John. John? Well, I think of John the Evangelist. John the Divine— if you're curious about the mystical. And, of course, John the Baptist comes to mind."

"Oh!" exclaimed Tripoli. "Yes. I should have thought of that."

"I don't get it," said the priest, smiling with mystification. "And why all these questions?"

"Well, I've been reading these books."

"What books?"

"Well, just certain old books I found," replied Tripoli evasively. He reached into his pocket and pulled out a piece of translucent paper onto which he had traced the inscription he had found at the very head of the first volume, on what might have been the title page. "I know you're a biblical scholar and…Can you read this?" he asked, handing the sheet across the desk.

The priest put on his reading glasses, unfolded the paper and studied the writing.

קאחדים הנאמנמ זהןלביב בצקבותינו שיזכו
קחפתבבכ צכ בתבי – חנכש חאלח. שומרי רוח
יקןפש שכ נצמת זסחגיקי אמיתות הצוכם האכה.
זשפחבת תמשׁין כדכזק כהפיץ אוך צכ התבק הזה,
יׁשצמו את דבד גזסה.

"Hmmm. Looks like ancient Hebrew."

"That's what I thought. Can you translate it?"

"Well, I *think* so…I studied it while I was in the seminary, but…" He squinted. "Let's see. It's addressed to…" he began haltingly, "…'to the chosen others who…who follow and are granted the right to gaze on these hallowed works, the keepers of…of the Sacred Spirit of Anterra, holders of these eternal truths." Without lifting his head, the old priest looked questioningly up at Tripoli over the rims of spectacles.

"Please, go on," he urged.

"'May this flame continue to burn and spread light on this planet, hear the word of Anterra.'"

"Anterra?" echoed Tripoli.

The priest sounded out the letters again. "Yes, An-ter-ra."

"Does that mean anything to you?"

"Anterra?" He shook his head and handed back the paper. "Never heard of it. This is from those books, I suppose?"

Tripoli nodded.

"And these books?"

"Well, they got me thinking…"

"About?"

"Oh, life and death. Love. Our purpose in being here on the earth— if there is any. Our responsibility to others. Other people. Other creatures. The planet itself."

"And what have you discovered?"

Tripoli hesitated to commit himself. "I'm not really sure. But I find myself thinking about things I haven't thought about before. I've always known that I was going to die—as a cop you see death a lot, face it every day. But suddenly now it's taken on a different aspect. I find it frightening and humbling, but also in an odd way liberating. If I can come to accept my mortality, feel it truly, then I become open to the things that may really be important. Do you know what I'm talking about?"

"Of course," said the priest. "You know there's a line in Hamlet…"

Tripoli shrugged. Except for a few selections in high school, he had never really read any Shakespeare.

"Hamlet says to his Horatio, 'The readiness is all.'"

Tripoli paused, thinking. "Yes, that's good. The readiness *is* all."

"It's about that boy, isn't it?" said the priest finally.

Tripoli couldn't mask his surprise. "What makes you say that?"

The cleric's face crinkled in a smile. "It doesn't take much to come to that conclusion. You'd have to be all but brain dead in this town, this country, not to have heard about him."

"The listening," uttered Tripoli.

"Yes, the listening," echoed the old man. He steepled his hands and stared thoughtfully up at the ceiling. "Well, I've been thinking about that myself. There's a parable in the Bible. In Matthew." He reached behind him and took the book off his shelf. "Christ talks about a sower who went forth to sow seeds." He wet his finger and thumbed through the book as he spoke. "Some seeds fall by the wayside and the birds come and devour them. Others fall upon rocky places where there's no earth and the seedlings soon get scorched by the sun. Still others land upon thorns and the thorns grow up and choke them. Ah, here we are…" he interrupted himself, then began to read: "'…and others fell upon the ground and yielded fruit, some a hundred-fold, some sixty, some thirty."

Tripoli looked at him eagerly. "You mean…?"

"'He that hath ears, let him hear.'"

"Oh…" uttered Tripoli.

"What's interesting is that the parable begins with 'Harken.' And then there are those last words." He intoned them again, this time ever more slowly. "'He that hath ears let him hear.' We assume that because the initiative is with the speaker that the message controls the hearer. But, Lou, it's just to the contrary. An appeal, even the appeal of Jesus, may be frustrated by unreceptiveness. The inability to listen."

"And you think the boy is a messiah?"

"No. Of course not. But…through the ages the Lord has, from time to time, as He has chosen them, employed His messengers. It's a question, of course, of our being open to listening. A question of the ground being prepared to accept the seeds of wisdom. Fertile and unchoked."

They spoke for a long hour after that. Then the priest walked Tripoli to the door of the church.

"If you want to talk further," said the priest, taking his hand, "I'm always here."

The faint but insistent tapping kept chewing into the edges of Molly's sleep. She rolled over away from the window and tried to bury herself into the pillow, but it kept drilling into her consciousness like a rodent gnawing at her ears.

"Huh?" She awoke with a start and shot upright in bed.

Her eyes went immediately to Daniel's cot. He was in a deep sleep. The noise, however, kept up and at last she realized it was coming from her window: a coin or key was being struck against the pane. The illuminated digits on her clock read 3:20. Cautiously, Molly separated the slats in the blinds and peeked out. At first, she couldn't recognize the man. Didn't expect to see him with the beginnings of a beard. Then she eased up the blind and asked, "What's up?" Tripoli motioned for her and she climbed out of bed and unlocked the front door.

"What's the trouble?" she asked, standing barefoot in the doorway. The linoleum was cold, and she was still fuzzy with sleep.

"No trouble," he said in a whisper, slipped in, and closed the door softly behind him. "I just wanted to talk to you."

"Huh? At three in the morning!"

"I just wanted to make sure Daniel's okay."

"Of course he is. He's sleeping."

"Good. Can I see him?"

He looked haggard. She glanced out the window and saw no sign of a car. "How'd you get here?"

"Oh, I was out walking…" he answered nebulously, "…and then just…just came by."

Molly took a hard look at him. His clothes were rumpled, the furrows in his face were deep, and the skin hung loose around his neck. Town was a good three miles away.

"Have you been drinking?" she asked.

"Of course not!" he retorted.

"I haven't seen you in ages."

"Yeah, I know. I've been busy."

"What's up? You don't look so good. Looks like you lost

weight," she said, surveying him. It looked as if he had shed pounds, and his skin had an unhealthy pallor as though he hadn't seen daylight in ages. And his eyes burnt with an intensity that frightened Molly. "Are you okay, Trip?"

"Yeah. Sure. Can I see him?" he asked again. "Just take a look at him. I won't wake him—I promise."

It was an odd request. "Cripes," said Molly. Shaking her head, she relented and led him towards the bedroom. She opened the door, and Tripoli tiptoed into the darkened room.

Daniel was sleeping deeply; his eyes were closed and his lids fluttered in dream. His features, nested in the pillow, were cast in a soft repose.

Tripoli went to the bed, knelt down at the edge, and bowed his head, staring down at the boy. He said nothing, did nothing, just knelt there in silence, his chin resting on his hand. It reminded Molly of those strange people who had been waiting for her, blocking her way to the office.

Daniel, as if sensing Tripoli's presence, smiled in his sleep. His face reminded Tripoli of angels one saw in frescoes painted on the ceilings of Italian churches. Tripoli reached out and lovingly stroked the little boy's cheek with his fingertips.

"I've got to get to sleep, Trip," whispered Molly into his ear, breaking the spell. "I've got a full day ahead of me."

Together, they slipped out of the bedroom. Tripoli took Molly's hand as they stood in the darkened kitchen. "We've got to protect him," he said, his voice soft and throaty.

"Well, of course!"

"Nurture his gifts."

"What are you talking about?"

"You can't send him to school," he said right out.

"Who...?"

"Daniel told me. He's worried. You can't do it."

"Of course I can. And I will. And I *have* to."

"Putting an exceptional boy like Daniel in an ordinary school is ludicrous. It's a recipe for disaster. Believe me. Look, I've got a much better idea. I've thought it all through. We don't have to get married right away if you don't want to. You could just move out with me. And Daniel loves my place. There's plenty of room. It's in the country. We'll fix it up together."

"Do we have to talk about this now, at *three* in the morning?"

"You can stay home with him."

"But I don't want to stay *home*. I like to work. I've got to have some kind of life too."

"Okay, then *I'll* stay home with him."

"And take care of him?"

"Sure," he said. "We can school him at home. I've got it all figured out."

"Oh, you're going to quit your job?"

"That's no problem. I've got a little bit of savings that'll carry us through until the spring. I've got lots of land. Then we'll start growing crops. The soil isn't the greatest, but we can grow enough for us and then some to sell. I was thinking of doing vegetables. Maybe beans and tomatoes. Some melons."

"Trip!"

"And we've already got some animals. They'll have babies. We've got milk. Cheese. There's wool."

She tried to interrupt, but he kept excitedly pushing on. The more he talked, the more he sounded like Danny. Like a little kid. The less like a life's partner.

"Trip, will you do me a favor? Just go home and go to sleep, *please*."

"The wild fires and hurricanes, the heat waves and floods, the crops that have failed in Canada and…I suddenly understand," he said with an intensity that frightened her. "The world's on the brink of catastrophe! And we've got to do something—"

She looked at him as if he were a stranger.

"The tornado that hit town," he pleaded, clutching both her hands in his. "You saw that with your own eyes, right?"

She realized that she had made the mistake of nodding, and that had launched him further. He started going on about some books he had found, about Anterra, the spirit of Anterra.

"Anterra?" she said.

"I'm a little punchy, I realize that. I haven't slept much. And maybe I'm not making perfect sense right now, but—"

"Well then go home and go to sleep."

"Daniel. You don't understand how important he is. He's the key. The link in the—"

"And let me go back to sleep, too, willya?"

She pushed him out the door, but he was still rambling on, even as she locked it behind him.

After he left, Molly couldn't go back to sleep, much as she needed to. Was Tripoli, she wondered, turning into another one of these fanatics who believed that Danny could make the lame walk and the blind see? Obviously he was going through a rough time, still blaming himself for the old man's death. School, she thought. Of course he had to go! Keep Danny at home? That would just isolate him further, make him yet more different. The poor boy needed a chance to live his life, make friends, play in a school yard, God's sake. Baseball. Basketball. Football. Molly didn't care what. And she wanted a life for him, not just for herself. She wanted him to dance and fall in love with a nice girl, have a decent job, not become a mystical goat herder. All she desired at that instant was to save him from the world, not burden him with the task of saving the world from itself. If it was burning up, that wasn't his making. Oh, dear God, she thought, help me do what's right.

"It just hit me!" said Rosie bolting upright in bed. She rolled over and shook Ed, who was sound asleep.

"Huh?" he said, slow to rouse. 'What the...What's going on?" He blinked in the darkness trying to focus.

"He's getting ready to take off again."

"Who?"

"Daniel. *Daniel!*'"

Ed raised himself up on an elbow. Yawned and scratched his chest.

"That's why he insisted that we walk over to the railroad beds."

"What time is it?" Ed squinted at the illuminated numerals on the clock. "Shit, four! Rosie, I've got to get up in another hour."

"Will you just listen to me!" Rosie turned on the light by the bed.

"Do I have any choice?" He blinked in the pain of the bright light. Hearing Rosie's heated voice, the babies started mewling for milk.

"If she puts him into school, he's gone." Rosie stumbled out of bed. Her feet and hands were swollen again. When she went to pick up the twins, she noticed that there was a new, large bruise on her arm. She found another on her leg, but couldn't remember injuring herself. "I've been spending some time alone with Daniel," she said as she brought the babies back into the bed. "Here, hang onto Freddy a second." She popped open one side of her nursing bra. "The things that little boy knows. The things he says..." She took Freddy back and brought the infant's hungry mouth to her nipple. In a moment she could feel the heaviness in her breasts being eagerly drained on both sides. "...The wisdom he has..."

Ed was already fast asleep, his breath wheezing through his lips.

chapter twenty-one

"You've tricked me!" cried Daniel, as a cluster of parents and children swept past the school entrance, turning to stare at him. Daniel dug his heels into the ground. "Please let me go!" He struggled to break loose from Molly's grip, but she hung on.

"We're just going go in to look and meet some of teachers."

"No, I can't." He was starting to cry. *"Please."*

"Oh, Honey," she said, bending down to bring him close. "But I told you we were going to go here."

"I don't care what you told me, I'm not going in."

Hoping to create the air of a festive occasion, Molly had taken Daniel to the Moosewood Restaurant for dinner. When she had first hinted at visiting the school, he hadn't really reacted and she guessed things might go smoothly. Daniel had seemed perfectly happy in the restaurant; he liked the Russian cabbage pie and the waiters who doted on him.

"We didn't order that," said Molly when Siddhartha, the cook, brought out double desserts—a heaping serving of fresh mango ice cream and a big slice of carrot cake, thick with nuts.

"This is on the house!" Siddhartha's white teeth glinted through his dark beard as he ceremoniously served the boy. "For our own Daniel."

"Mmmm, it's good," said Daniel looking up with a full mouth of the homemade ice cream. "Can I have some of that cake, too?"

He pointed with his fork.

That evening, the Ithaca School District was scheduled to hold its annual system-wide registration and Molly, after much deliberation, had decided to enroll Daniel in the South Hill School on Hudson Street. It seemed the perfect elementary school. It was right in town, within walking distance of her office, yet sufficiently removed from most of the city traffic; a small school in a quiet residential neighborhood of older, well-kept homes, a solid brick structure that felt safe and secure. And they had a guard and an electronically controlled door. No strangers got in. No little children wandered out.

"We're just going to go and take a good look at the school," she had said as they left Moosewood, trying to prepare him. "And maybe talk to one of the teachers."

"They're going to try and keep me there and never let me out." He had started to balk on the street. "For years!"

"Oh, don't be silly. It isn't a jail," she urged him along. "All children go to school. And you'll be out and free, every afternoon. And the weekends will be all—"

"They're going to teach me things I don't want to learn."

"How can you say that if you've never been there?"

"I know," he had said, looking her deep in the eye. "I just know!"

Molly glanced around as more people brushed past them at the school doors. "You're going to make lots of new friends here and have plenty of fun."

He turned his head away.

"Now stop acting foolish." Some of the parents with their little kids in tow stopped to gape at Daniel and Molly. "Come on, Sweetie," she whispered in his ear, "Everybody's looking at us. Don't make a scene."

"I don't care!" he whispered back.

"We're not going to the dentist. Just look at all the other chil-dren. How excited they are."

"I'm not a child!" he objected.

"You've still got lots of things you have to learn."

"But not here."

Rising to her full height, Molly took both hands and scooted him forward. "One way or another you're going in," she said finally. He started to resist again, but she was adamant and finally he relented, following her into the building with head bowed, his lips set in a miserable pout.

The brightly lit gym was already crowded with dozens of par-ents and children milling about, their eager voices echoing off the polished wood floors. There were tables set up for the various classes, and the school's teachers had turned out for the occasion.

Dianne Lifsey spotted them and, waving, pushed her way through the crowd. "Well, hello, Molly!" she piped.

"Hello, Mrs. Driscoll," said little Stevie when Mrs. Lifsey poked him. He seemed to Molly a little overdressed for the occasion in his white shirt and bright red bow tie. "Hey Danny," he grinned. "'member me?"

Daniel was in too much of a funk to notice him or anyone else.

"And how is our famous Daniel doing?" inquired Mrs. Lifsey, leaning over to get a closer look. She was almost breathing in his face. "I'll bet Daniel will be in Stevie's class."

Daniel, who was studying his shoes, flushed a deep crimson.

"Come on," Molly nudged, "at least say hello."

"Hello," he muttered, grinding the toe of his shoe into the floor.

Molly could feel his hand shaking in hers. Painful as it was, there was no way around it, she knew. He was going to have to go to school and negotiate social situations with other kids if he wasn't going to grow up to be a freak. And she needed to hold down a job. It was as simple as that.

Another set of parents with a child joined them. Then another. Before Molly realized it, they were encircled by a small but smiling crowd. The people all muttering, Daniel, Daniel.

"You have to excuse us," she said, and took Daniel over to the school nurse, who was the first stop.

"Oh, this is the Daniel I've heard about," she said with a big, toothy smile. "Can he really predict weather?"

"Please," said Molly, pointing to the papers on the table.

"Oh, yes, of course," said the nurse becoming all business. She put on her glasses and reviewed Daniel's vaccination records. "Let's see…he'll need a polio and…and a triple vaccine booster this year."

On another line, the school secretary checked Daniel's birth certificate, recorded Molly's address and phone number, both at home and work. "We need an alternate emergency number." She kept looking at Daniel very curiously.

Molly gave Rosie's address and number

Standing tight at Molly's side, Daniel seemed to shrivel as the woman took down the pertinent data of his life.

"Oh, come on now," Molly tickled him under his arm, trying to get Daniel to lighten up. "Can't you see how everyone is so happy to see you here?" But he just pulled away, looking pained and worried.

"I think…" said the school secretary, searching through her files. "Yes, you'll need to go to room 112. Just down the corridor and to the left. Mrs. Scocroft will be doing the interview and evaluation."

"I gotta take a pee, bad!" said Daniel as they walked down the corridor.

There was a men's room and a women's, and Molly didn't know which to chose. She didn't dare let him go unescorted—not the strange way he was acting just now.

"In here," she said, holding the door for him.

"But it says 'Women.' I can't!"

"It's okay." One of the mothers passed around her and went into the rest room. "Come on. It's fine."

She took him into a stall and stood behind him as he unzipped his fly and fished out his little thing. In the next stall the woman was letting out a torrential gush, but Daniel, poised over the bowl, was so tense he couldn't let go.

"Can't we go home," he pleaded, turning around.

"Pee already," she said as the neighboring toilet flushed.

When they got to the classroom, Mrs. Scocroft was waiting for them. Her face lit up when she recognized the new pupil.

"Oh, you're *that* Danny!" she exclaimed. She was much younger than Molly, had her hair tied in a pony tail, and appeared so kind and warm that Molly fervently hoped she would be Daniel's teacher.

A father with a cute little girl in a frilly dress came into the room and stood waiting behind them. When Daniel turned, the man winked and waved. He bent down, whispered something to his daughter, and the little girl kept straining to see Daniel, who kept shielding himself in front of Molly.

"We need to get a sense of his development for placement purposes," explained Mrs. Scocroft. Then she turned to Daniel and smiled at him kindly. "Well now, Danny…"

"Daniel," he corrected, his head still down.

"Oh, excuse me. 'Daniel.' Yes, that's much nicer. It's more grownup, isn't it?"

Daniel finally looked up at her, and Molly breathed a sigh of relief.

"Now, Daniel, do you know your birth date?"

"December fourteenth."

"Excellent! And do you know where you live?"

Of course Daniel knew. He lived in a trailer.

"Yes, but where is the trailer?"

"On the planet Earth."

The teacher broke out in laughter. "That's very funny," she said. "Do you know any other funny jokes?"

Daniel didn't know what she meant.

"Do you like playing with other children?" asked the woman hopefully.

"Playing? You mean like *games?*"

"Well, yes…"

"No," responded Daniel flatly. "Not really."

Two other prospective kindergartners accompanied by their parents entered the room and got in line to wait their turn, and Molly could feel Daniel tightening. The cute little girl who stood behind Daniel kept waving to him, trying to catch his eye, but he would have none of it. Molly worried that if he kept this up, they would end by placing him in a group of developmentally stunted kids.

"Danny's very smart, really," Molly turned back to the teacher. "He's just a little shy. But he's *very* interested in books. All kinds of books," she went on hastily.

"I hear Daniel knows a lot about weather."

"Yes. But he's especially interested in animals. And plants. Anything to do with nature. Right, Danny?" She tugged his hand, and he nodded obediently.

"Well," responded the teacher, still trying to draw Daniel in. "Would you like to learn how to really read those books? You know, by the time Christmas comes you'll know *all* the letters, and maybe even how to read and write some words. Now how does that sound?"

The books became all consuming. It was hard going, but Tripoli sat at his kitchen table working his way from one volume to the next, trying to garner some sense of it in language he was comfortable with. Though Tripoli was able to decipher the sections that were in relatively modern English, he could at best guess at the contents of those that looked to be in Middle or Old English.

Some of the volumes, he found, dealt primarily with observations and calculation of natural phenomena: how weather patterns coalesced and swirled over the globe, predictions for the chaotic behavior of frontal systems, of wind speed and cloud cover and rain fall. There were diagrams of what looked like the jet stream with arrows indicating its seasonal movements. Tripoli had no idea what the equations and diagrams implied, but it was clear that some kind of calculus was being employed to solve sophisticated problems that modern scientists with their computer models had only begun to touch.

In one section, Tripoli found detailed accounts of how various creatures migrated, how their senses were keyed into the angle of the sun, how pigeons utilized the magnetic field of the earth to navigate their way home, how bees performed dances to inform the other workers in their colonies about the location of a new source of nectar. And all this, he realized enthralled, had already been discovered long before the establishment of modern science. Most intriguing to Tripoli were the careful tabulations marking the onset and end of the growing seasons. They were keyed to the blossoming of specific flowers and these entries were closely correlated with migration patterns.

For countless centuries, at least two thousand years, the authors had been tracking fluctuations in the climate. There were variations in temperature, up and down, periods of cooling and warming observed around the globe. Though scientists could no doubt observe the end result today, what they lacked was the baseline. And the prehistory was all here in the books, the data that science could at best only infer from tree rings or signs buried in the rocks and soil.

But it was the relatively recent entries that riveted Tripoli's attention. Apparently made in the early twentieth century, the authors had noted that global temperatures were steadily rising. What astounded Tripoli was that at this early date the authors had the foresight to see that, as a result of continuing human activity, temperatures in the future were going to rise at an accelerating rate. And that the regularity in the patterns of rainfall would begin to vary in ever-increasing wild oscillations. They were calling for droughts where there had been an abundance of water. Floods in what had formerly been deserts. If things were allowed to continue, not only would the quality of life suffer, but there would be severe dislocations: crop failures and famines with, inevitably, political instability and war, vast migrations of desperate people in search of habitat and food.

And not only would the planet become progressively less capable of sustaining any significant human population, but countless life forms would be rapidly extinguished as weed species crowded them out of their ecological niches. Catastrophe could be averted, noted the authors, only if humans drastically changed the patterns of their lives. From what Tripoli could discern, it all appeared to revolve around energy, its generation and storage and use. And buried in these arcane books lay the very prescriptions for survival—if one could decipher them.

The other volumes dealt with humanistic issues, about how and why people behaved as they did when gathered in groups. There was a model proposed for "a just society," a democratic structure in which each individual's unique talents were to be identified and recognized. Under the plan, no adult was to be underutilized or mismatched in vocation; the promise of each child was to be given the full opportunity to develop and flourish.

Tripoli's reading kept him leaping back and forth both temporally and across the span of books scattered on his table. In the late afternoon, as the sun was throwing long shadows across his kitchen, he discovered a huge collection of stories about the encounters its authors had had with other people, living creatures, and cosmic phenomena. Taken together, these stories seemed almost like a handbook for living with the *real* rules of life given by example—not the sort of thing, he mused, that he had been taught in school.

Tripoli was so engrossed that he rarely left the table. He forgot to eat, hardly slept. Coffee became his constant companion, and the only times he got up were when his bladder was so painfully full he could no longer concentrate.

The books, taken together, were interconnected, linked almost like a complex piece of software. There were branches and bifurcations that led Tripoli from one volume to the next, then looped back again through a third, as if the numerous writers had been holding a dialogue among themselves stretching across a wide span of time. In one of the later tomes, Tripoli was particularly fascinated to discover that the authors had developed indices that could be employed to measure the state of a civilization, to determine if society was healthy, in decline, or perhaps even dead. The indicators keyed in on everything from the accumulation of refuse to declines in everyday civility. They looked at how a society treated its most vulnerable citizens; examined a culture's architecture, gauging its scale in relation to humans and the surrounding natural world. One of the primary indicators, however, was a measure of the ability of a society's citizens to listen to each other and truly hear what was being said. It evaluated by gradation the ability of individuals to stand motionless for prolonged periods, receptive to their surroundings.

When Tripoli finally took a long-needed break, he stepped out into his yard. The night was cool and overcast; a heavy fog had settled around his house obscuring all light. He stood perfectly still and stared blankly out into the night until, suddenly, he was struck by something he had never noticed before. Even here in Newfield, in the country miles from the city, there was a constant, almost subsonic rumble. He could feel it through the soles of his feet. It was the massive weight of trucks on the move, machines drumming, billions of people shod in hard shoes rushing about, their feet pounding the earth.

When the phone rang in the morning, Tripoli ignored it. He turned from the book he was reading and stood at the kitchen window, watching the lambs as they frolicked around the enclosure, their tails twiddling contentedly. He was still thinking about his discussion with the old priest. The man, who seemed as much a theologian as a cleric, had found through his own studies that most holy men became enlightened through a series of traumatic events, the experiences culminating in a state of extreme tension that ultimately transformed them.

"Some people go insane," the priest had explained, "some people become prophets...and some people can't tell the difference." Many of them, when called, were reluctant to go forth. Many were of ordinary lineage, born into the most modest of circumstances.

Tripoli's phone kept ringing. He shifted his gaze back into the kitchen, his eyes falling on the books interleaved with slips of paper serving as bookmarks. The table was littered with crumbs, pieces of dried toast, and piles of hand-scribbled notes. He had gone as far as he could, he realized, absorbed as much as he could, but now he had hit the wall of incomprehension. Although with his limited powers he had barely scratched the surface, the message within these works was, nevertheless, now abundantly clear: when humanity's deafness to simple common sense is allowed to reign, the implications for the world can only be catastrophic.

The telephone rang on incessantly.

"All right, all right already," he said picking it up.

"Is this Lou Tripoli?" inquired a woman's voice.

It took him but an instant to recognize it.

"Rosie?" Tripoli's voice registered his surprise.

"Look, I'm sorry to call you at home like this…"

As with most of the cops at IPD, Tripoli's number was unlisted and he was surprised that Rosie had found it.

"When she wasn't looking this morning, I went through Molly's address book," Rosie confessed. "I mean I wouldn't do this normally, but—well, I'm getting kind of desperate. If she puts Daniel in school, he'll be gone again. But this time it'll be for good. I can just feel it." She told him about the walk they had taken along the old railroad beds. "Daniel knows his way around and could be miles away before anybody knows it. I tried to tell Molly but she won't listen to me. But if Daniel takes off into the woods…this time he has nowhere to go. He's just a little boy. And he'll starve!"

"Okay, what do you propose?" he asked.

"Yeah! That's the word." Rosie gave a high, nervous laugh.

"Huh?"

"Propose."

Tired as he was, Tripoli had to laugh, too.

"I'm serious," Rosie went on. "You live out in the country. You love each other. And Daniel's really crazy about you—he keeps telling me about you. And your farm. He loves you. I mean, what more do you need?"

"And you think I haven't tried?"

"So try again," she urged. "If Daniel runs off…I keep thinking of what it'll do to Molly. What it might do to all of us."

"Oh?"

"You don't have to be a rocket scientist to figure things out. You've got those books."

"*What?*" he asked astounded. "How did you know?"

"Curly Donahue's sister is married to Ed's first cousin. Small town, huh?" Rosie laughed.

Tripoli was speechless. "Yeah," he said finally. "Small town, busy tongues. So, what else do you know?"

"I've known Daniel since the day he was born. I've been spend-ing time with him. Just the two of us alone. And I can tell you he's been changed. Spiritually changed."

"But Molly doesn't see it."

"Of course she sees it! It's just that she's in complete denial. If we can protect Daniel, keep him here safe, with us, one day that boy is going to change the world."

Rosie seemed to have gained an insight that he had reached only by studying the books. Reluctantly, Tripoli finally told her about all he had discovered. Everything. About the young Matthew. His teacher in Florida. About the ancient books and their implications of an impending calamity.

"My God, of course The weather *is* going crazy. I keep seeing things on television. There are these terrible fires. And today I heard how people's crops in South Africa are being devoured by these clouds of insects. I keep thinking, well it's far away and it doesn't really affect me. But it does and it will. And not just me but my kids. Things may be getting out of control, but at least we can do *some-thing* here."

"Like what? Kidnap the boy?"

"I was thinking. You're a cop."

"Oh, am I supposed to arrest Molly?"

"No, no! Listen to me. You post a guard. Somebody sits there. Right in the class with him. Doesn't take his eyes off Daniel—you know that he's going to take off the first minute somebody turns their back."

"But—"

"You've got cops, don't you? A whole station house full of them. You could rotate. Everybody takes a turn. Once every two weeks."

Tripoli imagined the Chief going for the idea. "Rosie, dear," he sighed indulgently. "Rosie—"

"I'm just talking about buying a little time. Till we can talk some sense into Molly. Look, this weekend is Labor Day. Then on Tuesday he starts school. Three days. That's not much time. We've got to take some action. Now!"

"Look, I gotta do something," said Rosie early Sunday morning as she bolted out the door, her hair flying in the wind. Outside it was so hot and dry, it felt as if she were in the desert.

"Hey, you can't just march up there!" Ed cried after her. But Rosie was already out of earshot.

She caught Mary Tilley, the South Hill principal, just as she was heading off to church. Mrs. Tilley was backing her big Lincoln out of the driveway when she spotted Rosie rushing toward her car.

"I'm sorry to bother you like this," said Rosie. "But if you could just give me a minute…" She hung onto to the edge of Mrs. Tilley's car and caught her breath. "It's about one of your new first graders."

Mrs. Tilley turned off the motor.

"It's Daniel. Daniel Driscoll."

"Oh, yes." Mrs. Tilley smiled. She immediately knew who the boy was. She had, of course, heard about the kidnapping and his subsequent return and a bit about the fuss people in town were making over the child. But it was quickly obvious to Rosie that she hadn't the faintest notion about how extraordinary Daniel really was. Leaning in through the open window, Rosie hurriedly tried to explain. "…and he's tuned in—in touch with life like no other human being. And he needs to be out in nature. He's not the kind of boy that you could keep confined in a classroom."

"Well," said Mrs. Tilley, cutting her off and smiling indulgently, "that's certainly very interesting."

"*Interesting?*" echoed Rosie.

"But you're not the mother."

"No. Of course not. But I've taken care of Daniel since he was born. And I know him as well as his mother. Maybe even better right now."

"We certainly would gladly talk with Danny's mother and discuss…"

Rosie refused to give up.

"Just listen, *please,*" she pleaded. "This has all happened once before. There was another boy just like him in Watertown and…"

As best she could, Rosie tried to relate all she had learned from Tripoli—about the boy called Matthew, the old books that had been discovered in his hut, the chain of the legacy that had been broken but might still be reparable.

"I'm sorry," said the woman, now eyeing Rosie warily. "I really have to go." She started her engine and, with a fixed smile, continued out of her driveway and hurried off to church.

When Molly awoke on Labor Day morning, the sky was black with oppressive low clouds and the air felt pregnant with a storm. Daniel was already up. He had put on his T-shirt and shorts from the day before and he was sitting listlessly in the kitchen with his head resting on the table.

"Maybe you want to work in your garden while I make us breakfast?" She stretched and yawned. "I think you need to water it again too," she said, hoping to spark him into activity. "It looks kind of dry."

Daniel didn't even bother to raise his head.

Ignoring his mood, Molly toasted some bagels and set out juice. She buttered a bagel and placed it in front of him. "Go on, take a nibble. It'll make you feel better."

"I've got a stomachache," he complained.

Finally he took a couple of bites.

But a few minutes later he was assaulted by a sudden case of diarrhea. As he sat perched on the toilet, she felt his forehead. He didn't have a fever. He wasn't particularly pale, either. Molly was sure she knew what it was: nerves. Sometimes when she was under stress it happened to her. The best strategy, she decided, was none. Don't make any fuss. The less said about school the better. When she thought about his starting on Tuesday, Molly found herself vacillating. She wanted to do the right thing for Danny, but what was right? Give up her job and find themselves back where they started? Penniless and on the edge? Or dependent on the whims and whiles of another person? There was no one she really could talk to, no one she could trust to have *only* Danny's interests at heart. Not Tripoli, nor Rosie, nor Larry. Everybody had their own agenda, and Tripoli had gone off the deep end.

Daniel went to his bed and lay there on his back, hands clasped and staring up at the ceiling.

"I was thinking we could go out to Little Tree Orchards." Molly stooped down and engulfed his hands in hers. Despite the heat they were icy cold. "They've got early apples, and we could pick a basket. Maybe make a nice pie. As long as the rain holds off." She shot a glance out the window at the leaden sky. "It looks a little grim out there, but we can give it a try."

Daniel sat up and stared out. "It won't rain," he said in a little voice while chewing on a corner of his thumb.

"Oh Honey, don't do that. You'll nibble off your finger," she said, trying to make a joke of it. Into her mind popped the image of a fox caught in a trap, trying to gnaw off its own foot.

So she dressed him in fresh clothes, piled him into the car, and they took off.

When Daniel saw the apple trees in the acres of orchard, he completely forgot his stomachache.

"Look how nice they are!"

In a minute he was high up in a tree, scampering from branch to branch selecting the best apples and carefully handing them down to Molly, who stood on a ladder.

"Be careful up there," she warned. "I don't want you falling down. Remember what happened on those monkey bars."

"I was little then," he piped. "How's this one?" He held out a large, well-formed apple flushed with red.

"Oooh, it's perfect. And get that giant one over there—you see it?"

The orchard was full of other families, children and their parents picking. A lot of the people kept roaming around, looking for better trees with bigger apples.

"Don't bruise them," warned Daniel as he climbed down into Molly's arms. "Then they won't keep. But if you're careful with them, you can make a hole in the ground and store them there all winter," he explained with earnest wide eyes.

Later, they took a hike around the outskirts of the orchard. Though the sun was obscured, the heat and mugginess of the day kept building. They cut through a cool pine forest that then opened into a large meadow. Grazing cows looked up, their heads turning to track them as they moved across the field. In the distance, Molly could still hear the high voices of children playing in the orchard.

"I know you're worried about school, Honey," she said finally.

He didn't answer.

They came to a fence and Daniel stretched apart the strands of barbed wire for Molly to slip through. Then she held them for him.

"Kids are always nervous about the first day of school," she went on. "I can still remember my mother taking me. Some of the kids were crying. One girl threw up all over her desk. Everybody was a little jumpy. But once we all settled in, we loved it. We had a really nice teacher."

They cut through a recently hayed field that was dry and bony. A young heifer came trotting up to them. Daniel petted it, then rubbed his nose against the calf's neck, drinking in its scent.

"I don't see why I have to go," he said without looking at Molly.

"But Darling, *everybody* has to go school. That's the way it is. It's the law. And try to understand, Sweetie. I've got to work. We need to make a living."

He turned to look at her and the neglected heifer poked him with its head.

"Darling," he ran her hands through his hair, "I've got to pay the rent every month."

"Hey," his eyes shone hopefully, "we could move out to Trip's?"

"But we'd still need to pay for ourselves. You can't always count on others, and Trip isn't a millionaire."

"Or we could build our own place," his face brightened. "I think I know how."

"Danny, Angel," she said, taking his face in her hands and kissing his lips. "You can't build your own health insurance or dental plan." She took his hand and they continued on, climbing down to a stream bed that was nearly dry. Daniel stooped down and washed his face in a pool of trapped water.

"It may not be perfect," she said, watching the water trickling through his hands, "but we've got to somehow live in the real world."

Daniel looked up at her, his face wet and glistening. "Is your magazine the real world?"

"Everything's the real world, Honey. The birds. The trees. But also the buildings. And the cars and streets are real. Even the mall you hate—that's real, too. Some of the real things we like, some not. But we've got to deal with them."

"Why?"

"*Why?* Sweetie-pie, we can't live on cattails and nuts. I've got a job and I like it. I like it a lot. I can't drag you to the office for the rest of your life. And school's not the end of the world. Give it a try."

"Why?"

"Can you please stop saying *why?* When you get to school you'll see why. And once the teachers get to know you, see how smart you are and how well you can read—why I'll bet you anything they'll jump you ahead. Maybe they'll put you right into second grade—or third grade even. Who knows? And you'll make good friends. You'll see." Molly tried her utmost to sound infectiously enthusiastic, but still it didn't catch.

"Oh, come on, Danny," she pleaded, "for my sake at least. Promise me that you'll at least try, huh?"

As they neared the edge of the orchard where Molly had parked her car, she noticed a young woman in a business suit and heels standing next to her old Chevy. The woman wore heavy makeup and lots of jewelry. She seemed to be wilting in the midday heat, but when she spotted Molly and Daniel, a look of relief spread over her face.

"Mrs. Driscoll?" she asked, approaching Molly.

Molly, taken by surprise, put down her basket of apples. "How did you know I was here?"

The woman fumbled in her purse. "I'm a producer with CBS." She handed Molly her business card. It was for a primetime magazine show hosted by Anne Snell, the famous movie star. Molly had seen the program a couple of times. "Hi, Daniel," said the producer, holding out her hand.

"Hello," said Daniel, smiling and shaking it.

Molly didn't like the looks of this. "I don't get it. How did you know we were here?"

The woman just smiled mysteriously. "Look, I'm sorry to bother you like this on the weekend, but it's the only way I've been able to get you."

The sun was broiling and Molly picked up the basket and carried it back towards the car.

"We're going to make an apple pie," Daniel chirped, tagging along. "You want a piece?"

"That would be wonderful," said the woman smiling at Daniel as she followed behind.

Molly turned and cut her with a look. "What is it you want?"

"We'd like to have Daniel appear on our show. We'd fly you both to Los Angeles, put you up in a first class hotel. You'd like that, wouldn't you?" she addressed Daniel.

"You talk to me, not him," said Molly, clipping the conversation short. "And I'm not interested."

"We'd be willing to pay travel and expenses and whatever else—"

"We're not going," she said, shoving the apples into the backseat.

"We're talking about ten thousand dollars." The woman turned to Daniel. "You'd like to be on television, wouldn't you?" she asked in a childish voice.

Molly didn't even wait for Daniel to open his mouth. "I'm not putting him on any television show."

"We're prepared, if necessary," said the woman eyeing her, "to go higher."

Molly opened the door for Daniel, and he climbed in on the passenger side. "I'm not putting him on some freak show."

"Please Mrs. Driscoll, our show is a very respected program. Last year we won two Emmys for news stories. Daniel would have exposure that—"

"His name is Danny. Danny, got it?"

"Twenty thousand," said the woman, apparently not one to mince words. "You could buy yourself a decent car," she said, looking down with a touch of disdain at Molly's wreck.

"I don't need a car. This one's fine. It's a classic. A collector's item, in fact," she added sarcastically.

"Twenty-five thousand. But that's as high as I'm authorized to go."

Molly looked at her. "You don't get it, do you? First of all, he doesn't go on any television shows. Secondly, if he did, you'd be wasting your money. You'd be disappointed. He doesn't do any tricks."

"We thought you'd like to visit L.A., but if you'd prefer I think we could convince Anne and a crew to come here and film it in Ithaca. Twenty-five thousand dollars," she said as Molly got into the car, "just to interview a little boy. And Anne Snell doesn't often travel for a shoot unless it's really important. And Daniel is."

"Thanks, but no thanks," she said, cranking the engine. It took four tries to get it going, and when it sputtered to life it left the woman in a cloud of blue, oily exhaust.

"Bye!" called Daniel leaning out the window.

Molly drove back to town in silence, the only sound was the wind whipping through the open windows. Slowly, the magnitude of money that the woman had been offering began to dawn on her. Who knew how much they were really prepared to spend. She thought about the slack it might buy her at work if Larry would grant her a leave, or just the prospect of having a nice chunk of cash sitting in the bank. The temptation, however, was only fleeting. Once they had him in the limelight on a big show like that, any chance of normalcy would be gone forever. No, she told herself, whatever the payoff, the price was just too high.

"Okay, let's first get all the ingredients together," said Molly when they were back in the trailer. The afternoon heat was merciless, and the trailer was baking. Turning on the oven was insanity, but she had to keep Daniel occupied. Keep his mind off school. "Now let's see, what do we need for the crust?"

"Flour."

"Exactly."

"And then some kind of butter or fat?"

"Why, you don't need my help, Honey."

"Yes, I do!" he laughed. He seemed to be his old happy self as he helped her peel the apples. For a little guy, he handled the sharp knife with ease. Molly knew where he had learned to do it.

"Now let's get the ingredients together."

"I'll get them," said Daniel, eagerly. He climbed up on the counter and took down the canister of flour from the high shelf. Then he handed Molly the sugar, jumped down, and started hunting through the lower cabinets for a pie plate.

"No, no, let it go for now. We've first got to get our dough going."

"Okay," he said, sticking his finger into the sugar to take a taste. "How do we do that?"

Daniel stood on a stool, watching as Molly carefully measured out the ingredients, the drops of perspiration dripping off her face into the dough. She showed him how to cut the butter into the flour, and let him add the cold water.

"You want to do the mixing?"

"Yeah!"

"All right, you mix this with your hands. Are they clean?"

Daniel started busily kneading.

Later, she let him roll out the dough. They were about to lay it into the pie plate when there was a knocking at the door.

"Hey, look," exclaimed Daniel, popping open the door. "It's Trip. And Aunt Rosie, too!"

The unlikely pair took Molly by surprise and Daniel, his smile fading, immediately sensed that something was up. Molly could feel all the buoyancy of the day leaking away and she was furious.

Tripoli pulled her aside. "We need to talk," he said in a subdued voice.

"But we're just in the middle of making a pie."

Daniel's eyes flashed from one adult to the next.

Tripoli had her by the elbow and was trying to get her out the door.

"Oh, look, an apple pie," cried Rosie a little too ardently for Molly's taste. "Why don't Daniel and I finish this while you two talk," said Rosie brightly, stepping over to the counter and taking charge. "Right, Daniel?"

Daniel stood still rooted by the door. "Are you going to talk about me?"

"Just good things," said Tripoli with a wink.

"So why can't I listen?" he asked, eyeing all three of them.

"Because you need to finish the pie, Darling," said Rosie, taking him by the shoulder and moving him back toward the kitchen. "Oh, look, the apples are all peeled already. We just need to slice them up a little more. Now, Daniel, where's the sugar?"

Tripoli got Molly out the door and closed it behind them.

"Do we have to go through this again?" she asked wearily as they stood in the front yard. She kept her gaze on Daniel's garden, couldn't even look him in the eye.

"Molly, I love you," he said soothingly. "You know that." He took his hand and stroked her cheek. His fingers felt unusually rough and calloused.

Finally, she looked at him. "Well, you're not treating me like you do. I spent the whole day trying to cheer Danny up and then...you and Rosie just keep battering me."

"If we do, it's because we love Daniel too."

A truck started up in front of the neighboring trailer. A moment later the Dolphs drove past, moving with deliberate slowness. Their heads were turned and they were staring boldly at Molly and Tripoli.

"You know, Trip," she said, watching the truck as it progressed down the lane, "I don't quite recognize you anymore. You're not the same person I used to know. And I'm not sure it's necessarily for the better."

"I've learned things. And I've changed, yes. I see things differently. I know things now that I didn't know before. Molly, I beg of
you, you've got to hear me out."

"Okay, out with it then," she said, impatiently. A rivulet of sweat
sluiced down from her temple, and she didn't even bother wiping it
away. "God, I hate this heat," she mumbled to herself. "Well?" She
turned back to Tripoli. "Go on already!"

"The Hermit," Tripoli began. This wasn't the way he wanted to
explain things, but these days he never seemed to be able to catch
Molly at the right moment. "There are a couple of things I didn't
tell you. We got a set of fingerprints from the old man before his
body disappeared from the morgue. The old man who took Daniel?
I know who he is—was."

Molly lifted an eyebrow, and Tripoli could see he was gaining
her attention.

"His name was Matthew. Matthew Roland. His name came up
as a missing person. *Twice.*"

"Huh?"

"He had disappeared as a little boy from his home in
Watertown."

"Watertown? So that's what—"

"He was just about Daniel's age when he vanished," Tripoli
pressed on. "Right out of school. Not a trace. He had lived alone
with his mother. A single woman. He was missing right through the
winter. The *whole* winter. In the spring, he suddenly came back.
Perfectly healthy and everything. Except…" He paused.

"Except?"

"Except he was changed. Radically changed."

Tripoli went on slowly, deliberately. He told Molly about his
conversation with the old sheriff in Watertown, his trip to Sarasota
to meet with Flossie Francis. Molly appeared surprised by the

lengths he had gone to, and Tripoli went on, relating everything he had subsequently learned. He took from his car the old clippings he had found in Watertown papers, the pictures of young Matthew he had borrowed from Mrs. Francis, and showed them to Molly.

She looked at the photos, then scanned the articles, her eyes always returning to the pictures. Little Matthew the first grader, standing with his class. Matthew with his teacher.

Finally she handed it all back. They could hear Rosie's voice coming from the trailer. She was showing Daniel how to grease the pie plate.

Tripoli told Molly about the birthmark, pointing to the mark on the boy's neck.

She squinted. "I don't see anything."

"God, it's right there," he said, trying to stem his anger. Obviously, she didn't want to see. "You're just not looking!"

"Okay, I see a dot."

"If you had a magnifying glass you could see—"

"Well, I don't."

"…it's a star. Just like Daniel's."

"All right," she said finally, looking back at Tripoli. "So what? Kids have birthmarks."

"So what?" He gaped at her incredulously.

"Anyway, this is different."

"What's different?"

"That was fifty, sixty years ago. A half century. These are different times. The situation is different. Danny's different."

"Oh, yeah?" His voice was now raised. Tripoli knew it, but couldn't help himself.

"Yeah! Nobody is going to be chaining him to a frigging desk. Nobody is keeping him prisoner."

"Molly!"

"Molly nothing!" Her eyes welled with tears. "Everybody is putting pressure on me. You. Larry. Rosie. The news people. Everybody in the whole damn world! But none of you really care about the little boy who is Danny! You just care about your own…"

"Molly," he said reaching out for her, but she pulled away, turned and stood hugging herself. "Molly, if Daniel takes off…if we lose Daniel, it'll be more than just your loss and mine. People are finally beginning to realize that there are crazy things going on with the weather. We're all in trouble. Serious trouble. People are scared and I think they're ready to listen to Daniel, change the way they live, make the sacrifices that are going to have to be made if we're to survive this."

Rosie, who had been keeping an eye on the exchange, rushed out to join them. Daniel tried to follow her, but she stopped him at the door. "You watch the pie!" she ordered, closed the door, and then stood with her back firmly against it.

"Oh," cried Molly, "Not you, too. Are you all going to gang up on me?" She continued to look angrily off into the distance.

"Yeah, me, too. For God's sake, you've got to listen to us."

"I'm not an unreasonable person," said Molly, a plaintive note creeping into her voice. "You think I haven't thought about this a gazillion times?"

When Rosie put her arms around Molly's shoulders, she didn't resist. "Come on, Molly. Nobody's saying that."

Molly eyes went to the trailer door. With a voice barely audible, she whispered, "You think I'm not terrified about putting Danny in school?"

Rosie and Tripoli waited quietly.

"Okay, he's a prophet. A saint. Whatever you want to call him. But that doesn't mean that he shouldn't go to school. It's all the more reason for him to go."

They continued to wait her out, and she knew that she would never have peace from them—or herself—unless she came to some accommodation.

"Look," she said finally, turning back. She caught her lower lip in the corner of her mouth and kept biting down. "I'll go with Danny to school. I'll stay there with him. I'll sit right next to him, if they'll let me. I'll take a week off. We'll see how it goes. If it looks like a disaster, I'll be the first to know, right?"

Rosie and Tripoli traded looks.

"That sounds reasonable," said Rosie finally.

Tripoli couldn't realistically hope for more. Not yet. It bought them time to win her over. "Sounds good to me," he said.

"I'll tell you one thing," said Molly, "Larry is not going to appreciate this. It's going to take more than a miracle to keep him from firing me." She thought again about that producer out at the orchard in her jewelry and high heels. A big lump of cash. No, she told herself, I can't. It'll only be trading short-term relief for major long-term trouble.

Molly hardly got any sleep that night. The air in the trailer was torrid and the bed clothes were sticking to her body. Tossing restlessly, she kept turning her pillow as it dampened with sweat. Outside, the air was inert, and every sound coming through her window seemed amplified—the frogs croaking in the nearby swamp, the crickets chirping. A couple in a nearby trailer were having a shouting match, and then the dogs in the park let up a howl. The whole place seemed on edge.

Molly kept drifting off to sleep only to awaken with a start. Her dreams were fragmented and chaotic, the barking gradually became a strident chorus. In one of her dreams, Rosie was yacking some nonsense about Danny's diapers not drying in the rain. *Diapers?* Larry was chasing her around the office, nagging about a lost picture of a snake that was to go in the magazine. Danny was standing on a television stage amidst a blaze of hot lights, pieces of him literally melting off as though he were made of wax. In the next instant, Tripoli was chasing around in his police car and Molly found herself in the front seat hanging on for dear life as they careened along the lip of Fall Creek Gorge. Below them, the turbulent water roared over the rocks.

In one of Molly's dreams, she was wandering alone in the night. It was pitch black. Suddenly a tiny corner of the sky turned bright. At first it was little more than a pinpoint of pale blue light with a tail like a comet. Then the light grew larger and brighter, its color changing to sharp pink, then searing yellow. It kept growing in intensity until it was blindingly bright. Moving across it was a tall but hunched figure she could only make out in silhouette. Then the light diminished and Molly could see that it was the dead Hermit. Although she had never set eyes on the man, she knew it was old Matthew. In her dream, Molly tried to speak to him. She called him "Father," and kept crying out to him. But the old man didn't hear; he kept shuffling ahead, leaning on his walking stick. Then, suddenly, he was gone and Molly awoke bathed in sweat to realize that she had been weeping in her sleep. When she rolled over on her side and looked over at Danny, she discovered him lying there in his bed wide awake, watching her.

"I'm sorry," he said in the tiniest of voices.

BOOK THREE

chapter twenty-two

Jerry Sisler had never seen the likes of it. Everywhere people seemed to be on the threshold of madness. At the diner, Kesh, who was working the cash register, snapped at him because he only had a twenty dollar bill for a cup of coffee. A fight broke out on the Northside. Then he had to rush over to the South to cover a stickup. You never got robberies or fights at seven in the morning.

All over the damn city automatic fire alarms were being spontaneously triggered, and the fire companies kept ferrying up and down the hills chasing phantom fires. As the sun sluggishly lifted itself over East Hill, the day got oppressively hotter. Without the faintest hint of a breeze, it felt to Sisler as though he were in a sealed cooker, the pressure building by the hour. His radio was acting erratically and he swore he could actually detect in his body the electrical field of a huge storm that was beginning to build. If only it would start to rain, he thought to himself, there'd finally be some relief.

On his way back to the station from yet another morning call, he had to pull over on the west end of State Street. Two well-dressed men stood in the parking lot near the magazine office trying to choke each other.

"What the hell is going on?" Sisler demanded, separating the two. Then he recognized them. It was Bruce Trumbell, the well-known trial lawyer, and Jason Fine, the landlord who owned half the rental properties in town.

"He tried to steal my parking space!" cried Trumbell.

"Like hell!" bellowed Fine, raising a fist. "I was here first!"

The lot was almost empty. Maybe four or five cars at most.

Molly pulled into the lot with Daniel just as Sisler was leaving. He slowed and waved to her from his car, but Molly didn't notice him.

"Let's make sure we have everything," she said as she turned off the motor. The day was a real stinker. It felt like a lid had been forced down on the city; she could taste droplets of diesel and half-burnt gasoline suspended in the air. She gathered up Daniel's school papers, his registration card, the sign-up sheet for lunch, his health questionnaire, and the permission form for field trips.

"We'd better take an umbrella," she said, turning her key and locking the steering column.

Daniel, who had refused breakfast, remained grim in the front seat, his belt still fastened. He was terribly pale and looked sick with anticipation.

"We'll leave the car here and walk up South Hill," she said. Maybe the exercise would relax him, open him up. After school, Molly would bring him back to the office and try to squeak in some work. Larry was so angry, he wouldn't even discuss it with her.

"Just do whatever you want," he had said when she had called him at home last night.

"Larry, I'll get the work done."

"We'll see about that."

"Come on, we'd better hurry or we'll be late." Molly grabbed her pocketbook and the papers. "Come on, Sweetie," she cajoled. "We'll have a good time, you'll see." Moving around the outside of the car, she opened the door for him. Daniel unsnapped his belt and reluctantly stepped out. His brow was furrowed, and he was chewing on the inside of his lip. To Molly, it looked as if he might be caught in a struggle with himself.

"Please don't look so grim," she pleaded. "I'm going to be with you the *whole* time. Who knows, maybe I'll learn something, too." She forced a laugh, but it sounded flat to her own ears.

Taking Daniel by the hand, she cut across the lot to Green Street. The morning traffic was heavy. Delivery trucks and commuters backed up by red lights. Passing the law office housed in an old Victorian, Molly noticed that all the trees lining the street, apparently stressed by the drought and heat, were prematurely turning color. They were red and gold and they reminded Molly of that fall day now almost a year ago, when Danny had disappeared. Then it had been a crazy cold day with freakish snows. A year and so much had transpired that it was hard to comprehend.

As they neared Aurora Street, Molly's handbag suddenly popped open, spilling the contents across the sidewalk. Lipstick and keys and change scattered everywhere. "Oh, God!" Releasing Daniel's hand, she bent down to hastily gather up her things.

Daniel stood watching.

"Here, can you hold these a second?" She handed him the papers as she hurriedly scooped everything back into her bag.

Suddenly, a violent, spiraling wind came up out of nowhere. It gusted down Green Street, raising a cloud of dust and litter in its path. The papers flew out of Daniel's hands, taking off like birds and fluttering down the walk. Molly chased them. She caught up with them a dozen yards later as they lay snared in a hedge and scooped them up. When she turned around, Daniel was gone.

Just moments after Daniel vanished, the heavens flashed and the skies suddenly burst open, the rain came down in blinding sheets.

"Danny! Danny!" shouted Molly as she raced deliriously up and down the length of Green Street, her cries drowned out by the thunder, her tears obscured by the unrelenting rain.

She ran into the photo shop, water streaming off her onto the clean white floors. "Did you see a little boy come by?" she cried, startling the salespeople. "He must have come right past here."

She checked with the people in the Indian restaurant and the Roma Pizzeria. The man in the cashier's booth at the Green Street parking ramp claimed he saw a kid running through the rain headed toward the Commons.

The rain-swept Commons was deserted. She doubled back to Green Street, leaping out into the middle of the roadway to wave down an approaching cop car. It screeched to a halt on the wet pavement, barely stopping before hitting her.

"Get on the radio!" she cried, beside herself with grief. "My boy. Danny. He's taken off!"

She ran back to the lot where her car stood parked, got in and turned the key. The starter kept cranking, but the wires were soaked and the engine refused to catch. She kept trying until the battery gave out, the starter groaning to a halt.

Molly dashed into the magazine office, grabbed Tasha's keys off her desk, and took her car. The rain was coming down so hard that the storm gutters were backing up and the water was now building up in the streets. Even with Tasha's wipers on high, she could barely make out the taillights of cars in front. Near Cayuga Street, traffic was tangled and she drove up on the sidewalk, weaving around the stalled cars. Running a series of red lights, she headed towards Aurora Street, her car throwing up a wake as if it were a speed boat. South Hill, she thought. He's headed up South Hill. Where else could he go? Halfway up the hill a tractor trailer stood jackknifed, blocking the highway. Damn! Every minute that Danny was gone only put more distance between them.

Backing blindly from the truck, she threw the car into drive, hit the gas, and swung a fast U-turn. The front tire smashed against the curb and went flat.

Abandoning Tasha's car, she ran through the rain down the street back towards the downtown. From the first pay phone, she called Tripoli.

"He's gone," she cried breathlessly.

"Huh? I can't—" Given the noise of the rain beating down on the shelter, he could hardly hear her.

"Danny's gone!" she screamed. "Gone for real!"

"I'm coming. I'm coming," he shouted, "Where are you?"

She stood in the downpour, oblivious to the rain, waiting for him.

Fifteen long minutes later, she saw in the distance a pair of flashing red lights and knew it was him.

"Get in," said Tripoli, popping the door.

"Oh my God," she wailed. "It's hopeless."

"Nothing is hopeless." He peeled out from the curb. "Hang on."

They went back up South Hill, using side streets. They checked the alleys and backyards, then drove all the way out to the state forest.

"I was a fool," she wept as he plowed through the storm. "An idiot."

"Stop blaming yourself."

"If only it would stop raining," she prayed. At least they could see. Poor Danny, she kept thinking. Cold and soaked in the rain.

But the rains didn't stop. It poured without respite the whole of that day as Tripoli, the police, and a crowd of volunteers dressed in blaze orange slickers combed the city and it's surroundings, their cries of, "Daniel, Daniel," echoing through the roadways, the fields, and forests farther out.

"All is not lost," he said, putting an arm around her as they stood that evening in the station house staring out the window at the wall of water.

"Who are we kidding?" she asked, her voice so weak Tripoli

could barely make it out.

By nightfall, the rising creeks in the county began to overflow their banks, flooding basements and washing out roads. With the continued runoff cascading down from the hills, once placid brooks turned into angry, roiling rivers, ripping huge trees from their banks and sending them hurtling down the rapids, trunks and roots smashing through steel bridges and isolating communities. The raging waters lifted barns off their moorings and swept them away into the lake. Electric poles toppled like matchsticks, shorting the lines and plunging the town into darkness. In the lowlands behind the Wegman's and Tops supermarkets, the water was rising so fast that soon the entire parking lot was submerged in two feet of water; carp and bass were swimming where cars and minivans used to park.

It never let up. In fact, it rained steadily, day after day after day. Yet, despite the weather, the search for the boy went on, even more extensively than when Daniel had first disappeared the previous fall. Tripoli, returning to active service, was given immediate charge of the operation and requisitioned as much manpower as the department could muster. He organized search parties of volunteers and had them slog their way through the surrounding woods, bogs, and fields. He called in professional trackers with bloodhounds. All that remained of old Matthew's hut was rubble, but still they combed every inch of the surrounding Danby Forest, now all but a water-logged marsh. Commandeering private boats, Tripoli had them scour the flooded areas in the event that Daniel had been stranded by the rising waters. They found survivors huddled on rooftops and clinging to trees, dead pets and bloated cattle floating in the muddy waters, but not a single sign of the missing boy.

The airwaves were filled with stories of Daniel's disappearance. The *Ithaca Journal* carried front-page stories requesting information; the local and national networks carried tales of the boy's second vanishing, but not a soul in the town or the country at large had seen the boy since he had left his mother on Green Street.

Four days later, when the worst of the storm was lifting, Tripoli ordered up a helicopter and kept it circling over the city and neighboring towns, its engines often roaring right through the drizzling nights. But still they found no trace, no trail, no sign of the boy.

Molly waited in the trailer, listening to the rain drumming dismally on the roof, listening and waiting as hope faded and the water level in the swamp behind her home continued to rise. The newer trailers near the park entrance became flooded and had to be abandoned. The deluge spared only the older units, like hers, that sat on the high ground in the rear.

Tripoli did his best to comfort Molly, but as the prospects for finding Daniel diminished, she became progressively more withdrawn, preoccupied. She started keeping a journal. In it she wrote about Daniel, describing in minute detail the child she had known from birth, and then went on to chronicle his return and the astounding transformation he had undergone while living with the Hermit. And she wrote about herself, confessing how, sitting encapsulated in her office, she had become detached not only from the outside world, but her own child. That in her quest for what she deemed indispensable to live she had become blinded to all that was good and beautiful, deaf to the quiet voice of common sense that was her little boy. For Molly, her journal was a way of sorting out her feelings and coming to grips with what she had done and what she would do, might do, could do.

Whenever Tripoli phoned, their conversations were abrupt. "I'm sorry. I can't talk right now," she would say and slip off the line. When he came to the trailer to see her, she kept him at the door. Most of the time she just sat slumped at the kitchen table staring out the window, lost in thought.

"I'm just not up to seeing anybody these days," she told Rosie, who kept banging on her trailer door until she finally opened up.

"Molly, darling," she said, managing to barrel her way in. "We need to talk."

"Sure," she said, "but just not right now."

"You've got to stop whipping yourself. Nobody's blaming you."

"Maybe, but I am."

Larry called a few times. To apologize, to commiserate, to plead with Molly to come back while she waited for Daniel to turn up again.

"You got to keep busy in the meanwhile. Keep yourself occupied until they find him," he said. "Just like you did before."

"Thanks," she muttered, "but no thanks." Nothing could have been further from Molly's mind than the magazine.

Tripoli kept coming by every day, hoping to pull Molly back into life, but she scarcely seemed to hear what he was saying.

"I'm getting really worried about her," Rosie confided in Tripoli when Molly locked her out of the trailer, speaking to her only with the chain on the door—and then but briefly. "She says she can't face anybody, but this…this is scary."

"I didn't listen to you. I didn't listen to Rosie, I didn't even listen to my own boy," said Molly as Tripoli stood outside in the drizzle insisting that she accept a soggy bag of groceries.

Each time Tripoli went shopping, he discovered that food prices had leaped upward, some items nearly doubling in a week. And it was not only the breads and cereals directly impacted by the failure of the grain crop, but meat and fish, dependent on feeds, were rising dramatically. Fruit and fresh vegetables were now essentially out of the reach of working families. Tripoli couldn't even find a bag of sugar in Wegman's, and he suspected that people were beginning to hoard basic supplies—which would only magnify the problem. And, as he stood in the rain hoping that Molly would accept the package, he kept hearing in his mind the voices of the books. It was as if the spirit of Anterra was talking to him across the ages, urging him to action. Do something. But do what? Was it too late?

In town there was a swirl of speculation about Daniel. He was out there alone in the woods with no one to turn to and nothing to eat. It was only a matter of time until he was dead—if he hadn't already succumbed to the drenching rains and hypothermia.

"And that boy knew something really important," said Howie Schultz, the postal carrier, as he stood under his umbrella sorting mail into the boxes that served the trailer park. "Something that could have stopped all this. Just look at how it's been raining. The wife's really scared. First that heat. Then these rains. I mean, what's the world coming to?"

"She drove him away!" said Mrs. Dolph bitterly, as she waited in the downpour for Howie to get to her social security check. "Some mother!"

"First she has the old man killed," remarked Mrs. Lifsey to her bridge circle, "then she chases away her poor little boy. For the second time!"

One morning, Molly looked out the window to see garbage spread all over the front of her yard. Often, when she answered the phone, she was greeted by the click of someone hanging up. Other times, anonymous voices cursed and threatened her. "You're not fit to be a mother!" hissed one female voice. "When he comes back, if he *ever* comes back," shouted an angry man, "I hope to hell the authorities take him away from you. "

Molly knew that they were right, that she was to blame, and so she kept those messages of anger and hate, dutifully recording them in her journal.

After the rains finally tapered off, there was an early hard frost in October and Molly finally ventured outside. Standing in front of her trailer, she stared down at the remains of Daniel's neglected garden.

Oozing tomatoes hung on withered vines, desiccated bean plants shivered in the wind. When she poked her hands into the soil, she pulled up sodden potatoes, half-rotten. This is all that remains of Danny, she thought, kneeling in the mud. This and memories.

Molly spent her time wandering the nearby hills, following familiar paths, every step reminding her of Danny. Day slid into meaningless day, time losing all definition as the trees turned barren, the fields and meadows took on mournful shades of gray and brown, and the sky, grim and low, cloaked the sun. Gone were the summer wild flowers; and Danny, too. How little it might have taken to keep Danny, she kept telling herself. Now he was out in the wilderness, alone, this time with no one to care for him or shield him from the brutality of this unforgiving climate.

"Since the day that Danny was born and Chuck deserted us," she wrote in her journal, "I've been so caught up in paying bills and going back to school, that I've never had—or allowed myself—the chance to stop and look up at a cloud, stand at night and stare up at the stars. Being productive does not always require running around in busy circles. Sometimes a person just needs to take a deep breath, stand still, and contemplate. Here was a little boy living with me, try-ing to teach his mother a little common sense. Was I always such a slow learner?"

One evening the phone rang, and Molly let it ring. When the answering machine picked up and she recognized Sandy's voice on the other end, she took the call.

"How are you doing, Molly?" Sandy inquired.

"Not so great, as you can imagine," she answered. "How are things at Larry's?"

It turned out that Sandy was no longer with the magazine. Molly was surprised.

"Apparently you haven't heard. After you left, things just fell apart."

There were cost overruns in printing the October edition, egregious editorial mistakes that never got caught, pages that were bound out of order. And creditors were suddenly demanding payment up front. Larry had apparently been living on the edge, and hiring the new people had pushed him into insolvency.

"It was as if the magazine were cursed," Sandy said. "First he fired the new people he had hired to replace you. Then he laid off Tasha. Then me. Finally Ben. I still can't believe how fast everything unraveled."

Larry Pierce had closed the doors to the magazine and filed for bankruptcy. The attorney handling the case was Alex Greenhut, by chance the same lawyer who had helped Molly obtain food stamps and welfare when she had been at the low point in her own life. From what Sandy had heard, Greenhut had tried his best to protect Larry, but there was no way to appease the creditors who were crying for blood. Not only was the magazine out of business, but Larry, as a result of his personal guarantees, was utterly ruined. Broke. In the end, he couldn't even pay his lawyer's bill.

Molly had some savings but she refused to touch them. She was keeping them for when Danny came back. It was getting colder and the propane company was now refusing to deliver gas until her bills were paid. She failed to pay the rent, and let the car insurance lapse. Whatever it took, Molly was determined to hang on, wait for Danny, ignore the angry stares and denunciations of her neighbors, hold out as long as she could.

Tripoli was persistent. Every evening, without fail, he appeared at Molly's place. Sometimes during the day, when he was near the east end of the city, he'd think of her and drive over to the trailer park. When Molly finally relented and let him in, he sat with her, sometimes for hours, asking nothing, just quietly holding her hand.

"I don't deserve your love," she murmured, head bowed and

unable to look him in the eye. "I never did. You're wasting it on me. Find someone else. Someone who'll make you happy."

He collected the garbage scattered across her lawn, straightened up the kitchen, and cooked her dinner.

"How can you ever forgive me, Trip?" she asked, "For not believing you, not trusting you."

"There's nothing to forgive," he said, holding her fragile frame tight. Through her thick sweater he could feel her ribs and vertebrae. "I only hope and pray that you can stop punishing yourself."

Some days were better, some decidedly worse. On the nights that threatened to be bad, Tripoli slept over, holding her close and kissing away her tears.

"What would I do without you?" she asked.

"Why don't you come to my place? Live with me," he gently urged.

"I can't. I can't leave here. Not until the day they evict me—and then they're going to have to drag me out bodily."

Tripoli offered to pay her rent and was secretly relieved when she refused. The sooner she was out of that place of misery, he believed, the better.

The arrival of November was greeted by bitter cold and snow, promising another harsh winter.

"Sometimes I dream about living in a warm climate," she said, shivering on a particularly frigid night. She was rationing heat, and by evening she was so chilled that even in bed with piles of blankets and Tripoli holding her she couldn't warm up. "It's so dreadful here. So hostile."

Tripoli thought about the tropics. He recalled his flight down to Sarasota to meet Matthew's old teacher, remembered the myriad of aquamarine pools, the endless miles of paved highways, the shopping malls, and the fast-food joints. "It's really beautiful here, if you just open your eyes and look around. The summer and winter, it's all part of a greater whole. Daniel saw what it was and loved it. He wanted us to love it, too."

She stared at him in the darkness. How different he sounded these days, how different from that down-to-earth detective she had first met in her trailer the night Danny disappeared from daycare. Then she thought about Kute Kids. Mrs. Oltz, long dead. Cheryl, who had locked poor little Danny in the basement. The magazine. It now all seemed like a couple of lifetimes ago. How could she have been so insensitive? So stubborn? So utterly deaf and blind?

In her journal, Molly revisited each and every error she had made since the moment she had spotted Danny wandering up the road back toward her trailer. If only it were possible to move back in time, she thought going back through the densely covered pages of her notebook. If only retracing her steps were as simple as this, how differently she would have handled everything. Might have. But then some fools never learn from their mistakes.

Secretly, Molly harbored the dream that one day she would look out the window and there would be Danny, just as before, bouncing happily up the road, a coarse wool sweater tossed over his shoulder. But it was just that, she knew, a dream. People didn't get second chances.

chapter twenty-three

That same day in September when Daniel disappeared, the books had vanished, too. Tripoli had come home late that night, exhausted and soaked to the bone, and noticed immediately that the books were missing from the kitchen table. All that remained were scattered dishes and crumbs, his pile of notes encircling the spot where the volumes had rested for weeks. Until now, he had never had anything of value in the house and hadn't even bothered locking the door. He kept kicking himself for being so lax. Why would anybody want to steal them? he wondered. Ultimately, when Matlin finally caught on that he had taken the books from the evidence room, there would be hell to pay. An independent investigator appointed by the governor was questioning everybody in town about the disappearance of the Hermit's body, and the books would be the next point of investigation. The noose was tightening. To hell with them, he thought. What could they do to him? In the grander scheme of things, measured against the wider flow of human events, their inquiry and his life were of minute significance.

For Molly's sake, Tripoli pushed on with the search, but his heart was no longer really in it. It was history repeating itself, Watertown revisited. Even if Daniel was still alive, he certainly would not be coming back. Wasn't it only once in a generation that people had a chance at enlightenment?

Tripoli returned to his regular routine as a city detective, focusing on the cases assigned to him. In his off time, he started working on his house again, though he wasn't quite sure why. He finished renovating the downstairs bathroom and began insulating and sheet-rocking the master bedroom upstairs. He replaced the worst of the leaky windows, weather-stripped the doors, and then made the barn tight for the approaching winter so the animals would have adequate shelter from the wind.

On a Thursday night, one of the young goats disappeared. It looked as if it had broken free through the fence, and after that Tripoli kept the animals confined to the barn until he had time to reinforce the enclosure. From a neighbor, he bought enough hay to last the winter and hauled heavy sacks of cracked corn and wheat out from town.

A week before Thanksgiving, Molly's telephone service was cut and the power company sent her a final warning. Even by stretching it, she now had barely enough propane to last a week.

"You can't live like this," said Tripoli as she sat in her kitchen huddled in blankets.

"Danny," was all Molly could utter. "My sweet Danny."

"He's fine," murmured Tripoli. "He's free. And he's where he wants to be. I know it. I just know it in my heart."

"If only," she said, biting her lip, "if only…"

Finally, Tripoli got Molly to agree to move out to his house. Her sudden willingness to leave the trailer took him by surprise. He came with a carload of empty cartons he had scavenged from the supermarkets and helped her pack her belongings. They boxed up all of Daniel's clothes. His favorite books. The microscope that Larry had given him. Then Tripoli helped her sort through the rest.

"Leave this," he said, stuffing things back into drawers. "And this. I got plenty of egg beaters. And who needs more can openers? This broom is shot. And forget this vacuum—maybe the next people can use it. Anyway, I got two." Molly didn't really care one way or the other. She just wanted to be certain they took all of Daniel's things. It took him a couple of trips to move everything; then he brought Molly out to the old farm house in Newfield.

"This is your home now," he said as he led her in through the kitchen door.

It was the first time she had ever been there. He took her upstairs. "I've got two bedrooms finished," he explained, showing her around. The place smelled of fresh paint and spackle. "You can have your own if you want. I'd understand. You could take the bigger one." He opened the door for her. "The only trouble is that the good bathroom is downstairs. I haven't begun to work on this one yet."

Molly walked around dumbstruck, gaping up at the high ceilings, running her hand over the newly refinished chestnut staircase. It was smooth and sleek. Compared to her place, everything here seemed bright and polished. The effort he had gone to, she realized, had been for her. Finally she found words. "Thank you. You're a good man," she said, looking him deep in the eye for the first time since Daniel had vanished. "And you've always been. Putting up with me like you've done…"

"No…" he said waving away the compliment though it felt genuine and good. "Nah…"

"It's going to be a real downer having a lead weight like me swinging around your neck."

"Sure, you're a pain in the ass," he said, pulling her to him with a smile. "But let's face it, you're going to be living with a dumb, depressed cop. Hey, I got a great idea! We can just depress the hell out of each other. I mean really get into it."

Molly had to smile. She said in a more serious vein, "Any time it gets to be too much and you feel like you want me to move, I want you to be truthful and just tell me."

"And we'll find you a nice trailer in the back of that park. Hey, come on now. This is for keeps."

He showed her around the property. Took her out to the barn. And there were the animals. Daniel's animals.

Thanksgiving came and they were invited over to Rosie and Ed's for the annual family bash. Molly kept trying to back out.

"I'm not quite up to facing people. Maybe next year," she hedged.

Tripoli didn't argue with her; but when the time came, he simply tossed Molly her coat and bundled her off into the car before she could really object.

The tiny house on Spencer Street was packed, the table longer this year than ever in the past. There were more cousins than usual, Molly noticed. Aunts and in-laws from out of town. Lots of kids racing noisily up and down the stairs. Rosie had trouble handling the dinner. She dropped a big casserole and Molly went into the kitchen to help her clean up the sweet potatoes and broken glass.

"I'm just a little at loose ends these days," confessed Rosie as Molly stooped down to help her scrape up the mess.

Using the dustpan as a shovel, Molly came eye-to-eye with her. Rosie, who had always been so round and busty, seemed thin and hollow-cheeked, a shell of her old buoyant self. "You don't look so good," she said finally.

"And I don't feel so great right now, either," she admitted. "Here, you can just toss the glass in this." She held out a paper bag and Molly dumped in the shards.

"You ought to go see a doctor," insisted Molly as she hunted for the broom.

"Yeah. Sure. Soon as I get some time," said Rosie, but Molly suspected she didn't mean it. With Ed working but still without insurance, the Greens were too poor to afford medical care, too rich for Medicaid.

Molly took over helping Rosie serve the dinner. Then Rosie's elderly aunt, Betty, came into the kitchen to lend a hand, too. And so did her cousin. Between the four, they got the dinner quickly on the table. Everything was there. Everything but the sweet potatoes.

The platters traveled down the long table, people helping themselves. At the far end, the twins sat propped up in baby seats next to Ed who was trying to keep both mouths busy with mashed bananas. The boys seemed large for their age, very alert and very active. Their big, dark eyes kept eagerly following the other children, and they reminded Molly of Danny when he was that age—the way she would have to aim a spoon at the moving target that was his mouth.

Molly remained subdued through the meal. Later, she took one of the babies from Ed and sat next to Rosie on the sofa. Studying the child's tiny fingers, she found herself gripped with an intense longing.

"Whatta you thinking about?" asked Rosie.

Molly turned to her and smiled wanly. "Oh, just about how nice little babies are. Just look at this wonderful, perfect, little hand."

Driving back out to the farm in Newfield, Molly sat quietly in the car recalling that previous, bleak Thanksgiving and how she had spent it alone imagining Danny's bones being gathered up by the police and submitted for a DNA test. But this, in its own cruel way, was worse, far worse. Without the old man, Daniel didn't have a chance. And this time it was her doing! There was no one else in the world to blame.

Without the lights of the city, the countryside seemed blanketed in unrelieved darkness. There was little to see but what was revealed by the cone of headlights: cold pavement with a light dusting of snow, naked trees, stretches of wind-whipped fields and blank emptiness. They drove on past a caved-in barn, a lone trailer with a bare porch light, an ancient truck without wheels abandoned at the edge of the road.

"I've made so many mistakes," whispered Molly in the darkness of the car. "What I wanted was for Danny to fit in. Fit in," she reiterated bitterly. "How could I have been so dumb?"

Tripoli didn't know what to say. At least she was finally talking. Since they had moved from the trailer and packed away Daniel's things into the attic, she hadn't uttered his name. Tripoli reached over and took her hand, held it as they traveled home together.

Molly spent her days fixing up the house. First she cleaned, giving the place a thorough scrubbing. The house had been long neglected; the kitchen was coated with an ancient layer of grime that predated Tripoli's occupancy; sometimes it took the flat blade of a spackling knife to peel up the layers of grease. But she kept at it. When the room felt sufficiently clean, she started painting, first the kitchen walls, then the worn faces of the cabinets.

Outside, the farmhouse the weather seemed ever more chaotic. Some days it was so cold that it was painful just to venture out for a quick armload of wood. Then suddenly, overnight, the temperature would start to rise and by noon it would be fifty, sometimes even sixty degrees. The snow would melt and Molly would be out in shirt sleeves cleaning up dead branches in the yard, only to wake up the next morning to see that a heavy snow storm had hit during the night.

Each evening, when Tripoli came home from the station, he found the kitchen table set and a warm meal ready and waiting. He would quickly tend to the animals, and then they would sit down to dinner. Molly made him soups with potatoes and leaks, spicy risottos, pastas with eggplant and mushrooms. She even started baking her own bread. It was all wonderfully tasty, all vegetarian—just terrific.

Molly started avidly reading the daily newspapers Triploi brought home from work. The papers were peppered with stories about the

extreme fluctuations in the weather patterns and the continued speculation about the effects of global warming. Of course, it got her
thinking about Daniel, who was never far from her thoughts.

"The warming," he had said, the day of the tornado, gazing up
at the big yacht perched on the top of West Hill.

"But *how* did you know?"

"I could feel it."

Molly wondered if she, too, could learn to sense the coming
weather. Could anyone? Was it somehow there if a person simply
opened his mind's eye, as Wally Schuman had written?

For the first time since moving out to the farm, Molly picked
up her journal, read back through it, then started writing in it again.
She wrote about her hike with Daniel through the ancient gorge
near Taughannock Falls and how he had known about the ice-age
glaciers that had created this remarkable topography, about the
Indians who had farmed this land and tended apple orchards. And
she recalled his ominous warning about what appeared to be tran-
spiring in the world around her. "Unless we do something," he had
warned, "something terrible is going to happen to us." Was it already
in progress? she wondered.

"What's that you're writing?" asked Tripoli one evening, coming
up from behind her as she sat hunched over her notebook.

"Oh, it's nothing," she said, quickly closing the book.

"Come on, let me see."

"Oh, it's just some random thoughts," she said, stuffing the book
behind her in the seat.

"I just hope to God you're not writing about me or our sex life,"
he said with a wink.

"Don't flatter yourself," she said with a faint smile.

On Daniel's sixth birthday, Tripoli decided to pay up Molly's
lapsed insurance. He also got her car relicensed, inspected, and back
on the road. "It's not good to be just stuck out here brooding," he

said, gently. "Maybe you want to get out a little bit."

Molly thought about Daniel's birthday. She had missed his fifth and now this one, too. Two birthdays in a row that poor Danny was without his mother. It got her thinking about his birthmark, and she dug out the photos of Matthew that Tripoli still hung on to. Enlarging the image with a magnifying glass, she all but gasped when she saw the striking similarity.

Molly mustered up the courage to face people again. The city was busy with last-minute Christmas shoppers. The downtown was strung with colored lights and decorations, and there were bell ringers in front of the bank and the sheepskin store. She picked up supplies from Bishop's hardware, and then went to Wegman's to relieve Tripoli from the grocery shopping. After her long absence, it seemed strange to be in traffic, to see people bustling around the stores, to bump into the students that clogged the aisles and check-out lines. Life continued to move on, she realized, with or without her. She could either become a part of it again, or remain aloof. A hermit, she thought, and then laughed sadly.

"I'm back driving my car," she wrote in her journal. "Maybe it's good for me to get out, but the car suddenly feels as big as a boat. I'm just another person just adding to the problem. What I wonder about is, what can I do now to lessen the harm that I've done? What would Danny want me to do?"

Molly finished painting the living room and then started on the dining room. Tripoli's farm house, she thought, was really a gem in the rough. The frame was constructed of heavy hand-hewn timbers, and the high-ceilinged rooms all had old chestnut trim and wainscoting. A handsome wooden staircase with beautiful hand-carved spindles led to the upstairs rooms, some of which were almost palatial in size. After years in a tiny trailer, it felt as though she were living in a mansion. And all the house needed, she saw, was some stripping and painting and polishing to bring out its inherent beauty.

In fact, the more she threw herself into work, the better she felt. Her strength was returning and she was gaining back the weight she had lost. And with these changes, the ardor she had felt for Tripoli slowly returned. She came to look forward to their lovemaking in the evenings after dinner or in the early mornings when they embraced in a state of blissful half-sleep. One Sunday they stayed in bed the entire day. They made love in the morning and then Tripoli brought her breakfast. They lounged in bed, reading the Sunday paper, then made love in the afternoon. Then did it yet again in the early evening when the sun had gone down and the stars twinkled through the bedroom window. Long after their lovemaking had exhausted them, Molly continued to cling to him as though, in the velvet darkness of winter, she were trying to absorb him.

"Do you think we're setting a record?" asked Tripoli with a laugh.

"Hush," she said, planting her fingers on his lips as if they might lose the moment. "Don't talk. No words. I just want to feel you."

Wally Schuman showed up on a Tuesday afternoon right before Christmas while Tripoli was still in town. It was the day of another heavy snow, and the driveway was so deep that he had to leave his car on the road. His red goatee was encrusted with ice and he looked frozen.

"Come in quick," said Molly, as the snow blew in through the door.

Stamping his feet and removing his boots, Wally explained that he had run into Tripoli in the courthouse and had inquired about how Molly was doing. "The roads didn't look so bad when I started out in town," he confessed, rubbing his red hands to get them warm.

After Molly made him some hot tea, he sat by the stove slowly drying out, steam coming off his wet clothes.

He started with what he had apparently come to say. "You

shouldn't be too hard on yourself about Daniel," he said, sipping the hot tea.

"I suppose what's done is done, and I can't undo it."

"Well, at the very least, I think Daniel got people thinking about the effects of their actions on the earth. And that's at least a start." He then went into the reason for his visit. The *Journal* was short staffed. Knowing that Molly had worked as an editor at the magazine and… "Well, I was wondering if you'd like to try your hand on a few pieces. I've got to warn you that it doesn't pay much."

"Did Tripoli put you up to this?"

He looked genuinely surprised. "No. No. This was my idea entirely."

"And I was the only writer in town that came to mind," she smiled and wondered if Tripoli had been sneaking looks at her journal. Deep down he was, after all, a nosy cop.

"Well," Wally admitted, "I do have another motive, too. I still think a lot about Danny…Daniel." He held his hands over the stove, stretching his fingers, examined them, and then shifted his gaze to Molly. "I'm convinced he was destined to return to the woods again," he said looking her in the eye. "Maybe not as early as this. Maybe not to face the forest alone. But I think that what happened to Daniel was not your doing," he said with a warm and generous smile. "And I think people need to understand that. And not just for your sake, but for the town's."

The change in Molly was obvious to Tripoli, though he didn't dare mention it for fear her state of well-being might simply evaporate. She seemed to be in a continuous state of metamorphosis. She certainly wasn't the same woman he had met that fateful day he had taken on the case of her missing son. The edges to her personality had been rounded, and in their place was a seamless acceptance of life and its changes, an understanding that its small pleasures were fleeting and could only be taken where and when one found them. Even Molly's body had changed, he noticed. Her thighs and hips had taken on more womanly contours. Her face was filling out and her breasts seemed larger, more firm. What should have alerted him, eluded him, Tripoli who had no such experience before.

"I want to get rid of my car," she said, and Tripoli looked at her surprised. "And I want you to get rid of yours, too. They're both just polluting wrecks on wheels."

"Okay," he smiled. "Do I take a horse and buggy to get to work?"

"No, but...do you think we could afford one of those new hybrid cars?"

"Well...yeah..." he scratched his head. "I suppose so. But what about mine? The Caprice belongs to the department."

"Get them to change, too."

"You mean the whole fleet?"

"Why not? This is a progressive town, right? They're always patting themselves on the back, saying how enlightened they are. Well, let them put their money where it counts."

"It's not going to be easy convincing Matlin."

"Go talk to the mayor. Common Council. You might be surprised."

"You go talk to them."

"Okay. I will. But first you talk to Matlin."

Tripoli swallowed.

"Oh, come on. You're not afraid of him, are you?"

"No," he replied quickly, "of course not."

They spent a quiet Christmas together. Tripoli had gone out and cut a small a tree, and they set it up and decorated it in the newly finished living room. She had knitted him a scarf and a pair of matching wool socks to go with it. Tripoli had dozens of gifts for her. Perfume and jewelry. A fancy nightgown that she couldn't use until spring. A set of bath oils and a couple of cookbooks that he had found on sale.

Jewelry, she thought, out here in the sticks? Perfume? Though the gifts were a little inappropriate, she knew his sentiments were sincere. After Christmas dinner, they lay on the rug in front of the fireplace watching the flames dance and talked quietly about Daniel.

"I wish Danny was with us," she said, looking at the tree. "He would have loved this. Just think of it," she added wistfully. "The three of us together. Here."

When Molly had finished sprucing up the dining room and stripped and varnished all the woodwork, she went back to town to get material for curtains. The room called for something cheerful, colorful, perhaps in yellow and green. She found the perfect fabric in a sheer material that was on sale, and bought enough for all the downstairs rooms.

Then she headed over to City Hall where she had a morning meeting with the mayor.

"Danny's mother, of course!" said Mayor Rankin getting to his feet to take Molly's hand. "Please. Please sit down." He offered her a chair. "I was going to call you, in fact. Chief Matlin called me about updating the fleet. It's funny how everything comes together at once," he leaned back in his chair and played with his mustache.

"Oh?" she said, trying to disguise her surprise.

"A year ago, six months ago, if I had suggested replacing those police car tanks I'd have been booed and thrown out of office. Now people seem to be receptive to the idea."

"Why's that?" she asked.

"I think it's a lot of things."

"Danny?"

"Well, yes. Among others. Certainly. Look, I'd like to ask a favor.

You could make my job a lot easier."

"What's that?"

"I'd like you speak to the Common Council."

"But...But..." Molly stuttered. "But I'm not a speaker."

"I think you'll do just fine. And what I'm hoping to propose is not just replacing police cars, but all city vehicles."

"Well, in that case..." said Molly.

"I knew you'd see it my way." Mayor Rankin smiled and led her to the door.

As she was coming out of City Hall, she passed her old boss hurrying up the street. For an instant, she almost didn't recognize him. Larry was clad in an expensive Italian suit largely hidden by a jauntily unbuttoned camel's hair coat. His hair was newly styled and brilliantly moussed. He was freshly tanned as if just back from a Caribbean vacation, and his skin seemed to glow. Hardly the down-at-the-heels businessman she might have anticipated, given Sandy's dire report.

"Larry," she gulped, unable to hide her surprise.

He looked at her for a moment. "Oh, Molly. Molly. How are you doing?" he exclaimed cheerfully, as if they had seen each other only a day ago. "How's everything going? Are you working these days?"

She shook her head.

"Just hanging out, eh?"

She nodded.

"What a waste of talent," he said with a smile she couldn't quite read. "I always had big expectations for you."

Strange, she thought, not a word about Danny. "I heard about the magazine," she finally ventured. "I'm sorry."

"Oh, that!" He flicked his hand and laughed. "That's already history. Didn't you hear? I've just opened up a new firm. Internet marketing. Things are taking off again. You know," he turned philosophical, "sometimes blessings come in disguise. You think you're on the right track and—whoops," he checked his watch. "I'm late for an appointment." He started to move off. "But I definitely want to talk to you. Might have a key place for you in the organization," he said, turning his head as he retreated into the distance. "How about lunch some time? Why don't you give me a call? We'll play catch-up. Gotta dash."

And then he was gone.

Molly liked living at the farmhouse. It took just a quick walk through Tripoli's field, and she was deep in the Connecticut Hill wilderness. It felt right being in the country, and crunching through the ice-layered forest gave her solace, a sense of connection with Danny. Often, she would find herself talking to him, as if Danny were still there, close to her. She would tell him about her new life on the farm, about the toasty wood stove they had in the kitchen, how they were fixing up the house, finishing up all the rooms. How there was so much space—not like the old trailer. How life here was good and wholesome, and how she wished he were here with her to enjoy it.

On cold days, when the sun came out and the wind on the hilltop fell to a calm, the winter air became so still that Molly found she could hear for miles. She could hear the scurrying of squirrels on the icy ground, could make out the snap of twigs as a trio of deer stepped gingerly, nearly out of sight, through the distant woods. Here, high on the crest of the hill, if she listened she could hear the very bowels of the earth itself groaning and shifting under her feet, ever in motion as it had been for eons. Sometimes, when she spoke to Danny, she swore she thought she could detect traces of his voice, feel his presence, sense his eyes upon her.

She recalled the walks they had taken together and how Danny had sprung to life when they fled the office for the outdoors. In her mind's eye, she could still see him climbing the high hill behind the trailer park and prancing like a deer through the deep grass and wild flowers of summer. How little it had taken to make him happy! What a terrible mistake she had made in not moving out here with him right from the beginning. Oh, how he would have loved it here, might have grown and thrived here. This, after all, had been their dream before her faintheartedness in the face of uncertainty had insinuated itself into their life. Now, day by day, her surroundings, she realized, were transforming her: her view of life, of love, even her sense of her body was now different. Her period had skipped a month and she began to wonder.

It was a walk one late afternoon that prompted Molly to take up Wally Schuman's suggestion. The rays of sun were slanting low through the trees, and, when she looked carefully at one of the low maples, she noticed for the first time it had no new buds. Examining the other trees, she found that many of them, invariably the maples and beech, were utterly devoid of buds. The discovery was frightening. It meant that many of the trees in the forest wouldn't be having leaves in the coming spring. Were they dead? she wondered. Had the summer heat and drought taken its toll? What would the woods look like in the spring?

Molly started by writing a small piece. In essence, most of it was excerpted from her journal. In it she wrote about life in the country, about the chickadees and nuthatches and bright red cardinals that came to Tripoli's feeder, about how the boughs of the tall spruce in front of the farmhouse, when heavy with snow, looked like the outstretched arms of an old man struggling to keep the load aloft. Of course, she wrote about Daniel, too. How he had been endowed with the wonderful ability to listen and sense all that was in the natural world around him. And she wrote about her discovery of the budless trees and how Danny, she now understood, had been sent by the old Hermit to warn of an impending calamity. That people, herself included, would have to change what they did or how they did it.

She sent the article to Wally Schuman and was surprised not so much that he published it, but by people's reactions. Her observations must have hit a responsive chord, because two days later there were a flurry of letters to the editor about her article. Upon close examination of the trees in their yards and woods, others around the county had also come upon the same worrisome phenomenon of budless trees. And it was not limited to just the maple and beeches, but to some species of birches, too. Molly's article, they wrote, had the ring of authenticity and truth, and, yes, Daniel had been right. All the respondents were hoping for further stories from Molly.

She did another piece. This one was solely about Daniel, recalling him as a small child, then describing in detail his return, his transformation, his incredible gifts. The headline for the piece was entitled, "Just Listen." This, too, brought a chorus of cheers.

"I knew it," said Wally on the phone. "And the Gannett Wire Service wants to carry your articles—with your permission, of course. Generally, we share with our other papers."

"Sure," said Molly.

"And it means a bit more money, too."

The prospect of being able to help pay her way at Tripoli's was inviting. So she sat down and wrote another article. This was about herself and was much harder to write. Almost confessional in tone, she examined her own situation while working for the magazine. "I was so terrified at the prospect of losing security that I allowed myself to become distracted from what was essential in life. I was so swamped with the informational noise of the everyday that my connections to the essentials of the earth had become severed. I had come to believe that fruit and vegetables grew in supermarkets, that milk was made in containers, and fish magically laid themselves glassy-eyed upon beds of ice. And all for me."

"So, what do we do now," she asked, "now that the dairy farmers don't have enough hay for their cows because of the summer drought, now that we've depleted the oceans of fish?"

A day after the article appeared nationally in the Gannett papers, Molly began receiving letters from all over the country. There were so many letters that Josh Miller, the mailman, couldn't leave them in the box and had to come all the way to the front door lugging a sack.

"Hey, you're getting famous," he said, slipping the bag off his shoulder and letting it fall at her feet with a grunt.

"Hardly," she laughed.

"Everybody I know here in Newfield still talks about Daniel. What with all the stuff that's happening, folks are scared."

"And you?"

"Geez," he took off his wool cap and scratched his bald head. "Of course. But what can I do? I'm just a lousy postman. Well, happy reading," he said and jumped into his jeep and headed off to the next farm.

Molly opened the sack and started eagerly reading the letters. A woman in Ohio wrote that over the last month she had been discovering the bodies of red-breasted nuthatches and pileated woodpeckers in the woods near where she lived. "I told my husband about it, but he says that sometimes birds just die. But these are hardy winter birds, and I've never seen anything like this in my thirty years of birding."

A country vet in Minnesota wrote that his small town had been experiencing an outbreak in rabies the likes of which he had never seen. He had already euthanized dozens of dogs and cats attacked by rabid animals. "I've been telling folks that the reason for the outbreak is that the population of skunks and raccoons has been going through the roof. Everywhere you go, you're just about tripping over them.

"My belief is that the previous mild winters we've been experiencing out here have let the rabbits and mice survive in big numbers. And since they are the primary food for the raccoons and skunks in the spring, the weather is at the source of this outbreak. Well, that's what I'm telling folks, but nobody's listening. Maybe you could mention something about it?"

There was a letter from a citrus farmer in the Florida panhandle; he and his neighbors were having a miserable crop because of poor pollination. The bee population had undergone an inexplicable die-off—and this time it wasn't mites.

Molly even had a letter from an Eskimo from Point Barrow, Alaska. Because the ice had closed so late this year, the whales didn't leave as usual, and now pack ice from the Arctic Ocean had moved in to close off their escape. He himself had counted over a dozen trapped whales milling around, frantically trying to find a way out of the bay.

"Interesting," said Tripoli when he came home and started reading the letters. "No one thing in itself is really proof but, speaking as a cop, altogether this gets pretty suspicious."

"Right, she continued his thought. "It's all anecdotal. But taken collectively, you start to get a pattern."

"So what are you going to do?"

"I'm not sure yet."

The Gannett office in Washington called to ask Molly if she would like to do a regular, weekly column. Molly was both flattered and intimidated.

"We thought we'd call it 'Just Listen.'"

Molly gave it a moment's thought. Thought about Danny, who had been gone six months. "Okay. Sure. Why not."

The column she submitted cited the surprising response she had gotten from her first article. Those letters spoke to her of a deep concern that was nationwide in scope. "I had always thought that environmental concerns were limited to a select few, the elite and fringe groups. But now I see that people all over the country, in all walks of life, really do care about the earth."

And for the next three days, Josh Miller found himself lugging even heavier sacks of mail up to Tripoli's farm.

By the time she took the microphone at the Common Council meeting, everybody in attendance at the overflowing session knew who she was.

"I'm a little nervous talking to so many people at once. So I hope you'll forgive me if I…if I…" She fumbled with her notes. "If I can't get my notes straight," she said, and the people laughed politely. Finally, she tossed her cards away. "Look, I'm not going to make this sound easy or cheap. We've got a chance right now to change the way we're living. Replacing all the city vehicles with more efficient cars means the city will probably have to float a new bond issue. Tax rates are going to go up. There's no way around it. But it's going to drastically reduce the amount of energy we use and the pollution we emit. Most important of all, we have a chance in this small town to set an example for the rest of the country. And we're not doing this just for ourselves. We're doing it for our children and their children."

Molly spoke with such passion, surprising even herself, that when she finished people were on their feet applauding.

Afterwards, she invited everybody out to see her new two-seater parked in front. "Every time I brake," she explained, "instead of heating up the brake pads, I turn a generator and it recharges the batteries that drive the electric motor. And it's a wonderful car to drive. And park. Just look at it," she said proudly.

When Molly's first check arrived from the paper, she decided to use it to continue fixing up the house. Molly, who had never given much thought to interior decoration, now took a surprising pleasure in it.

She hung curtains and rearranged the furniture. She found some old antiques hidden in the far reaches of the attic: a table that they moved into the dining room and an old chest that was perfect for their bedroom. Here was a realm where one had some control, she thought, where life had definition, tasks had beginnings and ends, and accomplishment could be measured by simply looking and seeing.

"I need some help," she said on a Saturday morning when Tripoli was home for the day. "I found an oak hall-tree hidden up in the barn."

"A what?"

"It's this thing you put in the hallway and hang coats and hats on."

"Oh, one of those."

"There's all this heavy junk in the way. I can't move it and I was hoping you could help."

"Yeah, sure!"

They went together out to the barn and Tripoli unlatched the door. It opened with a creak.

"Oh shit!" he suddenly exclaimed.

"What's the matter?"

"Another animal is missing! Wait," he said, moving in, Molly right behind him. "Let me count." He counted as they kept milling around.

"Are you sure?"

"Of course I'm sure!"

He searched all through the interior of the barn, went behind the bales of hay, everywhere a yearling sheep might have hidden. "It's a lamb. I'm missing a lamb. Damn. It was the littlest one, too."

Together they hunted all over the farm, then trudged through the deep snow on the adjacent land. There was no a sign of the lamb. Not even tracks.

"Someone's stealing them. It's obvious," he said over dinner a week later, after still another lamb vanished. "Some neighbor is having lamb chops at our expense!"

"What are you going to do?" asked Molly, coming back from the stove with a second helping of spinach lasagna. "Sleep out there with a gun?"

"Well, the thought had occurred to me."

"Come on, Trip," she said, serving him.

"Enough. Enough," he held up his hand as she mounded the pasta on his plate. "Hey, you trying to make me fat?"

"Not a chance. You're too busy running around. Don't worry. But if you really want something to worry about—"

"What?"

"My period," she said. "It's four weeks late. My breasts are swollen."

It took him a moment, and then a smile spread on his face. "Interesting," he said finally.

"Is that all you have to say?"

"You know, I was beginning to wonder. You seemed kind of different."

"Boy, for a cop you really are slow." She punched him playfully in the shoulder.

"A baby," he muttered softly to himself. "A son."

"Or a daughter."

"Whatever. I'm not particular. I'll accept any flavor at this stage in my life." He got up, took her in his arms, and kissed her. Running his hands over her belly he claimed he could already feel the baby. He bent down and put his ear to her stomach and swore he could hear a tiny heart beating. "How wonderful!" he murmured.

Long before Tripoli arose to go to work, Molly was up. She built a fire in the downstairs stove and sat alone in the darkness, waiting for the light of dawn, listening to the wind howling around the farmhouse. The morning was cold, colder than it had been all of December. The previous night, the temperature had plunged to five below and the thermometer had hardly budged above zero level as the day began. All through the dawn, the wind kept buffeting the house, rocking it gently and causing its heavy timbers to groan as though it were an old ship at sea.

Later, as Tripoli stood shaving, he looked in the mirror and saw Molly standing in the doorway watching him.

"What's up?" he asked without turning. The lines in her face were deep and there was a terrible aura of sorrow about her.

"I've always felt that somehow Danny was alive," she said, her voice barely audible. "But now I don't think so."

"What do you mean?" he asked, just as she started to weep. She came into his arms and burrowed her face into his neck, smearing shaving foam on her cheek and hair. In the deathly cold, the swaying birch tree outside the bathroom window creaked with each gust like something in pain.

"There's no way he could survive this. No human being could."

Downstairs in the kitchen, the coals in the stove burned red hot, whipped by the draft from the chimney. The panes in the old windows shuddered. The entire house seemed to be crying out for relief.

"I think that this new baby is meant as a substitute," she said finally. "To replace Danny."

"Don't be silly." He stroked her head, took his towel and wiped off the soap. "People are allowed to have more than one child, you know. God doesn't play bait and switch. Daniel's okay."

"How can you say that?" she asked looking up at him with reddened eyes.

"I don't know," he said, "But I just got this feeling."

"There's no way. You're trying to console me."

"No. Never."

"Yourself then."

"You have to have a little faith."

"Faith in what?"

Over breakfast, she sat motionless over her coffee. "You'd better go. You're going to be late. Again."

But he couldn't leave her, not like this. He got up from the table and opened the door to the stove to toss in a piece of wood. The air rushed in, sending up a hail of sparks. "If you think about all that has happened," he said turning to her as he knelt in front of the stove, his face glowing in the heat, "you begin to realize that it all goes beyond anything we can really comprehend—–or imagine. I really and truly believe we'll see Daniel again."

"Oh, how I wish I could believe that." She turned and looked out the window. The sky turned black and a gale of wind-whipped snow blew past, obscuring the barn. Then, almost as quickly, a break appeared in the clouds and a column of bright sun beamed through. Molly watched it dance over the land, illuminating everything in its path. "You're right. I don't understand anything. Why Danny, of all the children in the world? And if this old man had all this wisdom, this message to bring—whatever it was—why didn't he just do it himself?"

"I've wondered about that, too," said Tripoli, getting up and standing behind her chair to gaze out on the wintry fields. "Daniel called him father. And John. And I kept thinking. John? John? His name wasn't John. But when I read those old books we found in the hut, I realized that there were pieces in there that looked like they were taken from the Bible. From the Koran. God only knows where else. It was like a synthesis of all religions. John? Yes, I thought. Of course. John the Baptist."

"Huh?" she turned to look up at him.

"Matthew thought of himself as John the Baptist. He was meant to teach and mentor Daniel, to baptize Daniel in the wealth of all this amassed knowledge."

"You mean the old man was…?"

"He *thought* he was." said Tripoli. "In any event, Daniel was the chosen one. He was the culmination, the very purpose of the legacy. The time is ripe. The world is floundering. It's in a precarious, unstable, sick state. It needs a quiet, intelligent voice. The old man, whoever he was in fact, chose Daniel for this role. You see, Daniel was meant to be of this world, and yet not of this world."

"What do you mean?"

"That's why he came back. Look, the old man was not against technology. Daniel told me how he had asked him about television and computers and cell phones. He knew all about them. And those old volumes were full of all kinds of neat devices, clever ways of pumping and impounding power, growing crops, harnessing wind and tidal forces, using renewable resources. The people in the chain of the legacy weren't primitives. Just the opposite. They were way ahead of us. In some sense, light years ahead. And Daniel was meant to be the bridge—between the old and the new. That's why Matthew let him come back. It was to be as much a part of his education as living in the woods." Tripoli became excited as he spoke, and his enthusiasm began to infect Molly.

"And now?" she asked, knowing what he was going to say but needing to hear it.

"Daniel *has* to live on. Don't you see, it's our only hope. The world's hope. If I didn't believe that, I don't think I could go on myself." He told her about Christ's parable of the soils that the priest had shared with him. About the good ground that bore fruit.

"That's all very nice," she said. "But all you have to do is look outside. How can he keep warm? What can he eat? He's still human, you know. And the ground is hardly 'good,' it's frozen solid!"

Molly hadn't seen Rosie since Thanksgiving, but she did keep in contact with her by phone. Rosie had suffered a bad bout with the flu and couldn't seem to shake it. The boys, on the other hand, were healthy and growing like crazy. Ed, she told her, was now working not only full time, but putting in overtime. "For once, everything's going great. If I can just get back on my feet, things'll be perfect."

"As soon as you're feeling better, we want to see you guys."

"Well, sure!" said Rosie. "Just give me a few more days. I'm dying to see what you've done to the place."

Molly then told her that she was expecting.

"Oh, that's wonderful!" exclaimed Rosie, "Better than wonderful. Hey, I'll bet Tripoli's tickled."

"I don't know if he's quite absorbed it yet."

"Maybe he's just in shock," said Rosie with a laugh.

"Having a baby is going to mean more of a change around here. I'm trying to envision him singing lullabies and changing diapers."

"He may even have to take off his gun when he comes home!"

Thank God, thought Tripoli, Molly was again back in the mainstream, working and talking to people. What they needed now, he felt, was to get more sociable. Invite and get invited.

They had Jerry Sisler and his wife, Tracy, out for dinner on a Friday evening. It was the payback for all the scrumptious dinners that Tracy had cooked for him while he was single.

Tracy was a perky blond who sported lots of jewelry dangling from her neck and wrists, and had a tendency to bubble with talk.

"This place used to be a wreck," exclaimed Tracy as she took in all the remodeling that Molly and Tripoli had made since she last had been out to the farm—it was just before Tripoli's divorce. "I can't believe this is the same house. I mean this place is amazing. It looks like a museum!"

When they sat down to dinner, Tracy brought up the subject of the old books.

"Books?" repeated Tripoli and looked hard at Sisler.

"It's hardly a secret," said Sisler with a shrug. "Everybody knows you have them. It's pretty obvious. Curly Donahue's been talking about it, and even I saw you carrying them out of the building.

"Boy, Molly, this is great soup," exclaimed Tripoli. "Got any more?" And, without waiting for a reply, he jumped up and dashed off to the kitchen.

On the last Friday in January, they finally had Rosie and Ed out to dinner. Rosie looked washed out after the flu, but put on a cheerful face.

All through the meal, Tripoli kept talking about his missing animals and the "rustlers."

"I think Trip is obsessing a little," Molly joked.

"Well, what do you expect?" said Rosie teasingly. "He's a cop, ain't he? They always got to catch their crook. Hey," she turned to Tripoli, "did you ever think it might be some poor, old, starving widow with six kids?"

"Yeah, one who's got a taste for shish kebob," Ed laughed with a full mouth. "Hmmm. This is good, Molly. What is it?"

"It's a vegetable casserole. Danny always liked it."

"Daniel," uttered Tripoli, and the mood at the table became somber. Outside, a coyote was baying into the night. The moon was nearly full and the land was bathed in an eerie white light. Almost in unison, all eyes went to the window.

"Hey," Ed said, suddenly breaking the silence. "Why don't you rig up something?"

"Huh?" said Tripoli.

"I'm still thinking about the sheep."

"Yeah," said Tripoli. "Right."

"You could make some kind of an alarm or something. You know, next time they come to swipe a lamb—boom!—you nail them."

"Hmmm…not a bad idea," agreed Tripoli, lost in thought.

"Hey," said Rosie turning on Ed. "What are you, planning on joining the force or something? Whose side are you on, anyway?"

"I was just speculating. That's all."

"What do you want him to do," asked Rosie, turning on her husband, "shoot some poor sucker because he takes a goat?"

What Ed and Rosie, and especially Molly, didn't know was that Tripoli was no longer certain that the animals were being stolen. What if they were just being reclaimed? His suspicions had been sparked shortly after the first goat went missing and grew as each new animal disappeared. It was almost good to be true, and Tripoli decided to keep the notion to himself. He certainly didn't want to raise Molly's hopes only to discover that the culprit was a thief after all.

Was it possible that young Daniel had already learned enough from the old man to survive a winter in the woods alone? Tripoli was afraid that if he let on what he suspected, people might begin scouring the woods searching for Daniel, driving him further away from the farmhouse and the animals he so desperately needed. However remote his theory, there was no way Tripoli could take that risk.

A cop needed to deal in solid facts, not just speculation, Tripoli told himself and he began work on an alarm that night. It was a very primitive arrangement. Nothing as sophisticated as a motion detector or an electronic switch. It was similar to what Tripoli had once concocted as a teenager to warn him and his brother when his parents were returning home on a Saturday night. He took a reel of fishing line, hooked it up to the barn door, and then led it into the downstairs living room. It was rigged up with a series of small pulleys so that when the barn door was opened, a tin can clanked to the downstairs floor.

"You must be joking," said Molly when Tripoli dragged a mattress and a gun—in case they really were being robbed—into the living room and settled in for the night.

"I'm deadly serious," he said.

"Please, Trip, come back to bed. I don't like sleeping alone."

"Well, come sleep down here with me then."

"Not on your life. And put that gun away. You're going to end up hurting someone."

"I'm not going to shoot anybody—unless I have to. You want me to go out there in the dark without a weapon? What happens if the other guy's armed? Hey, we're living out here in the boonies. I don't want to scare you, but you never know what kind of nut is out there roaming around in these woods."

"I'm not scared. I just want us to go to sleep. Please, Trip."

"Just till I get the perp."

"How long is that going to take?"

"As long as necessary."

It was cold on the floor—hard, too. Not anywhere near as comfortable as the queen-sized bed upstairs where Molly lay. But he slept at his post on Sunday night. Then on Monday. Then Tuesday and Wednesday.

"Once you make up your mind about something…" Molly said over breakfast. She didn't need to finish the sentence.

"Tenacity," he said, solemnly shaking his head. "That's what makes a good cop."

"Great!" she said. "Enjoy yourself!"

It wasn't easy sleeping down there. He couldn't quite let go and relax. He even slept with his clothes on, his shoes and gun strategically placed on the floor within reach of his right hand.

On Tripoli's birthday, they had dinner and then went to see a movie, some English period piece about virtue and virginity, and

Tripoli slept through most of it. As they drove back, the night was moonless and it started to snow. The snow stuck, and, light and fluffy, the flakes kept tumbling down. Tripoli went to bed around midnight, exhausted from the long week of restless sleep, and fell into a deep, snoring slumber.

Somewhere in the depths of the night, the can hit the floor with a loud clank. Tripoli awoke with a start, sitting up abruptly. Jumping to his feet, he forgot his gun and shoes, and in his rush to the door took a wrong turn and ended up walking blindly into a sharp corner. A second later, as the dullness turned to pain, he could feel a trickle of warm blood dripping down his face.

Going back to the bed, he groped in the dark for his shoes, but couldn't find them. He located his gun by stepping on it. By the time he got to the door, the can had already risen. The barn door was shut, and someone was moving off into the darkness.

Tripoli scampered barefoot out into the snow. For a moment, he couldn't quite believe his eyes. In the near distance, he could make out the figure of a stately old man with long, flowing hair and a beard. He had one of the ewes on a line and was trying to drag it forward. Behind the animal followed a smaller figure, a little boy, pushing. Tripoli stopped dead in his tracks. He stood riveted, his weapon dangling at his side, watching the slow procession advance through the scrim of falling snow. Tripoli was frozen by shock, and overcome by a deep sense of love… of relief. The old man was alive. And he was still there, watching over Daniel.

As the faint figures began to move off into the woods, his feet suddenly felt cold and he stepped back into the shelter of the porch. Now he could tell Molly, he thought. How would he tell her? Should he wake her now? Turning to go in, he found himself face to face with Molly standing in the darkened doorway.

"Oh," she gasped as she spotted the figures that were beginning to dissolve into the distant line of trees. She started to move, to chase out into the night after them, but suddenly caught herself and held back, holding on to one of the columns of the porch for support.

Tripoli came up behind her. He slipped his arm around her waist, felt her shivering, and pulled her close. They stood there in silence long after the boy and old man had vanished into the night. Then, finally, they went back into the warmth of the kitchen, Tripoli closing the door softly behind them.

For the longest moment they stood together in the darkness, holding each other.

"The old Hermit's alive," uttered Molly, shaking her head in disbelief. She could hardly see through her tears. "And Danny—he really *is* safe."

"And he'll be back," murmured Tripoli tenderly.

"You think so?"

"You'll see. He'll be back because he loves you and because he was meant to come back."

"Do you really believe that?"

"Yes. With all my heart. Daniel has a job to do. An important one."

Molly turned to look out the window. It was pitch black outside, and though she couldn't see anything, she kept staring. "He's going to change the world, isn't he?" she said, her eyes still fixed on the window.

Tripoli nodded as he stroked her wet cheek.

"Somehow, I've got to help him. And I keep wondering about what I should be doing? What I can do to lessen the harm that's been done? What would Danny want me to do?"

"I think you're doing it already," he murmured.

In the weeks that followed, Daniel did come back. March remained fierce and Molly, knowing that there would not be much food to gather in the deepening snow, left something in the barn each night.

On occasion the food would sit there, accumulating for a few days, only to vanish suddenly. Wrapped in hay so they wouldn't freeze, Molly left sacks of potatoes and onions, bags of nuts, and the casseroles and dishes that she cooked for Trip and knew that Danny would relish. She was dying to tell Rosie what had happened that February night, but Tripoli remained adamant.

"Please, don't mention this to *anyone*," he had warned the morning after their discovery. He finished buttoning a crisp white shirt and then hunted for a tie with some green in it to match his pants. There was a break in the clouds and the sun was streaming into the bedroom. "Least of all Rosie."

"But that's not right! You know how much Rosie—"

"Yeah, I know she loves Daniel, but she also loves to talk. If anybody finds out that he's here somewhere in the woods, this place will be crawling with people and they'll drive him further away. Do you want that?"

"No, but Rosie's been almost like a mother to him."

"Why take the chance?"

Though she was bursting to tell, Molly kept their secret, contenting herself with the knowledge that Danny was safe and near at hand.

Once when she went out to check in the morning, Molly found a series of small, clearly marked footprints in the snow leading from the barn. The poor kid was still wearing those sneakers she had bought him at the mall. In this weather his feet must be freezing, she thought, and hurried to town. Three days later, to her relief, the pair of lined hiking boots she had left were missing, and the next week when she again discovered small prints at the mouth of the barn, they bore the unmistakable tread of those new boots.

"Just give him space," Tripoli had counseled. But much as she tried, Molly often found that she simply couldn't resist following those boot tracks. She pursued them as they wound up hills and plunged down into gullies, cut across open fields and snaked through dense forests. Sometimes they went for miles, but then she would discover that either the snow had blown over or Daniel had followed a running stream or they just mysteriously ended as if he had become weightless and taken off into the air. She felt a tinge of guilt tracking him as she did, knowing that if he wanted to see her, needed to see her, he could have done so without effort. It was just that she craved to see him, longed to touch him and hold him in her arms—if only for a moment.

"You sound funny these days," remarked Rosie when they spoke on the phone. "What's up?"

"Funny?"

"Just…well strange. It's like you're hiding something?"

"There's nothing to hide," she sputtered. "Nothing at all. I've just been so darn busy with my column. People keep calling and writing."

"If you don't want to talk, I'm not going to pressure you."

"Rosie, come on. You're just imagining things," she said, feeling terrible. It wasn't quite so much a lie as an omission, Molly tried to console herself, but, in fact, she had erected a barrier between them which Rosie, her dearest friend, detected and which Molly abhorred.

Molly baked and cooked for Daniel and the old man, attempted to anticipate what it was that they might need or desire to eat. She tried to imagine the old man biting into a piece of her homemade bread. Molly thought of the supplies as missives she was addressing to old Matthew. Surely by now he understood her message.

"If you're going out to the barn, take this, too," she said as Tripoli pulled on his padded parka. It was a loaf of fresh bread, still warm and wrapped in a towel.

"Hey, how do we know they're not opening a store and selling this stuff," he chuckled. He now had his arms heaped high with two new sleeping bags and a week's supply of food. And, as he stepped out into the wind-whipped winter evening, Molly tried not to think about Daniel in the cold but rather living in the warmth of the old man's love, living with the father he never had. But soon Daniel would have a brother or sister, and that, too, would change things. For the first time in her life, Molly truly looked to the future, prepared for what it had to offer and ready to embrace it.

chapter twenty-four

In the spring, Tripoli and Molly made a garden. Although it got warm early and flowers bloomed and migratory birds arrived weeks ahead of schedule, a driving wind kept blowing over their hilltop farm. It so threatened their seedlings that Tripoli hastily erected a barrier to shelter the fragile plants. Watering the dusty soil and babying the young plants brought to mind Daniel's prolific garden carved out of the unyielding soil around the trailer. By now, Molly was so big she found it hard to bend over: she weeded and thinned the beets and carrots crawling forward on all fours.

"Hey, come on, Darling, you shouldn't be doing this kind of work anymore," said Tripoli, stooping down so his face came level with hers. "Let me," he whispered.

"No, no, I like doing it."

"But the baby," he said. "I don't want anything to happen."

"Don't worry," she laughed, "I've been through this once before."

He kissed her brow and her lips. He tasted the salt on her neck, then he went back to work.

Like a man possessed, Tripoli kept tilling the soil and expanding the garden, appending row upon row. He put in two dozen additional tomato plants, did five long rows of corn, placing them beside hills of squash and cucumbers. Then he made a second planting of beans, placing them in tight proximity to the corn. Close to the marigolds he clustered peppers and eggplants, cabbage and brussels spouts, using the very methods of companion planting that he had seen Daniel employ in his tiny garden. When Molly wiped the sweat from her face to discover him stringing yet another line, she asked, "What are you planning to do? Feed the whole of humanity? We're only two, you know."

"No, no," he corrected. "Three. No four. No wait, five!" He laughed, then watched Molly as she returned to cultivating the row and thought how perfect the moment was. Together they had created something good and honest and lasting. Who would have thought it?

Molly turned to catch him staring at her. "What are you looking at?" she asked, a half-smile on her face.

"You, Darling. You."

May, June, July, and August were busy months for the two of them.

Early each morning before heading into work, Tripoli was in the garden, harvesting the first crops, loading them into his new car to make his daily drop-off at the local soup kitchen and pantry run by the church.

"Lou, these are absolutely amazing," said the old priest, taking a fresh potato from the basket and hefting it in his hand. It must have weighed a good pound or more. While other gardens were being infested with insects or withering in the hot, driving winds, their garden was producing vegetables the size and taste of which were the talk of the town. "What's the secret?"

"No secret at all. Just following some of Daniel's rules."

"Well, you're making a lot of families very happy."

Molly was writing, but she was also traveling. She was given invitations to speak all around the state. She addressed government groups, women's clubs, unions—whoever wanted her to speak or was willing to listen. In the middle of her eighth month, so big she was hardly able to sit behind the wheel, she drove to Albany and spent two days meeting with state legislators.

When she got back late that night she was beaming.

"I met with the governor!" she exclaimed when Tripoli came out to help her in with her bag. "We had dinner!" She told Tripoli how she had spent three hours with the governor trying to convince him that he should lead a drive to resurrect the rail system, getting him to imagine a high-speed train running down the spine of the state; what it would do for the economy, what it would do for his image, how the history books would hail his efforts. "And there I was in the governor's mansion. Me. Molly Driscoll. A nobody. Having dinner with him! Just the two of us."

"Were there candles and soft music?" he asked, and she laughed. "I mean, maybe I should be jealous?"

Her water broke early in the morning. It happened on the seventh of September, a good week before the doctors had planned to induce labor and do her C-section. The pains began only minutes later. The contractions were sharp and hard. They seemed more intense than she remembered them when she had started labor with Danny. Then she noticed she was bleeding. At first it was just a trickle, then it came in a steady flow, bright red, oxygenated blood running out of her.

Tripoli was immediately on the phone, calling her obstetrician who notified the hospital. Then he bundled Molly into the car. Now she was losing blood even faster. It felt like it was gushing and, despite the pads, the car seat was completely soaked.

"Don't worry. Don't worry," he kept repeating as he swerved down the curves to town, siren and lights going full blast. He tried to imagine losing the baby, losing her, and knew it was beyond any-thing he could humanly bear.

"It'll be okay," she said, smiling weakly. The contractions were coming, intense and close now. It all seemed too fast, too early. Please, dear God, she whispered, let me keep this one.

A team of nurses and two trauma doctors were waiting for her in the emergency room. Tripoli was shunted aside and told to wait as the staff drew the curtains around her. After a hasty examination, Molly was rushed directly into surgery without even a chance for him to say anything more than to wish her luck.

Tripoli was left to pace the waiting room, weaving between the others who sat in their orange plastic chairs staring blankly up at the game show running on the overhead TV. After an hour, he couldn't take it any longer and, placing himself in the corridor leading to the surgery, started cornering nurses and staff every time one of them came through the double doors leading to the operating suites.

"Molly Driscoll," he kept saying. "How's she doing? And the baby? Is it okay?"

No one seemed to know. Or wanted to talk. He wasn't sure which.

Finally, one of the nurses headed into the surgical unit stopped to talk to him.

"Don't worry," she said, adjusting her scrubs. "You've got Dr. Wozniak. He's the best there is."

Tripoli looked as if he were going to cry, and she placed her hand on his shoulder. "Please, just go back into the waiting room. We'll call you as soon as we know anything. I promise."

It was hours before Dr. Wozniak appeared through the double doors. The man looked exhausted. His face was furrowed, there were splotches of blood on his green scrubs, and his gait was ominously slow. Tripoli leapt to his feet. At first the doctor failed to notice him, and it seemed to take an extraordinary time for him to close the short distance separating them.

"Oh," said the doctor, startled when Tripoli took hold of his arm.

"Well?"

"She's lost an awful lot of blood," he said, the furrow between his eyebrows deepening, "but I think she'll be okay. We've now got her stabilized."

"And the baby?" he hung onto the doctor's arm. "The baby!"

"A girl," said Wozniak, covering Tripoli's hand with his. "A nice, plump little daughter. Seven pounds, two ounces and a professional screamer."

When they let Tripoli in to see her, Molly lay in bed, her eyes shut, her skin as white as the linens. Slowly she opened her eyes, saw him, and then smiled a little. "Good police work, Trip," she said through lips that were dried and cracked.

A young nurse brought her the baby and placed it in Molly's arms. When Tripoli saw his child, he lost control and started to weep. Molly was crying too, and the nurse slipped discreetly out of the room.

"You did it!" he said, his voice choked as he examined the infant swaddled in a blanket. The baby was round faced and fine featured, a layer of silky, dark hair covering her head. She was beautiful. Perfect.

"You don't know how much I love you," he said the next day as he watched Molly nurse for the first time, the baby drinking eagerly at her breast. The color had returned to Molly's face, and she was propped up in bed, looking clearly victorious.

Gazing up from the suckling infant, she smiled at him. "Yes, I know," she said, and there was a radiance on her face that gave her the look of a young girl. Four days later, they released her from the hospital with strict instructions not to climb stairs or exert herself in any other way until she was fully healed.

"What do doctors know?" she laughed as she gingerly made her way up the flight to their bedroom. "What am I supposed to do, sleep on a mattress on the living room floor?"

Tripoli cooked, did the laundry, and cleaned the house, but it was impossible keeping Molly confined to bed. Every day she gained more strength; even the doctor was surprised at how quickly she recovered.

"Come on, already, I'm not exactly an invalid," she objected when Tripoli insisted on waxing the floors in the kitchen. "Give me that mop willya?"

They called the little girl Rachel, and Molly never let her out of her sight. She had surprisingly delicate features and a heart-shaped face like Molly's with a pouty little bow-shaped mouth. Her fingers were long and fine and, when Molly nursed her, studying her closely, she could see that Rachel's eyes and wide brow were clearly Tripoli's. The baby was also blessed with a happy disposition, hardly ever complaining. Indeed, she always seemed to be smiling.

A week after her release, Trip bought her a new computer and Molly was back working on her articles. The inbox on her computer was daily filled with emails from a contingent of volunteers strategically placed around the globe. A network had organized itself spontaneously, and Molly, somehow the rallying point, suddenly found herself acting as the clearing house. Daily observations on the flora and fauna flowed into her computer from everywhere. Her database was getting so comprehensive, the observations so accurate and incisive, that scientists were beginning to contact *her* for data.

The energy companies that sold fossil fuels were still insisting that the fears of global warming were being fed by alarmists, but it didn't take much fancy research on Molly's part to see otherwise. In less than two years, the mean annual global surface temperature had jumped nearly a full degree. Her observers, which included physicians, were reporting a recent surge in vector-borne and infectious diseases, especially in tropical and subtropical regions. The warm weather was intensifying the transmission of malaria, and there were explosive outbreaks of dengue, hantavirus, and cholera.

Scientists who had been observing the ice sheet in West Antarctica were now writing to her with warnings that, because of rapid melting, huge portions of the shelf were in danger of breaking loose.

"The massive ice sheet," wrote a Harvard geophysicist in his email, "sits suspended on bedrock above the sea. According to my calculations, if it drops into the ocean, it can and will set up a soliton—a massive and destructive wave—that will inundate coastal areas around the world and leave ocean levels permanently raised."

As she continued to receive such news, Molly's writing took on a new urgency and her column, "Just Listen," now syndicated daily in papers across the country, was experiencing a burgeoning readership.

"Another three major papers in Europe and two in Asia just signed on," exclaimed Wally Schuman during their regularly scheduled morning phone conference. He had stepped down from his management position at the paper and was now devoting himself to Molly's column as well as a nonprofit organization he had created and called "The Daniel Foundation." Unsolicited donations were coming in every day to support the research and development of innovative energy-saving appliances. The fund had already helped a number of inventors to start building prototypes and apply for patents. Molly's column was helping that effort in no small measure.

"Just keep doing what you've been doing," Wally urged. "People need to hear what you have to say. It's exactly what Daniel would want you to do." Wally, however, like most everyone else in town, was convinced that Daniel was now long dead.

Each day, when Molly sat down to write, she envisioned her readership as an audience of two: Danny and the old man. There was still hope. If people would just modify their habits, lessen their consumption, she urged, the earth's warming could be arrested, maybe even reversed. But it had to happen now.

Then, a large fire broke out in the northern Amazon where Brazil and Venezuela met. The rain forest there had turned tinder dry, and all it took was a bolt of lightning to set the jungle ablaze. In a matter of days, it covered several hundred thousand acres and sent up a black pall of smoke that swirled around the rotating globe. When Tripoli left in the morning for work, Molly could see that the sky was encased in a thick, brown haze. That same evening, the sunset began far earlier than normal. It was unnaturally brilliant, a flaring reddish-orange that looked like a laser-light show and lasted for more than an hour.

In town, Tripoli noticed how the people kept staring up at the menacingly brown sky as though mesmerized. "I didn't worry about it before," said Kesh in the diner, pouring Tripoli a second cup of coffee at lunch. "But did you see that sky today? This is serious shit. I've a grandchild on the way. What kind of world am I bringing that kid into?"

In Washington, the government was still debating about what action to take. Leaders in capitals from Paris to Berlin to Tokyo seemed paralyzed. An unplanned experiment was being carried out on the Earth, it's outcome unforeseen, yet nobody could agree on anything.

Yet every day without fail visitors appeared on Molly's doorstep. There were locals, but also people from New York and Chicago and as far away as Oregon.

"I'd like to do something," said a troubled woman from Anaheim, "something to lessen the harm that I've done. What would Daniel want me to do?"

"You're doing it already, just by coming here," said Molly by way of encouragement and the woman smiled. "You've been watching, you've been listening, you see. Now go back now and talk to people, organize them, rally them to put pressure on their elected officials." The woman left energized and Molly was taken by how little it sometimes took to galvanize people.

Josh Miller was now delivering three and sometimes four heavy sacks of mail every day. Her readers sent faxes and emails, and the newspaper was besieged with urgent calls all asking for Molly's help. All she knew was that the political leaders weren't listening to the people, and the people weren't listening to each other.

"It was just like Daniel said," said a frightened Mrs. Ruzicka, appearing unannounced at the farm early one morning. Molly hadn't seen the woman since the day that Daniel had disappeared and Molly had questioned little Kevin at the mall. Hefty Mrs. Ruzicka had bicycled all the way from town to say, "If only Daniel and that old man were alive. They could have helped. I'm sure. People would have listened to them. My husband and I certainly would have."

Molly knew that bad news, like good, came in droves. It was Ed's call that confirmed her deepest fear.

"It's Rosie." His voice was breaking. "You know that dry cough she had. And the way she was always tired." He couldn't go on, and didn't have to. Molly could guess. "I kept pleading with her to go the doctor, but…"

"Where's she now?"

"Up at the hospital. She's really sick. I'm back home with the twins. I don't quite know what to do."

Molly called Tripoli, who came straight home. She left him with little Rachel and went straight to the hospital.

They had Rosie in a semi-private room, screened off from the other occupant. When Molly saw her, she could hardly believe what she saw. Rosie's skin was completely yellowed. Her cheeks looked as though they had collapsed. She was being catheterized, and they had bottles of saline and drugs plugged into her arm.

Rosie slowly turned her head, and when she noticed Molly standing at the foot of her bed she gave a weak smile. "Liver cancer," she said hoarsely.

Molly, unable to speak, took her hand.

"Just like I thought," said Rosie. "Every day when I worked at that body shop they were poisoning me." Then she started to cry quietly. "I wanted so bad to see my boys grow up and now I'll never have the chance."

Molly wanted to say that it wasn't like that at all, that Rosie would survive this, but even without talking to the doctors she could see it wasn't true. She couldn't even brave the lie. So she sat with Rosie silently holding her hand, sat with her for a couple of hours until Rosie drifted off to sleep.

Molly's mind was in turmoil. She worried about the twins, tried to envision what would happen to them in Rosie's absence and who would care for them. She felt heartsick. Wrapped up in her own problems, her pregnancy, and her writing and her life with Tripoli, she had neglected Rosie. She knew Rosie hadn't been well, yet she hadn't bothered to visit her, making do with phone calls. And then there was that lie, that wall she had erected.

She headed down the Trumansburg Road back into town, cut over the inlet bridge, and drove to Spencer Street.

Ed was beside himself. "They told us it's bad. Very bad. She doesn't have much time left." He broke down and wept in the kitchen, sopping up his tears with Rosie's apron that lay abandoned on the counter. "I love her so much, and now…I don't know how I can go on," he confessed. He had to look after Rosie, keep on working, take care of the babies. He was trying to get one of Rosie's cousins to lend a hand. Or somebody in his family.

"We'll help. You don't need to worry about that. Trip and I are here. You can count on us."

Weekdays, while Ed held down his job, Molly had three children. Three pairs of diapers to change. Two sets of bottles and meals to prepare while she nursed Rachel. Mounds of dirty laundry that needed washing.

Nevertheless, with Tripoli's help, she squeaked in time to keep reading and writing. "I couldn't manage all this without you," she said, following Tripoli as he carried out the heavy basket of laundry to hang on the line.

"I didn't exactly plan to spend half my life running a daycare," he said, wrestling a sheet, a clothes pin in his teeth. "But you gotta do what you can. Poor Rosie."

Ed came by each night after visiting Rosie at the hospital and picked up the twins. Often, however, he was so exhausted that he crashed right there on their sofa, too tired to even eat, and they tip-toed around him, letting him sleep the night.

Rosie came home from the hospital and her Aunt Betty took care of her days, leaving Ed to manage her care at night. When Molly went to see her, she was now so weak she couldn't even get out of bed to urinate, and had to ask for a bedpan. It was hard to fathom the speed with which she was wasting away. Ed kept besieging the doctors. What about chemotherapy? he kept asking. Okay, if not that, then a liver transplant. But the cancer had already spread to her adjoining organs, to Rosie's spleen and pancreas. It also appeared to be metastasizing into her bones and spine leaving Rosie in almost constant pain.

Finally, Molly suggested to Ed that he consider moving her to the hospice.

"*Hospice?*" he repeated with a shudder. It meant the end of the road, and he couldn't bring himself to even contemplate the prospect. Molly realized that the trip had already been started a long time ago.

In order to be home to help Molly during the day, Tripoli pulled as much night duty as he could. In the city, the deadening heat lingered on through the long fall nights, and cruising the streets at three in the morning, Tripoli could still see people sitting on their stoops and porches dressed in sweaty undershirts and shorts trying to catch the relief of a breeze. Paradoxically, crime in the city was down. There were fewer stickups and burglaries, fewer domestics and assaults. People were just too wrung out from the heat to fight, steal, or otherwise disturb the peace.

Tripoli spent the hours of daybreak watering the garden and picking the daily crop while Molly and the baby still slept in the silent house. He was thankful that they had a good, deep-drilled well. Other peoples' wells had run dry and they were hauling water from the lake—a once pure and glacially deep lake that was now sprouting smelly algal blooms along the shore.

In his pocket, Tripoli still carried the tracing he had made from the old Hermit's book. And when, moving through town in the dead of night, he started thinking about the fish gasping in the lake, about his neighbors squeezed by food prices as they struggled to put meals on the table for their kids, when he permitted his horizon to expand and consider the problems of people elsewhere in the state, the country, the world, he would take out that piece of paper, unfold it and run his fingers over those ancient Hebrew letters.

To the chosen others who follow and are granted the right to gaze on these hallowed works, the keepers of the Sacred Spirit of Anterra, holders of these eternal truths. May this flame continue to burn and spread light on this planet, hear the word of Anterra.

Smoothing that wrinkled paper as it lay on his lap, Tripoli felt a surge of comfort…and hope. For Anterra, he began to realize, was the divine spirit of the world, both mother of the earth and father of the sky, the keeper of mountains and oceans, the protector of humankind and nature. Anterra had been defiled and forgotten and now lay seriously ill. More than ever, people desperately needed direction, someone to remind them of their fundamental connection to this spirit, of their absolute dependency on the earth and their venerable responsibility to it…to what the books had called Anterra.

One morning, instead of going home, Tripoli took a detour and drove out to the Danby Forest. As he walked through the woods, the sun was just rising up over the lip of the horizon, and the birds were beginning to chirp. When he came upon the site of old Matthew's hut, he was taken aback by the sight of people. There were nearly two dozen of them, both men and women. They were gathered in a large circle around the remains of the building. The rubble, entangled now in brush and weeds, stood illuminated in a shaft of the red fiery light penetrating the opening in the forest. Someone had laid bouquets of wild flowers on the remains of the hut. There were rows of candles burning in little glass jars. And the people, their heads bowed, were praying, the low hum of their voices resonating through the forest. Tripoli's skin broke out in goosebumps and, before they could notice him, he silently slipped away.

Rosie's twins had started walking and, when Tripoli was left in charge, he had his hands full. One of the twins would take off towards the kitchen, while the other would head for the stairs, as if they had worked out some diversionary ploy. They would hoist themselves up on a chair and pull dishes off the table, yank books off the shelves, and dump food out of the refrigerator, spilling whole pitchers of juice and jars of jam. Nothing was safe from their eager clutches. They were intensely curious, and whenever Tripoli turned away for a second they were riffling through Molly's papers or banging away on her computer.

But they were cute and cuddly, and Tripoli would lie on the floor making crazy animal sounds as they climbed all over him laughing with excitement. And Tripoli couldn't get enough of Rachel. He loved to hold her, fascinated by her face and fingers and toes. He sang to her, held long conversations with his little daughter, and swore that she understood every word. She was so tiny and delicate that it was hard for him to believe that one day she was going to be a big girl, a teenager, much less a grown woman. He loved her smell and, when he had her up on the changing table, he would bury his nose into her belly and drink in the sweet scent of milk and powder and baby—somehow he just couldn't get enough of it.

Molly was going full speed in all directions. She had three kids, a garden that was producing food faster than it could be eaten or canned, a husband who needed to be loved, and a dear friend who was dying. Nevertheless, she managed to carve out chunks of time to keep updating her database and continue her correspondence, encourage Wally Schuman and his foundation, and write her column. These days it was dense with suggestions of things ordinary people could do to lessen their impact on the ecology, simple things like turning off lights when not needed, walking instead of driving short distances, using bicycles instead of cars, fans instead of air conditioners, heat pumps in lieu of furnaces. "Small actions by large numbers of people," she wrote, "end up having sizable effects."

Ed relented and Rosie, clearly in the final stages of her illness, was moved to the hospice. It was an attractive, gray wooden building with peaked roofs that sat high on King Road. It was decorated in restful shades of purples and pinks, and hanging on the walls were paintings and photographs of Ithaca's natural beauties by local artists. The place had lots of comfortable, well-worn furniture, wicker chairs, and stuffed sofas. Wrought iron plant holders filled with greenery hung everywhere. There was even a piano. And off to one side sat a kitchen where the staff would prepare whatever the resident desired—if they could eat.

They gave Rosie a corner room which had large windows and an outside deck. On the days when Rosie felt up to it, they would wheel out her bed and let her lie in the shade to gaze out on the rolling hills.

Rosie was sleeping more and more each day, and on some occasions Molly would sit with her, reading a book as Rosie slept through the visit.

The staff was very protective of Rosie, and there were bad days when she couldn't face people. Then they turned away all visitors, including Molly and Ed.

They gave Rosie drugs to mitigate the pain, as much as she felt she needed—though sometimes she refused all medication. "I want to be alive for the time that's left." And though she had more pain, her caretakers honored those wishes, too.

"There's something I've wanted to tell you," said Molly one late afternoon. She had managed to get Rosie to take a few spoonfuls of warm cereal, and was dabbing her lips with a tissue. The fall sun was slanting in through the windows and Rosie just looked straight at her with those big, dark eyes of hers, the whites yellowed with jaundice.

"Danny's alive," she said succinctly.

Rosie became very still, her brow wrinkling as she took in the news. "Oh…oh my," she sighed, the muscles in her face relaxed as a surge of relief flooded her face.

Molly then told her about the night they had spotted him and the old man leading the ewe from the barn, about the boots and food she had left him, about his vanishing tracks.

"You couldn't have given me happier news," said Rosie, gathering her strength and pulling herself upright in bed with such vigor that it alarmed Molly. "You know, I always knew he was alive. I was just afraid of upsetting you."

"Oh, Rosie," she said, clutching her and starting to weep. "I'm sorry I didn't tell you sooner. We were worried about telling anybody."

"Of course!"

"Can you ever forgive me?"

"Forgive you?" she said, and stroked Molly hair. "What's to forgive?"

Whenever he could, Ed brought the twins over to the hospice so Rosie could see and touch them, witness how they were growing, healthy and happy.

For each passing day, Rosie was becoming progressively slower to respond and Molly could see how she seemed to be almost deliberately detaching herself from her surroundings. She required increasing help for each movement of her body, and Molly had to support her head just so she could sip a little cool water.

Then, Rosie started refusing all food.

"I'm tired. I've had enough," she said, and Molly could actually see that her friend was preparing to die. She spoke less and more infrequently. Sometimes she merely opened her eyes, searched for Molly or Ed and then, spotting them, wordlessly closed her eyes again.

Late in the afternoon on the sixteenth day of October, while Molly was sitting with her, Rosie suddenly awoke with a start, a look of surprise on her face as though she had just made a discovery. She stared straight at Molly and there was brightness, a burning in her eyes that looked to Molly like ecstasy.

"Molly," said Rosie. She spoke so softly that Molly could barely hear her. Her breathing was light, her chest hardly rising or falling. A gurgling noise came with each breath and though she was smiling, Molly became alarmed.

She pulled close to Rosie. Her body was now all just raw, leathery skin and painful bones, and Molly was careful not to jar her as she tenderly encircled her friend with her arms. "Yes, darling," she said.

Rosie smiled, and her face was nothing but teeth and eyes and burning eyes. "Promise me…" she began. Then she closed her eyes and her breathing became ever more quick and shallow, like the fluttering of bird's heart.

"Yes, yes?" said Molly, but Rosie was slipping away.

Molly ran and got a nurse.

The nurse called Ed, and he was there in less than ten minutes. By the time he got to the hospice, however, she was already dead. When he saw that Rosie was gone, he crumbled into convulsions of inconsolable tears. Molly, who had been waiting quietly there with Rosie finally started to cry, too. They wept in each other arms, and Molly understood what the promise was.

"Last week, as you probably read," began Molly in her column that appeared around the country in the October twenty-second papers, "a large piece of the Ross ice shelf the size of the state of Montana broke off and slid into the Pacific Ocean. There was a massive wave that swamped coastal dwellings from Chile to the islands of the South Pacific. The Maldives off the coast in Africa no longer exist. In a matter of hours, the Marshall Islands lost 80 percent of their land mass. The low-lying countries of Europe and Southeast Asia are imperiled. In Holland, the sea level has risen to the point where the first storm surge could drive it over the dikes and flood the entire country. The governor of Florida has declared a state of emergency; New Orleans and countless other southern coastal towns and cities are in danger. It will take months just to calculate the loss of life. Uncounted millions have lost their homes, their agricultural lands, and their means of livelihood. The less obvious but long-term effects are incalculable: salt water intrusion threatens drinking supplies, the mouths of rivers are backing up against the high sea and will undoubtedly cause flooding in the near future; the infrastructure of ports and sewage systems, roads and bridges, constructed on the basis of previous sea levels, are now worthless. The list goes on and on."

"This is all too much for any person to grasp. When I learned all this my reaction was probably like most people's: numbness. The whole thing seems dreamlike, an abstraction. Maybe I could understand it intellectually, but I could not quite feel it in my heart.

"At about the same time that this wave of devastation began spreading across the globe, a dear childhood friend of mine died. Rosie was a young woman, a loving mother and good wife, an honest and caring human being. She felt that her cancer had been triggered by a work-related exposure to organic solvents in an auto body shop. I tend to believe she was right.

"After her death, I spent a lot of time walking in the countryside near my home, trying to pull things together, trying to make the connection between the wave and my friend Rosie.

"I thought about all the cars in our county, one hundred million, certainly more. The number of cars in the world—how many hundreds of millions of them are there? I did a little multiplication. Each car dripping oil, leaking a little gas, and the drips and spills became a flood, a wave. I thought of the time I damaged my car and had a fender replaced, the body repainted, and then I understood. In some small way I caused Rosie's death. In some small but significant way, I precipitated that killing wave.

"For me, guilt isn't the answer. It accomplishes nothing. And it's getting awfully late for that. My son Danny had been trying to tell me something, but my life was too noisy, too busy for me to hear. I regret that, but I'm listening now. It's a promise I've made to Danny and myself. A promise I made to my dear friend Rosie."

On Sunday morning, a week after Rosie's funeral, Molly was working in the garden. The Indian summer had continued with no sign of frost, and she was harvesting the last of the fall crops. Ed had the twins for the day, Tripoli was covering the weekend shift, and she finally had some free time.

Keeping the baby close, Molly placed her in the shade of the birch tree as she set to work. It had rained the day before, and in the early morning the earth smelt fresh. Although Tripoli had already brought in some of the tomatoes and started a sauce, there were lots large ripe ones remaining and she started gathering them.

Baby Rachel seemed content to lie under the tree, staring up at the sky and watching the birds flitting through the branch tops. When Molly finished gathering tomatoes, she started in on the late crop of beans that needed picking. Thanks to Tripoli's persistent watering, the beans were long and thick and juicy, so plentiful that a single plant took nearly five minutes to pick clean.

With the sharpness of her nail, Molly snipped off each bean, tossing it into the swelling pile. Someone in a house far down the road was chopping wood, and she could hear each blow of the axe. The sun was hot, and when she licked her upper lip it tasted salty of sweat. Reaching the end of the row, she heard the phone ringing in the house. It kept ringing until the answering machine picked up. A moment later it was ringing again. Then again, and she realized someone was urgently trying to reach her.

With Rachel in one arm, she made it to the phone on the fourth try. It was Tripoli on the other end.

"Molly!" he gasped. He sounded like he was winded.

"What's the matter?"

"Come to town. Quick."

"What's up?"

"You're not going to believe this." He was on his cell phone and running. "Somebody spotted Daniel and the Hermit coming in to town. Try to get to South Hill as fast as you can. Can you handle the baby?"

"Danny?"

"Yeah. Yeah!"

She ran for the car.

As she entered the valley, she came upon crowds of people hurrying into town. They were not only in cars, but on foot, riding bikes, and pushing strollers. It took her ten long minutes just to creep towards Green Street. Was there some mistake? she wondered. Could all these people be wrong? The days and months since Daniel had disappeared seemed endless. Did she dare hope she would see her son again? Touch him? Hold him?

By the time she got to Cayuga Street, traffic was at a dead standstill. In their haste, people were double-parking, some were simply leaving their cars in the road. Lifting Rachel from her baby seat, Molly got out of her car and stood for a moment in the stream of people. The citizenry appeared to be streaming in from all directions. They were sweeping in from the north and south flats, and Molly could make out an unending wave of people pouring down from East Hill. Everybody, it seemed, was converging on the east end of town.

As Molly moved ahead, she caught sight of familiar faces. Stan Goldberg, who owned Bishop's Hardware, flashed a broad smile and gave her a big thumbs-up. Harry Gesslein, the president of the bank, who she had only met once in her life, greeted her with a hearty pat on the back as if she were an old friend. Sandy, who was standing on the hood of a car, spotted Molly over the sea of bobbing heads and waved. She cupped her hands and shouted something, but Molly couldn't make it out above the hubbub of the crowd. What was Danny doing at this end of town? Molly wondered as she joined the crowd and hurried to the base of South Hill. And how did everybody know?

There were uniformed cops everywhere, city and state police and sheriff's deputies, hopelessly trying to contain the mob and keep the roadway open.

"Have you seen Tripoli?" she asked Officer Paolangeli, who was trying to move an ambulance through the throng.

"Up the hill," he gestured, pushing aside a group of teens. Someone had fainted in the heat and the ambulance was trying to reach them.

As she neared the focal point, the crowd became incredibly dense and Molly had to fight her way in, shielding Rachel with her arms as she inched forward. How would she ever find Tripoli in all this? she wondered, wedging herself through the midst of the crowd.

"Excuse me. Excuse me," Molly kept saying. "Could you please let me through."

The air felt hot and heavy and was pungent with the smell of baking pavement and diesel. The trees on the side of the road were yellow and brown, and when a wind blew down the street the leaves fluttered down, settling on the people like confetti. Everybody was standing on tiptoes, craning their necks trying to see. People had their kids propped up on their shoulders and were pointing. "Look. Look!" they were saying.

She spotted Tripoli not far from the head of the crowd.

"Trip! Trip!" she shouted, and he barreled his way through to her, taking the baby from her.

"Come on," he said, and, holding Rachel above the press of the crowd, moved further up the incline, Molly following tightly in his wake.

Then, suddenly, the sea of people ahead of them began to part, opening a path down the hill. The sound of loud cheers and applause washed backwards like a wave. Some people fell to their knees and for the first time Molly finally caught a glimpse of the street ahead. When she did, her heart leaped and she let out a cry of surprise. There was Danny, coming down the hill. And he had the Hermit by the hand, leading him into town. His hair had grown full and long and curly again, and in the midday sun it glinted like a golden halo. His walk was slow and measured, his bearing regal and confident. And there was a look on his face that spoke of goodness and peace and wisdom. My God, he's beautiful, she thought as the noise suddenly died and the crowd fell into an unearthly hush. And in that instant she saw Danny not through the skewed lens of a mother's eye, but as others saw him, might see him, would certainly come to view him in the future when he would be a strong and wise young man, a man of vision and learning.

Molly squeezed Tripoli's arm and, as he turned to smile at her, she thought of his foresight and conviction, and knew that everything he had said would truly come to pass. She thought of poor Rosie and how from the very beginning she had recognized Danny's promise, knew all along that he was still alive and would return to the people when they were finally ready, ready to listen.

The crowd closed ranks behind the boy and old man and finally Danny was standing right in front of them, encircled by the people.

"Hello Mother," he smiled, triggering in Molly shivers of delight. "Hello, Trip. Hello, little sister." He reached up and stroked the baby's head. The baby laughed.

"Daniel," uttered Molly, falling to her knees and hugging him. "Daniel."

Tripoli wrapped his arms around them, pulling them all into a tight circle.

"This is my friend, John," said the boy, pointing. "We've come home."

The old man smiled warmly and held out a calloused hand. Molly took it, clasped it, and brought it gratefully to her lips.

afterword

The novels that I've written seem to fall into two distinct categories. There are those that write themselves. An example of that is my novel *Baby,* which magically spilled forth upon the page. Then there are those books which are sheer agony, that require repeated rewrites. This novel is the perfect example. It went through four (or is it five, I prefer to forget) complete rebirths, each time almost a different story.

I'd like to say that I did this with no help, but the reality is that that I relied on many friends. How do I even begin expressing my thanks?

My gratitude goes to Linda Johanson for helping with the first pass. Then to Don Smith who once again took time from a busy law practice to read and toss out ideas. Josh Goldman, a gifted physics student at Cornell, who started off by copyediting and then surprised me with his ability to analyze plot. I'm eternally indebted to my dear friend and novelist Tony Caputi who spent countless hours helping me fine-tune this book.

Additional thanks go to Allen MacNeill, biologist, for his fertile ideas and expert help. To Tom Corey and Alan Friedlander for their readings and comments. To Cornell University and my colleagues in the Physics Department who been so supportive over the years, enabling me to pursue my alternate career of writing and filmmaking.

Thanks also to Lt. Beau Saul of the Ithaca Police Department (a one time student of mine who lets me ride shotgun in his squad car), who read this book and checked it for procedural accuracy.

Liza Dawson, my agent, believed in this book already in its earlier incarnations and was instrumental in convincing me to do those last painful rewrites. Thanks Liza.

Hillel Black, my editor, was enormously helpful in his reading and suggestions, always available when I needed him.

And then there is Gunilla, who has ridden with me through a wild and crazy life, who has willingly and stoically read and corrected all my books (even typed them before the advent of computers, poor woman). Needless to say, she has been instrumental in any successes that I have had.

If there are others who I have omitted mentioning, I hope they will pardon this lapse. I humbly confess that the creative process does not occur in a vacuum.

About the Author

Robert Lieberman is the author of several novels, including *Perfect People, Baby, Ten Days to Murmansk, Goobersville Breakdown, Intimate Details,* and *Paradise Rezoned.* He is also a physicist and professor of mathematics at Cornell University and an independent filmmaker. His films include *Green Lights, Faces in a Famine,* and *BoyceBall.*